The Angel of Amar

Cletus R. Willems

The Angel of Amar
All Rights Reserved
Copyright © 2015 Cletus R. Willems

ISBN-13:
978-0692335482
ISBN-10:
069233548X

PRINTED IN THE UNITED STATES OF AMERICA

Cover Design: SelfPubBookCovers.com/Daniela
Author Photograph by Bradford W. Wilcox

For my Mother and Father

CONTENTS

Prologue	Five	1
Chapter 1	Divergent Paths	7
Chapter 2	Made Flesh Again After Death	35
Chapter 3	Angelic Visions	57
Chapter 4	A Candle in the Darkest Night	81
Chapter 5	Settling and Searching	105
Chapter 6	How I Spent My Family Vacation	123
Chapter 7	A Wedding in Lake Forest	149
Chapter 8	A Toast to Love	177
Chapter 9	Foreign Connections	181
Chapter 10	Elementary, My Dear Watson	201
Chapter 11	Azume	227
Chapter 12	Angels and Demons Among us	247
Chapter 13	Painful Recollections	271
Chapter 14	Timing is Everything	295
Chapter 15	A Good Day at the Office	311
Chapter 16	A Memorable Holiday	335
Chapter 17	Liberty Leading Lives Past	355
Chapter 18	Cosmic Justice	379
Chapter 19	Capri Boy	405
EPILOGUE	A Final Gift	419
Select Characters		427
Author's note		430

"I am confident that there truly is such a thing as living again, that the living spring from the dead, and that the souls of the dead are in existence."
Socrates

"My life often seemed to me like a story that has no beginning and no end . . . I could well imagine that I might have lived in former centuries and encountered questions I was not yet able to answer; that I had been born again because I had not fulfilled the task given to me."
Carl Jung

PROLOGUE
Five
Fairfax County, Virginia, 1946

The sleeping man started with a jerk when a disturbing vision emerged from a dream, sending a shiver down his spine. This delighted Dr. Edmund Wright. *Excellent, almost like clockwork each evening after two hour's sleep. I can work with that.*

The patient awoke and the psychiatrist took his vitals, but Project Chatter number 5 remained unresponsive throughout, staring upward from the bed, preoccupied with a slide show of unknown people, places and events flashing through his mind. Known as "Five" to the staff, and recently as John Redford to most others, only four men knew his actual name and all were committed to maintaining the secret.

Five was in an isolated government facility soon to be placed under control of the new Central Intelligence Agency. Wright ran the Special Projects Ward at the covert facility, and had worked on strange cases during his brief tenure, but none this odd. The challenge had engaged him, and he'd developed an unusually strong—if not entirely professional—attachment to his charge. *He's endured so much, yet his strength shines through. Rare for someone so ill. With his looks, he could hardly be more attractive.*

The official record detailed Five's condition upon admission the previous year: "Chatter 5 is a Caucasian male presumably in his late twenties. He stands sixty-nine and one-half inches tall and weighs one hundred and seventeen pounds. He has hazel eyes and a short, broad face with high cheekbones, and a wide jaw with a pronounced cleft chin. He has thick, brown hair and eyebrows, and a distinctive four-inch long, recessed birthmark on the interior aspect of his left bicep. He's unkempt, malnourished, and critically ill.

The subject worked as a scientist on the Manhattan Project, and his condition is said to have resulted from an accident during an experiment conducted near the war's end. Details of the incident are classified top-secret and unavailable, and the subject's true identity is unknown.

Initial admission goals are restoration of the subject's physical health and determination of his intelligence level. Secondary goals include achieving functional intelligence, ascertaining his identity, and incorporating all compiled data into the Chatter database. Discharge will be considered if the stated goals are met, if compatible with national security guidelines. Any inquiries and all progress reports regarding the subject are to be be directed to Deputy Administrator Brant Frey, exclusively."

Five entered the government facility in deplorable condition. His arms, legs and back were covered with numerous wounds, open sores and scabs in various stages of healing, and when standing he hunched over markedly, unable or unwilling to lift his head. His entire body twitched and shook spastically, randomly, when he wasn't otherwise staring ahead vacantly, lethargic if not catatonic, seemingly impervious to speech and other stimuli. He was feverish and yellow skinned with jaundice, which would later be linked to an infection in his central nervous system.

Wright met with Frey demanding an explanation. He confided—strictly off the record—that Five had been "treated" with a large number and eclectic mixture of drugs with known, often conflicting effects, ranging from anesthetic and sedative to euphoric and hallucinogenic. The administered drugs included opiates, such as morphine and heroin, barbiturates, cannabinoids, atropine, mescaline, and amides of lysergic acid.

Frey said it had been part of a misguided attempt to restore the subject to normalcy by shocking his system, and the mistake had been compounded by his use in field testing before implementing rigorous treatment and measurement standards. "The men responsible have been punished and discharged," Frey lied. "We don't tolerate such gross negligence in our operations."

"Who was responsible? If they didn't measure results and compile the data they didn't accomplish anything. What kind of idiots would think they were being productive?"

Frey didn't respond. The responsible parties weren't idiots. Frey had given Daniel Stegger, slated to become the CIA Director of Science and Technology—a brilliant man, but also something of a loose cannon— free reign to deal with the subject.

Stegger believed science could answer any questions worth asking, and men wasted their time pondering abstractions such as morality, righteousness and propriety. This view added to his visceral hatred of Redford, who'd possessed moral convictions he lacked and been dismayed by the decisions made in using the atomic bomb. Stegger couldn't understand how such a man had surpassed his own work on Manhattan, and for a time been applauded by the directors instead of him. He'd thought them all fools not to recognize that his views threatened scientific progress.

He'd hated Redford because he thought he diminished science, but also because he'd made him feel inferior; so he'd delighted in punishing him in a feigned effort to learn his identity—actually didn't give a shit about Redford's real name, saw nothing in that for himself. His thoughts were more basic—*Too bad Redford can't appreciate the irony of being brain-fried just like we fried the Japs in Hiroshima and Nagasaki that made his simple heart bleed.*

Wright managed to restore Five's physical health after months of diligent work, but he remained mentally absent. He needed Five to communicate to regain his mental prowess, and he surmised that excessive stimulation coupled with one additional drug might help.

Sodium thiopental (ST) had been discovered in the 1930's, by a chemist foreseeing multiple uses for the short-duration barbiturate. It could be used as an anesthetic, could induce comas, could reduce brain swelling, and could even be used for euthanasia. It also decreased higher cortical brain function, causing many subjects to release their repressed memories. Having studied ST at Harvard Medical College, Wright saw promise in its versatility.

During Five's sleep, his muscles tensed and breathing fluctuated as he moved into Rapid Eye Movement or REM state (when the brain paralyzes the body allowing dreams to occur). And the startling dreams which woke him regularly appeared at fairly predictable times, thirty minutes after REM and two hours after falling asleep. Since he resisted interaction while conscious, Wright hoped REM paralysis and the consistent timing of his dreams could be used to overcome resistance and access his mind's storehouse.

He selected sound recordings for their stimulant value, and he had them played day and night within Five's hearing, with greatly amplified volume during his periods of REM sleep. The recordings ranged from classical music to lectures in chemistry and physics, and included provocative subjects such as dream interpretation.

Five didn't respond to the recordings' stimuli by itself. Then in late 1946, Wright introduced ST into his intravenous line when he transitioned to REM. Almost precisely two hours later he woke, with the sound of *Haydyn's Fire Symphony* blasting away. After locating Wright with his eyes, he spoke for the first time since his admission, asking, "Where am I? . . Who am I?"

"You're in a hospital in Virginia, but I don't know who you are, we'll have to discover that together," replied Wright, elated.

"What's a Virginia?" asked Five, his eyes darting about wildly.

Wright tried explaining, but Five had stared off as if uninterested and unaware even of what his questions meant, as if they'd sprung from latent retained memory like babbling—it seemed the road to discovery would be quite lengthy.

Wright knew medical science tended to be absolute, materialistic, skeptical and unyielding, viewing patients as machines able to be repaired simply by consulting something like a manual. Yet, similar conditions treated similarly often led to very different outcomes. Wright interpreted this to mean that the best men of science needed to be artists, and artistry would be required to find the singular part of Five defying measurement, the fundamental core needing repair.

God knew he'd try his best. But he realized success depended upon Five's destiny as much as his efforts. He might well end up senseless and wrapped in a blanket in an asylum, or emerge stronger and wiser, perhaps capable of instructing others. *When all is said and done,* he thought, *we all dance to a mysterious tune.*

At home later the day Five first spoke, Wright sipped a Bourbon Manhattan, set it down on the table beside him and stretched his legs out along the length of his lounge chair. Looking at the dense forest before him, he could identify many trees, but he settled on the most impressive, a seventy-five foot hemlock spruce with a diameter of three feet. It towered above the others alongside a stream flowing down from the Appalachian Mountain Range. He'd examined it closely once and knew it stood tall and unwavering despite its roots being seriously disrupted long before by a rock slide that would have killed lesser stock. He greatly admired the inherent strength enabling it to thrive despite such adversity.

He fished in his drink for the cherry. He secured it from beneath the ice cubes, popped it into his mouth and licked his fingers. Content and fortified, he began thinking of different methods he might use to release Five's indomitable essence. He'd redouble his efforts in the morning.

1.

Divergent Paths

Washington, D.C., 1952

Daniel Stegger walked north on Fourteenth Street in Washington, D.C. in early December, topcoat folded over his arm. He looked formidable in a British-cut vested suit with the tip of a white handkerchief peeking out of his suit coat pocket. He ignored the clatter of buses and streetcars and the roaring engines and horns of cars, hordes of government workers fleeing the District for the weekend. *Subways will be needed soon*, he reflected, *and that'll bring even more opportunity. Nothing can slow the government expansion.* His meeting with the Secretary had gone very well. *Soon we'll be able to steal even more. Damn*, he mused, *it's almost too easy. God bless the USA!*

Crossing Pennsylvania Avenue, he headed straight for the Willard Hotel. Once inside, he circled the Round Robin Bar and was greeted warmly by the familiar bartender. He asked for his usual, a vodka martini, and settled down in his favorite black leather booth, beneath drawings of Grover Cleveland and Ulysses Grant. He'd arrived early to savor the ambience, missing his favorite gathering spot as much as he could miss anything. They'd hatched so many plots there—*if only the walls could talk!*

A tall, fortyish man wearing a sashed topcoat and sunglasses sauntered into the room, shook hands with the bartender and ordered his own usual cocktail. Approaching the corner booth, he slowed while staring intently at Stegger, looking for a sign. He stopped a few feet away, stretched his hands out, said "Ta-da!" and leaned over to shake hands. "You bastard, Stegger, I can tell by that Cheshire grin. Pulled it off, didn't you?"

"All twelve million, Brant, signed, sealed, and ready for delivery next week. A barely noticeable dent in a seventy-one billion dollar budget. Thanks to the Ruskies, it's like fish in a barrel, courtesy of the Defense Procurement Act of the Eighty-Second Congress. So take your coat off. Stay awhile, and put those glasses away. You look like a goddamned secret agent."

" I don't look covert?"

"More like a neon sign blinking 'spy here, spy here'"!

They pronounced "God bless Ike" in unison, clinked their glasses together, munched on olives and breadsticks, and spoke of the good fortune that made such a sweet deal possible.

"So, Brant, I was a Democrat this morning, should I register as a Republican before the Inauguration?"

"It won't matter so long as you show the new pols our money. *Our* money, right Daniel?"

Stegger reached down into his briefcase and withdrew a large manila envelope. He handed it to Frey. "Inside is an embossed certificate for forty percent of DRS Energy Applications, Inc. You'll want to hold onto that. Suitable for framing, but I don't recommend it—very un-spy like. The initial value of your shares will be just under three million, all fully marketable thirty days after the public offering. Not to mention two hundred and fifty large ones already in *your* Swiss account."

"Excellent, but short of expectations. Did Mr. Secretary bargain for extra juice?"

"He did, the greedy bastard. But this one should actually make money—we'll make up the difference in eighteen months. Hell, it might even create some jobs and save us from the commies."

The two first met in the latter days of work on the Manhattan Project while Stegger served as a scientist and Frey as head of military security. Recognizing their mutual greed, they bonded quickly and plotted to be installed together in the upper echelon of the planned Central Intelligence Agency, soon to be known simply as "the Company." There they implemented self-serving plans, doing it so masterfully that their compatriots saw only what they wanted to portray: two devoted public servants, loyal, unquestioning, and willing to take on the most challenging assignments. They were admired especially for leaving desk jobs to dirty their hands in the field.

After they'd become established within the Company, Daniel felt bored dealing with bureaucratic obstacles, administrative minutia, and tedious management issues. He also felt stymied by policies he thought he should be dictating as Director of Science and Technology. (Such as its unwillingness to fabricate larger bombs even while the Russians were hell-bent on developing a seventy-five megaton hydrogen device, five thousand times the explosive power of Hiroshima's Little Boy.) Needing an adrenaline fix, he convinced Frey they could expand their Company influence by spending more time in the field. Besides, he'd argued, it'd make them more empathetic managers. So for two years, they found the excitement Daniel craved in up-close and personal encounters with coups, rebellions, and assassinations.

Their first major in-field project, Operation Free Choice, involved the 1949 Italian elections. Ostensibly acting in counter espionage, Frey and Daniel worked to counteract the communists who threatened American business interests preferring the status quo. They purchased votes, conducted counter-propaganda publicity, and disrupted anti-American factions. When their efforts appeared insufficient to stem the communist tide, they adopted stronger tactic to convince opposition candidates to withdraw from elections at inopportune times.

Frey and Stegger were ensconced in a cellar near Piazza Campo de Fiore in Rome one morning, along with two Italian operatives and two captive communist candidates. The candidates were gagged and bound, secured on narrow wooden benches placed side by side. They remained stoic, and when threatened by the Americans disguised under hoods, told them to kiss ass, Italy would decide who ran its affairs, not foreigners without the balls to show their faces like real men. Their defiance was anticipated and more persuasive methods planned, but Daniel improvised off script, exceeding all expectations.

"Eeny, meeny, miny, moe," he'd rhymed while pointing back and forth between the two bound men. "Catch a commie by his toe, eeny, meeny, miny, moe . . . Well, Emilio, this isn't your lucky day. You're going to be the message and your compatriot will be the messenger." Then he instructed the locals to strip Emilio naked from the waist down and immobilize him.

It wasn't so much what he did that disturbed Frey—he'd already seen more than a lifetime of suffering and gore by then—but Daniel's mood swings throughout were troublesome. He appeared on the verge of madness one moment and fully rational the next, interspersing precise and deliberate actions with seemingly impulsive acts of unusual cruelty, often curiously detached, as if an observer not personally responsible for the mayhem.

Stegger shed his hood, looked Emilio in the eye and said *"Ora si vede un uomo,"* *Now you see a man.* Then he'd smiled and said, *"E necessario?"*

"Vaffanculo!" Emilio spat back through the cloth stretched across his mouth, the meaning of his barely audible response abundantly clear. Daniel responded to the obscenity with a grin and then   by producing a large, razor-sharp knife.

"Speaking of fucking," he'd said, pointing the tip of the knife toward the man's crotch, "How do you say . . . *Come se dice,* 'eunuch' *en Italiano?"*

"Eunuco," Paolo replied, shaking his head in mock sympathy. *"Molto triste, molto triste,"* *very sad* indeed.

Daniel bent over the helpless man nose to nose, peering into his eyes with the sort of detachment one might expect from a physician examining blood vessels with an opthalmoscope as he looked for signs of hypertension. He'd seemed unaware Emilio was unable to conceal his fear any longer and needed little encouragement to capitulate. As he watched Daniel looking down at the bound captive, Frey imagined a switch being thrown and transforming him. For a moment he wondered if Daniel was having a mental meltdown.

"Look at me . . . *guardami!*" Daniel shouted. "*Recordare chi ha fatto questo!*" Indeed, Emilio would certainly never forget the man brutalizing him.

Leaning over Emilio's naked lower torso, Daniel sliced the flesh of both thighs with studied precision, placing symmetrical three-inch long gashes that instantly drew blood. He'd focused intently on the task, sliding the knife slowly, oblivious to the man's squirming and muffled cries, and counting aloud for each methodical cut. Then he'd moved the knife to just below the captive man's scrotum and, as if being especially considerate, gently moved his penis up and away with the back of one hand. He'd paused for what seemed an eternity to Emilio, who trembled noticeably while tears rolled down his face and he begged through his gag. "*Non ancora,*" not yet, Daniel replied flatly.

Moving from the unfortunate man's genitals to his feet, secured in place near the end of the table, Daniel stood upright, pursed his lips and ran his thumb and forefinger across them as if in deep thought. "Six divided by two is three," he'd muttered as if having solved a difficult equation, just before severing the two smallest toes of Emilio's left foot with one swift movement of the knife. The others in the room gaped and Emilio screamed into his gag while Daniel merely lifted his head and seemed to regard Emilio's full-bodied bucking with curious interest. "Paolo, tell him to stop being such a baby . . . Ask him which other toe he doesn't need since it has to add up to three." He crossed his arms in apparent patience, waiting while Paolo tried to engage the weeping man who struggled mindlessly against his bindings, unintelligible in his pain. "Never mind, we don't have all day," Daniel said, before quickly severing the large toe on Emilio's right foot, causing his bladder to let loose as he passed out.

"Jesus Christ, the little boy pissed himself. Wrap up his feet and throw some water on his face. We're not finished yet."

Daniel moved over to address the captive on the second bench and he began moving the knife in tiny circles, inches above his face.

"*Tutto quello che vuoi, Tutto quello che vuoi!*" the terrified man screamed repeatedly while staring at the knife and squirming. "*Prego, per l'amore di Dio!*"

"I'm no fool. Words are easy. I've heard people promise they'll do anything before, but without a vivid reminder they always seem to forget." Daniel grasped the man's hair, pulled his head back and drew a thin gash across his scalp under his thick hair from ear to ear. Blood flowing down his face, the man howled and begged him to stop.

"Paolo, tell him they *will* withdraw their candidacy by noon tomorrow. And let him know I don't believe in that 'for love of God' shit, only *el diablo*. I know where they live and Emilio won't be running away too fast after today. If they cross me on this or try to blame us in any way, I'll find them no matter where they hide. Then I'll make both of them eunuchs and cut their sons' nuts off for good measure."

Over time, the players and places changed while Daniel's cruelty continued unabated. He engaged in cold-blooded murders in Greece and Ecuador, and he participated in atrocities in Iran while helping overthrow Mossadegh in favor of the Shah. Outrageous and obscene conduct in those venues reportedly included electric shock, and human flailing in a grotesque technique that might have shamed even the Gestapo. "It's fascinating," Daniel told Frey when asked about the reports, "but nothing is so revealing of a man's character as his reaction near the limits of tolerable pain."

Frey continued playing the role of Stegger's best friend, which he was as far as that went, but the extent of his cruelty concerned him. Daniel was so damn bright, so glib and charming, so clever and deceptive, that it took insight over time to see his genuine character beneath the veneer. Once he did, Frey feared he was psychotic, and he became concerned his excesses would become uncontrollable and compromise both of them.

To put some distance between them, Frey detailed how much more money could be stolen if he remained inside the Company and Daniel worked on the outside, in consulting entities feeding off intelligence funding. Their third venture, DRS Energy Applications, was an offspring of the concept, and it had worked so easily that even more promising ventures were soon underway.

Daniel realized why Frey really wanted him out, but it suited him fine. He disliked working in a public organization, resented the oversight and the accountability of being judged by those he considered his inferiors. He also recognized that, even if he were to become Company Director, he'd be subject to the whims of the Congress, and he thought politicians were among the most inferior of all men. Besides, he'd been excited by the prospect of using the mind control techniques developed in projects Chatter and MKULTRA, but those would fall out of favor once Truman left office.

As a youngster, Daniel had behaved as a loving and devoted son to his parents while despising them; he'd feigned interest in religion so a pastor would help educate him; he'd pretended to be dedicated to his grandfather's business so he could steal it; and he'd acted like a caring husband and father merely to appear normal. Such role-playing had served him well, making him a fortune and bestowing the power accompanying money, but he thought *enough already*. He'd sanitize his Company record, leave with a sterling reputation intact, and after that, the hell with games. It was time to be the real Daniel Stegger, powerful, ruthless, and beholding to no one. Of course, he'd continue lying and deceiving others since no workman should ever waste his best tools.

His resignation surprised many and disappointed the Director who tried changing his mind. Stegger confided in earnest tones that the work and travel had taken too great a toll and had caused his divorce. He claimed to miss his family life, said he wanted to try to resuscitate his marriage.

Frey and Stegger drank excessively the night they met at the Willard. They ate dinner and reminisced about the beginning of their relationship. "Whatever happened to Asshole Jack?" Daniel asked, while cutting into a rare steak. "I lost track of him when I moved on to weaponry after he got weird."

They'd dealt with Stegger's fellow Manhattan scientist, John Redford, in one of their earliest capers. It had been peanuts in the grand scheme of things, but Frey went along to curry Daniel's favor. He knew how much Daniel hated "Asshole Jack" for being too straight laced and principled.

"Weird doesn't even come close to describing his rambling. Speaking only in Latin, for Christ's sake. Odd that he concocted such fantasies when he couldn't even remember his own name. It'd be a piece of cake breaking him with today's tools, but it's just as well Groves and Donovan worked it out—it kept the OSS mess and your payback secret. Too much digging would have made our escapades harder—still, I would have enjoyed hearing what those old war horses had on each other to make them keep the peace."

"What happened to the sap?"

"Sap for sure. All that 'for God and country' bullshit. Goes to show what sacrifice gets you from your grateful nation."

"Never catch me there while the big boys are looking out for number one. Very short-sighted for someone supposedly so bright. Did they terminate him once he was brain-fried?"

"No. They reprogrammed him with the Ludlow technique. Substituted the fake Redford identity for his own. They used his work on the Hill for continuity. Easier since he'd already been playing the role. So now the braniac from West Virginia is a science professor at Columbia."

"Sounds like a loose end. Should we handle it?"

"We don't need the attention. He's still catalogued in MKULTRA. But it's been a long time and he's Professor Zombie. The poor bastard wouldn't know his mother if she enrolled in his class."

"Poor bastard, my ass. Serves the self-righteous prick right."

"You really hated him, always calling him Asshole Jack."

"I despise people who think they're hot shit and are always spouting off. He acted so superior."

"Wait a second, what about us?" asked Frey, his index finger pointed upward, eyes twinkling with merriment. "Aren't we hot shit? Don't we always lets others know it?"

"That's different," Daniel laughed, "when it's so goddamned apparent!" Lifting their glasses of Chateau Lafitte Rothschild '36, they toasted themselves once again. Passing on dessert, they told the waiter that, as usual, they craved something sweeter to finish the evening. Five minutes later, the concierge came to their table and traded two keys for fifty dollars Daniel slipped into his palm.

"Thank you Charles."

"It's always my pleasure, sir, thank you. I believe you'll have a delightful evening. 702 is your room, Mr. Stegger." He knew Daniel preferred brunettes.

"Don't hurt your back, Daniel," Frey joked as they called for an elevator.

"Brant, I'm a flawless, long endurance machine. Never fear."

Frey gave him a thumbs-up, knew it was true. He'd never known anyone as sexually obsessed as Daniel. Since his divorce, he'd been hell-bent on setting promiscuity records on four continents. There wasn't a Mrs. Right for Daniel Stegger, but there was usually a Miss Tonight.

———

John Redford raced up the stone steps two at a time, leather satchel clasped to his topcoat, driving rain dripping from his fedora, his shoes and socks soaked. Dodging around a statue of Minerva, he'd imagined the Goddess of Wisdom shaking her head, dismayed that anyone could forget an umbrella in springtime New York. Moving toward the entry, he focused on the steps dancing around the puddles, pleased by his dexterity. Meanwhile, a young woman huddled beneath an umbrella and clutching a folder full of papers emerged from behind a column and headed down the steps in his direction. They collided, and she landed on her bottom with legs akimbo.

Glaring at him as he darted about trying to capture her umbrella, she'd yelled, "Get the papers"! It pained her to see her students' final exams scattered about, pages wind-whipped open and sopping, a full semester's recounting of knowledge dripping away.

Feeling her limbs and moving her neck in circles to assess her injuries, she rose reassured and moved into shelter beneath the columned portico as he crisscrossed the steps gathering her things, stumbling and slipping in haste and stammering apologies. "I-I-I'm so sorry! Forgive me, I-I-I'll get everything! Please, st-st-stay there. Let me do it, it's all my fault!"

"There are fourteen exams . . . I need them all!"

The physics professor sat down on the wet marble, holding his topcoat above his head while cradling the drenched exams between his chest and knees. Nudging the merged pages apart with his fingertips, he counted until satisfied. He flipped his coat over his shoulder, rose and approached the young woman.

"I think I have them all. You said fourteen? Are you all right? May I call a doctor? Obviously it's entirely my fault. I'm sorry for being so reckless . . . How can I make it up to you?"

"I'll be fine," she replied, as she scrutinized the test papers and noted the many illegible pages. "Our students will be delighted to receive A's by default."

John Redford removed his hat, tilted his head downward and ran a hand through his thick and wavy brown hair. "I'm really sorry, I-I-

I . . . " He raised his head, looked into her eyes and immediately forgot what he intended to say. That memorable moment, and the entire evening in 1949, beginning with their collision near Columbia University's library and ending with mutual infatuation fueled by a lengthy conversation over coffee, would remain a cherished memory for both throughout their lives.

When knocked off her feet that day, twenty-three year old Rosabella Tassi was a teaching assistant at Barnard College, having recently received a Master's degree for her thesis, *Urbanism in Imperial Rome*. She'd planned on pursuing her doctorate until meeting John. She hadn't originally intended to pursue an academic career, had always assumed she'd marry and raise a large family. But she wasn't one to compromise and it had appeared unlikely she'd ever meet her perfect man: hers had to be intelligent and engaging with a pleasant appearance; he had to be sensitive and empathetic; he had to have integrity and strong moral values; and he needed a purposeful and significant career, but one kept in perspective. He also needed to be especially tolerant to overlook the idiosyncrasies of her high-strung family; moreover he had to be Catholic or Momma would never approve.

Her upbringing had been far different than most other Ivy League students of the time. Her parents emigrated from Italy, arriving in Boston off a boat from Civitavecchia, the port of Rome. The family moved to Hazleton, Pennsylvania shortly before her birth, and they opened up an Italian delicatessen in the immigrant-rich city. The idea was a good one, but the venture ate up the family savings quickly and failed, largely because her father loved alcohol far more than storekeeping. His baby daughter, Rosabella, who'd always be known as Rose, never got to know him since Amadeo Tassi died at thirty-one, a month before her second birthday. He died from pneumonia after deciding to sleep in a snowdrift one night rather than return home to face his wife's wrath. Francesca, a practical woman with five children to raise, had been reduced to rifling through her drunken husband's pockets for leftover coins, and lamenting his reckless sociability. Many mourners at Amadeo's wake were genuinely saddened realizing thereafter they'd have to buy their own drinks when toasting Italia at Molinaro's Marche Bar.

Rose inherited a cagy intellect and survival instinct from her mother. Even while pallbearers lowered Amadeo into the ground at Our Lady of Pompeii Cemetery, Francesca's scented letter sailed overseas to Signor Antonio Ridolfi in Rivitolo, Italy. Francesca remembered that he'd adored her throughout their childhood and had mournfully watched her marry while watching longingly from behind a cypress tree. True to her proactive nature, she wrote to him after Amadeo's death describing her plight persuasively: "My sorrow and loneliness is profound. So young and full of life and with so much love to give, but where shall I find comfort now? Think of me, my special friend, and pray for me now and then."

In early 1931, Antonio rejected a prayerful approach and traveled to America with Hazleton in his sights. Determined to provide earthly solace to the beautiful widow, he was undeterred by assuming financial responsibility for a woman with five children.

Francesca was equally undeterred by her lack of love, so they wed and began a tolerable life together. Francesca achieved her goal of keeping the family intact, safe and comfortable, even if in a just-getting-by Depression-era sort of way, and Antonio had a dutiful wife to attend to his needs.

The entire family contributed. Antonio worked as a security guard at night and slept during the day while Francesca handled affairs on the homefront. The children did all they could, including walking miles of railroad track and retrieving pieces of coal to sell to those even more needy. Even as a young child, on summertime dawns Rose would be trucked off to onion farms to pick weeds for twelve cents a day. Her earnings, like those of all the children, were deposited into Antonio's exclusive cache, the so-called "family pot" resting atop his bedroom dresser.

Momma Tassi recognized that the well-educated suffered far less than others during the Depression, so despite having only three grades of formal education, she relentlessly advocated advanced education for her children. She considered high school a necessity and spoke of those completing college as if worthy of a monument. Her youngest children, Marino and Rose, absorbed her persistent message and earned top grades, scholarships, and even post-graduate degrees from prestigious schools. This garnered them Momma's acclaim but estranged them from their underachieving siblings. Resentment surfaced whenever family discussions shifted to money, the siblings contending the two overachievers knew nothing of genuine earning since they didn't even break a sweat while making a living, unlike "real laborers."

Family resources were adequate because of Momma's thriftiness, ambition and business savvy. She planned and plotted and schemed to earn money by cleaning homes, scrubbing floors, taking in laundry, selling garden vegetables and homemade rosaries, and by providing room and board for passing strangers. Years later, even when relatively prosperous, money continued to dominate family conversations. How could it not, with copies of *The Wall Street Journal* stacked up next to the icebox for reference? Momma read the paper daily to track investments she made with funds diverted from Pa's pot or the meager food allowance he parceled out while complaining about her extravagant spending.

Food played a preeminent role in Rose's early life. Abundant meals were common, no matter what else needed be sacrificed. This overemphasis arose from Francesca's emotional needs: affirming deliverance from abject hardship; maintaining family unity in the new world; asserting control over at least one large part of life; and retaining belief in the real and imagined virtues of life back in the old country. Momma Francesca truly believed, as she'd often remark, "What you *mangiare* tells everyone everything they need to know about you." So her meals could never be ordinary.

When thinking of home, enduring images and sensations sprang into Rose's mind: a large pot full of rich, red sauce simmering on a backburner; an oversized, well-dented aluminum cooking vessel up front, its top rattling as boiling water awaited an immersion of homemade pasta; the tart taste and smell of lettuce, arugula and radishes sprinkled with vinegar and oil; Pa's homemade red wine in dark green bottles placed on opposite ends of the table, sediment-filled bottoms compelling a steady-handed, slow pour imparting the aroma of fermented fruit; mashed potatoes infused with bacon, green beans, and chunks of garlic; roasted blackbirds lined up wing to wing in a pan, their vacant eyes staring ahead as they bathed in a mixture of their juices, butter, oil, and wine, the luscious cacciatore sauce awaiting a covert swipe of crusty bread, a frantic scraping of the delicious, hardening rue at the pan's bottom the moment Momma turned her head.

Rose learned lifetime lessons while listening, arguing, laughing and gossiping during family meals amidst the dramatic encounters which outsiders often found unsettling.

Believing he came from a small family, John felt unaccustomed to the strident tone of loudly voiced opinions, and Rose worried how it would go when he met her family on Thanksgiving. But he passed his test flawlessly even before the pumpkin pie made its way to the table.

"Have enough to eat?" Rose asked with a chuckle as they drove back to New York.

"Let's see, I started with that luscious salami and cheese bread, and then had three different meats plus the turkey and stuffing, mashed potatoes, sweet potatoes, green beans, two casseroles, carrots, jello, salad, and ravioli. But there were only four or five desserts, besides fruits, cheeses and roast chestnuts. Were they holding out on me?"

"It's always *abbondanza* at home!"

"Did the Pilgrims eat pasta on Thanksgiving?"

"Must have, you can't have a holiday without it . . . Did it remind you of your mother's meals?"

Rose regretted the reference immediately. It'd been a lovely day and she usually avoided the troubling subject.

"I have only a slight recollection of even her. I know her maiden name was Moldari, Italian enough, but I don't remember anything about our meals. I don't even remember being in China! Your family has so many interesting stories—I wish I had some memories to share."

"We'll make our own," Rose said, scooting even closer to him on the seat of his Nash. She changed the subject. "My family's a bit loud, don't you think?"

"No one will ever call them pretentious! Actually, once I realized Dante and Ernie weren't really going to duke it out across the table I enjoyed the dynamics."

"I'm proud of you, John, although you were a bit unmanly declining the blackbird's head. That's the tastiest part!"

"I didn't see you digging in, Wonder Woman."

"I know. I'm all talk. Their bones are too tiny and I can't stand picking out the buckshot with my tongue. I tried once. Tore the head off with my mouth like a peasant, truly gross! You made a prudent choice.

But I admired you standing your ground in the conversation. You disarmed them by being soft-spoken. They try to win arguments with volume. Notice the picture hanging over the sofa?"

"I was afraid to ask. I thought it might be a ritual for a dead relative."

"It's FDR. Been that way ever since his speech to Congress after Pearl Harbor. We sat around the radio listening, and Momma became furious when she realized he was breaking his promise to keep us out of the war. She turned his picture against the wall and it's been like that ever since. She thinks war is always wrong, and insists on keeping it that way to remind us."

"She seems strong-willed."

"I know no one stronger."

" Was my response about converting okay?"

"Perfect. Did you really mean it?"

"Absolutely, I'd become a Buddhist for us to marry so Catholic is no big deal. Besides, it's about time. However did my Italian mother became Presbyterian? There must have been tremors in the Vatican when she converted—my father must have been one persuasive preacher."

Rose expressed her love for John passionately. (Understandable for a descendant of Torquato Tasso, an infamous and intemperate sixteenth-century poet from Sorrento whose intensity led to confinement in an insane asylum.) The power of her feelings allowed her to overlook John's quirks, most notably his unusual shyness, his disdain for physicians, and his odd amnesia.

She was cautious and skeptical at first, but she came to understand and gauge it relatively unimportant given the breadth of her love. It seemed almost as if it made her nearly perfect man more attractive, like a hero in a dime store novel whose one flaw adds an intriguing aura of mystery. One memorable evening at Spark's Steakhouse in midtown Manhattan, John candidly discussed his memory problems.

"I don't quite understand why you can't remember," Rose had asked, and John, ever the teacher, did his best to explain.

"Memory is the cognitive ability to register and store data gathered through sensory input for access and output on demand. It's effortless for most everyone when dealing with short-term matters using sensory memory, like viewing a flame and recognizing fire and its heat, or hearing a certain noise and understanding a door was being shut. I don't have difficulties in that regard anymore, even if it also requires using long-term memory since I relearned the basics fairly easily. It's as if that's embedded in my senses."

"Long-term memory being ?"

"It's the ability to retain and recall far greater amounts of information, what's been accumulated over much longer periods of time, for most extending throughout one's entire lifetime."

"Like knowing the color of the sky is blue or in your example, remembering fire is associated with heat based on past sensory experiences?"

"Exactly. My problem stems from some defect in a sub-system of the brain's long-term memory retrieval system caused by an accident. The flaw interferes with my ability to recall non-sensory information even though it's lodged firmly somewhere in my subconscious. I know it's there, because otherwise unexplainable and recurring data used to be released involuntarily in my dreams regularly, and also while I was awake, in something like visions coming on randomly and without context."

"Whoa, slow down."

"Okay. Well, I remember very little of my past before roughly late 1946, except for some details of my work on the Manhattan Project—some of which I regained rather quickly. I suspect those memories were more engrained and accessible because they're intertwined with scientific knowledge, grounded in mathematical reasoning and logic, fundamental processes less subject to distortion because they lack an emotional component.

By contrast, I've had to be told about my prior personal life and even then I'm not sure I actually remember it even now. It's more like viewing a photograph and thinking you remember the event although you really only remember seeing the depiction before . . . Is that confusing?"

"A little, but it's intriguing. Tell me about those visions you say you used to have while you were awake."

"Vivid incidents used to pop into my mind at random times for no discernible reason and they'd disappear as quickly as they came on, before I could anayze them and piece together their meaning. It's like going into a theater and not knowing what's playing. Then, after watching the middle of the film for two minutes you walk out. You're aware of what you saw, but you can't put the scene into any meaningful context."

"So you know what you saw, but not what it means."

"Essentially, although I knew it was personally significant in some way, like a déjà vu experience with visions apparently quite troubling and unpleasant."

"You said 'used to' pop into your mind."

"Right, before I finished treating with a government psychiatrist, a doctor named Edmund Wright."

"You said 'apparently' unpleasant, don't you remember them even now?"

"I also lost those bad memories when I was cured, so I only know what Dr. Wright told me before my discharge: He said they were strange, intense, inexplicable events, like fleeing and being injured and being . . . being involved with unknown individuals in a variety of unpleasant ways. Really, it sounded like the dreams were as vague and ambiguous as many Freud reported. Wright told me about them very generally in case they recurred." Withdrawing a well-worn card from his wallet, he handed it to Rose. "He gave me this so I could call him for further treatment if it ever became a problem again." The card read "Dr. Edmund Wright, Falls Church, Virginia, Olympic (OL) 658-3388."

"I haven't felt any need and honestly can't imagine I'd ever call him. I'm through with doctors. I've wasted enough time with them and am overdue to make up that lost time and look forward, like to *our* life together."

"I suppose I understand that, but what about this accident? Are they certain it's the cause? I mean, is it possible it's somehow congenital?"

"My darling, subtle Rose . . . No, don't protest, I love you for it! It's definitely not congenital so you can be sure our children will be safe! My amnesia is due to trauma and chemical exposure. I lived a normal life until an experiment went bad in Los Alamos."

"What kind of experiment?"

"I don't know the details except that it happened near the end of the war and I was the lone survivor. It's classified top-secret so I wasn't told much else."

"But if you were injured surely someone had to tell you . . . " John reached out and squeezed her hands. "Rose, sweetheart, top-secret means top-secret and I haven't held a security clearance since the Project. They can't tell me any of it until it's declassified. That's just how it is, how I had to know it would have been when I signed up for Manhattan. I'm just grateful they helped me recover."

"It doesn't seem right. I mean, they were responsible somehow! Maybe if they told you exactly what happened you might . . . "

"I could have died, but they saved my life and brought me through a difficult recovery and rehabilitated me. I owe them more than I can repay, and at least I learned how I came to have these memory gaps so I can move forward with my life.

I'm told it involved exposure to a large number of unusual chemicals, hardly an unheard of risk for a scientist. The exposure damaged my medial temporal lobe, probably the amygdala and the midline diencephalic region as well, also likely the mammillary bodies of the hypothalamus."

"What does that mean in plain English?"

"Just that chemicals damaged various parts of my brain. Precisely which and the mechanics of the damage couldn't be determined without an autopsy. I firmly rejected any suggestion they do one immediately to be more precise!"

"John, I . . . "

"It's all right Rose, you can laugh, and now I can joke about it too. Stop, don't get all teary-eyed on me. It's not that bad, not something we can't overcome together."

John told Rose he'd been rushed into emergency treatment at a military hospital in Virginia, the best facility available, where he'd been treated for nearly three years. During his treatment he'd experienced persistent, random dreams and visions until they'd finally disappeared and he'd been cured. He'd recaptured all of his scientific knowledge and expertise and intellectual proficiency, and although selective, his post treatment memory was outstanding. The government helped him obtain a doctorate from Columbia, largely due to his exceptional work on the Manhattan Project, and it helped him secure his position there as a Professor of Physics.

John told Rose what he understood of his upbringing as the only child of Presbyterian missionary parents killed in China: He'd been raised and homeschooled overseas except for attending high school at a military academy in Lake Geneva, Wisconsin; he'd studied at West Virginia University, graduating in 1942, with a degree in physics before working on the Project as an assistant to General Leslie Groves; and he'd been an eye witness to both the Trinity experiment and the bombing of Hiroshima.

Rose had asked about relatives. "None that are living, and all my friends postdate my discharge. I undoubtedly had friends in China and at West Virginia, but who knows? Honestly, I've been told I was shy and something of a loner, so combing through records of people to find 'friends' seemed pointless. Then too, once I became involved in the Project we were up on the Hill in New Mexico, isolated from the world."

"Surely you had time there when you socialized and may have shared something of your past."

"Perhaps, but not likely enough to be helpful. Scientists are a boring and obsessive lot who discuss esoteric concepts easily, but not personal lives and backgrounds. Remember too, that Manhattan required working six plus days a week on an accelerated schedule racing against the Germans. After leaving there I spent more than three years in a hospital while the others moved on so I lost track of all of them. I lost my clearance and . . . and I fell far behind . . . "

Coming around the table, Rose hugged John and kissed his neck. He'd leaned back and smiled. "I'll be all right, sweet Rose."

She'd whispered in his ear, "I love you John. We'll make up for it with new memories, enough to fill more than one lifetime." Loving

John for the purity and goodness of his spirit, of which she was absolutely certain, she didn't believe it possible anything she might some day learn of his past could tarnish his endearing essence.

One thing John hadn't told Rose before proposing was that he had access to a large amount of money. With her family's obsession, it took some time for her to accept the idea that they'd be wealthy. "How much?" she'd asked.

"To be perfectly honest, I've never known or cared since it's invested and safe and growing and my trustee deposits whatever I need in my bank account when I need it. He says it's adequate to last well through our grandchildren's lifetimes unless we become reckless spendthrifts!"

"The Trustee must know something of your background?"

"No, he's only a corporate fiduciary, an investment banker who manages assets allocated according to sealed court instructions. Apparently the Trust prohibits me from investing any of it myself. Anyway, it's only money."

"Goodness, John, I had no idea your father was rich, I mean for a missionary . . . I . . . how . . . Why didn't you tell me sooner?"

"Rose, I don't think it's from my father. It has to be the government assisting me because of the accident. All of the records are sealed by a court and the government is the only one I know who could do that. It's likely part of a fund for victims of unusual types of government service. That would explain why it's so large. It's the government charitably taking care of its own, another reason to be grateful and not push for irrelevant details. The money will make our life together a little easier. Please, don't change your mind because I have too much money!"

She'd playfully hit him with her purse and hugged him. "I always like when they say 'for richer or poorer.' I'll still marry you, Mr. Rockefeller, but you have to promise you won't ever let my family know you're wealthy. I'd never hear the end of it. " John agreed and he never did.

John converted and they married. Buoyed by Rose's love, he underwent a notable transformation as his shyness receded. He no longer lectured from carefully prepared and detailed notes. Instead, he began speaking freely away from the security behind a podium. He paced back and forth rapidly across the lecture hall stage, using Socratic give and take, mixing history and humanities with science, actually looking students in the eye while lecturing, arguing with enthusiasm and encouraging them—professors trying to emulate his teaching transformation sat through his classes. And whenever in Hazleton at the Tassi home, he proved able to out-eat and out-argue the Tassi men. He listened calmly to their jibes and shed them like rain. He never let them know he recognized some truth in such as Dante's oft used dismissive comment: "He's a professor, for Christ's sake, what the hell does he know?" Indeed, he realized there was far too much he didn't know.

Soon after their marriage, the Redfords moved into The Dakota, an imposing residential building off of Central Park West. Their son, Absalom John Redford ("Abe"), arrived in 1950, and they began the delightful task of filling up their large home.

2.

Made Flesh Again After Death

Fairfax County, Virginia, 1946

When Five first spoke it thrilled Dr. Edmund Wright, even if only done by habit without comprehension. Seven additional months of diligent work would be needed until they reached their first substantial breakthrough. It came while they prepared to watch *Serving through Science*, a weekly television program Wright had introduced into their therapy sessions.

Wright turned the TV on early and a children's show was playing. He rose to turn it off, but Five shouted, "Leave it!" Shocked, he froze, waiting for him to speak again and then Five said simply, "That's a dragon."

"Yes, yes it is. It's Kukla, Fran and Ollie, and the dragon is named Oliver J. Dragon."

"Like dragons . . . talk later."

"No, no, let's talk now! This is a great development, please . . . "

"Later," he repeated, focusing on the show. After it ended, he moved to a seat near the window and stared looking out. "Need think," he muttered, shutting everything out, trying to make sense of his existence. The following day he spoke at length and proved to be soft-spoken and stoic. "Don't know who be or where from or why here. Hope know, but maybe no find. No want bad night in head. I know you help, thank."

Wright explained as well as he could, but Five lacked vocabulary and context. Concepts like treatment, government, war, family, even basic concepts of right and wrong, were often confusing. Wright tried reading to him, but it proceeded too slowly to be productive since Five misunderstood too much and his vocabulary was too limited. Frustrated, he began engaging in self-destructive behavior, gouging his skin, punching his hands into walls, chewing his nails to the quick, and once even deliberately falling while running. It seemed pain triggered a greater degree of awareness, forcing Wright into a delicate balancing act—he needed to sedate Five periodically to reduce the risk of serious injury even while dulling his senses.

Dreams also slowed his restoration. He cried out in his sleep in both distress and joy, but the source of his outburst remained locked away and unexpressed. They tried to discuss his dreams, even attempted sketching them, as Five turned out to be artistic, but he became easily distracted: He'd suddenly lose focus and stop to gaze at ordinary objects as if they were wondrous things, seemingly transfixed by such as a clear, glass coffee cup.

While sketching a dream's image one morning, Five suddenly flung the pencil aside, looked around, fingered his clothing, and swiveled about wildly while speaking rapidly in what they eventually determined was classical Latin. He became angry at Wright for not understanding him, pointed to his clothing and exclaimed, *"Quid est in inferno!" What the hell is this?* Then, *"Quid hic ixuta me redire cupio?" Why are you keeping me here when I long to return home?*

He became combative, refused food and drink, and had to be restrained, only calming down when made to understand otherwise he'd be tied down and fed through a tube. After he continued speaking exclusively in Latin for four days, Wright hired a translator for the obsolete language.

As overseer of the facility and one of those responsible for Five's condition, Brant Frey followed his treatment closely. When he read Wright's account of the treatment plan, he guffawed, laughing so hard he had to wipe his eyes. *Good God,* he thought, *that wacky, tabacky, fucking shrink, our Haaavaard trained psychiatrist, is as loony as his patient. Nutcase spews out a few foreign words and he hires a goddamned translator from Georgetown who believes the nutjob's claim to be from ancient Rome "carries many hallmarks of authenticity." Are they all crazy?*

The actual transcript of Professor Dante Franceschini's interview made the matter appear less hilarious. The reknowned scholar thought Five's account remarkable, and he'd marveled at his flawless use of the ancient language and his apparent historical accuracy.

Franceschini began by introducing himself and explaining as best he could where and when they were, and assuring Five he had no enemies nearby, only friends anxious to help. He understood they were healers anxious to determine who he was and how he'd come to be there, and after accommodations were reached, his restraints were removed. Then Five spoke easily and deliberately throughout five sessions which lasted over the course of a week.

"Quintus Tullius Varo sicut et cognitus sum. Libet occurrere grammaticus homo," he began in a strong and distinctive voice captured on a wire recording, not sounding at all like Five. *"My name is Quintus Tullius Varo. It pleases me to meet a literate man."* Varo then recounted the story of a life unlike any in the twentieth century.

"Addressing me as Five is inappropriate since I'm generally known as Varo, although sometimes I am also called 'Dreamer,' although not always fondly. I am forty-eight years of age, having been born on . . . "

"Slower please, Varo," interrupted the Professor; "dates are more difficult for me. Did you say *Dies Saturni, xxv Julius XLIV?*"

"Yes, *Saturday, July 25, 44.*"

"Do you have any idea of today's date?"

"No. The last date I'm certain of was April 18, 93. I remember it because I'd been preparing for a court appearance on April 27. Last I recall, it was just past dawn and I was outside Tibur walking along the river Anio, watching it flow rapidly near its descent from the falls. I recall reflecting upon its ultimate destination in Rome, thinking how dramatic the contrast between the hearty flow near my villa and the dying trickle from Aqua Appia as it refills the Aventine baths in that noisy and overburdened city. Yet I felt myself unburdened, exhilarated and joyous being held in nature's grasp despite my dreary dispute with cowardly Frontinus. I heard some foreign sound and turned toward it, and then all my thoughts vanished and I found myself here. I see you're puzzled, Dante. Perhaps I should start nearer my beginnings ? All right then.

I spent my childhood in Puteoli, the principal port of Campani, where we lived in a flat overlooking the Bay. My father kept a store below us and rented rooms above to freemen who worked for him whenever he sailed to replenish his stock, which seemed like always to a child missing his strong presence. We were plebeians, but well-off due to father's trade and gift for bargaining. He imported Corinthian bronze and Alexandrian tapestries, and he dealt large shipments of Egyptian corn, nearly priceless whenever local crops failed, which happened quite often then. As with most fathers, he wanted me to adopt his trade, so at eight years of age I accompanied him to Alexandria. As a native Campanian with Sabine roots, I confess to being rebellious and questioning, and after that voyage I realized there were not enough denarii in the Empire to convince me to spend my life on the unruly Sea.

Father disliked religion and we rarely sacrificed, but he preceded every business journey with an offering of incense and wine to Hercules, the god of commerce. Our round trip to Alexandria took eighteen days and I spent it observing, but also feeling ill, bored or terrified while pretending enthusiasm for his sake. He suspected this, and it likely made my career choice more palatable. My father knew unenthusiastic labor yields mediocre results. Still, you need to know of the trip to know of Varo since its lessons have guided me throughout my life.

I was enthralled watching the multi-colored Sea rise up to meet the dawn's first piercing rays of light, revealing dark-skinned moors attired in white jallabiya robes with checkered hattahs on their heads casting their nets off of small papyrus reed boats and waving to us on our massive vessel. That night, I lay on deck looking up at the countless expanse of stars, trying to understand what gave me such pause. Sometime after I reached maturity, I understood—We Romans mastered transportation and controlled the world, allowing us to cross the Sea and return quickly with enormous quantities of food and goods, yet our purpose and means mirrored that of Moors catching fish with boats and nets since before the invention of the wheel. How many generations saw the very same break of dawn and expanse of night sky during that time? How many more would experience it before we improved upon the task perhaps by doing it only somewhat more swiftly? What more proof is needed that human life and achievement is a fleeting, meaningless pinpoint in the expansive scope of all things? I believed thereafter that existence required a less temporal reality for its validation, grounded in spirituality I contend, and I have continued searching for it ever since.

I admit to being an unusual man as many have noted. Yet, we can only be true to ourselves, can only meet our own expectations. Do I digress too much? Is this adequately helpful? All right, then I'll continue.

We encountered an unseasonable, great storm on our return and would likely have capsized but for the ballast of our enormous load of grain. Curiosity drew me topside during the maelstrom, when but for an unseen hand propelling me into the fitting, I would have been swept overboard to my doom. Truth is truth, so I tell you that I dreamt that evening and met my savior who assured me I would never be alone. That lovely, angelic presence has watched over and guided me ever since, protecting me when she could and comforting me through my trials and my greatest sorrow, the untimely loss of my beloved Atia. She reassures me I will ultimately understand our purpose, that such is Jupiter's plan for me. She tells me even now that this present tribulation is also a necessary part of my journey.

Relaxing with my father on the deck on one moonlit night, I decided to share my thoughts and vision with him despite the risk of ridicule, for he could be blunt and straightforward when addressing impractical matters. He listened intently and looked back into my eyes, remaining silent for a long time until he finally hung his head in thought. Eventually, he looked up and took my hands in his. He said, 'Varo, my son, you will be an honest man I am certain, but you will always be a dreamer. I know not what that portends for you, except that you must not work at my trade. I could command otherwise, but to what end? Should we both be miserable? My great-great-grandfather is said to have also been a man of consuming visions, although I confess I know not its impact upon him. Yet it is clearly what you must endure, just as money and wealth and security are what direct your simple father. Gods do what they will with us and why I do not know. Each day I only know how little I truly understand.'

I squeezed my father's hands in gratitude and he responded with an act wholly out of character. He reached into his woolen undertunic and withdrew a silver tetradrachm given him by his own father, a three-hundred year old coin bearing the image of Alexander the Great, a treasure I had long admired. Tears filled my eyes as he placed it in my hand and told me, 'My father gave me this for good fortune, and now I give it to you, my firstborn, my dreamer. Wherever your dreams lead you, may good fortune follow.' His gesture moved me and the coin has remained with me always, until I found myself in this strange place after my world vanished."

As Varo, Five continued his account of the Roman's life through many more hours of translation until his life's story was fully told. He awoke the morning of the day after the final session, as if it had never happened, with no recollection of the episode, and speaking exclusively in English once again.

Franceschini pled with Wright. "Let me show the transcripts to one of our Roman scholars, someone better able . . ."

"Can't do it. I asked and they refused."

"If I can make a copy or take notes I'll research it myself."

"Sorry, Professor. I suggested that too, but they said no."

"Why not? Good lord, how could this have anything to do with national security?"

"I don't know, but they won't chance it. Besides, they don't see the point. They believe he's demented and details are unimportant if he actually believes he's from the first century. They're probably right that pursuing it won't lead to his actual identity."

"We can't stop now! Who knows what we might learn? It makes me wonder how much your superiors actually care about helping him."

Wright knew the professor hit upon it. Frey didn't care about Five's recovery. He'd approved the translator to pacify him, believing nothing would come from it. Still, Wright knew he had to continue working through Frey. If he went over his head he'd be dismissed and any chance for Five's recovery would be greatly diminished.

Psychosis was a simple answer, and Wright used it. "I think he's delusional, believing he's an ancient Roman trapped in a twentieth-century body. Whatever, there's nothing else for you to do."

"My God, man, don't give up so easily! This is an incredible example of . . . "

"Sorry, Professor, I did what I could. I appreciate your help and I'll call you if he reverts to Latin. Meanwhile, I know you'll be tempted to discuss his case, but my superiors specifically instructed me to tell you they'll prosecute if you breach your confidentiality agreement. They're very adamant about that."

Running out of ideas, Wright set aside his skepticism and decided to try hypnosis, knowing an international authority and one of its most reknowned proponents practiced in nearby Charlottesville.

Born in Canada in 1920, Graham Steadman Cowell possessed a brilliant mind honed to perfection through voracious study. During a bed-ridden childhood, he'd read every book within reach, most provided by a Scottish lawyer father who'd taught him to appreciate disciplined research and study. He'd inherited his mother's extensive interest in theosophy, speculation about the nature of the soul based upon insight into the nature of God, along with her fascination with paranormal phenomena.

He'd earned degrees in biochemistry and medicine from the University of Edinburgh, graduating at the top of each class. Thereafter, he held a series of positions in various hospitals as his interests led him from the study of psychosomatic illnesses to researching the interplay of memory, repressed thought, and induced recall. He experimented with psychedelic drugs, including LSD and mescaline, as part of his research, and he claimed they'd imparted unmatched serenity and unique insight.

Cowell was tall and thin, with graying dark hair combed into a high wave, and he wore oversized dark-rimmed glasses which rested atop a long, beak-like nose. He had thin and narrow lips, and he always dressed impeccably, usually in a three-piece vested suit. He reminded one of a fashionable stork, but his intense gaze and the power of his deep, deliberate, and clipped voice dispelled this initial impression. His patrician air intimidated most, and he was a serious and blunt man. Articulate, charismatic, and determined, he seemed destined for greatness.

By 1945, Cowell had spearheaded a worldwide effort to secure medical acceptance for past life regression, a practice of using hypnosis to recover what proponents believed to be memories of past lives. Wright didn't believe the Varo tale meant that Five was living another incarnation, rather he thought most likely it stemmed from a type of cryptomesia, perhaps from having once been a historian, or an avid student of Latin and ancient Rome. Regardless, he found himself floundering, required help, and had exhausted every conventional treatment method he could find. And he believed Cowell would find the uncommon case intriguing and challenging enough to warrant his attention.

Critics begrudgingly acknowledged the rigor of Cowell's methods, but some ridiculed his work because he would not be dissuaded from a logical conclusion no matter how unorthodox it appeared. He knew that many recollections released under hypnosis could be attributed to cryptomesia or to confabulation: cryptomesia being the recounting of information once learned but forgotten and recalled from the unconscious mind as if a completely new thought; and confabulation being the presentation of false information as true due to the proponent's steadfast belief in its veracity. Yet in some instances, he found that memories couldn't be explained by either, and if believing they weren't false or distorted, he had no problem accepting reincarnation as a logical and acceptable answer.

The extent of theological and philosophical support Cowell found for reincarnation, literally "being made flesh again after death," was overwhelming, including recognition of the concept in virtually every human culture throughout history. As a well-trained biochemist, Cowell knew that while science could not determine how personality and consciousness could migrate from one body to another, neither could science find a means of disproving the possibility.

Cowell held a tenured position in the University of Virginia Department of Psychiatry, where he'd established the world's only academic department dedicated to the study of prior life memories and paranormal phenomena. There he met with Wright.

"Did you have a chance to review the agreement I sent?"

"I did. I ran it by counsel and have a green light if I want to take on the work. But tell me, why should I sign something exposing me to potential prosecution? Besides, it's quite a stretch to envision how my services might relate to national security issues."

"That's one reason I wanted to meet and explain the situation. I for one never thought I'd end up in security work myself—life is nothing if not twists and turns, hey Doctor?"

"Indeed, Dr. Wright, indeed."

"I've been a psychiatrist for eight years and I'll never see another patient like this no matter how long I practice. He served his country well on the Manhattan Project, a top-secret matter if ever there was one, but he's paid a great price for his service. Well, the thing is that finally we're making real progress, finally communicating with each other, but imagine, he went from not speaking, to speaking fractured and childish English, then to speaking only ancient Latin, and now again to speaking solely English."

"An American?"

"As apple pie, and a formally brilliant scientist."

"You say he spoke Latin which hasn't been used colloquially for fifteen hundred years? Are you certain it wasn't one of a hundred variants of languages with Latin roots?"

"We compared his speech with many of them, some so remote they're only found in isolated mountain towns in Romania. A Latin scholar confirmed it and then elicited a lengthy tale of an ancient lifetime told entirely in Latin."

"Hmmm, about this agreement, why should I subject myself to it?"

"I'm also a civilian, and I've had a similar agreement for years. It's only a minor variation of the patient-physician confidentiality obligation, and it may sound corny, but it's a small price to pay to keep us safe, loose lips and all of that."

"Whatever does it have to do with intelligence or the CIA?"

"His condition was caused by an ultra top-secret experiment that went wrong, so no one knows what he could reveal unwittingly once he opens up."

"A secret experiment caused an American scientist to lose his identity and speak Latin?"

"That's the meat of it."

"Very strange, well, I do admit it's intriguing, no doubt not an everyday opportunity. I don't suppose it could hurt. And you say I can terminate the arrangement if it becomes uncomfortable?"

"Absolutely. You can terminate it anytime without further obligation. Really, please help. It's far beyond my skill set. I need someone like you who can . . . "

"Your flattery is wasted on me, Wright. I'm not here because of my ego. I agreed to this meeting because I was directed to be here."

"I thought you'd find this case interesting. I never thought . . . "

"Don't be defensive. This has nothing to do with you, you're probably a fine psychiatrist. May I be candid?"

"Of course, what's said between us stays . . . "

"Good. Well, the fact is that UVA has grants with Defense since they're keen on the military use of hypnosis and mind-control. So, I couldn't jeopardize our funding by refusing to meet. Regardless, it's interesting and I'll help. But there are problems with your approach. Let's take them one at a time, shall we?

First, there's the matter of hypnosis itself, which I've been trying to restrict in my regimine, largely because of the risk of contamination. I've found that past life memories are more reliable if induced according to a well-considered scientific protocol, rather than by verbal cues and questions that could easily suggest false memories. So, although I use a modified version of Hull's method, even my finest effort could contaminate a sample. That means that first I need to be certain it's essential, so give me a rundown."

Wright detailed the information available to him while Cowell sat back smoking his pipe. He never interrupted, merely waved his free hand back and forth from time to time, impatiently prodding Wright to speak more rapidly.

He absorbed everything. "Intriguing, and what have you learned from his co-workers on the Manhattan Project?"

"I can't speak to them because of national security concerns."

"Good God, man, do they think you're a magician? They haven't given you much to work with, have they? On the other hand, knowing so little makes this an unusual case since there's very little risk of contamination. So, hypnosis should work.

All right then, I'm onboard with these ground rules: first, as to collaboration, you need to understand I must be alone with the patient without a chance of your presence tainting his recall."

"Graham, I've been struggling with his problems for a long time. I absolutely need to be there. I can tell you whenever . . . "

"Sorry, Wright, I won't relent on the point. Your emotional involvement is evident and could be problematic. Don't worry, I value your input and I'll wire record our sessions. At the appropriate time you'll hear everything we discuss.

In the meantime don't tell him anything other than I'll be acting as a consulting psychiatrist, agreed?"

"What choice do I have? When can you begin?"

"Just one more thing. The sessions have to be offsite, obviously. Security is up to you, but it has to be a controlled, neutral and fresh setting, unrelated to his confinement."

"That can be arranged. I'll need a week."

"Let's say two weeks from Tuesday at seven sharp."

They met in a nondescript office complex and Wright introduced Cowell as a specialist in amnesia. Cowell began by giving Five a thorough physical examination, and he spent a considerable time probing the four-inch recessed birthmark on the inside of his left bicep. Cowell believed birthmarks and scars were not always random but sometimes could be linked to past life memories.

In inducing hypnosis, Cowell spoke in a slow and steady monotone, creating a soothing rhythm. He began by adopting a gentle demeanor when introduced, and by consistently lowering the tone of their conversation until the patient ended up reclining at a forty-five degree angle on a comfortable couch. He did it so masterfully that he could induce a full hypnotic state within three minutes of reaching the couch. He proved his skill to skeptics once by delivering a patient through open-heart surgery without using anesthesia.

The most challenging aspect of the process was constructing a means of unloosing true memories while avoiding contaminated or false information. Cowell believed memories resided in select brain cells so that he needed to find the stimulus for only that particular cell to unlock the genuine memory storehouse. The artful trick was identifying the right key.

In reviewing Wright's work, Cowell noted an obvious error he needed to work around: while Wright had been appropriate and professional, he'd attempted to use his pre-existing relationship with Five as a platform allowing increased trust and candor. Cowell felt that guaranteed inaccurate results since the subject would attempt to meet his expectations in an attempt to sustain their emotional connection. So he decided to approach Five, an innocent and wide-eyed subject, on a far different and more basic level, one rooted in childhood. He knew maturity modulated behavior and mandated convention, while before it everyone went through a period of naïve, blunt, and forthright honesty. He thought if he could tap into Five's childhood subconscious, he could coax out his uninhibited essence. So he'd approach him as if they were two children meeting for the first time.

Heightening the pitch of his deep voice and speaking in a soft, gentle and simple manner, Cowell said, "Hi, I'm glad we can be alone to play together. My best friends call me Hammie. Do they really call you Five? That sounds like a number instead of a name. What would you like me to call you? . . Can't you hear me? . . .Won't you tell me your name, please? Let's be friends . . . If we're friends we can play together and share things. Everyone likes to play. Don't you want to play with me?"

Meeting silence, Cowell continued speaking like a child and asking repetitive questions for more than an hour, during which time Five only sighed in response. After that, Cowell sang a child's song, adding an appropriate lisp and giggle each time he finished its refrain. "The itsy bitsy spider climbed up the waterspout, down came the rain and washed the spider out, out came the sun and dried up all the rain, so the itsy bitsy spider climbed up the spout again."

 Cowell repeated it several times over, creating a persistent and compelling rhythm. Then he stopped abruptly and asked, "Do you like secrets? I do. I have lots of them, and I'll tell you my very best if you tell me yours. It'll be fun! Please, if you don't talk to me I'll feel all alone, and who wants that? Yuck! We all need friends to share with. My stomach hurts when I don't have friends to share with and I feel all alone. It makes me so sad. Sometimes it even makes me cry."

After a long period of silence, Five's eyes moistened. He crossed his arms across his chest and began rocking back and forth. When he stopped, he placed his palms on his knees, looked up at Cowell and said, "You're nice, and I'd like to be your friend. But I'm not like other kids, really, not at all. I'm not nice."

"Sure you are. We all have the same . . . "

"No, I'm different. You won't want to be friends with me."

"Sure I will."

"But it's bad. I'm not even sure who I am or which secret to tell you. I have so many."

Listening to Five, Cowell thought of multiple personality disorder (MPS), a condition caused by trauma too painful to assimilate into one's consciousness. MPS shows itself in the adoption of a number of separate personalities, each with distinct memories struggling for control, and each with particular gestures and mannerisms. Under hypnosis, the different identities often switch and respond uniquely to the therapist's requests, competing for attention. It seemed a possible explanation for the rendition of being an ancient Roman, but Five lacked the compulsions and rituals, eating disorders and other symptoms usually associated with MPS.

"How many of you are there? Which of you want to be friends with me?"

"You don't understand. It's not like that," Five replied, "there's only one of me, but I'm really different sometimes. It's like I remember doing different things at many different times, but they're all mixed up in my head. I even say things I don't understand, like big words from old people. But sometimes I know what they mean since I'm the one saying them. Does that sound crazy?"

Perhaps schizophrenic, thought Cowell. "No, not at all, it's different, but so what? I'm different, too. Once I stayed in my bed for two years and read books to pretend I was a different person doing things in places far away. That's one of my secrets, and it sounds like you too.

I think you should tell me the very first secret you can remember."

"That's easy, but it's not a nice one. It shows I'm bad."

"Friends share everything, even bad things, and more than anything else I want to be your friend."

"Why? You're nice. I'll bet you have lots of friends."

"I need one really good friend to talk to since it makes me feel better when I share things. It's funny, but lots of times I find out my friends have done the same things I have! We all make mistakes! But we learn from the bad things and try not to do them again. You're nice, I can see that. Tell me your bad secret, I won't tell anyone else. It'll be just between us. I know it'll make you feel better cuz sharing always helps!"

Five paused for a long while until he blurted out, "I had a friend I liked, really a friend I loved. I loved her more than anything. She was pretty and sweet and kind. She seemed like an angel . . . but . . . How could I? She looked right in my eyes . . . she wanted to . . . but I-I-I hurt her. How could I do that? After that no one will ever think I'm nice again. No one wants to be friends with someone who hurts people."

"I still want to be your friend. It's all right. Help me understand. Tell me who you hurt."

"Not just hurt . . . killed." He pointed to the birthmark on the inside of his left bicep. "They hurt me here first . . . It happened a long time ago but I'll always remember it."

The two spoke for hours that day, and for hours more during six additional sessions. Numerous, unrelated events sprang from the subject's subconscious: he related details about a primitive life and the death of a young woman; he described events from a childhood in Wisconsin and a period of military service; he described a life in ancient Rome and a passionate love ended long ago but resumed centuries later; he described events in New Mexico and in Virginia. Some accounts were unbelievable and full of obscure information, impossible to verify. Others were credible, familiar and clearly accurate. Some accounts were riveting, some extraordinary, some heartwarming, and some described obvious criminal misconduct.

Although pressured into taking on the work, Cowell found it exhilarating, and when work captured his imagination and appealed to his penchant for the paranormal nothing pleased him more. But if some of these convincingly conveyed accounts were true, it placed him in a difficult, perhaps dangerous position.

Members of the CIA and possibly Wright as well, appeared to have engaged in serious criminal activity, while certain other accounts might be explainable only by reincarnation. Yet, it would require government resources to verify much of the information, and besides, how could he even mention reincarnation again without throwing another bone to his many critics?

He needed proof. Additionally, he needed to think through the implications of the confidentiality agreement and his risk of being prosecuted, as well as any possible impact on the government funding his program required. He had to consider it all carefully and thoroughly, remaining scientific and prudent.

He retained everything the subject revealed in wire recordings produced during their sessions, while the subject left with no recollection of what he'd revealed under hypnosis. Cowell had refused to share anything of substance with Wright initially. He'd been concerned he could be part of the criminal misconduct despite his obvious love for the patient. Ultimately, he concluded that while Wright may have suspected something about the truth of Five's mistreatment, he wasn't likely culpable. And if his instincts about him were correct, they might be able to work together to gather the information needed to verify Five's disclosures.

After his final, lengthy session with Five, Cowell met with an expectant and anxious Wright. "Let's make ourselves comfortable while I share my impressions and preliminary conclusions. I'd like to see if we can agree what needs be done with this extraordinary young man."

3.

Angelic Visions

New York City, 1961

By his fortieth birthday, John Redford had achieved more than most men aspire to in a lifetime. He'd married an intelligent, attentive woman, fathered five precocious children and enjoyed the company of caring and interesting friends. He benefited from a large trust fund and his family wanted for nothing while living comfortably in the world's most exciting city. He taught physics at Columbia and could be satisfied knowing he'd served his country with his work on the Manhattan Project. Yet, he became unsettled and depressed when the disturbing dreams and visions he'd managed to suppress for a decade recurred. Ironically they started up again at his favorite place on earth, Yankee Stadium.

John tried to share his love of baseball with Rose. "Sweetheart, it's a microcosm of life! Every game has moments that matter only to a few, while certain games are considered momentous by millions. Sound decisions and timing are critical, and skill gained by untold hours of repetitive practice can sometimes overcome great physical advantage. A game's drama and conflict are sometimes resolved joyfully, but one might end with a painful loss—even the best players fail at bat nearly seven times out of ten—but there's always a chance for redemption in the next game or next at bat.

Blind luck may dictate the outcome of a contest, but regardless, precise records are kept of each game played. Those who do well are rewarded and the very best are memorialized, if deemed worthy, while the worst are disdained and quickly forgotten. It's a divine game!"

"Johnny, my man-child, I love your enthusiasm, but I'll take tennis for sport and opera for drama. Abe and Mark will share your obsession. What choice do they have with balls, gloves, caps, and pennants festooning their rooms already?"

"Wait until they see the house that Ruth built!"

"They might become Dodger fans."

"Better they be atheists!"

The gods smiled on Yankee fans in 1956: Mickey Mantle won the Triple Crown in batting, and the Yanks bested their cross-bridge rivals in the World Series. When these wondrous happenings first appeared possible, John's colleague, Michael Thomas, treated him to a front row seat as a birthday present for his thirty-fifth birthday.

Thomas, known as "Big Mike" by most due to a prodigious appetite that belied his average size, shared John's love for the Yankees, and the present was an annual event. A single play in the 1956 game guaranteed John would always remember the otherwise routine outing against the lowly Senators.

Billy Hunter, a shortstop from Punxsutawney, Pennsylvania, dove in the dirt to knock down a blazing shot bounding between him and the third baseman. Kneeling and arching his back, he threw a sidearm rocket cross-field, besting the batter by a foot. Applause erupted over the remarkable play and Hunter doffed his cap in acknowledgement, exposing thick, greased-back black hair.

Big Mike slapped John on the back exclaiming, "Wow, talk about slick!"

Slick! The word slammed into his head with explosive force. Feeling dizzy, thinking he might faint, John grabbed a railing to steady himself. His breathing became labored and he felt a chill. Plopping down, he closed his eyes and his mind searched for a face matching the provocative word. He imagined an oval face with a pointed nose and small eyes under thick black hair, but he couldn't quite identify it as Fritz "Slick" Retzling, his closest friend and neighbor throughout childhood. With his eyes shut, his thoughts drifted, and he pictured a small home with a rocker on its porch, he imagined bells chiming, he envisioned a steeple, the inside of a church, an altar, and the statue of a dragon. Then, just on the cusp of remembering his family home and nearby St. George Church, a familiar voice returned him to the ballpark.

"John . . . John, can you hear me?"

"Hey buddy, should I call a doctor?" asked a beer vendor.

"I-I'm all right."

"You look awful. You're pale and shaking, I should take you . . . "

"No! I'll be fine. I skipped breakfast so it's probably just low blood sugar." He knew his visions had reappeared, but he refused to share the problem. Knowing he suffered from unwelcome visions randomly popping into his mind could make even a friend question his stability.

The color returned to John's face and he broke into a grin. "I'm fine, only a little lightheaded."

"Are you sure? It'd be no problem if . . . "

"Ya, I'm sure. Hot dogs and beer will take care of it . . . Besides, we still have our bet: you absolutely cannot eat a hot dog every inning! Plus, we're only up by three so these bums could make a game of it yet."

"You're certain? I mean you looked . . . "

"I'm sure. Look at me man, handsome as ever, right? Just a passing thing. I'm fit as a fiddle."

The crisis passed and they ate through a sixteen to two drubbing, kept box scores and discussed post-season prospects. Preoccupied throughout the game, John welcomed the subway rattle which overcame all conversation on the trip home. He tried to focus and make sense of the word "slick," but he couldn't.

In the days that followed, additional visions assaulted him both in his sleep and during waking hours. Try as he might, he couldn't fit the wide-ranging episodic glimpses into a coherent whole. In one, he was barefoot on a beach, sensing the feel of sand between his toes as he skipped stones across grayish water that ran to the horizon. He wasn't alone, but he didn't know who stood beside him, only that they were childhood friends. But his friend was quite different than him, something like Huck Finn to his Tom Sawyer.

In another, he pictured himself watching an old newscast and being surprised that President Roosevelt looked like an old man vainly trying to duplicate his powerful iconic image, with his face tilted upward and a cigarette holder held between his lips and his chin thrust confidently outward. But Roosevelt looked frail, fatigued and weary, his face well-lined and his hair very thin and silvery white. He sensed having been only an arm's length away as Roosevelt made that pose sometime before, recalled thinking him unexpectedly old then too, although remembering his strong and reassuring voice.

One night he awoke bathed in sweat, feeling the imminence of death, sensing he sped forward in an aircraft about to crash, clenching his hands and anticipating the impact, all the while assaulted by a disgusting stench like the exposed innards of a slaughtered beast. He woke Rose when he'd cried out, but by then she'd become all too familiar with his nighttime visions.

In his most detailed and vivid dream, he saw himself resting on the edge of a garden pond, surrounded by plants and sculptures. He was in an open courtyard surrounded on three sides by columns, a structure he immediately recognized as a distinctive Roman style peristyle. Oil lamps flickered and the pond water rippled as it accepted the flow of water from a pitcher resting across the legs of a bare-breasted, sculpted woman. He knew her as a Danaid, one of fifty daughters of a king, each of whom had murdered one of fifty sons of his rival for revenge on the day they all married. In atonement, the daughters were sentenced to fill leaking jugs with water for all eternity.

His dream included a distinct feeling of warming as the early morning sun warded off the night's chill. The murmur of running water soothed him and added to his palpable feeling of fulfillment. He'd raised his face upward to the sky and murmured, "Praise You," in gratitude while a slave girl hurriedly shuffled toward him to place a swaddled bundle at his feet. He'd responded swiftly, with certainty borne out of fervent regard for his wife, his Atia. He knew her desire no matter the child's gender or health, so he'd picked the infant up in his arms and lifted him toward Jupiter, decreeing he should live.

The cinematic-style vision of an event in some ancient time mystified him. He had no idea of its genesis, believing he'd never been in Europe, let alone Italy or Rome. As always, he discussed it with Rose, hopeful she could lend some insight since Imperial Rome had been the focus of her master's thesis. "We talked about the Danaids during the Ancient Legends showing at the Museum, but we didn't discuss fathers accepting their children. I knew of the custom of course—Roman children were their father's property, and left to die if he wouldn't accept them—but I never wrote about it. Perhaps you heard about it in some class and Mary's birth triggered the vision."

"I don't think so. I never cared too much for history. I essentially studied science and mathematics to the exclusion of everything else. But the thing is, it wasn't like I'd merely heard about it. It wasn't an ordinary dream. I felt certain I was actually reliving it!"

"John, obviously you're not having ordinary dreams. They're recurring because of the past you've forgotten. You have to stop trying to piece everything together by yourself. You need to get some professional help or otherwise you'll continue flailing away and only frustrating yourself without getting closer to the truth."

Rose suggested, "Why not call Dr. Wright? Isn't that why you have the card with his number?"

"No, I won't call him or any other shrink! I might have a phobia, but I'm simply not. I spent enough time treating with him while my colleagues from Los Alamos moved on to greater accomplishments. Science is a young man's game, and I've lost too much time already. I wouldn't be just a college professor now if I hadn't . . . "

"At least let me call him. He said you should call if . . . "

"No! Obviously he didn't solve it then. I can't imagine why I should think he could now. I may be struggling, but I'm more alive now than I ever was after leaving him. Sooner or later something will shake loose a memory we can decipher. We're as capable as any shrink of making sense of this."

Rose and John spent intimate days together they called dates, when they focused only on each other and left all distractions behind. This often included brunch, a walk in Central Park, and browsing through the Metropolitan Museum of Art. In 1958, they spent one such Sunday viewing the exhibit, *Centuries of Angels in Art*.

"This is wonderful! It's amazing how angels have fascinated people for centuries. I've never taken them very seriously, maybe I'm too skeptical. Does that make me a bad Catholic or is it optional, like not eating meat on Fridays? Father Farrell said it's not a mortal sin if you eat less than a quarter pound of meat."

"You're not serious, Rose! He claims the size of the portion matters?"

"He says less than a quarter pound doesn't constitute the grievous matter needed for a mortal sin."

"Wouldn't it depend on the size of the sinner? I mean, isn't a quarter pound weightier, excuse the pun, for someone who's skinny? I wonder who watches the scales for God. Really, how silly, maybe I'll become a Presbyterian again . . . Don't hit me! I'm just kidding . . . This brochure is really interesting. Listen: "Angels appear in Genesis without wings when Jacob dreams of a ladder used to travel between heaven and earth, and Isaiah describes angels as having six wings, many eyes, and multiple faces. This divergence led theologians to conclude there were several types of angels. The topic was hotly debated, including how many angels could fit on the head of a pin, until 1259, when Aquinas postulated that angels are intellect without matter, able to assume shapes and appearances at will when interacting with mankind. This postulate is accepted by the vast majority of the world's most practiced religions, as well as many lesser belief systems.""

"Tell me honestly, do you think you've ever seen an angel?"

"Sure, whenever I look at you."

"You're a sweetie!"

"Rosie, you need to know, if you are considering taking on a different earthly appearance as part of your angelic duties, that I prefer a less traditional angel. Beautiful of course, but I don't care for that androgynous, boy-or-girl type of thing. I like a classical feminine shape, and," he bent over to whisper, "one with sensitive, soft, well-rounded breasts . . . and large is fine. But no wings, wings could definitely get in the way."

Rose wagged her finger playfully. "Johnny Redford, you have a one-track mind. Is that what I love about you?"

"Seriously, someone has to be really special to encounter an angel, like Gideon or those at Christ's tomb, or Mary when Gabriel told her she was pregnant. I think any interaction we'd have with angels would have to be more subtle, with them more difficult to recognize. The bible says something about not being aware . . . "

"Hebrews Thirteen says we 'entertain angels unaware,' which makes sense. If they were too apparent there wouldn't be room for skepticism since we'd all be intimidated, and goodbye free will. You're such a good man I'll wager you're guided by an angel unaware."

"Stop, you'll make me blush!"

"Good, mission accomplished. I like seeing you all hot and bothered—you still turn red after all these years!" Rose pulled him close and laid her head aside his chest. She whispered, "Speaking of hot and bothered and sensitive breasts and all, did you know that the angels in *Paradise Lost* ate and drank and had sex? Lots of passionate sex. I have a great idea. We'll find a hotel and discuss the matter intently. Times a wasting for child number four!"

John planted a brotherly kiss on her head. "Tell you what, we'll finish up here and cab home. Nanny can watch the kids a bit longer and we'll continue this discussion in our bedroom. My interest has definitely been piqued!"

"It's a deal, big boy."

They moved toward the end of the exhibit. "Item 226 is next," said Rose and she began reading aloud from the brochure. "Simply entitled *Angel*, this oil on canvas work by Abbott Handerson Thayer was completed in 1887. The artist's model for his visionary angel, was his eleven-year-old daughter, Mary, shown resplendent in a Grecian style gown. Thayer's work conveys a mystical feeling and symbolizes the lure of spirituality, its subject not being entirely of this world, but rather ethereally transcendent, a creature for all time, at once innocent and vulnerable, stalwart and poised. Thayer intended the portrait to express his belief that his artistic mission was a calling from God to show the attainment of spiritual truth . . ."

She realized she'd been reading to herself. John stood motionless ten feet away, staring open mouthed at a three-foot-high painting set in a gilded, gold-frame, displayed on an easel against a sky-blue velvet background. Rose joined him in examining the painting marked "Number 226, *Angel,* Abbott Handerson Thayer, 1887."

Thayer's angel wore a vaguely pink tinged, flowing, Grecian style gown dipping down from her shoulders to a fold above her bosom and a loose belt at mid-torso. Her smooth, pale arms were splayed downward in an inverted V as an apparently welcoming gesture. She wore two very large, feathery white wings which filled most of the canvas from her elbows upward, but for a small depiction of blue sky above her head. Her thick auburn hair flowed down smoothly, and tucked behind her head above her neck, with a few stray strands on the sides and at her forehead imparting a sense of reality. Her face was delicate, with high cheekbones and a cupid shaped, rosy mouth, and her wide, dark eyes looked away, as if she were pondering something captivating and otherworldly. The bottom tip of her ear, her slim, delicate neck, a slight expanse of her chest and her long arms from shoulder down, were naked and suggestive although she looked like a girl just become a woman.

Rose admired the artist's skill. She was impressed by the subtle contrast between the angel's pale complexion and her feathery wings, and by the skill shown in creating a haunting and complex mood using only a single, simple subject. Although appearing truly angelic and innocent, *Angel* also appeared adequately appealing and seductive enough to refocus a man's thoughts. Rose turned to John who looked mesmerized. "John . . . "

"Shhh, just a moment," he responded, unwilling even to turn his eyes away from the portrait. Rose felt rudely dismissed and she moved to a nearby bench where she sat sulking.

After an uncomfortably long time, others noticed John frozen in place. An attendant approached Rose and asked, "Excuse me madam, but is he all right? He hasn't moved for some time."

"He's an absent-minded professor who tends to obsess. There's time until closing isn't there? Thank you, but he's fine."

Thirty minutes passed until John averted his gaze and looked around as if startled. He spotted an angry Rose, but he disarmed her with his excitement. "It's amazing, Rosie! I know her! I know her face as well as my own! I can't place her, but I'm certain she's part of my past somehow."

"John, it's just a painting, not an exact likeness. The model was eleven years old in 1887, so she would have been forty-five when you were born. How could you know her? Maybe you knew her daughter or more likely just someone who resembles her."

"Rose, humor me, I know her! Let's hurry, this fits!"

"Hurry where? Did you forget about our assignation?"

"Our what?"

"Our heavy date, our sexual encounter, our love-making, what do you think I mean, you dope."

"It's early. We'll have time for everything! But first, let's go to the library and see what we can learn."

They did find time for both, but only their assignation proved satisfying. Nothing at the library shed any light on what became of Mary Thayer after modeling for her father in a subsequent painting, *My Children,* completed in 1897. After lovemaking, Rose rested her head on the crook of John's arm while he looked up at the ceiling wondering how this image fit into his past.

A book on nineteenth century art included a reproduction of the painting that John studied for hours without gaining any further insight. So he decided to visit the source.

"Thanks for keeping me company, Big Mike, anybody else would think I'm crazy."

"Like I don't? Just kidding. It's a great day for a drive and teaching's become so boring I think I'm happier than my students when I cancel. I've always wanted to visit Dublin anyway, although I had Ireland in mind! Any good pubs up there?"

"Guaranteed, they're essential for New Hampshire winters."

Thrilled by the interest of two professors from Columbia, the curator of the Thayer museum told them what he could of the father and daughter before directing them to a large cache of family correspondence exchanged between 1875 and 1946. After three hours of reading, they learned that the angelic-looking Mary Thayer Birch had not lived a heavenly life. She'd married poorly against her father's warnings and been abandoned by her husband. Beset by financial woes, she'd moved frequently, living for a time in venues as wide ranging as Trinidad and Tobago, England and Arizona. Usually in poor health, she'd died in 1933, at the age of fifty-seven, when John was twelve. Her remains were buried in Denver in an unmarked grave, and her only child, Elsie Birch Reeves, had last been seen in Washington, D.C. Elsie would have been twelve years old when John was born.

There appeared no possible connection between Mary Thayer or her daughter Elsie and John's service on the Manhattan Project, his accident and amnesia or anything he could imagine of his past.

"Could *Angel* be a doppelganger?" he wondered aloud.

"Remind me what that is."

"It's an exact double of a living person. Really, what else could she be? Her age is all wrong otherwise, and with three billion people in the world someone out there has to look exactly like her."

"This helps you how?"

"You're right. It doesn't. So what if someone out there looks exactly like a subject in a painting."

"John, take it from a friend. Start drinking a lot more and thinking about this BS less. I'm half-serious. Take up martinis and forget this "I knew her somewhere" crap. You've got a great wife, a good life and a family to enjoy. Who cares what happened sometime before that has nothing to do with you now? Don't drive yourself batty. Look ahead, not behind you!"

John appreciated the advice, but it wasn't so easy. Big Mike couldn't appreciate the sense of emptiness that came from not being grounded by a recalled past. Knowing so little of his life before 1946, except for parts of the Manhattan Project, his life lacked an emotional context and richness he craved, felt like nothing more than some stranger's story, interesting but essentially irrelevant. He had no recollection of being raised by missionary parents killed in China, of attending a military academy in Lake Geneva, Wisconsin, or of graduating from West Virginia University before beginning his work with General Leslie Groves, Project Director of Manhattan. So whatever the precise details, such "facts" were unsatisfactory and couldn't alleviate the misery and discontent that came from not knowing whether he'd journeyed well or poorly from his roots.

A week after returning from New Hampshire, John returned to the Met and discovered that the exhibit featuring *Angel* had been replaced by one celebrating life in Medieval England. Disappointed and with scant interest, John moved quickly through it, until eyeing a sixteenth century woodcut entitled the *Lyfe of St. George*. While looking at the image of the mounted saint wielding a lance and sword, about to dispatch a fearsome dragon, he felt his neck twinge and then begin to tighten. The sensation moved upward into his head and it began throbbing in pain. The pain grew until he was forced to clap his hands over his ears, wondering if he was having a stroke. It lessened gradually until he began hearing unintelligible, faint mutterings. These became louder, and then recognizable as random words which repeated over and over again. He listened to their insistent rhythm and began mouthing the five distinct words aloud, "George, Libya, Atia, azume, the maid . . . George, Libya, Atia, azume, the maid." Stumbling to a bench, he wrote them down on his brochure.

Two words obviously referred to St. George the crusader whose famous exploits had occurred in Libya, but he'd been looking at a woodcut of the saint so that made sense. Then he recalled his first vision in Yankee Stadium, and remembered the sound of church bells and seeing a dragon near an altar. *Was it a church dedicated to St. George? All right*, he thought, *say it's St. George Church. Where is it and what does it mean?*

Again there'd been the name Atia, an Italian and Roman name, the name of his supposed wife in the mysterious vision of fathering a son in some ancient place. But he didn't remember ever knowing anyone with her name. He couldn't imagine whatever an azume was, nor could he make sense of "the maid." *Could azume be a name, maybe the name of a maid like "Azume the maid?"* Regardless, it meant nothing to him.

Studying the scribbled words, he mouthed the refrain. He stared up at the image of the saint, focused on the lance raised to pierce the dragon, thought of the terrible pain it would inflict and . . .The woodcut disappeared from his sight, replaced by a statue of a howling and bleeding dragon at the very moment of being stuck by a lance wielded by a helmeted St. George, with flowing blond locks that made him resemble an iconic Jesus. The vision delivered a bolt of realization as he realized the statute he imagined then had been real, and in a familiar St. George Church. Instantly, he knew he'd been staring at it before, a long time ago, while kneeling in a pew and praying; he'd been praying while agonized, distressed, and obsessed with the vision of a girl who'd been the very image of Mary Thayer—not a mystical angel but rather an actual living girl—and he knew with absolute certainty that the object of his obsession had been just eleven years old.

He broke into a sweat and felt a sharp pain in his abdomen, as if kicked in the stomach. Then he pictured the girl flat on her back beneath him, with a flower tucked behind her ear . . . his mind rebelled at the vision and he pictured her as he preferred: alive in the sunlight, holding his hand, exhilarated and full of hope despite their fright, while they ran together until reaching the edge of a cliff and leaping off of it together.

Then he saw himself floating alone, high above the earth, shaking his head frantically to dispel a vile stench assaulting him. He recalled the sensation of nausea, at the very edge of tolerance, but then he'd seen her again. But he'd seen her as an actual angel, one who looked remarkably like both the girl and like Mary Thayer. And the angel had been kneeling with her head bowed low and her hair hanging down while she wept. She'd begun to speak and he strained to recall her words, but then *no, oh God, no,* he thought, *she wasn't weeping, she'd been standing upright, fully naked with water flowing down her beautiful shoulders, down across her breasts and over her shapely ass.* And he recalled he'd been watching, leering at her, enraptured by her loveliness after her emergence from water, like a pond somewhere, and she'd turned to face him.

He again saw her smile and heard her laugh aloud in a low, throaty, and wanton way, unashamed and welcoming his lustful gaze. His eyes had devoured her, feasting on the swell of her breasts and the widening of her hips, imagining the sensuous feel of the wispy hair spread out in a triangle between her thighs. He again knew he'd been hardened by his desire and imagination, been overwhelmed, eager to stroke her hair and caress her, determined to lay with her, and he'd pressed forward driven and ready. But he'd thought of that flower tucked neatly behind her ear and his lust had been dampened. He recalled too that she'd been pleading with him to let her live, but as he'd really always known but suppressed so often, he knew despite her pleas, he'd placed his hands around her graceful neck and squeezed together until he heard the ugly, cracking sound of her bones breaking as all life left her.

John felt undone and exhausted, as if whipped to the brink by the full and definitive recognition of what he'd known deep in his subconscious, what he'd managed to repress but never really quashed—what he'd dismissed as an unreal possibility for his entire life—while gazing into the beguiling, pleading eyes of a woman who looked exactly like the portrait of *Angel* at some unknown time and place during his adolescence, he'd killed her by choking her life away. There could be no doubt.

The horror of it tore at him and filled him with guilt. The idea that he'd lusted for a girl-woman repulsed him with its obscenity. He felt ill instantly, and he moved to a nearby trashcan. *How fitting,* he thought, as he vomited, choked, and spat, trying to disgorge what he could never hope to be rid of, the reality that he was a cold-blooded murderer. He finished emptying his stomach and wiping his face, then he fled from the Museum and ran aimlessly into Central Park.

Thereafter, when the visions John once welcomed as windows into his past recurred, they reminded him that he was despicable. He tried concealing the memory and his feeling, but that deception opened a chasm between him and Rose, adding betrayal of their pledged honesty to his list of sins. He also began wondering who else he'd victimized and conveniently forgotten. Professor John A.

Redford, respected scientist and educator, devoted father, loving husband and good friend, could add pervert, pedophile and murderer to his resume. Despicable!

Over the next few years, John drifted from Rose, his family, friends and professional life. His lectures deteriorated until they regularly included awkward mid-sentence silences while he stood frozen and glassy-eyed. What once might have been charitably forgiven as stereotypical, eccentric brilliance came to be seen as sad, uncontrollable blackouts, origin unknown.

By 1961, the Chair had had enough, and being unable to persuade John to seek professional help—he blamed his behavior on stress over his inability to complete an article on subatomic particles—he asked Big Mike to intervene. Resignation would be best, the Chair said, tenured firings were unpleasant and messy. He worried too, that any public airing of John's condition could jeopardize the government funding his department needed to thrive.

John's difficulties were old news to Rose. She'd tried everything to halt his decline including contacting Dr. Wright. But the psychiatrist's phone had been disconnected and she'd been unable to locate him. John's withdrawal put her into such a depressed state that she began receiving the psychiatric treatment he continued to refuse.

John spent his free time in his office scouring books, researching Thayer and his art, Italian history, unsolved murders, dragons, philosophy, and the astounding number of churches named St. George. They were found in every state in cities large and small, and in denominations including Episcopal, Catholic, Presbyterian, Greek Orthodox and Ukrainian, all in New York City alone. They were so plentiful he'd not have been surprised to find a St. George Synagogue.

Rose and their children receded in importance as he tried researching his way to self-forgiveness. He loved them all, but then his attention had to be captured for him to become engaged. Since child rearing and running the household used up Rose's energy, she began ignoring him, resenting the growing distance. She couldn't continue living a married life that made her feel fortunate if he'd just listen politely to her reporting the family news.

Mary was four when John underwent his change, and Lizzy and Timmy—twins who were "the fourth child" Rose wanted to conceive on the day he saw Thayer's *Angel*—turned two in 1961. So the youngest never knew their father otherwise and his disinterest didn't especially trouble them, sadly it seemed normal. But the two oldest, Abe at eleven and Mark at eight, suffered along with Rose. They missed the daddy who'd tickled, wrestled, and roughhoused with them, and now they played ball with friends without any tips from their first coach. They asked why he didn't love them anymore, but Rose assured them it wasn't so, Daddy just needed to solve a problem in his mind. The bright children nodded politely, but soon stopped asking. It only mattered that they felt irrelevant.

Rose missed the friends they no longer saw since it'd become too awkward. Their "dates" also stopped along with any semblance of a love life. John never felt quite in the mood for sex and only responded half-heartedly to Rose when she became uncomfortably aggressive. He seemed content resting on his back in bed, mentally off somewhere until his snoring announced another day's shut down. Rose loved John and his suffering pained her, but she foresaw she might need to separate from him rather than risk harm to their children.

Rose accepted Big Mike's invitation for lunch. "How is everything at home?" he began, already sensing the answer.

"Nothing's changed. John acts like he's sleepwalking and refuses to have any serious conversation with me. We're like office workers chit-chatting around a water cooler. I have more stimulating discussions with the maid."

"I'm sorry, Rose. It's been a long time for you and the kids."

"The little guys are fine and honestly it's gotten a little better for Abe and Mark now that they're more involved at school and with their friends. We're all adjusting to Daddy being the oddball father."

"Don't forget that your friends are prepared to help however possible. Just say the word."

"Thanks, I know. You've all been great. You call and we have lunch and everyone's supportive and all, but it means nothing to John. Lately he's started losing weight, and he sleeps poorly, usually thrashing about in a cold sweat. I'm sure he's clinically depressed and can't focus enough to accept help . . . I'm sure it's not any better at Columbia."

"No, the Chair says something needs to be done. Well, here I am. I've got an idea, but selfishly I don't like it. Still, desperate times and all. I'm thinking a fresh start might help overcome the years of bad memories in New York. It's none of my business, but it depends a bit on your finances. Still, I'm sure we could find a way to help . . . "

"That's not an issue. Tell me what you're thinking."

By the time they finished their almond cookies and espresso, Rose agreed that relocating was worth considering. John was so passive he'd go along with any coherent plan she advocated. Northwestern had an excellent reputation and Mike assured her they could make the calls necessary for him to secure an appropriate position there. The children were young enough to be uprooted without serious objections and moving away from her family in Pennsylvania was no longer an issue. Since Momma's death her siblings had frequently urged her to divorce John. No matter the children, they contended she shouldn't stay married to a man who'd so obviously lost it. But even her own siblings didn't understand the extent of her loyalty. Rosabella Tassi Redford wasn't a shrinking violet that bailed out when the going got rough. It might be getting closer, but she hadn't quit just yet.

She'd never been to Chicago, but a college friend lived in Lake Forest and said life there couldn't be beat. You gave up some New York culture and sophistication, but the place doesn't assault you like Manhattan. She said there was no better place to raise a family.

John said he'd think it over, but he was only being polite. His obsessive search had reached his own saturation point. He detested living a lie by trying to fathom how he could espouse such high standards of morality and still murder an innocent woman. It justified self-punishment equal to his self-loathing. The loss of his disagreeable presence would release his family from pain. They'd start anew with a man worthy of them since Rose surely would rebound with a new husband. Attractive, young, passionate and rich, she met the time-tested formula for remarriage. Perhaps too, as physics taught, since matter and energy occupied the same scale the next stage of his transformation might find him being a source of positive energy.

He thought *there are worse ways to depart life than with the sweet smell of bitter almond.* But for cyanide to work well his stomach had to be empty or death could be painful and delayed for hours. So John didn't eat one morning; all he needed to do was ingest one and a half grams of KCN dissolved in a glass of water. He'd wait five minutes, pour it down his throat, be unconscious in a minute and dead in less than an hour.

He'd leave simply, and relieve everyone. He wouldn't leave a sappy parting message. *What use are the self-serving words of a man whose life has been constructed upon such colossal deceit?*

So, on a pleasant summer day John Redford strolled down Tenth Avenue in New York walking to Columbia University one last time, intent on securing the simple white compound that would bring him the everlasting peace found in nothingness.

4.

A Candle in the Darkest Night

New York City, 1961

John Redford decided to stop at his office for a nostalgic farewell. Sitting amidst stacks of papers and half-finished books, he turned the radio on by habit while looking at his childrens' drawings, innocent expressions of love taped to the wall near a gold-framed picture of Rose—all youthful joy and beauty, leaning against a tree and laughing. The memory stung. How had it come to this?

He recognized a familiar song, one they'd played repeatedly while lounging on the floor of their apartment, imagining their future. He'd rubbed Rose's belly and voiced his hopes for the child snuggled inside. Now, Frankie Laine's emotional wail made him tremble. He folded his arms and pulled at his shoulders as if trying to hold himself together. The lyrics spoke of not being afraid, of finding hope in the darkest night. When had he lost such faith?

He sobbed, wondering why a loving Creator would place this burden upon him. Wasn't he devout enough? Reflecting on her picture, he marveled that Rose hadn't left him. Despite his brooding and his gloomy disposition, she remained stalwart and committed. He had only to reach out to her and she would respond with comfort and guidance, like a guardian angel, always nearby and sustaining. *Good God, how obvious. I'm wallowing in self-pity, forgetting what Rose never has, what the song insists: We never walk alone.*

And God gave me tools to navigate difficult times, not to bail out when things get rough!

He became angry. *Damn it, I'm not insane. I don't understand it, but murder isn't in my nature, and neither is suicide. There has to be some explanation why I killed her.* His anger made him feel a glimmer of hope, he only needed to . . . The phone interrupted him mid-analysis. He hesitated, but answered it on the fifth ring. He didn't recognize the voice or the name, but the message seemed a godsend.

"If you only knew what I've been struggling with! Ya, of course I'll meet but . . . I don't understand who . . . all right, I'll look at them, but why . . . I see. Two hours then . . . ya, Minerva's statute in front of Low Library. Thank you, thank you so much, you can't imagine what this means!"

John raced to his faculty box, unlocked it and withdrew a large envelope with a typed note affixed by his secretary. "Professor, this was dropped off Friday by an older gent who wanted to see you, but he wouldn't give me his name. So I didn't give him your home number. He said he'd call later. I hope I did the right thing? Hope you enjoy the weekend! Barb."

John tore it open and found a calling card. "Walter McFarland, Director of Project Engineering, Sperry Rand Corporation, 6395 Parkleigh Road, Darien, Connecticut." Under the card were several photographs clipped together along with a small note reading "Six." Flipping through the five 8 X 10 photographs, he double checked, wondering why there were five rather than six photos as the note suggested. McFarland had said the photos might help, but not to worry otherwise, he'd explain it all when they met.

The first photograph showed a home viewed from across a narrow street. The small, wooden dwelling had a brick front porch, with two columns aside the stairs and an overstuffed rocker in its corner. John's pulse raced, recognizing it as the same house he'd imagined years before in Yankee Stadium. But he couldn't place the modest home, a standard type looking like it might be found anywhere in America.

The second photo showed a circular driveway lined with lush plantings fronting a tile-roofed, Mexican colonial-style building. Interlocking letters on the entry door spelled out "CCC," and a smiling, uniformed Negro stood nearby with his hand raised to the brim of his hat as if in greeting. It meant nothing to him.

In the third photograph, a distinguished man wearing the uniform of a three star general sat behind a desk with his hands entwined, looking at the camera with a solemn expression. He looked to be in his late fifties, had a full head of thick, white hair, and a plaque on the desk identified him as Major General William J. Donovan. John didn't think he'd met Donovan, but he knew him by reputation. He was a Columbia legend, an All-American in football who earned the nickname "Wild Bill" because of his unique running style. He attended Columbia Law School, served as a member of the University's Board of Regents, and served as a United States Ambassador to somewhere in Asia, he thinks perhaps Siam.

Obviously, he held a high position during the War although John was sure he wasn't involved with the Project in Los Alamos.

The fourth picture was of poor quality, a partial image produced by folding the original in a hurried attempt to copy it. The standard World War Two Air Corps photo depicted a combat crew with their aircraft. The faces of the two standing officers and the airmen squatting down in front of them were distinct but unfamiliar. The crew wore cold weather flight gear, and the number 114 was visible on the runway, but little else distinguished the photograph. The slab sides of the plane's fuselage confirm it was a B-24 Liberator, derisively referred to as the flying coffin because of the high number of fatalities inflicted upon its flight crews.

The middle airman wore a cocky smirk, as if anxious to start a fight or hurl an insult, while the other enlistees looked bored or tired. John was struck by how young all the men in the photo appeared, smooth-faced and bright-eyed. The officer on the right sported a brimmed cap and was staring straight ahead, clearly uncomfortable posing. The other officer . . . *God Almighty,* he'd gasped, *the other officer looks just like I must have looked twenty years ago, The expression and the cleft chin are the same I see in every family photograph, the same one I see in my mirror when I'm shaving every morning. But the posture is all wrong. This guy exudes self-confidence and I've been told repeatedly how unusually shy and withdrawn I was at that age.*

The fifth picture was clearly the most current. Captioned "CIA Reception, 1959," it showed President Dwight Eisenhower shaking hands with a gaunt-looking man surrounded by a crowd of twenty-some applauding others. John closely examined the honoree but didn't recognize him. *I don't get it, the CIA deals with spies and that sure as hell doesn't have anything to do with me. Manhattan was top secret obviously, but the CIA didn't even exist until after the war.*

Leaving his office thirty minutes early, John craved insight like a desert wanderer wants water. He hoped McFarland would arrive early for their meeting.

Walking through the Upper West Side of New York, Walter McFarland felt better than he had in years—maybe like fifty years earlier when he became an Eagle Scout by completing other good deeds. He'd always prided himself on his integrity, strong moral sense and code of honor, attributes learned from his father, General Alfred McFarland, a righteous rock of a man ideally suited for his stint as West Point Superintendent. His premature death had created a void in Walter's life which he tried to fill by emulating him. But viewing his father through a child's eyes, he far outdid the General, enduring frequent migraine headaches for his effort. His reputation as a dignified and rigid man who would always do his duty made him Donovan's choice to be Special Operations Director for the OSS, the country's wartime intelligence agency. Despite his reputation for being unorthodox, Wild Bill knew that intelligence work often brought out the worst in men, requiring a disciplinarian to keep them under tow; he knew there would be hell to pay if men wielding such unbridled power felt enabled to use any means to complete a mission.

No venture in American history had been more critical and urgent than the Manhattan Project. So when Roosevelt asked for an internal spy to safeguard it from sabotage, Donovan agreed to procure one without question and without requiring any formal assurances. Not an eyebrow had been raised while agreeing to conduct a covert, illegal, domestic espionage mission inside the most carefully protected project in history. It turned out well, of course, since the bomb came to be developed and used without interference, but Roosevelt's death showed the recklessness of relying on a man who couldn't be President forever.

Harry Truman was a small man with a complex who'd disliked the charismatic, urbane, and imperious Roosevelt who'd always seemed larger than life. When he'd learned the OSS and Roosevelt had hidden the very existence of the Manhattan Project from him, he'd felt like the village idiot and responded by quickly moving to disband the OSS and punish its leadership. Considering the attack unjustified and wholly political, McFarland felt justified using deceit to defend the organization, himself and Donovan. Regrettably, this had necessitated cutting loose the man they'd planted inside as John Redford.

Collateral damage is always part of high-stakes warfare when there aren't many viable options, and if the shit had hit the fan they risked lengthy prison terms. Of course, if Roosevelt had survived, he'd have met with the Senate Intelligence chairman and resolved everything on the QT simply and with a wink. It had been his fourth term, after all, and he'd have been treated like a victorious king.

Sixtus Peeters had been an easy choice as their spy. He was a natural-born teacher with scientific knowledge and the idealism needed to accept the sacrifices that came with being reported MIA while using an alias. It had worked well, since he'd earned Groves's confidence and helped produce the bomb, but no one foresaw either Roosevelt's death or Redford's unfortunate and untimely objection to using the weapon.

Peeters's fate stung more than most, because he'd been so bright and determined, so noble, confident, and dedicated. Such men were discarded reluctantly, and McFarland never attended a Good Friday service without feeling guilty when the minister recounted Judas's betrayal kiss in Gethsemane. Now he would remove the taint on their honor. *This is for us, Wild Bill. God rest your soul, we both thought well of the boy.*

McFarland was staying in midtown New York and he took in a play the evening before calling Redford. He'd planned to ride the subway all the way to Columbia, but it rattled, shook, and smelled, and being early, he emerged at Seventy-Ninth Street, a mile from their rendezvous point.

Strolling in the sunlight was delightful, and crossing Eightieth Street heading north on Amsterdam, he reminisced about his early years in the City. Those were the halcyon days after his wife transferred to Barnard while he finished up at Columbia, giving the newlyweds a chance to share adventures in the world's greatest city.

They'd frequented east side delis and flea markets, museums, and the Park. God, he missed Jane, and with no children had been terribly lonesome for over a year. He'd thought perhaps he might move back to Manhattan after retiring. Where else could someone feel so alive?

He also missed Donovan. They'd been an efficient team and as close as brothers. He'd hurried to Walter Reed Hospital when Wild Bill had his final stroke, anxious for one last visit. It had been a nostalgic, heartfelt and cleansing session, and they'd discussed their regret that things with Peeters had gotten so far out of hand.

McFarland put off contacting him while caring for Jane throughout her last illness. But after she passed away, he had no excuses or anything left to lose. Only five other men knew how Six Peeters had been passed off as John Redford: Roosevelt, Donovan, Walt Radmutz, Brant Frey, and Groves. Donovan neutralized Groves with the dirt they had on him, and Groves hadn't been involved or known how the spy had been mistreated after he cut him loose. With all the rest dead, it was time to tell Redford the tale so he might finally return home.

McFarland had kept some photographs and documents for his personal protection when he'd retired, knowing how such high-stakes affairs sometimes turned inward. He'd added a recent picture from the CIA reception honoring Frey, and left copies of them all at Redford's office, as an icebreaker of sorts. He'd hoped Redford would recall some of the details before he had to spell it all out, it could get uncomfortable and he couldn't know how he'd react—He might not understand that they'd been well-intentioned and honorable men throughout. He'd glanced at his watch, anticipating they would meet in twenty minutes.

———

Tall and handsome at sixteen, Nathaniel Stegger could have passed for his father at the same age. *God forgive me*, thought his mother, Abigail, for disliking the resemblance nearly as much as her son's arrogant disrespect. He could be disarmingly charming when it suited him, but she might only ask where he was going and he'd as likely tell her to screw off as be civil. She was grateful he'd be leaving soon since he brought constant tension into the home. She could usually ignore his disagreeable presence, having mastered the technique during her marriage, but it pained her to see her daughter, Alexandra, suffer, wondering what she'd done to cause her twin to treat her so poorly.

The children had seemed unscathed when their parents divorced in 1948, and they moved from Daniel's Gold Coast mansion in Chicago to Lake Forest. Its green fields and woodlands and their mother's supportive friends made it feel like a homecoming. They were a tight threesome then, not missing the father who'd become a stranger. They'd carry on without him they insisted, would be like *The Three Musketeers*.

Their solidarity crumbled after Nathaniel reached puberty and began treating them like inferiors. *It's just a phase*, advised Gail's *psychiatrist: he's struggling with identity, blinded by testosterone, coping with his father's absence,* blah, blah, and blah. But she knew it'd been inevitable and feared it would be lasting. He had too much of his father in him, and Daniel drew out the worst. She'd been unable to resist and forced to watch it happen. Daniel wielded such power that he'd have crushed her without a second thought if she'd interfered.

The change began when, after years of absenteeism marked by only a few visits, phone calls, and report card reviews from afar, Daniel told her he would be reconnecting with Nate.

His command came in a letter delivered on Nate's twelfth birthday. "He needs a real man's guidance to learn how the world works. We don't want him to become a sissy. I'll visit with him when I'm in Chicago, during the summers and whenever I can bring him along on business. You needn't fret about me interfering with you and your daughter. Tell her anything you like. She's nothing to me, she's just like you, enough said. All arrangements will be handled via my man James. Tell Nathaniel he has no choice in the matter, but I can assure him he'll enjoy the time spent with me."

Before then Nate had been respectful, following convention and showing deference to adults. He'd remained modest although especially bright and capable, having advanced two grades through high school and completing coursework at Northwestern even before he turned eleven. He'd been sensitive, appropriate and deferential then. Whenever they'd played games like Risk and Scrabble, although he competed fiercely and never lost, he'd encourage them, suggesting how difficult it had been for him to win. He'd often teased Alexie by remarking on her good looks, saying she'd need armed guards to chase the boys away and that he'd be her protector. He'd always been genuinely concerned about their welfare and they both expected he'd be their lifelong champion.

After just one summer with his father in Colorado, Nathaniel changed so much that their friends stopped asking about him. He'd become so arrogant that those who'd once admired him preferred forgetting him entirely.

Leaving for college, Nate hugged Alexie and told her he'd miss her, but she didn't believe him and she was right. When Gail instinctively reached out for a parting embrace, Nate held her at arm's length, glaring at her through his cold, hazel eyes. He said, "I've lost my respect for you. After father's accident you never asked me how he was or expressed any sympathy for him. That's despicable."

"You don't understand, Nate. You don't really know . . . "

"You're so predictable. I knew what you'd say. I also know Daniel Stegger is a self-made millionaire respected by thousands of people, including many far more important than you!"

"Nate, please . . . I d-don't want . . . "

"It's Nathaniel, not Nate, and you will hear me out!" he boomed, holding her tightly and frightening her as he spat out his words. "All you have is due to my father. So next time you're kneeling in your fucking pew, pretending your goddamned brainwaves are in touch with something up in the sky—whoop, whoop—ask the wizard behind the screen why you have everything you could ever want. You live like a queen with your tennis and bridge and country club bullshit while the man you betrayed is stuck in a wheelchair busting his ass to provide it all."

"Betrayed? What are you talking about?"

"Is 'adultery' more palatable?"

"Nate, Nathaniel, I never, I swear . . . my God, how could you imagine such a terrible thing?"

"I'm not stupid, Mother. I know what you were up to behind his back in New Mexico, and . . . No, take your damn hands off of me! Goodbye, Mother!"

With that parting shot, on August 8, 1961, Nathaniel left home for the University of Colorado, intent on pursuing a law degree. With perfect grades and a barrel full of accolades, Nathaniel could have gone to any college and studied anything, but this seemed ideal. He'd be a thousand miles away from his mother and close to his wise and powerful father, following his advice.

Daniel had taught him, "History makes it all predictable. We're the Romans of today, and just as with Rome, our dominance has led to unparalleled prosperity which is shared with the unproductive 'plebes' of today. They'll inevitably complain that the wealthy have too great a share of the prosperity, and to remedy such 'injustice,' politicians will gain votes and power by redistributing to the dependent. Finally, with so much to waste and the citizenry having so little in common, the supposedly neutral law will become the sole refuge and forum for all disputes. Learn to game the legal system and you won't ever have to bust your ass the way I did. Clever lawyers can steal what others busted their asses for, and the idiots will never realize what's happening. Trust me. The system will be so complex and so full of money that it'll be like catching fish in a barrel. God bless the USA!"

———

"You goddamn klutz!" Daniel screamed when the scalding coffee dripped onto his hand. "Get out of my sight, you bitch! James, . . . James! Get your black ass in here."

By 1961, James Jackson had served Stegger for nearly twenty years, living a life unimaginable when he first started working at the Palmer House fetching things for wealthy white folks. He owed Stegger for seeing something special in him, arranging his training and elevating his lot, but he hated the man nonetheless.

Before his accident, Stegger was rarely home while James tended to his mansion overlooking Lake Shore Drive in Chicago. Wielding the power of his rich master, the black son of a dishwasher felt like the ruler of a kingdom, waited on hand and foot and enjoying such extraordinary perks as the sexual favors of dutiful maids, even if they needed to be shared with his boss. He did whatever he was asked without question, and with the use of a virtually unlimited checkbook. The expenditures were so large that Jackson briefly considered skimming some of the cash for a rainy day. But his father didn't raise no dummy, and upon reflection he decided being discovered would likely cost him his life, let alone his gravy train.

He'd learned from his father to "take what ya can from whitey, but know de mark, some don't take any shit and dey bedder left alone." James knew no one who took less shit than Stegger.

"She'll be gone within the hour, sir," said James as he applied salve to the burn.

"Damn right, bad enough I'm in this fucking contraption and now with a bum hand to boot. Goddammit start hiring better people!"

"Yes, sir, I assure you I'll do better next time."

He made an Old Fashioned for Stegger and wheeled him out onto the porch overlooking Grand Lake. The splendid view of forest and mountain across the clear water could soothe the foulest mood. The attraction of this aspect of Colorado was evident, but with Stegger wheelchair-dependent and rarely away, James began thinking of the place as fancy slave quarters, while his life before the accident couldn't have been sweeter.

The Chicago winter of 1958 was to blame. What began as a mist of powdery flakes turned into one of the city's notorious storms, and before long nothing was visible outside the brownstone except for the dull light of a total whiteout when twenty-two inches of snow fell in twelve hours, shutting down most everything. Even while preparing a welcoming fire, James assumed Stegger wouldn't be coming home that evening. But he learned he was wrong when the hospital phoned near midnight.

Fighting through waist-high snowdrifts, head under his hat and walking into the gusts of a raging wind, Stegger stepped into a rapidly moving snowplow as it turned a corner onto State Street just a few blocks from home. Tossed backward into the air, he landed awkwardly and fractured his left leg. Unfortunately, this was of minor importance compared with the injury to his back; before hitting the ground, he'd been tossed against a light pole, fracturing his vertebrae at the T-10 segment of his spine. By the time he finished rehabilitation five months later, he knew that it would require a miracle for him to ever take another normal step. But such luck as he had, his injury was incomplete, his legs were paralyzed, but he retained normal respiratory function and upper body strength; he could move independently from his wheelchair with use of his arms, and he'd retained full bladder control and sexual function.

Stegger battled depression, but he perked himself up before leaving the hospital by utilizing several private "nurses" to confirm his retained sexual prowess—more than ever, he craved sex to confirm his self-worth.

He maintained an office and home in Chicago, but began spending most of his time in Colorado. Set in the woods and barely visible from the town, his extravagant Grand Lake lodge could only be reached by an isolated, private road. Living there gave him a sense of security his new vulnerability demanded. Few knew where he lived, and no one ever visited him except for his son, his longtime attorney Arlen Christensen, his business colleague, Brant Frey, and prostitutes James procured.

———

In 1959, Frey paid his last visit to Stegger. Surprisingly, Stegger felt genuinely nostalgic over the impending death of his only real friend.

"We're quite a pair, Stegger. Fucking cancer man and the gimp!"

"Gimp your ass, Frey. I'll bet I can still toss you off this porch— not that I would Mr. High and Mighty, respectable, Presidential Honoree, sir."

"Ike has no clue how much money we stole when . . . " Frey began until he started coughing with a raspy, wheezing sound. Stegger reached out to steady him, holding his arm tenderly.

Frey took a drink of water, lit a cigarette, inhaled and coughed again. "All the shit we pulled and dead vegetable leaves kill me, go figure."

"I told you to quit years ago . . . dumb shit!"

"Thanks for reminding me . . . asshole!"

After insulting each other, the two men began laughing and continued until tears flowed. It had been years since Stegger laughed so hard, but the irony of their situation struck him as hilarious: having escaped revolts and uprisings, atrocities and violent conflict, the two soldiers of fortune were reduced to their sorry state in ordinary and wholly unexpected ways.

"A snowplow!" roared Frey, his gaunt face suddenly alive with laughter, "I can't believe you walked into a fucking snowplow!"

Sipping their third martini, they mellowed as they enjoyed the spectacular sunset over Arapaho National Forest. "I'm going out like that sunset, Daniel. I figure I've got about a month left. You'll like working with Brad when I'm gone. He gets it, and he's a rising star. I'll be surprised if he's not Director someday. He inherits everything, so the transition will be seamless and all the capital you'll need will still be available. Wouldn't it be a gas if someday the boys worked together? Stegger and Frey reborn!"

Stegger gestured at the box beside him. "Thanks for bringing your files. I worried they might be a problem."

"I thought about leaving them with Brad, but it's too much for him now. You'll know what to dispose of and what to leverage for the next score—no one does it better than you. I want you to teach my son how to bust balls."

"I will," Daniel said earnestly, "I'll make him tougher than you. You were a little weak sometimes, but still, I couldn't have asked for a better partner."

Stegger reached into the three-foot square box holding thirty-some multicolored folders, along with films and sound recordings, all materials related to projects they'd worked on over the preceding fifteen years. The materials detailed bribery, kickbacks, and sweetheart deals, four scams currently underway, and several interesting OSS and CIA matters.

"That's funny," Daniel said, leafing through a blue folder. "Three hundred grand to Senator Reynolds for sponsoring the Tailgate legislation, with another fifty to make sure the Rocky Mountain National Park surrounded my piece of heaven here. 'I'll make sure your nearest neighbor is miles away,' he promised."

Their glasses clinked together a final time and Frey said, "I remember thinking, Jesus Christ, a politician who keeps his word, what could be more unlikely!"

Frey died at his Maryland home three weeks after his visit. Going through his files sometime later, Daniel focused on one labeled "Sixtus Peeters," and realized it concerned the spy he'd only known as Jack Redford. Learning of his background for the first time Stegger reflected, *Imagine, a genuine war hero, what a waste, ending up not knowing his own name and teaching. Nice career choice, could anything be more boring? And the clueless Boy Scout wasn't just from the Midwest, but from Kenosha, just seven miles from my hometown. What a small world. "Sixtus," no wonder he turned out to be so naïve and foolish. What were his parents thinking giving him that handle?*

He also noted seven three-inch spools of wire recordings labeled "Sixtus Peeters." He hadn't seen recordings like that in more than ten years. He'd find an old player and listen to them when he had some spare time. He knew Frey liked to dictate when his thoughts were fresh, so he assumed they were nothing more than his initial thoughts later transcribed into the hard copy file materials.

In 1961, Fritz "Slick" Retzling looked ten years older than his actual forty years. He'd been in great physical shape when first released from prison, but idleness and alcohol added weight and rounded out his oval face to give him jowls and a double chin. His jet-black hair had faded to a greasy gray, but it remained thick enough to be worn long and swept back slick. He took great pride in his hair knowing many school classmates were balding, and he felt certain his cool locks scored him a few chicks.

Slick lived alone above a bar off Fifty-Second street in Kenosha, not far from his childhood home. His mother was still alive, but he seldom visited her. He found her depressingly old and he hated possibly seeing her neighbors, Anna Peeters and her daughter Agnes. They reminded him of his best childhood bud, Sixtus. He regretted that they'd parted on bad terms when Six refused to give him an alibi, and he ended up going to the joint for a hit and run death before Six got wasted in that stupid war in Romania, some goddamn place he'd never even heard of before.

Slick followed a similar routine most days. He'd get up late, take a walk, have a few beers, and catch some sleep in the afternoon or listen to a ball game. When the Motors first shift got out he'd meet his working buds at their bar de jour and drink till he got blotto and stumbled back to his place. The routine varied if he got lucky with some skank, found an odd job to replenish his funds, or hung out with his best buddy, Hans.

Hans Stegger II had been his cellmate at Waupun Correctional during his eight years there. Hans came from a large Danish family in Racine that had once been very wealthy. Hans claimed he'd been a normal sort of guy until his family lost all its money because they were "screwed in the ass big time by that son of a bitching lowlife cousin Daniel." Slick wondered about that, thinking it didn't make sense that someone could get as crazy nutty as Hans just because they lost all their money. After all, he had nothing but still thought of himself as perfectly normal.

Barely six feet tall, Hans's wiry, thin frame masked formidable strength and power. "It's the eye of the tiger," he explained. "I tense up my shoulders and shut my eyes, then I scrunch my neck and imagine power flowing through my body from my toes up, like a wave right to my fists, then whammo, I'm fuckin invincible, man!" Slick saw Hans do exactly that several times, thought it a wonder to behold, like a Captain America superhero sort of thing, except his bud didn't need any special serum.

Slick first saw the eye of the tiger in full force when a large farm boy from Fort Atkinson made the mistake of deciding to pick on Hans shortly after the fool arrived, trying to rep himself but not knowing who was who in the joint. Five prisoners watched as the two squared off in a quiet area near the laundry and the contrast seemed comical at first. Four inches taller and at least seventy-five pounds heavier, Farm Boy seemed to have good reason to be cocky. "Okay, little man, come and get a piece of me," he'd growled. Hans stood five feet away saying nothing, just smiling. Then he held his hands up, meaning "just wait," shut his eyes and scrunched his body down. When he opened them and stood up straight again, he had a crazed look that shivered Farm Boy and made the hair on Slick's arms rise. In a split second he'd crossed the distance between them and transferred all his force into a concentrated right hook that audibly cracked Farm Boy's jaw when it launched into him. After he fell to his knees, Hans grabbed his head in the crook of his arm and pummeled it with his fist repeatedly until all his energy was dissipated, continuing well after all the life left Farm Boy.

When they discovered his corpse, no one would say how it'd happened and prison life continued like always except no one messed with Hans or Slick, the bud of "The Man." After that, Slick would do anything to please Hans.

On parole, Hans popped every available drug and partied with abandon. Slick loved it, felt wholly alive when hanging with him, drawing vicarious energy from his scary, animal intensity. When Hans directed his focus on some woman in a bar, she'd invariably be drawn to him like a moth to a flame. This created leftovers for Slick who wasn't fussy about who he bedded or who had been there before or when. They bet on how many women they would share when they went on their road trip once Hans got "his payback shit" together. Slick couldn't wait, life in K-town had become boring. It would be a parole violation, but what the hey, life was short. Anyway, they were too lucky to get caught. Plus, he had a disability he could use as an excuse for his next screw-up.

At a recent probation hearing, Judge Schroeder had ordered Slick to undergo testing, and no shit, they found out he had a reading problem called dyslexia. Those damn nuns at St. George didn't have a clue, had treated him like a dimwit because they were too stupid to spot it. Yet that sweetheart doctor in Milwaukee figured it out in like twenty minutes. Where had she been when he needed her? If his problem had been discovered in grade school, he could've been a popular and smart guy. He thought he might even have kept up with Six and gone to the University of Wisconsin rather than to the slammer after driving down that stupid bitch who didn't know enough to look out when crossing the street. On the other hand, he was still upright and Six was pushing up tulips.

Sent to St. Mary's Hospital in Milwaukee for evaluation, Slick had been startled by the white-coated woman who walked into the examination room. "Hello, I'm Doctor Adalia Weber, I'm a resident physician here and I've been asked to evaluate your condition."

"Bullshit! Get out, who are you really?"

"Excuse me?"

"You're too gorgeous to be a doctor," he blurted out. *My God,* he thought, *tall and blonde with legs up to her ass—how does my hair look?*

She laughed in a light, sweet, and melodious voice. "Well, thank you for that, but really, I'm a physician and I'm here to evaluate you for the court. Is that alright with you?"

"Sure," he said, "you can be my doctor anytime!"

She handed him a piece of paper onto which she'd written, "Apples are different than pears, but both are fruits," in large block letters. "Can you read this?" she asked.

He recognized "apples" and "pears" but couldn't make much out of it otherwise. Then she asked him a series of questions and he answered yes to each one: "Have you ever been labeled lazy; been told you're not trying hard enough; ever felt dumb; ever seemed to zone out or daydream; ever complained of headaches, dizziness or stomach aches while reading; ever felt confused by letters, numbers or words; ever have difficulty putting thoughts into words or have trouble learning the alphabet, etc.?"

He felt good answering yes to all her questions. She seemed to understand him and he liked agreeing with her. She said, "Mr. Retzling, you've done a fine job of making it this far in life with such a significant disability. I'm recommending you as an outstanding candidate for reading therapy. Please consider it. If you follow the plan rigorously it'll make your life easier. Now, don't hesitate to call me if you have any questions or need follow-up assistance." She touched his arm, "God bless you and be well."

He felt the young doctor expressed as much concern for his well-being as anyone had in years. It reminded him of the kindness his neighbor Mr. Peeters had shown including him in his conversations with Six all those nights on the Peeters's front porch during his childhood. "Outstanding candidate," she'd said, "don't hesitate to call me." Obviously she liked his hair.

Slick wasn't the type to take advice, and he didn't undertake the recommended therapy. *Why bother,* he thought, *I've gotten this far in life well enough.* Besides, he was too old, and he could still make out most of the words that really mattered, words like tavern and Schlitz and store, and he always recognized the names of people he knew and had painstakingly memorized. A follow-up meeting with Doctor Weber might be nice, but he'd continue drinking for his therapy.

5.

Settling and Searching

Evanston, Illinois, 1964

The bite of the wind whipping off Lake Michigan no longer bothered Redford. After three years in Illinois, he felt like a Midwesterner, the cold helping his blood move and his brain work. Twice a week he stopped at the Student Union, read the Sun Times with coffee and a donut, and headed to his office to prepare for his lecture. Later, and on his free days, he'd meet with students and colleagues, read journals, and work on his latest publication, *An Analysis of the Anomalies of Dark Matter*. All in all, he enjoyed a comfortable routine far different from that of his latter years at Columbia. The teaching position at Northwestern had worked out well.

Vague thoughts of his mysterious past intruded periodically, but Xanax let him sleep through the night without any troubling dreams. The turning point had been the McFarland tragedy.

Walter McFarland had never arrived for their meeting. John had paced back and forth while waiting, unable to imagine what had gone wrong, since McFarland had been eager to meet. He went to the subway stop several times to make certain the trains were still running, but after three hours he gave up and went on a bender in despair.

When the doorman brought him to his doorway at 3:30 a.m., his appearance was frightening: his mussed hair pointed in several directions, except above his right temple where matted blood held it firmly in place; his eyes were bloodshot; his cheek black and blue; and one sleeve of his suit coat was missing along with his right shoe. Dried vomit speckled his cheek, with a singular piece moving up and down in a disgusting rhythm as he tried to speak.

Rose had never seen her impeccable husband in such a condition, but the Dakota's doorman reassured her. "Don't worry, Madam, it isn't serious. I've seen others in a similar state. He just needs a thorough scrubbing and time to sleep it off. A cabbie found him outside the Dublin House leaning against a light pole with his arm around the shoulder of another dru . . . er, inebriated gentlemen. It seems they had a scuffle that ended with them being tossed into the street."

As John told her later, he'd hoisted a number of boilermakers to drown his crushed hopes, and had ended up on a barstool next to another Yankee fan. He recalled engaging in a heated debate about the relative skill of Yankee pitcher Bullet Bob Turley before John had confided, apropos of nothing, that he didn't know his own name. His drinking buddy opined he was full of shit, everybody knew who they were, and John remembered throwing the first punch then. Apparently the men had reconciled, because they'd been singing *My Wild Irish Rose,* linked arm in arm with the fellow when the cabbie arrived.

He slept late the following day, popped some aspirin, and began searching for McFarland. He called Sperry Rand, but the staff didn't know his whereabouts. *He's been cutting back,* they said, *we don't expect him for another week. He's using vacation time before his retirement. When he calls in we'll give him your message.*

A riot had broken out near Columbia the evening they were to meet, and with a queasy sense of foreboding John called the NYPD. They didn't know anything of a man named McFarland, but they wondered about his query. When the detective asked why they were meeting when he couldn't even describe him, John hung up. He couldn't find a good way to say he was meeting a stranger to learn his own name.

He pestered the staff at Sperry Rand, and after three weeks without hearing from him they too became concerned. Their Vice-President of Public Affairs traced McFarland to a midtown hotel where he'd last been seen leaving to see the play *Bye, Bye Birdie*. The hotel management called the NYPD when he'd failed to check out on schedule while leaving his belongings behind. But the routine complaint garnered little attention. When the executive had called the police a week later, they suggested he should check with the morgue since an unidentified elderly man had been found in a dumpster.

Dressed in a Savile Row suit, the executive followed an assistant coroner through a refrigerated room lined with rows of five-shelf pallets set side by side. Human remains were deposited on each shelf, each corpse marked with a yellow tag on its big toe. Seeing so many stiffs in one place unsettled the executive and he held his well-tailored arms inward while passing down the narrow rows, shallow-breathing against the disagreeable odor. The assistant stopped, and after glancing at three tags, he read one in the second row off the floor, "John Doe, July 10, 1961." Turning to the executive he asked, "Is this your man?"

Stepping up, he leaned over and looked into a blank, sickly-yellow face with a droopy chin atop a swollen body, crudely stitched autopsy cuts making the corpse appear a botched Frankenstein. Stitches ran across his hairline and from his crotch up to mid-torso where they branched into a Y extending to both shoulders. Multiple gashes about the palm of his right hand suggested he'd held it up in a futile effort to thwart a knife-wielding attacker.

"Y-y-yes, that's McFarland," he gasped. He'd known him well enough to be certain.

"Are you sure?"

"Y-yes," he muttered, turning away. *Yes*, he thought, fleeing the crypt, *no doubt that was former Army Colonel Walter McFarland, a man of great accomplishment and exceptional grace, reduced to a disgusting mess with less dignity than a side of beef.*

McFarland had been strolling to Low Library, recalling a New York when one could walk safely anywhere on the Upper West Side. But Eighty-Fourth Street between Amsterdam and Columbus had changed dramatically while accommodating immigrants lured by cheap housing. McFarland unwittingly walked down a street *The Times* had deemed the worst block in Manhattan, "a gathering place of drunks, narcotics addicts and sexual perverts." Still, all might have gone well enough had he passed through the hood a bit earlier.

But he'd had the misfortune of arriving just after police fired warning shots to dispel a huge street brawl.

The deterrent failed, and the alignment of the moon and stars was such that four hundred of New York's worst surged from their tenements to vent the frustration of their miserable lives. Police and unfamiliar others who appeared easy marks suffered their rage, and McFarland's age, race, and spiffy clothes made him a prominent target. Four street toughs drug him into an alley where they abused and scorned him while relieving him of his possessions. In one final, unfortunate and officious pronouncement, McFarland, ever the Army officer, suggested his assailants were in big trouble since justice would triumph over their obscene knavery. Feeling disrespected, they drew switchblades and stabbed him repeatedly, taunting him before tossing him into a garbage bin to die. "Wise-ass old mutha fucka," jibed a fifteen-year-old, "let's see if da rats in dat bin can gib ya some a dat justice, honkey."

The thugs bemoaned the injustice visited upon them when, rifling through his pockets, briefcase and wallet, they found only $64.00 in cash, $150.00 in American Express Traveler's checks, his identification, and a folder marked "Peeters." After perusing the contents of the folder they threw the "worthless pile of shit" into the Hudson River.

The contents swallowed up included a report card from St. George School in Kenosha, Wisconsin with glowing comments from a teacher, a picture of Sixtus Peeters as a young man in cap and gown standing proudly on Bascolm Hill in Madison as the university class valedictorian, a Lieutenant's commission in the Army Air Corps, and an award for navigational excellence. It also contained a photo of a beautiful Italian woman with Mount Vesuvius and the Bay of Naples in the background. The photo captured the thugs attention long enough for them to concur they would have taken turns "nailing her" if she'd been there in the flesh.

John went to Connecticut for McFarland's funeral, but he didn't recognize anyone there. He listened for clues when the minister spoke of the decedent's wartime work in the OSS, but he touted its importance without disclosing any details. John spoke with his niece, the executrix, who listened sympathetically when he showed her the photos. None of them meant anything to her, although she recognized Donovan and the Congressional Country Club in Bethesda. "I'm certain that's it since the interlocking C's are their symbol. I went there for lunch with Uncle Walt. He enjoyed his wartime service, fondly recalled its memories, and spoke of people who'd passed through when they'd headquartered there—inspiring and selfless men. I'm sure that's the same Negro gentleman who opened the door for us. No man had ever tipped his hat to me before then and it seemed so gallant!

I recognize General Donovan. I never met him, but I've seen him in pictures and heard so much about him that I feel like I knew him . . . No, I don't remember any names."

John believed McFarland's death was an omen more than a coincidence, and he believed, for the first time, that he might never learn his identity. He decided to take Big Mike's advice and focus on what he had rather than what he wanted. Besides, Rose had been right so often that it seemed time for him to follow her lead.

She'd relentlessly pushed him to take the post at Northwestern, especially when she thought he might be suicidal. She'd sought out Father Farrell then, and he implored her to give it "a little more time and more prayer, for the love of God." Being devout, she obeyed and prayed, thought John's response to McFarland's death confirmed God's mysterious ways, something like dawn arising from the darkness.

McFarland's murder also demonstrated how common inner city violence had become in America. The failure to assimilate disparate segments of the population threatened the country's solidarity as middle-class Americans fearing civil disorder fled from the cities into the suburbs. The murder of McFarland helped convince the Redfords to join the exodus and rehabilitate John in the relative calm of northeastern Illinois.

Still, Rose agreed the airman in the picture had to be John as a young man, and it intrigued her while giving him hope. They reached a compromise which they wrote up as an actual contract: she agreed to tolerate his search as long as it remained manageable and secondary in importance to his career and their family, something like a hobby. In return, John agreed to be candid and share everything he learned with her. He also agreed to limit his efforts to mutually agreeable times with a checklist including deadlines for completion. For enforcement, he agreed to consult a psychiatrist of her choice if he violated the understanding. John hated the penalty clause, but committed to preserve his marriage. He crossed his fingers on only one item. Until he understood it fully, he'd never tell Rose he'd killed a girl who looked like Mary Thayer, the model for *Angel*.

The first checklist item proved easy. No soldier with the name of John Absalom Redford had served in the military in World War Two.

After accepting the position at Northwestern, they flew to Chicago to purchase a home. Rose dictated its terms: it had to be gracious, comfortable and spacious enough for their large family, and also adequately rewarding for her past travails. She settled on one she considered ideal, extravagant, but key to refocusing John, a sanctuary without any of the sensual assaults of Manhattan.

The home was one of the finest in the Chicagoland area, a stone walled, slate-roofed mansion in the French Chateau style. It had six bedrooms and baths, vegetable and wine cellars, a library and a conservatory. Rose especially liked the two-story library, picturing herself on a sofa devouring novels while the children were in school. And the kitchen would be perfect for the entertaining she intended to resume, with granite islands and a sitting area with a fireplace overlooking the backyard.

A short commute from Evanston, the property rested on eight acres with access from a road serving only two other estates. Entry was from the north, through a decorative iron gate in a ten-foot stone wall, opening to evergreens blocking any outside view of the home. The winding drive turned east from the entry along the wall, before wrapping back west around the evergreens for a view of the imposing home. It then ran one hundred yards to a circular drive and beyond to a three car garage.

The estate included one hundred feet of Lake Michigan frontage, reached by steps between an erosion barrier descending fifty feet to the beach. Adjacent homes were only visible when leaves had fallen, and then only by difficult views from the third floor.

An oaken deck behind the home spanned its width, affording a splendid seasonal view over a manicured lawn bordered with flowers including violet iris, white and pink hydrangea, and yellow and orange hibiscus, all interspersed with greenery of multiple shades. At the end of the fifty-yard expanse were bright white and yellow daylilies fronting tangled forest underbrush leading to linden, hornbeam, maple and oak trees. Sunlight warmed the deck until dusk when it struggled to reach the home through the trees, sporadic rays casting shadows that could often deceive one's eyes.

Set in a densely forested parcel, the home was well suited for a "Lake Forest" address. John deferred entirely to Rose in the choice, realizing all he owed her for his long period of self-absorption—too bad if his Trustee raised an eyebrow over the price.

———

In 1962, with his family housed, decorating and exploring their new home, John took advantage of a lull to check off the next item on his hobby list, a trip to West Virginia.

Crossing the mountains south of Pittsburgh and following the Monongahela into Morgantown, John noted that the University occupied a splendid setting atop a small town in mountains next to the river, and he felt certain that he'd never seen it before. Making his way to White Hall and the Physics Department, he met with their longest tenured faculty member.

"This is a charming campus, Doctor Iacovo."

"It is. Enough to keep me content for nearly thirty years. My, how time flies! I was raised on the eastern shore and imagined the whole country flat as a pancake next to an ocean until I came here as an undergraduate. Have you visited with us before?"

John ignored the question. "Since I was passing this way on my trip to D.C., our Chair suggested I see whether we have any research of mutual interest. Your academic focus is . . . forgive me, what is it exactly?"

"It's the relationship of neutron stars to general relativity. They're amazing platforms for studying the interstellar media and plasma physics. Do you have anything similar in the works, Doctor Redford?"

"Our man Chrisakos recently published an article on using tokamoks to create fusion energy by heating confined plasma. I'll ask if there may be some opportunity for collaboration."

"Good, good, there may well be some overlap!"

They discussed toroidal reactors used in thermonuclear experiments until John switched the subject entirely. "I know this seems odd, but I'm not sure whether I've been here before. I hoped you might help. I thought my name might be familiar."

"It's one reason I looked forward to meeting you. I worked closely with a man named John Redford before the war. The chap's middle name was Absalom, as unforgettable as him. You seem near my age, close to the same age he would have been. Are you related, or are there simply packs of scientists named Redford mucking about?"

"You said 'would have been' close to my age?"

"Redford passed away just before beginning the doctoral program, a real tragedy and genuine loss. He had a first-rate mind. He would have been our undergraduate valedictorian, but he declined because of his anxiety issues."

"You're certain?"

"Of what?"

"That this John Redford died."

"Well, of course I am. We were . . . just a minute, Doctor Redford, what's this all about?"

He paused for a moment, looked Iacovo in the eyes and asked, "Please, sir, humor me. Take your time and look at me very closely. What if I told you I was the same John Absalom Redford who graduated from here in 1942 with a degree in Physics?"

Iacovo guffawed. "Then I'd say one of us is out of his wits and I can assure you it isn't me!"

John described his lack of memory in general terms while Iacovo left no doubt he wasn't the brilliant scientist he'd known at the University. "I can't imagine anyone confusing you with him. There's a vague resemblance, but obvious differences, pardon me, such as the cleft in your chin, and your hair is far thicker, even then he'd begun balding. He was so shy he killed himself to avoid the anxiety of simply working in a team setting. He would never have a conversation such as this with someone he'd only just met, he was far too introverted."

A day later, John stood over the actual John Redford's grave in a tiny cemetery in Parsons, West Virginia, wondering why Doctor Wright and the government had deceived him. It took a high level of covert effort to place him in Los Alamos under a false name, but it was evident someone had, which explained Donovan, McFarland, and the OSS involvement. Still, it made no sense. If he'd been a qualified scientist assisting in the work, what was the point? The CIA photo was even more puzzling since the Company didn't even exist until after the war.

Anger rose up in him. Why would they disguise him as a social misfit? It couldn't have been to hide his killing of a young woman since they'd never knowingly use someone like that in such a sensitive position. He thought, *That lying bastard Edmund Wright would know*, but all he'd learned in D.C. was that Wright couldn't be found and the hospital where he'd been treated had become an inaccessible CIA facility.

He went to the elegant Congressional Country Club in Bethesda and discovered that the she-crab soup and service were both excellent. He wouldn't even have been admitted into the exclusive place without dropping McFarland's name and revealing his stint in Los Alamos. Delighted to have something of a celebrity grace his establishment, the manager picked up his tab and toasted the bomb's success. John learned that every vestige of the OSS time there had been removed but for a commemorative plaque. He also learned that General Leslie Groves was about to publish a book telling the inside story of the Project, and the manager said he looked forward to reading about John in it.

When his visions first struck anew, John didn't think Groves would be helpful. They'd only first met when he interviewed him as John Redford, and Groves wasn't the type to chitchat with his underlings about personal matters. John also knew Groves had returned to Washington right after the bomb was used against Japan, before his accident, and he'd already retired from the military when John underwent treatment in Virginia.

He first thought to contact Groves when he learned he'd also been employed by Sperry Rand, leaving the company only two months before McFarland's death. He learned that, in fact, Groves would have attended the funeral but for being in Australia. Although he'd certainly never been part of the OSS, he had to know those in the OSS leadership positions, and he may have known why McFarland had contacted him.

He called, left messages, and appeared unannounced at Groves's Maryland home. Ignored and rebuffed, he followed up with letters explaining his dilemma and asked McFarland's niece to intervene, but all for naught. He couldn't understand it. He recalled working well with Groves and couldn't remember a single disagreement during their eighteen months together. He wondered if perhaps Groves suffered from some sort of mental disability.

John devoured Groves's book upon its release, but it fell far short of its tantalizing title, *Now It Can Be Told*. It disclosed few details not already in the public domain. It focused instead on Project planning and logistics and Groves's emotional response to Trinity's success. Most significantly, the book mentioned many key players he'd worked with, but John wasn't mentioned anywhere, either by name or by function. It didn't make any sense. He'd been deeply involved, helped deliver the plutonium for Trinity, discovered Stegger's error jeopardizing production, and had even been one of the few witnesses at Hiroshima. His omission had to be purposeful, but why?

Groves's health deteriorated shortly after his retirement from Sperry Rand, and he died of heart disease without ever responding to Redford. His health issues dominated his final years, and beyond that, he had no interest in revisiting his profound disappointment at having been deceived by Peeters and the OSS.

When the war ended, the Russian threat sounded a call to arms. Americans began imagining the horror of the Ruskies bombing their cities, so the government designated anything remotely related to atomic energy as restricted to protect national security interests. The need to balance that restriction against the public clamor for details, and the government's desire to trumpet its achievement, led to *The Smyth Report*.

Meant to disclose some secrets and establish guidelines for further disclosures, and released only after approval by seven separate commissions and by President Truman, the Report called for disclosure of anything "benefitting the general welfare." It said, the "people of the country must be informed if they are to discharge their responsibilities wisely." But deciding who would determine what to disclose delayed any significant release of data for the next fifty years, placing unsurmountable obstacles in the path of victims like John Redford with a genuine need for details.

The system designed to filter information before its release became a bureaucrat's wet dream: multi-layered and separate units known by an alphabet of acronyms played intersecting, conflicting, and indiscernible roles. These included the DOD, AEC, ERDA, NRC, MED, LASL, COD, JCAE, NAS, ASCP, TEP, and DOE—all to protect the USA from the USSR. From 1945 until 1994, forty-four million pages of documents were withheld, being designated secret, top-secret, ultra-top-secret, confidential, official eyes-only, highest, restricted and restricted-restricted. Bulletins, pamphlets, reports, panels, committees, commissions, offices, services, classification groups, classification review groups and comprehensive review programs all dictated protocols for treatment of the information.

With that and with declassification policies also restricted, little helpful information could be accessed by anyone not employed by the government or holding a security clearance.

John turned to the law for help getting through the bureaucratic complexity. In 1963, he engaged Chicago attorneys with a branch office in Washington, D.C. After receiving a hefty retainer, they confidently assured him they'd discover how Wright, McFarland, Donovan, the OSS and the CIA were involved, how he came to be a beneficiary of a sizeable trust, and why he'd been given a dead man's identity.

The trust issue seemed simplest, and his lawyers soon determined the source wasn't government compensation as John had believed, but rather funds originally set aside by Stephen Harkness of New York, a deceased major shareholder of Standard Oil. But to their astonishment, they couldn't find out why he'd been included. The names of all trust beneficiaries were protected by a court order that could only be broken by showing trustee fraud, a practically impossible hurdle. The attorney had never heard of such a daunting restriction and he confidently said it could be overcome.

In three years, the law firm generated thousands of pages of research and court pleadings, sent stacks of letters, made innumerable telephone calls, and visited with well-developed contacts in many government agencies. Yet their efforts produced nothing but orders of Courts from the Southern District of New York and the Second Circuit requiring both John and his agents to "cease and desist" from further efforts to undermine the Attorney

General of the United States by seeking information protected for national security purposes.

The lawyers did learn that the CIA had employed Dr. Edmund Wright after he completed his psychiatric residency, but they couldn't find a trace of him after he surrendered his medical license in 1948 for undisclosed reasons.

John parted company with his lawyers, who recommended he put the matter behind him until time loosened government tongues. "Barring that," his primary lawyer advised, "there are extra-legal approaches, like investigators working alongside the system. Their unconventional ways are said to be helpful. We can't vouch for them and our firm would never recommend one, but I'll write down a name that's supposedly the best of the lot. I'm not recommending him, mind you," he concluded with a wink. John filed the information away until the urge to uncover his past stirred within him once again.

6.

How I Spent My Family Vacation

England, 1965

"Is it just him?" Rose asked while watching their teenage son, Abe. Leg resting atop a bench, he held his entwined hands across his knee, straining to hold his shoulders and back straight as he pretended contemplating far-off matters of far more interest than anything in Trafalgar Square. The act was a hard sell, with the Square filled with flower children engaged in every conceivable antic. Meanwhile, his nerdy brother and oblivious sister called at him, but he stood his ground. He'd spotted two Carnaby Street birds wearing tie-dyed, vibrant sheaths, with white boots reaching high up on their long legs, and he knew they were checking him out too.

"Abe, Abe, look at me!" shouted Mary. He coolly ignored her, while considering the downside of family vacations. *I'd probably get lucky if I were here alone.*

"All the boys want to be Steve McQueen," observed John. "Look at him and think *The Great Escape*. Actually, he may be on to something, I've noticed two very . . . young girls eyeing him. They're heading toward him now."

"You're a dirty old man, Redford. You noticed? More like you're transfixed. Another half inch and their behinds would be on full display."

"I see London, I see France, I see hippies' underpants! Be a sport, Rose, we came here for stimulating sights."

"I'll give you stimulation. You need to talk to your son. These girls are so brazen. How am I going to explain 'Free Love' to Mary?"

Sexual revolution aside, the trip had been outstanding. After leaving Heathrow, they'd headed for the country, knowing nothing outside London would satisfy the kids after a few days in the exciting city. They'd experienced serious family bonding, singing along to the sounds of the British invasion while driving in a van, playing darts and experiencing pub life, and visiting Stonehenge, Blenheim Palace, and a series of castles. They even joined an impromptu celebration in Liverpool, lucky to be there the day the Queen anointed the Fab Four as Members of the Order of the British Empire. "It's not the sort of award given every day," Abe tried explaining to his presumably obtuse parents.

The first three weeks passed quickly. They missed Lizzy and Timmy, but they were perfectly content at home playing with Nanny Allison. Their turn would come next. It had already been a struggle convincing Abe to come along. Soon the older children would rather be bored at home than in London with their parents.

Parliament was visible from their suite at the Savoy, and "the best Dad ever" scored four tickets for the premiere of *Help*! John had surprised Rose with his patience, since she knew full well that he had an ulterior motive in visiting England. But other than studying maps, making a few calls and talking with locals, he'd ignored his "hobby," easily convincing Rose he'd earned a chance to explore on his own while they toured London.

John had a scientist's sense of statistical probability, and it had steered him to the East of England. With four days set aside, he drove from London, reviewing his thought process.

The words that flooded his mind at the Met (George, Libya, Atia, azume, the maid) were of no help by themselves. But he found envouragement in two of the photos left by McFarland: the one of the CIA reception (if he could somehow penetrate the Company), and the photograph of a B-24 aircrew, since he surmised he had to be the confident-looking young officer in the photo.

Most of the history of B-24 usage remained classified even twenty years after the war, but soldiers' memoirs provided clues, and he'd supplemented those by visiting VFW posts across the Midwest. He'd learned there hadn't been any master compilation of pictures of the crews even though such photos were taken routinely. This meant the chance of finding a photo identifying a particular crew was a matter of blind luck. He'd tried anyway, spent hours looking through similar photos in private collections, VFW posts and in libraries, including the Library of Congress, but none he found matched his photo.

He'd learned that the Defense Department requested funding by touting its wartime successes, and supporting data was published in the Congressional Record. So he spent two days in Washington reviewing the Record, and he uncovered some suggestive facts: Eighteen thousand B-24 aircraft were flown during the war and in every branch of service, but two-thirds were used by the Air Corps; (this matched the photo since one officer's brimmed cap appeared to bear the Air Corps insignia); the B-24 had been known as the workhorse of the Eighth Army because it was used most often by that branch in bombing Germany, and more than ninety percent of their missions originated from the East of England; and most B-24s were produced at the Ford plant in Willow Run, Michigan, beginning in October, 1942, with the greatest production being of the H model, placed into service shortly before June, 1943.

Upon enlarging the aircrew photo, he'd noticed a fragment of an emblem on the latch of a flight bag beside a crewman. The bottom of the emblem showed part of a curved line appearing to be part of a full circle, with the v-shaped tip of a star reaching to the inside of the upper curve. Such an encircled star had been the emblem of the Eighth Air Force, but the words "Eighth Air Force" were first inserted around the circle upon group realignment in January, 1944, and those words were missing from the photo.

John surmised, from all the data, that he'd most likely been a crewmember of an H model B-24 produced shortly before June, 1943, and flew from one of roughly fifty English bases before January, 1944. The speculation meshed perfectly with the certainty that he'd reported to Los Alamos as John Redford in the spring of 1944, after reportedly being killed in action.

The single clue to a particular base was the marker number 114 on the runway. Since no base had adequate traffic to require more than two runways, it couldn't be a ground control designation. This made it either a directional heading or a coded identifier. But compass headings typically consisted of two numbers rounded off to the nearest tenth of a degree, so 114 wasn't directional unless an extra digit had been added for an unknown reason. The number four likely didn't mean anything alone, but the first number one could have represented the primary runway, with the following fourteen representing a 140 degree heading, a runway running southeast to northwest. But he rejected this line of thinking as too convoluted, learning Air Corps pilots were trained on conventional runways.

He decided a coded numbering system must have been used for identifying specific bases. This made sense since geographic names and markings could have compromised security. Unfortunately, this made the number useless unless he found an index linking base numbers to locations, and he hadn't learned of such an index anywhere. Still, he'd search through the East of England for that unknown base. He had nothing to lose.

In Martlesham, he stopped for petrol next to the Golden Goose Gift Shoppe and spoke with the proprietor. "I served in the Air Corps on a nearby base during the war, but everything looks much different now. Would you know where I might find a wartime base?"

"Reminiscing, hey? Well, you lads did one hell of a job for us, so you're surely welcome back. You must mean RAF Martlesham Heath. Lord, weren't those the times! We'll never forget what you Yanks did, and you well knew how to party. All the merchants missed you after the war—too quiet nowadays. Oh, righto. Just stay east on Main Road until you get to A 12, then turn left five hundred yards and you're there. You'll be disappointed though. They ran

RAF fighters from there for a time after the war, but it was sold off about five years ago. Now it's an Industrial Park with nothing left of the place but a bit of runway concrete. Lord, those were the days! Come back and I'll buy you a pint."

"That's very kind of you. But do you know where I might find anything showing how it appeared during the war?"

"They aerial map now, but didn't back then. And there's no museum or such that I know of, though there's talk of starting one in East Anglia. I don't know of any personal collections, but I'll ask around. Maybe the RAF has something, otherwise I couldn't say."

John repeated the process several times and discovered that abandoned air bases had been transformed into grass-covered fields, housing developments, golf courses, Blackhawk missile sites, or like one outside Kimbolton, into a private flying club. There an aerial map displayed operable runways throughout the Region, and after studying it, John caught a break.

Directing him toward the longest remaining runway, a glider pilot explained, "You take A 140 ta Attleborough and turn . . . hmm, hey Watkins, do ya go east or west twa Banham passin 112 on A 140?"

John interrupted. "Excuse me, did you say 112?"

"Sure, 112, Shimpling."

"What's that?"

"Tis the nearest railway stop."

"Is there a 114?"

"Twas, I'm certain. The stations always bin known by their numbers til Labour saw votes cud be had creatin useless jobs makin signs painted with quaint names like Shimpling Shire, tho never been a shire! I still use numbers jest ta piss em."

"Do you have any idea where 114 would have been?"

"Itda ben two stops more." He pointed on a map, "Here, right on the edgea Wymondham."

"Was there an airfield there during the war?"

"Dudn't know tho I'm sure they flew out a Hethel close to 114. Check at The Green Dragon Inn in Wymondham. It's been there forever, someone there oughta know. I've not gan for years, but sure ta find good food and great ale for ya trouble."

At the curve in a lane in the middle of Wymondham, John found The Green Dragon Inn. He would have passed by if he'd been any less determined. What once had been a quaint and very old Tudor structure with a thatched roof had been butchered. The replacement roof had asphalt where there had once been thatch, and the building's front was clad in bright, gold-colored siding. It bore an oversized sign of a dumb-looking dragon with cartoonish eyes in a huge head, with a jutting chin and a mouth drawn into a crooked grin. Its misshaped form included tiny wings, a ballooning yellow belly and an arrow-tipped, short tail. The pathetic looking creature held a flowing banner reading "Puff," and a caption touting the place as the "Home of the Atomic Bar."

John saw a blinking neon sign reading "Open for Lunch," and he entered through a glass turnstile suitable for a Macy's. He found himself in a room bathed in artificial light so bright it rivaled a sunlit beach. Light reflected off a glossy white linoleum floor and silver-aluminum tables in yellow vinyl booths. It reminded him of the Kitchen of the Future at the World's Fair, except far more garish.

A thin, shoulder-length haired man wearing a paisley shirt and white bellbottoms waved at John from behind a bar. A sign above the bar displayed what was meant to represent the nucleus of an atom, white and blue balls combined in a mass and surrounded by orbiting electrons. "Welcome, man," he called out, waving at two dozen empty booths and generously inviting John to sit anywhere. "Hang in there, Dee-Dee will be with you pronto."

Dee-Dee appeared from behind a swinging door wearing a sleeveless, one-piece, white vinyl sheath with a duplicate of the atomic symbol on her torso, like a bull's eye. She smiled broadly while walking robotically and he couldn't resist noting, "That looks too stiff to be comfortable."

She responded with a fluttering of mascara-laden eyelashes. "It pays the bills, ya know, and the teddies dig it. Come back tonight and you'll see the strobes flashing off me behind while I walk away shaking it." She turned around, shook her rear end and bent over to reveal neon yellow panties. "Whee . . . cool, huh? And whatever you spill wipes off." She giggled, "Well, on my dress that is. I'm what you might call an expert at cleaning up spills!"

John wondered what he was doing there. "Don't give me a heart attack, Dee-Dee, old guys like me head home before nightfall."

"Nights are best for the lights, but anytime at all will do," she said while leaning in close. "I'll show you what you've been missing. You're not that old, believe me you won't regret it!"

John leaned back. "Look, Dee-Dee, you're a beautiful girl and all, but don't misunderstand. I'm trying to find an air base where I was stationed as a soldier in World War Two, and it . . . and well, I've come a long way . . . "

Dee-Dee's expression flashed from ditzy to serious and back so quickly that he wondered if he'd imagined it. She bounced up and exclaimed, "Think about lunch first!" Bowing over in front of him, she used both hands to place a menu on the table. Staring into his eyes, she tilted her head and then began lowering it very slowly. When she'd lowered it down to table level she winked again. "Be back, miss me," she announced before popping up and skipping off.

"Isn't she something?" asked the proprietor, who hurried over to the booth and sat himself down across from John.

"She's something else."

"What brings you here? You're not British."

"I'm American, an Air Corps vet. I'm checking out the old airfields, something of a nostalgia tour."

"Mind if I see your passport?"

"Really, for lunch?"

"Don't fret, you'll get it back," he said with hand outstretched. "No biggie, I'll explain."

John withdrew and handed over his passport. As the man studied it, John studied him in turn. He noticed crow's feet aside his eyes and streaks of gray running through his hair. He looked like he'd covered lots of miles, and John added years to his first guess, reckoned him over forty.

"An educator from Illinois, well, welcome back, Professor," he said, passing it back. "I needed to be sure you weren't with the Canadian gestapo. I left home on less than stellar terms—it's a nation of tight-asses. I'm Moe Cantwell, I own this joint." He held out his hand and the men shook.

"What do you think of my place, Redford, incredible right?"

"It truly is hard to believe."

"Planned it all," he said proudly, "although I'm a modest sort, I have to admit its perfect. You should have seen it before, like a thousand years old, a dump from the jolly old England days. Hello, what do you say old chap and all such BS." He laughed aloud, enjoying his wit. "I wanted a vision for the sixties, not Dickens for Christ's sake. It needed pizazz to rope in the youngsters and then bam, it hit me! I thought 'the Jetsons,' like a gateway to the future. Now when we run gigs on weekends we turn them away at the door. Everyone wants to see the next group before they hit the big time. Stop by Friday, Banks and Rutherford will be here, great sound, but not yet together. A cool name would help. I told them go with 'Genesis,' like 'the beginning,' neato, huh?"

"Very neato, Mr. Cantwell, but I'm not much for music. Actually, I came here because . . . "

"Call me Moe!"

"Sure, Moe, what I was . . . "

"Try the shepherd's pie with a pint of bitter, guaranteed to please. I kept the old recipes. I mean, what the f, we needed something for the older farts, no offense. But we added burgers and dogs. Maybe you'd rather a Chicago dog?"

"No, a shepherd's will be fine. But I have some questions I'd like to ask."

"Shoot away, man."

"How long have you owned this place?"

"I bought it in sixty-one, right after Barnsey died."

"Barnsey?"

"Michael Barnes, the longtime owner and my uncle, a large, gregarious chap who drank until it killed him. He had the big one rolling a barrel into the bar. I'm strictly a pot type, that alcohol can kill you, man. Hey, no offense friend, it's cool if you quaff a pint or two."

"No offense taken . . . friend."

"Aunt Emma wanted it kept in the family. So being the only relative with abundant cash, I moved back from Toronto and bought it. I ran a bar in Canada before it became too hot for me to stay there. Did I tell you the Canucks are tight-asses?"

"Do you know anything about the war years?"

"No, I was only sixteen when it started, too young to serve. "

"I mean, do you have any idea what it was like here back then, here near the Inn?"

"No, not really, we moved to Canada before it began. Daddio split, thinking the Jerries would soon be marching in."

Dee-Dee returned and stood listening, then coughed to interrupt. She laboriously wrote down "Table three, Number One" on a notepad after Cantwell told her John wanted the number one. When she turned away, Cantwell reached up under her vinyl skirt and squeezed her behind. "You're the most, hot stuff!" She gave out a high-pitched giggle and bounced away.

"She can be too talkative sometimes, but she really is the best."

"I can see that."

"See indeed!" He winked. "Did you *see* anything you like, Professor? Everything here is available, friend, and price is never an issue. Fair is my middle name. Dee-Dee's dance card is full every night, but it's quiet now. How's bout after lunch, after a little ale loosens you up, I slide you in, if you catch my drift."

"Ummm . . . I appreciate the offer, Moe, but no thanks. Really, I'm just here to . . . "

"Just think about it, Yank. She'll make your parts spin. One toke and she becomes an animal. Nothing is off-limits, nothing at all!"

"Really, no thanks, I just want some information and was told to try here. Besides, I'm married."

"Geez, Professor, who isn't married? We're not talking a relationship here! I respect your restraint, but I'm just saying watch her and think about it, let it play on your mind. No charge for looking."

Moe promised to ask around while John ate his lunch, if he'd promise to consider savoring Dee-Dee. But everyone on the Inn's staff postdated the war, and he apparently learned very little. Moe did report that all the structures on airbase 114, Hethel Field, had been demolished and the runways resurfaced for use as a testing ground for Lotus automobiles.

When Moe moved back to the bar, Dee-Dee came with the bill and leaned in close. He noted seriousness in her expression as she whispered, "Please, tell Moe you want to be with me. We won't do anything, but you'll save me from a beating. I'll tell you what you want to know. Trust me. I can help. Act like we're flirting, please!" She stood up and laughed, mussed his hair and exclaimed, "Well, aren't you the devil!" Scampering away she shouted, "See you soon!" over her shoulder.

Running up to him, Cantwell suggested an hour with Dee-Dee could be had at "a once in a lifetime special price, for wartimes' sake." John wondered what working for him must be like, and also if he was being conned. His feelings became sympathetic when he realized the price of her favors was less than the price of a baseball game.

"Sure, why not?" he said, reaching for his wallet. Cantwell grinned, delighted by his apparently successful pimp.

"Good man, you won't regret it! The bitch will teach you things you won't forget. Enjoy!"

Dee-Dee locked the door of a windowless room behind them. In the comically red light, he spotted only washcloths and a basin of water atop a dresser, a pitcher and two glasses, a single bed with the covers down and, *my God*, he thought, a double-wide swing hanging from a five-hundred-year-old beam in the ceiling. He couldn't imagine what toys were tucked away in the dresser.

Dee-Dee put her fingertips to her lips, and touched them to his cheek. "Thank you, now come and sit by me, sir."

Transformed and demure, Dee-Dee sat on the bed with her hands on closed knees, John beside her. "You seem like someone I can trust."

"I'd like to think so. I'm here because it seemed you needed me."

"You're protecting me, sir, there's no doubt, but I can help you too. I need to vent sometimes to know I still feel something other than that out there. I hate what I do and, it's complicated, since I think I hate Moe too, but still, I mean . . . "

"Dee-Dee, look, I . . . "

"Every now and then I need to do something just because it's right, you know, to prove I can do the right thing. Does that make sense?"

"Of course, but why are you . . ."

"Did you ever hear of Bergen-Belsen? Moe wouldn't know it if it bit him in the ass."

John knew of the concentration camp in Lower Saxony, Germany. It'd been used largely as a holding and transfer depot for war prisoners or Jews valuable enough to be exchanged for German prisoners. It had no gas chambers, but more than fifty thousand internees died there of disease or starvation, most notably Anne Frank of Amsterdam.

"My parents survived that hellhole. They went there in cattle cars after being captured in Warsaw. They were selected for what the Germans called 'Sonderbehandlung,' special treatment," she said, spitting it out. "They were emaciated and among the dead and dying spread across an acre of foul dirt when American troops liberated them in 1945."

Dee-Dee spoke in a soft monotone about her parent's resettlement in England, their rebirth and joy in hers, her failure to meet their expectations, and her drug addiction. Her eyes were moist with emotion when she finished her story. "They're gone now, but they always told me America's compassion and sacrifice gave them back their lives." Dee-Dee wrapped her arms around him and nuzzled his neck saying repeatedly, "Thank you, thank you."

He was embarrassed. She had no idea what he'd done during the war, yet she showered him with gratitude. He would have been rightfully proud had he known he was a hero and he'd sacrificed his identity for the war, but Dee-Dee's parents had been wrong. It wasn't the compassion and sacrifice of America, but rather that of ordinary men, selfless soldiers, who liberated places like Bergen-Belsen and allowed the hopeless to regain their lives.

"When Moe bought the Inn, it was filled with memorabilia accumulated over generations, with many items from the war when it was a hangout for the Hethel men. He told me to throw all the 'old time historical shit' out, but I didn't. I gave it to an old-timer who'd been a regular for years before Moe raped the place. I'd never defied Moe before then, and knew if he learned I gave something away for nothing he'd have beaten me silly. But it made me feel alive to make the old man so happy."

"Can you tell me where to find him?"

"Yes, but you can't tell Moe!"

"I'd never tell him . . . Dee-Dee, you're a gem. There must be some way I can thank you. But tell me why it is you still . . . "

"It's complicated, and I'm not sure. Moe's a bastard, but still, he's my bastard, if that makes any sense. But if you want to thank me, just tell Moe I'm the very best you've ever had."

"Of course I will. I'm so very grateful." Then she told him where he could find the old-timer.

She said, "We still have twenty minutes. I'd like to prove I really am the best."

"Dee-Dee, no, no, I'm sorry, you're very attractive and I'm grateful, but I just can't . . . "

She stood up, opened her robe and threw it on the floor. He jumped away, startled, while she giggled. She turned and messed up the sheets, came over and stood next to him, resting her head against his chest for a time. After the hour expired, she led him to the door and kissed him on the forehead while he stood as far away from her as possible, making her laugh again. "Just my luck, all the nice guys are taken." Gesturing to her body and the bed, she said, "Moe wouldn't believe us otherwise."

Moe ran over from the bar and grabbed John after he exited the room, as he waved back to Dee-Dee, who stood leaning stark naked against the doorjamb and waving in turn.

"Well?" he asked.

"You're a lucky man, Moe. She's far and away the very best I've ever had. I'll try to get back here whenever I can."

"No special price next time, Professor. This was my one-time patriotic gesture. Full price now that you've had a taste."

"God and country today, right?"

"Huh?"

Unable to resist, John added, "Moe, perhaps I can teach you something. Your atomic symbol," he pointed, "is supposed to represent uranium?"

"Sure, man, every dummy knows you need uranium for atomic power."

"Well, trust me on this one: a uranium atom has ninty-two protons and ninety-two electrons, of which six are valence electrons. And, of course, the uranium nucleus binds between 141 and 146 neutrons, establishing six isotopes, with the most common being uranium 238 with 146 neutrons, and uranium 235 with 143 neutrons."

"Man, that's heavy. What does it mean?"

"It means your place isn't quite perfect. In parlance you can appreciate, your atomic symbol is dog shit. Look it up and make it accurate." John clapped him on the back. "See you . . . friend!"

Forty minutes after leaving The Green Dragon Inn, John sat at a table in the home of Harold Williams, a loquacious older gentleman and former regular patron of the Inn.

"She's a peach, Redford. I would have paid anything for these memories, but she only asked that I keep it secret. Of course, I'd never speak to the moron anyway. It's an odd world where a woman like her is with such as him. What sort of idiot makes a monstrosity out of a treasure? Even now, you be sitting at my favorite table from the Inn . . . Lord, the memories! Barnes be spinning in his grave knowing his Inn has become a whorehouse for music druggies." He directed a stream of spit into the center of a spittoon. "No respect for memories, that damned Canadian. We asked the Commission to deny his permit, but he paid every one of those jackasses off! He's a cash kind of man, making pounds off the backs of ladies."

As the sole survivor of an Inn foursome, Williams enjoyed sharing his memories and airing gripes. His mind was intact, and he regaled John with wartime stories illustrated by memorabilia spread out on the table. There were many photos, mostly pin-holed, old and discolored, including shots of wartime Hethel Field, its planes, and airmen and mechanics in uniform. A cigar box contained feathered darts, a menu in a velvet folder, and a framed newspaper showing Churchill with a cigar in one hand, holding the other high above his head with his fingers forming a V underneath a headline screaming VICTORY!

Williams left the room to retrieve a large commemorative plaque festooned with red, white, and blue ribbons. He read the inscription aloud, "With gratitude to Master Innkeeper Michael Barnes for making The Green Dragon Inn a home away from home for the valiant warriors of Hethel Field who gallantly served . . . "

John's eyes drifted to a photo amidst the many spread out on the table, one showing three men standing with arms intertwined, laughing. The large and rotund man on the right clasped a flag with a cross, while the man on the left held his head high, resting his right hand on his hip and grinning with self-confident ease. John's heart leapt as he recognized the same officer shown in his photo of the crew, him! He grabbed it and looked more closely, turned it over to see a handwritten date "June 26, 1943." *No question at all, I was here twenty-two years ago!* He interrupted. "Please, Mr. Williams, excuse me, I'm sorry, but please tell me about this photo?"

Williams held it close and squinted from behind his spectacles as he tried making a withdrawal from his memory bank. Eventually he said, "That's Barnes holding the flag, and that's poor old . . . hmm,.." He pointed to the broad-nosed, tall, balding man in the middle. "It's umm, Murray, no not Murray, Murphy, no not Murphy . . . Merrill, yes, that's it, it's Colonel Merrill. A most affable chap who loved the Inn. A good man whose death stung us. Stress, they said, and I could believe it, what with welcoming all those men and watching them go off to die. Poor bloke, so young and all.

The third man was another Yank, but I only saw him a few times and never really knew him. I remember he fascinated Barnes with an odd take on dragons, something about good versus evil, not killing them and all. It excited Barnes so much he'd planned some sort of debate on St. George's Day. I never really quite understood it all, but it had to do with the saint and that's his flag he be holding."

John recalled the words from the Met: George for St. George, and Libya, where St. George slew a dragon. An obvious connection.

"What else can you remember about the American on the left?"

"Like I said, Redford, I only saw him a couple of times. I never really knew him."

"Please, sir, it's very important. Please take all the time you need. Is it possible you might remember his name?"

Williams ran his hand through his hair, scratched his eyelid, rubbed his chin, folded his arms across his chest and leaned back thinking. "He was killed in the war," he finally replied, "sometime before Merrill died. I remember being told it happened in a raid on some oil fields in Europe. They took it poorly, and Barnes stopped the idea of the debates, although he hung St. George's flag up for years. But I'm sorry, I can't recall his name."

Williams could add nothing further and knew of no other sources. They exchanged numbers, and Williams promised to pass along anything he uncovered. Before leaving, John asked Williams to look at him closely and tell him if he could guess why he was so interested in the unidentified Yank. After staring at him for a time, Williams said he had no idea. John asked if perhaps he resembled the man in the photo, and Williams responded with a hearty laugh. "That's a good one, Redford, maybe, maybe not. A man my age thinks everyone younger than fifty looks about the same, like a baby. How I'd love to trade places with you kids!"

Back in London, packing to return home, John received a call from Williams. "Hello, Redford! Glad I caught you before your trip back across the pond, cheaper than long distance, hey? Well, I've thought about it long and hard, even kept me awake racking my brain for a spell. Finally, the name came to me like a vision. Not all of it, but something." John thought Williams might have fallen asleep mid-thought when a period of excruciating silence followed. "All right then, I'm sure of it," he said finally, "the name of the man you're looking for is Peter, I've no doubt!"

"Peter . . ?"

"Yes, like the apostle, like the rock."

"Do you have idea what his surname could be?"

"No, Peter is all that came to me. I probably never knew him by anything else, but maybe that will help."

Flying back to the States, John was hopeful. The task had narrowed. All he had to do was search through the Army's records to find an airman named Peter something who'd been killed in the war. How difficult could it be?

———

"Not hard at all really," said Nathaniel Stegger. "It's more like an endurance contest, what with only one test in each course. Yale Law Review, here I come!"

"Will you be Editor in Chief?"

"Next year, I'm sure I'll get it."

"What about after graduation?"

"Anything I want, but I'll start with government service. As a wise man once told me, "Go . . . ""

"Where the money is," Daniel finished. They touched their glasses and laughed together. "You're an excellent son!"

"Mother would beg to differ. Every few weeks she sends the same sappy letter, the old and boring 'why don't you ever get in touch' routine. She's persistent. After four years you'd think she'd take the hint."

"She'll never give up . . . I remember how hard she tried to get me back," Daniel lied. "Finally, after years of persistent letters I had to be totally blunt and told her to fuck off. I told her she'd had her chance. I said, go back to your lover boy, bitch."

"Who was he, Dad? Who'd she have the affair with?"

"A second-rate player, a pretentious asshole who chased the ladies while the rest of us busted our stones twenty-four seven!"

"What was his name?"

Too close for comfort, Daniel thought. *Damn, should not have had that third martini!* He couldn't give his son the actual name of someone from the Hill—if Nathaniel checked it out he'd know it had all been bullshit. *Miss Goody Two Shoes would never have had an affair.* He'd concocted the story of her betrayal to turn son against mother, and it'd worked to perfection. It gave him the clear sailing needed to make Nathaniel his alter ego. He'd grown increasingly conscious of his mortality as he'd matured; if he couldn't live forever, at least he could live vicariously through his son after his death.

"Come on, tell me his name."

Inspired, Daniel responded, "Sixtus Peeters."

Daniel had no idea Gail and Peeters actually met on a train in 1943, and were so taken with each other that they'd thought of marrying. Daniel only knew he'd hated Peeters from the start; his ego would never permit him to think she could have loved another man more than him.

"Sixtus, get out, what kind of a name is that?"

Daniel congratulated himself on his impulsive choice. The file from Frey proved Peeters had really been in Los Alamos. It also solidified his status as the ultimate badass, and was untraceable, too. The name Redford couldn't be found anywhere in the file so his lie could never be unmasked. He thought, *I'm so brilliant it almost scares me sometimes.*

"Old-time shit, hard to believe, isn't it? Grab another drink, I'll be right back."

Daniel wheeled over to a set of six-paneled doors next to his office, the same style as throughout his home except that these opened up into a vault large enough for him to roll into. He went in and retrieved the folder labeled "Sixtus Peeters."

"Someday, when you're ready for it, I'll show you all my files, but this makes an excellent starting point. It shows the lengths a real man will go to maintain his honor. When I exact revenge, I have only one speed, what Brant always called my 'balls out' mode. I'm proud of it just like you'll be when you're the man." His father amazed Nathaniel. Despite his disability, he remained the most formidable man he knew. In college he'd set aside *The Art of War,* a book a professor called an essential primer, because his father routinely taught more than the book ever could.

"If injury should be done, it must be so severe the victim won't consider revenge. So first I considered the supposedly ultimate punishment, but I recognized that death ends all suffering and is often insufficient. So I came up with a more creative approach." Daniel smiled and leaned back with his eyes closed, projecting utter contentment. Nathaniel watched, spellbound, until his father opened his eyes suddenly and pointed at him. "Quick, tell me what you were thinking!"

"I-I I guess I was thinking how much you enjoy recalling what you did to him."

"Precisely! And its recollection is sweet because I still have conscious knowledge of the past. I remember what the son of a bitch did and how I responded, and that gives me a sense of accomplishment and fulfillment. Realizing that process applies to most everything in life, I deprived him of ever experiencing such satisfaction by erasing portions of his long-term memory.

Without knowing his identity or past he has very little to reflect upon. His emotions are shallow and primal. His parents, childhood, friends, accomplishments, likes and dislikes, have all vanished along with any sense of accomplishment, appreciation or the fulfillment they allow. He's a shell going through life like an automaton, conscious enough to know he's out of step but unable to do anything about it. He's like that Charlie Gordon in *Flowers for*

Algernon, with a past just out of reach and the terrible pain of his loss eating away at him. It's an excruciating punishment that'll torment him for a lifetime."

He said that Peeters lived aimlessly under an assumed name, but was so clueless he barely knew his ass from his elbow. "Let me tell you what we didn't record in the file—a marvelous use of science and chemistry. Okay, well first Brant and I . . . "

Daniel regaled Nathaniel with a false account of catching Gail and John as lovers and heroically exposing the bastard as a spy. He claimed he was supported throughout by Enrico Fermi, who if still living would have told his son of their friendship and mutual admiration. Daniel said the tricky part had been incorporating Peeters into Project Chatter, the mind-control study, so that he could exact his punishment under the pretense of mind control research. It took persuasion he said, possible only because of his own high status.

Nathaniel might have been less impressed to discover that Daniel hated Peeters for eclipsing him and had been cruel and destructive, with no other goal in mind. Peeters's amnesia had been only a lucky and unintended break, allowing the crime to go undetected.

Daniel never told Nathaniel the truth, but it might not have made any difference, since deceit came as easily to him as to his father. Daniel had molded him so he had no values or basis to distinguish right from wrong; he saw only aids and obstacles to whatever end he desired. It was as if when violently raping Gail, Daniel had thrust all his evil into the egg that produced his son, while all her goodness had been used up protecting the egg that produced his daughter.

In describing Peeters as an automaton, Daniel unwittingly had described Nathaniel, who knew only the feelings programmed into him by his father. Like cells dividing imperceptibly at the beginning of a cancer, those instilled feelings lay quiet in the innermost part of him, simmering slowly but steadily, awaiting the time when they would burst outward with terrible force.

7.

A Wedding in Lake Forest

Lake Forest, Illinois, 1968

Gail Stegger walked down the aisle on the arm of her brother Harold Marshall while music filled the church. Red roses paired with white lilacs symbolizing innocence, the heady scent overpowering her already overloaded senses. She passed by handsome ushers, imposing in morning coats, and friends nodding from pews decorated with bows and candles. It bespoke a Midwestern American Camelot, a romantic setting evoking impossible love. *Impossible for some,* she thought, fighting off nausea although she'd passed on breakfast. *Dear God,* she prayed, *don't let me make a fool of myself!*

Despite eight months to prepare and twenty-six years to forget, a sort of jealousy simmered inside as Gail looked about with a painted smile. Fortunately, she took comfort being at St. Mary's, the familiar refuge where she'd attended mass, clung to Hal during their father's funeral, and celebrated when he married Adalia Weber.

Adie had graduated from Marquette University School of Medicine, and interned at the University of Chicago Hospitals where she'd met Hal, an irresistibly kind surgeon. He'd been attracted by her intelligence and beauty, and by the rare enthusiasm of those who live each day as if it's their last.

Adie's mother, Katya, had confronted the Nazis and successfully fled Germany, but the price of liberation had been high: suffering, abuse, rape, and death, all of which Adie never forgot. But she'd also learned that determination could carry a person from the abyss to survival and far beyond.

As a German immigrant with scant knowledge of English, Katya had mastered it regardless, including enough difficult medical jargon to become the Director of Surgical Care at St. Mary's School of Nursing. At the same time, she had raised two remarkable girls, Adie, and Rachel, a young woman already nationally reputed.

Adie completed her residency in Milwaukee, obtaining the credentials required to open a private practice. She planned to honor her deceased, adopted brother, Hanny, by treating developmentally disabled children. Marrying Hal brought her to Lake Forest. There she found a best friend in her sister-in-law, Gail.

Adie loved Gail's irrepressible spirit, remarkable after such a disastrous marriage. As her confidant, Adie alone understood why Gail's emotions were so conflicted on her daughter's wedding day.

Adie never seemed to have a bad day, and appeared a nearly ideal woman. Intelligent, professional, tall and lovely, calm and unflappable, she held her arms around two wide-eyed and precious daughters dressed in princess pink chiffon, their blonde hair hanging down in curls, waving hello to Daddy and Auntie Gail as they approached walking down the aisle.

Katya Weber shared the first row pew on the bride's side with Adie's family and her adopted daughter, Rachel. Nearing sixty, Katya's breathtaking, youthful loveliness had dimmed yet remained discernible, but her steely blue eyes had come to dominate her looks; eyes reflecting the inner strength and determination of the strongest-willed woman Gail had ever known.

Watching Hal approach reminded Katya of the best of her late husband, who'd been idealistic, incorruptible, and caring before swept away in the Nazi madness. It also resurrected thoughts of sweet Hanny, the disabled boy she'd rescued and effectively adopted. *He would have loved this spectacle, I can picture him grinning ear to ear, dancing in heaven and sharing our happiness.*

Gail anticipated the bridal party's promenade. The women in beautiful gowns with flowered garlands in their hair and the men virile and handsome—all beguiling in that fleeting time granted youth upon the cusp of maturity, a singular and momentary time of unquestioned promise. She knew she'd cry and chew her lip while watching them and gauging her personal loss.

Neither the bride's father nor her brother were invited. Daniel's absence was understandable since he'd effectively given Alexie away long before. Gail often begged him to consider Alexie's feelings and give her some attention over the years, but he'd laughed at all her entreaties. In their last conversation ever he'd said, "I'm not a phony. Why pretend I give a damn about her any more than I do about you? What part of 'I don't give a shit' don't you understand? Devote *your* life to her, you dumb bitches deserve each other."

Gail thought to invite Nathaniel solely for the sake of propriety, since it seemed wrong to exclude the bride's twin brother. But Alexie adamantly refused, and Gail deferred to her, even while unaware of the reason Alexie reacted so strongly.

Alexie had missed Nathaniel once, and the thought of him not being at her weding formerly would have been unimaginable. But after they met for lunch shortly before her engagement, she preferred thinking of him as dead and buried.

She'd leapt into his arms when they met at The Berghoff. He'd grown to become an attractive, confident, and strong-looking man, and he'd been dressed impeccably in a pinstriped suit with a silk regimental tie. He appeared larger than she'd remembered, as if grown into the protector they'd foreseen as children. She clung to him, trying to pull him closer as if compressing their years of separation. But when he pushed her away and held her by the shoulders as if in judgment, she saw the same cold look evident in every photograph of their father. He smirked, as if amused by a private thought, as she wiped her eyes and hurriedly sat down, embarrassed by her display. He'd met her heartfelt greeting, "Oh, Nate, how I've missed you," with a hollow, "Well, hello there."

He said, "You're quite attractive, Alexandra, looking very much like mother before she got so old-looking. But you should dress less old-fashioned and more stylishly."

She'd reddened at his rudeness, having given a great deal of thought to her appearance. Her long dark hair was parted in the middle, framing her face and laying softly upon her shoulders. She wore a brown and white diamond print dress with half sleeves, cinched at the waist and cut several inches above her knees, attractively highlighting her long and well-shaped legs. "Old-fashioned?" she'd replied, wondering whatever he'd meant.

"You have nice breasts. You should highlight them and show some cleavage. I mean, you're not a little girl anymore."

"W-w-who are you to tell me . . !"

"Whoa, relax, just a helpful hint from your brother. Forget I said anything, okay? How about we start over?"

"All right, start."

"I thought we should reconnect, since I'm sure we think about similar things. Besides, we can help each other going forward, what with the divorce and our parents not getting any younger and all."

"You don't make sense. You're the one who disconnected from us! I don't have any idea who you are, Nate, I'd like . . . "

"I'm not called Nate. I'm not a child. My name is Nathaniel."

"All right, Nathaniel, but I'm still Alexie. Name aside, I need to know who you are. In four years you never wrote, returned my calls, or acknowledged my existence. Who abandons their twin like that? We shared everything, even called ourselves the three musketeers.'"

He smirked again.

"What's so funny, for God's sake? Do you know how irritating that is? I'm not sure I even want to reconnect with you!"

"All right Alexie, calm down. Let's take our time and order first. Apparently, there's a lot of ground to cover. We need to ease into this reunion thing. We're probably trying too hard. Sustenance and a drink should take the edge off." He opened up and scanned the menu. "Everything is good here, right? Maybe I'll try the schnitzel.

I've had it other places, but I remember this as the best. Those Nazis really know how to cook!" He added, "No pun intended!"

She glared at him, astounded. "Why give me such a look? I didn't mean to be funny, but what's the big deal? You're not a Jew-lover, are you? You wouldn't be if you spent the time I did at Yale. Father was right, the tribe pushes their way into everything."

She moved her chair back to leave, but Nathaniel caught her by the arm. "Look, I'm sorry. Don't leave, please . . . I guess I can be too outspoken at times, but I thought I could speak freely with my sister. Look, I promise to be good! Please stay, there are things we need to discuss. I'll be more sensitive, okay? What say we have a drink and start over?"

Crossing her arms, she asked, "What is it you need to tell me?"

"It's about Mother."

The waiter approached to take their drink order. Alexie ordered a root beer and Nathaniel asked for a large stein of the house brew. After the waiter left, they remained silent for a time, and his gaze made Alexie uncomfortable. She shifted in her seat. *Is he leering at me?* "What do you need to tell me?" she'd asked quickly.

"First, let me answer your question and tell you who I am: I'm a lawyer and a new member of the Colorado Bar, and I'm moving to D.C., to Maryland, actually. I'm going to work as assistant counsel to the Senate Intelligence Committee. There's an increased emphasis on foreign affairs with trouble brewing in Vietnam, and Father helped me get into the intelligence loop. So I'm an up-and-coming lawyer entering public service. You'll probably need a good lawyer sometime, so keep me in mind. I'll always have a special price for my loving sister!"

Alexie ignored the odd remark. "You're telling me what you do, not who you are. What do you care about? I'd like to know since our relationship obviously doesn't much concern you."

"Don't be so judgmental. I'm a lawyer and I care about the law and being successful. I care about people—I like them to see things my way. Like everyone else, I like having my needs met. We're not children anymore, Alexie. We know how the world works, and what else is there? In the end, what matters is the here and now, where you live and what you have, recognition, finding whatever pleasure you can, and, of course, certain relationships. That's all. That's how father lives. Why not emulate him? He's an amazing man."

"Seriously, you want to emulate someone who abandoned his kids? Don't you get it? You're not focused on anything lasting, you're focused on *things,* and fleeting moments. What's inside you is what matters, like the values that motivate you. What you've mentioned is so shallow. Is that what you are inside? Is that why you could walk away from us so easily?"

"That's not what I am, Alexie, and it wasn't easy. By the way, you need to know that Father encouraged me to go into public service."

"Since when did he care about anyone else?"

"He's in a wheelchair, Alexie, so go easy. You don't really know him. Or me."

"Whose fault is that?"

"You're right, but it's complicated. I've tried to have him reach out to you," he lied, "but it's hard for him—he said you remind him too much of Mother. Anyway, we all make choices, some are easy and others are hard, but life is all about moving forward—like my entry into public service. That shows something lasting, doesn't it? I'm concerned about other people, so I'll help out by working for the government! Maybe you're just upset that I'm not focusing on certain people. Maybe you're jealous!"

"Oh, I get it, it's my problem. You ignored me because you're such a humanitarian. Spare me, Nathaniel. I'm not stupid."

"Don't be so negative. I'm really glad we're together again and able to have a serious conversation. I forgot how cute you are when you get fired up, so passionate, just like when we were children."

The waiter delivered another stein of beer and Nathaniel drank half of it in one swig. He burped and smiled at Alexie. "Good suds, you should have some to help you relax."

"What did you want to tell me about Mother?"

"Okay, well here's the thing: I'm worried you might get hurt. My advice is that you put some distance between you. I'm certain she cheated on father. I even know the guy's name. It was in New Mexico during the war." Alexie looked back at him, shaking her head slowly in disgust. He continued, more rapidly, "I also know what Father did to the bastard who screwed her and it wasn't pretty, but so far he's let her walk away, like some goddamn princess. Well, that's not his style, and he might decide to give her what she has coming. If you're too close you never know what could happen."

"You're unbelieveable! Are you crazy, *our mother*? I know Mother and it isn't possible! Are you threatening me? Is that what this is all about?"

"No, no, Alexie, you misunderstand, we need to communicate better." He reached over and put his hands on hers again. "I'm here because we need to be closer, but this thing with Mother keeps getting in the way. Don't be so critical, I love you, really I do. I think of everything we've been through . . . and of course I remember the three musketeers. We'd have been fine, a real family, if Mother only hadn't ruined it when she . . . she decided . . . " He lost his train of thought and a distant look crossed his face.

She laid her hands in her lap, leaned back, and examined him as he finished his beer. *There's something wrong with him. His remarks are so raw and crude, insensitive, and scattered, then out of nowhere he says he loves me! I wonder if he's on drugs.*

He looked her up and down, then asked, apropos of nothing, "Do you have a boyfriend?"

"What kind of question is that? What does it matter to you?"

He leaned forward toward her and began to whisper, forcing her to lean toward him to hear above the roomful of conversation. With a distinct slur, she heard some of it. "I'm asking, because . . . if you . . . with your hot looks I'll bet you're doing him . . . and if our mother's betrayal doesn't bother . . . then you should do me, too. We'd be much closer then . . . so let's go up . . ."

Alexie thought she must have misunderstood. But he sat back, leering at her and licking his lips with his tongue. The reality of his filthy proposal registered. She leapt to her feet, frightened and alarmed, knocking a water glass to the floor and drawing the attention of the other diners. She screamed at him, "Doing him! What kind of a sick mind do you have? You're disgusting, you pig! You aren't my brother anymore!" She grabbed her mug and threw the root beer in his face. "You're insane. You're scum!"

She stormed from the Berghoff, furious and bewildered. *How is it possible?* She decided no matter, she'd never speak to him again. She wouldn't tell her mother about their meeting, better she never found out that her once wonderful son had become a beast.

Alexie knew her mother. She was so moral she'd always refused to even discuss her failed marriage or criticize their father. "You're bright," she'd said, "make your judgments based on what you know, but don't involve me. Adults shouldn't discuss their intimate matters with their children. It's enough for you to understand that although our relationship failed God blessed us with you."

After the divorce, Gail turned down many offers to date. She'd seemed more willing lately, perhaps after you marry, she'd told Alexie. She appeared content with teaching, community and church work, competitive tennis and bridge; yet, Alexie knew better, often seeing Gail sitting alone late at night holding an open book in her hand while staring off into the distance as if searching.

———

John Redford first met Varo "Tolo" Rivitolo in 1966 when he appeared at his office after his lecture on Big Bang nucleosynthesis.

After being assured he wasn't intruding, Tolo asked if they might discuss a dilemma he'd alluded to in the lecture: why did the densities of baryons, calculated by nucleosynthesis, appear to be less than the observed mass of the universe based on its calculated expansion? It was especially insightful for an undergraduate, and one day a similar question would lead to the discovery of dark matter.

Tolo spoke English flawlessly with a Midwestern accent, and it shocked John to learn he was actually an Italian exchange student enrolled at Northwestern for only one semester. He wasn't enrolled in his class either, just auditing it "because it sounded interesting."

"I'm sorry to seem so surprised, but you sound like a local. I worked with Doctor Fermi—not that there's anything wrong with an accent—and it's just that he . . . "

"I understand completely. It's due to my mother speaking to me almost exclusively in English to maintain her proficiency, and so I'd grow up bilingual. After I learned how important accents were, I tried perfecting Midwestern speech, since Fermi, Trinity, and the University of Chicago are all wrapped up together in my goals."

John looked confused. Tolo continued, "I'm sorry, sometimes I throw scrambled thoughts out. It's just funny that you'd mention Fermi since he's such a god in my country. I've loved science since I first wondered why spilt milk vanished. I was consumed by wanting to know how everything worked. So I wanted to come to the States, like my idol did, ever since I studied his diffusion equation which led to Trinity and all that followed it. I thought if I spoke like a

Midwesterner it might give me an edge for the University of Chicago."

"Yet, you're at Northwestern studying liberal arts, not physics. What am I missing?"

Tolo responded as he often did with a quote, "Voltaire said, 'while each player must accept the cards life deals him, once in hand he alone decides how to play them to win the game.' So, I was in Pisa, studying physics at Scuola Normale Superiore . . . "

"Tough to get into, where Fermi began, right?"

"Yes on both counts. But the problem is that Fermi *is* a god in Italy, so every aspiring physicist shares the same dream. Because I-I . . . I'm embarrassed Doctor Redford, here we just met and I've intruded and I'm rambling on about myself! I'm sorry."

John was well-regarded for his willingness to counsel students who reached out to him. This proved difficult with students who had the desire but not the ability to grasp the abstractions of physics. John knew such students were unwittingly wasting time until finding a suitable career path. But every now and then a student with a facile mind and extraordinary intellect appeared, reminding him of the excitement he'd first felt when considering the material world and the allure and intrigue of science. Within thirty minutes, John recognized Tolo as the sort of student he'd been, and beyond that, he experienced a strange sense of familiarity, like one feels when first meeting someone and sensing a link, in an intuitive, déjà vu sort of way.

"No, no, Tolo, don't be embarrassed. I'm genuinely interested. I'm a pinochle player and I always like to hear about playing cards!"

Tolo told of being raised in southern Italy by his aunt after his unwed mother's death, and having drifted abroad after high school, exploring the rough streets of the Middle East, from Istanbul to New Delhi. Relying on his wits for survival, he overcame his self-pity and adopted an eclectic and aggressive approach to life, combining ideas from Zen Buddhism, Descartes, and the Beatles. Bearded and much thinner, Tolo returned to Amantea to regain his strength on his aunt's pasta and sausage while preparing for the implausible: acing the difficult examination that earned its top finisher a scholarship to the prestigious Scuola Normale Superiore ("SNS") in Pisa.

Against the expectations of most, Tolo finished first in the competition and enrolled in SNS to study Physics in 1964. He enjoyed his studies, but found the arbitrary rules and aristocratic system of the school stifling. Politics and seniority seemed far more important than talent, and his unconventional background made it unlikely he'd receive recommendations to an institution like the University of Chicago.

"Candidly, Doctor Redford, the biggest problem I had was being a bastard from southern Italy. Most Italians believe that part of the country backward, and also that patrician roots are essential for upward mobility. Not having a father's name was enough to keep me out of SNS, but for my test score. But I held a card I played in an oblique fashion. You see, my scholarship allowed a single semester abroad, which everyone assumed would be used to study physics. But I found a loophole that allowed it to be used in a wholly unrelated field. So, when Northwestern advertised for a foreign undergraduate in their eastern philosophies program, I applied and impressed their visiting Dean with my English and grasp of Hindu, being sure to quote passages from the Vedic Scriptures in our conversation! So, phase one of my 'Follow-Fermi Plan' succeeded, and here I am in Chicagoland!"

Tolo's mention of the Vedic Scriptures seemed vaguely familiar to John. In fact, they'd been a staple of his real father, Alexander, who claimed the ancient concepts supported the theory of reincarnation. He said, "Amazing, tell me about phase two!"

"I'm still working on it," Tolo replied, "I visited with a professor at Chicago last month." It occurred to John, whether Tolo intended it to be suggestive or not, that he could help, and ultimately he did. He recommended him to a colleague who assisted him in obtaining a fully paid scholarship to complete his undergraduate studies at Northwestern. They hoped Tolo would consider their graduate program the equal of Chicago's and remain there. He did, and when he married, Tolo had been pursuing his doctorate with John as his mentor. John hadn't met Tolo's fiancée by the time of his wedding, but he would have met her at the celebration if he hadn't declined the invitation because of a planned trip to San Francisco the same day.

When the stirring *Triumphal March* from *Aida* began, Gail saw Eda Monteduro catch her nephew's eye and wink. The surrogate mother held her thumb up and shook it back and forth in rich appreciation, a joyful display lifting Gail's spirits. She shrugged off her personal sadness. Alexie deserved a magical day even if fate had denied Gail her own.

The ceremony went well and the priest made the traditional introduction. "It gives me great pleasure to present to you for the first time ever, Mr. and Mrs. Varo Rivitolo!" At that very moment, the sun passed from behind a cloud and streamed through the amber-colored windows designed to glorify Christ's resurrection. The glow cast upon the newlyweds delighted the attendees, except for Gail whose gasp vanished in their applause. She felt faint when the glorious, golden light masked the dark complexion and hair Tolo had inherited from his mother and instead highlighted his paternal heritage: a wide-jawed and symmetrical face, favored with high cheekbones and a cleft chin, piercing hazel-colored eyes, thick eyebrows and wavy hair.

Tolo caught Gail's eye while walking toward her to express his gratitude for their beautiful wedding. Watching his easygoing and athletic stride, she saw his father in it as well, and for a moment she could imagine that her intended, Sixtus Peeters, had returned from the dead for a wondrous reunion.

———

Gail had wanted Alexie to appreciate the world's diversity, so when St. Xavier College established its summer program in Rome, she'd seen it as an ideal opportunity, since Alexie could gain exposure to the world while being chaperoned by the watchful nuns from her all girl's school. But Alexie's last letter from Europe made her head whirl. She would have flown to Italy that very day if Alexie wasn't already heading home.

Alexie attracted boys easily, *but how in the world?* She'd hyperventilated, and a knot formed in her stomach. She held the letter as if a mystical object, asking why God seemed intent on tormenting her.

"Mom, I met a wonderful young man in Rome, our guide in the Vatican Museum. I know what you're thinking, but don't worry, it's just his summer job. He's a brilliant student studying to be a scientist! He's Italian, but his father was American and he speaks perfect English. He's kind and considerate and handsome and charming, but in a low-key and modest, very endearing way. Best of all, he's enrolling at Northwestern for his senior year starting in September. It's too perfect, like destiny and I know now what it means when they say 'head over heels' in love! I can hear you saying 'don't rush it!!' But you needn't worry, I'm listening! We'll have a year to get to know each other and for you to get to know him too. I'll make sure this isn't *Rome Adventure* calling before I jump in, and of course I need to know what you think of him. His name is Varo Rivitolo but he's called Tolo, isn't that cute?

It's unusual and I'll explain it all when I'm home, but because of some Italian custom he doesn't carry the name of his father, an American airman named Sixtus Peeters who died near the end of the war."

Gail reread the paragraph and its stunning words over and over again. Finally, certain she wasn't hallucinating, she thought through every possibility and came up with nothing but blanks. She popped two aspirin and called Adie. She had to share her story with her confidant and seek her advice. It made no sense, the Army had reported Six killed in action during the Ploesti raid, more than a year before this Tolo was born, and she'd mourned his death along with his entire family!

———

After returning from England, John began searching for a soldier named Peter. But no source listed airmen by first names, nor had the Eighth Air Force catalogued any helpful data. When it became part of the Strategic Air Command in 1946, the Eighth left its history behind. So while new information surfaced periodically after the war, all John had to start with was an Honor Roll of casualties prepared state by state, by county and alphabetically by surname. The Honor Roll gave their serial numbers and ranks, but not their birthplaces, addresses, or given names, only the first initials of nearly three hundred thousand honorees.

Peter was the twenty-third most popular name in the States during the war, borne by nine men per thousand. So, John had to review the names in forty-eight separate directories to ferret out about 2,700 individuals with the first initial "P." If such a name was listed KIA in the Army Air Corps, he would have to travel to a specific county to find the survivors to determine if their relative had been named Peter. If so, he'd show them the photograph of the aircrew to see if it included their relative. It was an incredibly daunting task, nonetheless, John produced an A list of 1,146 names. Beginning with number 573, he began working his way forward by proximity to Chicago. He'd visited twenty-six counties before Rose said she'd had enough even if he hadn't. He needed to forget it, find a gofer to take over the task, or see a shrink. In response, he contacted the licensed investigator recommended by his former lawyer.

Giovanni Conforti worked out of four rooms in a building with a faded façade in a dreary neighborhood surrounded by railroad lines and truck yards. Ascending the stairway for their meeting, John passed signs for "Lulu's Exotic Dance Classes," and "Mel's Bookkeeping and Chiropractic Offices," all of which shared a floor with "G. Conforti, P.I."

The door had a peephole and clouded glass. After several knocks, a pleasant female voice sung out, "Who is it?"

"John Redford. I have an appointment to see Mr. Conforti."

"For what time?"

"Two forty-five."

"You're early."

"I thought . . . " The door was opened by an attractive, twenty-some year old with a dazzling smile. "We needed to be certain it was you, professor, come in. Mr. Conforti will be with you in a few minutes. I'm Elise. May I get you something, iced tea perhaps?"

The bangs of her shoulder length, reddish-blond hair hung down to the top of her eyebrows. Her sleeveless dress had a ruffled white top cut straight across the neckline with a high waisted pink bottom beginning just beneath her bosom and flowing down to a hem inches above her knees. Her long legs were highlighted by white boots reaching mid-calf, she wore the faintest hint of makeup, and two very large silver hoop earrings. She could have been a fashion model.

The PI's large reception room displayed three white six-paneled doors leading to the inner sanctum, on a half-circle behind an ultra-modern glass and silver aluminum reception desk. The waiting area had rose-colored swivel chairs and a cream-colored couch grouped around a glass coffee table resting on a white shag rug on a glossy hardwood floor. The high walls were adorned with brightly-colored artwork contrasting with their starkness. The stylish space would have been equally in place on Mars as in the dilapidated building on La Salle Street.

Elise led John into Conforti's office, and he noted papers stacked on a table in a crowded work area that included a corkboard wall covered with photos, diagrams, and notes, a tabletop holding four phones, and a copying machine. The remainder of the office appeared as uncluttered and impressive as the reception area, although larger. On the plain white wall behind Conforti hung a magnificent abstract painting with rigid geometric shapes that seemed to leap from it as if three dimensional; a Mondrian, John was certain, an early composition and very valuable. Conforti reached across the desk and shook his hand. He spoke slowly and deliberately, voicing concern which seemed genuine.

"Thank you for coming in. I've read your summary and studied the photographs. I can hardly imagine what an ordeal this has been for you. I know it's no consolation to any client, but what you've described is interesting and a case I'd very much like to tackle. It's complex to be sure, but honestly, I'm also certain I can help."

"If only it were so easy, Mr. Conforti, I've been trying to understand these issues for years."

"Please, call me Gio. May I call you John?"

"By all means."

"All right, John, don't misunderstand, it won't be easy but we'll get it done. I've been doing this for thirty years, and whenever there's adequate capital to pay informants, answers are available. You said money wasn't an issue, within reason of course?"

"Correct. But I have two preliminary questions I need answered."

"Fire away."

"Will any of your work break the law? I'm no angel, but I can't be part of something illegal, and there is a restraining order in place."

"An excellent question, John, so let me be clear: First, I'd never ask you to be part of anything illegal since I'm licensed as an investigator. If I were found to have engaged in such activities my license would be lost and I might be imprisoned. So, I'm not going to jeopardize my livelihood. Everything is on the up and up, but my methods are proprietary. No one will know exactly what I do to reach the finish line, but we'll get there and you won't be complicit in any way. As for the courts' orders, well, they leave me more than enough wiggle room since I'm not a party with notice of the lawsuit. Do you understand what I'm saying?"

He regarded the mixed message carefully. Short and trim, the fiftyish-looking man seemed self-assured and conventional. Well-groomed and casually but elegantly dressed, he appeared he might well be a business lawyer or banker. He clearly looked successful and his office bespoke discipline and efficiency as well. Along with the pseudo-recommendation from his attorney, Conforti enjoyed a reputation for success. *What harm can there be in trying him out?*

"I understand. But can you tell me why your office is here? It's so out of place it's . . . of course, that's it, isn't it?"

"Exactly, there's advantage to be had tucking yourself away and hiding in plain sight. Seriously, being a chameleon is helpful. Sometimes a bon vivant is needed, but usually an average Joe can learn what he needs over a brew at the neighborhood bar while a smoothie remains clueless. But, let's get to it, the meter's running. Tell me . . . "

John answered all his questions and told him all he'd done following his checklist. He only omitted mentioning the five words he'd imagined in the museum. They had no evidentiary value, and he didn't want to be thought of as a lunatic. And of course, he didn't reveal that he'd murdered a mysterious young woman.

John detailed his contacts with seventeen co-workers from the Manhattan Project, all of whom confirmed his good working relationship with Groves. None could say what had happened after he'd left Los Alamos for Japan, only that he'd been an exceptionally capable co-worker who'd faded away after he left about the same time they had all moved on.

John described his visits to West Virginia and Bethesda, and to Northwestern Military Academy in Lake Geneva. No one had recognized him there, since the 1930's staff was long gone. His class portrait listed his name, but reported him absent when taken. Even scouring his supposed classmates' faces with a magnifying glass, he hadn't recognized any of them. He'd traced one former teacher to a nursing home in St. Louis, but the man's mental state was such that he hadn't a clue whether John had been a staff member, visitor, or blood relative when they'd met.

John also showed Conforti the picture of himself in England, supposedly as an officer with the first name of Peter, and he detailed the efforts he'd made to learn his surname.

"I admire your logic and persistence, but I'm going to begin with the intelligence angle. Donovan and McFarland were in the OSS when it operated out of the Congressional Country Club, so McFarland likely was going to explain how it tied into this Peter fellow, who really does look like you. Plus, you were working on a secret experiment which means intelligence had to be involved in some way, and you were treated in a Virginia hospital that's now part of the CIA. It makes Wright's disappearance very intriguing. I wonder whether he knew you were someone other than Redford?

I'll begin in D.C. and follow up if need be where you left off looking for this Peter. Meanwhile, go about your business. If you take another vacation, enjoy the sights but leave the digging to me. The worst thing we can do is give mixed signals by doing conflicting work. I'll be in touch when I find anything noteworthy."

Growing up in Cicero, Gio Conforti had been called "Puzzles" for a hobby he loved although it bored his friends. He'd found it exhilarating to begin with a table full of oddly-shaped geometric pieces and, through patience and inspiration, work through them until experiencing the accomplishment of sliding the last piece into place. He'd started as a child with a fifteen large-pieced beauty showing Elmer Fudd chasing Bugs Bunny with a shotgun, and moved on through art and idyllic American scenery to his all-time favorite, a nine-square-foot, seven-thousand-piece, pure white monster framed in his home. The faux art caused double takes, but was intended to remind him that every puzzle could be solved. He now had a great chance to prove it, in a notable challenge with a guaranteed fee.

Conforti began with "Frank," a well-placed source in Washington, D.C. They met for dinner at The Cedar Knoll Inn, a tourist's favorite overlooking the Potomac just north of Mount Vernon. Frank made the pedestrian choice, although they usually were far more extravagant whenever Gio had a client footing the bill.

"Okay, Frank, what's with this? I'm buying for Christ's sake! Are you sick, on a diet, or what?"

"Look around, Gio, tell me what you see."

"Every Georgie Washington fan with a camera is here and with kids too—probably looking for a cherry tree—well duh, okay, no one from the CIA is here."

"Right, they'd rather be dead than be seen in this tourist trap. That's important now that your boy's lawyer mucked it up big time. You can't imagine how hot it got when his lawyers went to Federal Court and took an appeal besides. So, now two cases are sealed for national security. Want to bet the Company files are stuck away in a vault somewhere if not already shredded?"

"But Frank, national security? Come on, beneficiaries on a trust account, 1945 records? National security my ass."

"I"m surprised at you, Gio. Does it have to make sense? Just makes it harder. Don't go naïve on me . . . I hear the Paella Valenciana is very good here."

"Is this about money, Frank? Are we negotiating here?"

"How long have we been doing this? Why are you busting my stones? I didn't take a vow of poverty and I've never been shy about remuneration. You'll know when I want more! Relax, I'll dig a little and do all that I can. Something may break loose since time works wonders. I just want you to know this ain't easy. Speaking of money, I assume you made my deposit?"

"I did, *Mr. Smith*. Really, I expected something more original."

"Innocuous and boring is how I like it."

They ate and spoke of the Company, of politics, and of losing the baseball Senators to Minnesota. After dinner over Irish coffee, Conforti handed Frank copies of the pictures Redford had received from McFarland. "Tell me if you recognize anything in these."

He went through them quickly, then more slowly a second time. "A real shitbox, don't know it, typical USA house, could be anywhere but the west coast. This is Wild Bill Donovan, obviously, hell of a reputation, old guard OSS and a maverick, but with friends in high places, dead. This is a typical World War Two send one to the folks aircrew pose, nothing special, thousands like it. This is the entrance to the Congressional Country Club in Bethesda. I've played there, tough course. Obviously ties into Donovan, who ran OSS war ops from there for a spell."

"Can you access those records?"

"Nah, old time stuff, pre-Company and Army controlled. I've got no reason to look into wartime Army records, besides the Army probably destroyed them in the 50's. But this one of the CIA reception has potential. I wasn't with the Company then, but I'll run it by my helpmate. It'll cost your client, but my pal would know since he was there. How urgent is it?"

"The meters running, so don't solve it too soon!" Gio laughed, "Seriously, whenever you can get it done."

"It'll be awhile. My man's in Southeast Asia, a little trouble brewing there you may have heard about. When he gets back we'll compare notes. What's the picture worth?"

"Two hundred bucks per face."

"Gio, don't go cheap on me, not when I have to share. Make it three fifty and include Eisenhower, I'm pretty sure I can verify it's him."

"You're a shameless mercenary!"

"Amen to that, time to ramp up the retirement fund."

"One last thing, I have a number for a physician forced out about 1948, Doctor Edmund Wright, a shrink." He handed Wright's calling card to Frank. "Number's out of service and he can't be found. I'd like to know why and when and where he is and all."

"Consider it as part of the work order."

Conforti's success as a PI sprang from having a network of informants willing to sell out for the right price. His best group was in D.C. because the volume of information in the capital kept growing along with the government's reach. His recruitment process was to meet a key player, find a way to empathize, send gifts, plant ideas, discuss money to be made, and sympathize by telling them they deserved a share of all the wealth around them. He played on egos, making sources feel they were his only important contact. When using lonely ladies, he found sex helped, like becoming their pimp. But he never was the first to suggest anyone should betray their employer. His hard and fast rule was that the idea had to come from them, and they had to set the price. Once they'd sold confidential information, he had them until they retired.

Frank had long been his best contact and also the hardest to score. It took two years to reach a deal, in part because Frank knew where he was heading when he started his pursuit, as befit a charter member of American Mensa. When he'd first made his pitch, Conforti thought he'd lost Frank, worried he might even report him. But the CIA proved no different than other companies in taking its good employees for granted. So, when politics trumped ability and Frank was passed over, he'd called Gio and traded stagnation for enrichment.

Conforti spent three weeks out east, two in D.C. with eight contacts, and side trips to West Virginia, New York City, and Columbia University. He verified that any records for Redford, between his interview with Groves for Los Alamos and his interview for a position at Columbia, had vanished. Anecdotal accounts of Redford revealed one fact of import: supposedly he'd vanished in disgrace after storming out of Los Alamos after some unspecified disagreement and insubordination related to use of the bomb; it was the sort of cover story which suggested intelligence was likely involved.

Drawing more blanks than usual, Conforti returned to Chicago. He identified the scientists he needed to interview, and then decided to try Redford's method of searching for men named Peter.

He spent two weeks in New England, an area full of Peters. He had an unproductive time showing the photo to clueless, aged relatives wondering what the hell he was up to. He went home after his twelfth strike out, a blank while searching for relatives of P. Denari, late of Essex County, Massachusetts.

In early 1968, Frank called with a progress report regarding Dr. Edmund Wright. He'd learned the well-respected shrink with a Harvard degree had shut down a private practice in New York and joined the Army in 1942, out of a sense of patriotism. Near war's end he'd taken over the Special Projects Ward of the intelligence group which later became the CIA, at a covert Virginia facility. There he compiled test data and treated 117 subjects over a four year period. It was clear the group included Redford, but Frank couldn't locate any index to identify the subjects in the projects which had been termed CHATTER before merging into MKULTRA.

Wright resigned in 1948 and surrendered his medical license "for undisclosed personal reasons," a forced exit due to his arrest for illicit conduct with his boyfriend six months earlier. He sold his Virginia home and moved to Greenwich Village, then skipped out on his lease in less than a year. He went to Brazil, disappearing there by dropping all licenses, memberships, and American contacts. Conforti had great confidence in his skills and he could go to South America to try, but he knew it was unlikely he'd find Wright in that big-ass country.

Frank needed input from his partner to determine the players in the CIA picture, but his return from Southeast Asia had been delayed. Redford would need to remain patient awhile longer.

8.

A Toast to Love

Salvador, Brazil, 1968

At three in the afternoon, Edmund Wright sat alone in the Estrelar Digno, a well-worn café bar in the Cidade Alta section of the city, situated on a cliff overlooking the Bay. Salvador had a reputation for friendly people which brought Wright there five years before, after years of aimless drifting throughout the country.

He'd settled down into a stable if boring routine, using his unlicensed medical skills to treat the poor Bahian people living nearby for minor ailments and such as syphilis, at all of five Real per pop, or more typically for a *benevolência* in return. He had what might generously be called friends, and a current lover, Thiago, but his lust for life had diminished dramatically, and nearing fifty he had the aura of a man twenty years older who'd been defeated by life and knew it.

Alcohol had been his longtime refuge from a haunting past, and recently he'd added cocaine to his treatment regimen. He loved the feeling of strength and competency it imparted, a flicker of how he'd felt when finishing up at Harvard, when it looked like life would only toss softballs his way. But since he didn't care to spend his remaining days in a Brazilian prison, he limited the cocaine, taking it slowly and carefully despite the allure. He knew that too much could lead to psychosis, and the reality he already sought to escape was crazy enough.

He ordered his standard starter, a *caipirinha* with a bowl of *moqueca,* the seafood stew he could never have too much of, and some *acaraje,* the marvelous bread you could smell being deep-fried from a block away. Sipping his drink, his mind wandered back, as usual, to his work for the CIA and the torment he'd felt over the death of the late, great Graham Cowell.

When Frey told him about Cowell's death he'd known instantly he'd been to blame, and the guilt still plagued him. His problem had been that he'd loved Five, even more than Phillip, so that when Cowell told him Five had been purposely brain-fried by CIA agents, including Frey, he'd taken it personally and passionately and confronted Frey. He'd unloaded all his frustration and given him a week to make amends before he went over his head. Dumb, blinded by love and compulsion, he'd paid the price big time, and Cowell had paid it as well.

A hit and run "accident" in Charlottesville, indeed. Frey had only shrugged and smirked when telling him, saying, "It's a shame, but sometimes bad things happen to good people who are in the wrong place at the wrong time." Of course, at the same time nearly everything related to Five disappeared or was altered, from CIA files and the subject's history to medical records and all of the recordings he'd never heard, the ones Cowell had made of his sessions with Five while he'd been under hypnosis—anything that might implicate Frey or the CIA in his criminal mistreatment, gone. Clearly Frey and his spooks had made the hit on Cowell in self-defense.

He'd fled, frightened, from the facility to the sanctuary of home, seeking solace, understanding, and compassion, and so stupid once again that he and Phillip had been arrested that very night, in their goddamn bedroom of all places, and charged with violating the Virginia law prohibiting sodomy.

The rest seemed inevitable. First, worst of all, he'd been forced to use Ludlow's Technique to reprogram Five to spend the rest of his life as John Redford, a shell of a man going through the motions of life without the emotional depth which came with genuine memory and knowledge of a past. Then, within six months, he was compelled to resign and turn in his medical license. He'd still had Phillip as a consolation, but he too ditched Wright soon after they moved to New York. Small wonder, both men were equally disgusted with the worthless wretch he'd become.

Wright had had little choice, really. Admittedly a devout coward, he'd been assured that otherwise he and Phillip would both die painfully and very slowly. And he knew by then how credible Frey was about making things bad for good people.

He'd slept poorly after that, would always wonder if his beloved patient would ever discover his real identity and find some contentment in his life. It would be very difficult, although not impossible. He had the intelligence to do it, perhaps the Ludlow Technique had flaws that could be overcome in time.

He knew "Redford" would have the financial resources to make everything easier, through a trust fund Frey said had been established to support him, a "fact" Wright reinforced in his reprogramming. Frey wasn't being charitable, just cautious, removing a source of possible conflict and allowing the patient to more easily fade away. Throwing money around had never been much of a problem for Frey and his ilk.

Wright asked for a double shot of *cachaca*, thinking he'd get blasted earlier than usual. Thiago probably wouldn't come home tonight at all. He seemed certain to leave him soon as well, so he might as well drink himself to death.

He'd come a long way from his days of promise at Harvard and his psychiatric residency at Massachusetts General Hospital, but all in the wrong direction. He never should have joined the government and the CIA, *public service my ass*, he thought, *covert bullshit without any regard for others. I can't ever return to the States, I couldn't stand the humiliation of knowing what everyone thinks of me back there. Anonymity is the only way to go.*

"Outro caipirinha, e desta vez torna-lo um triplo," he said to the bartender. *Another caipirinha, and this time make it a triple.* He'd drink a toast to love, what a bitch it could be.

9.

Foreign Connections

Chicago, Illinois, 1968

Tolo's features were so similar to Six's at the same age that Gail never doubted his paternity, but being over six feet tall and olive-skinned, any current resemblance would likely be overlooked by others. So, she decided not to disclose her relationship with his father, rather than risk interfering with her daughter's budding relationship with Tolo.

Tolo's upbringing had been difficult. He'd been raised by his aunt in impoverished circumstances after his mother's death during his childhood. So, by his adolescence, he only knew of his parents chiefly through their unusual stories as told to him by others: they'd been swept up in wartime romance after his mother, a ferocious partisan fighter, rescued his father not long after he'd been shot down in combat; his father, a scientist as well as a soldier, had been important enough to be rescued so he could return to the States to work on some highly secretive wartime project, apparently losing his life in the effort.

"It's so tragic," explained Alexie, "His father didn't know Atia was pregnant, although he promised to return for her after the war. But she never heard from him again, and had no way of contacting him. She pestered American authorities until some officials went to Italy to tell her he'd died in a top-secret experiment involving materials so toxic the victims' bodies couldn't even be returned to their families for burial. Can you imagine?"

Gail couldn't. The whole story seemed odd, and out of character for the man she was sure she'd known. She had no doubt he'd truly loved her. *How can it be he impregnated this Atia woman and never contacted either of us again? Could we both have misjudged him so completely? A secret experiment with no body to be buried, how bizarre, what's that all about? If officials travelled to Italy to tell this Atia, why didn't they contact the Peeters? Surely I would have heard from them otherwise.*

Six had hailed from nearby Kenosha, Wisconsin. *He'd been so proud of his upbringing there, why wouldn't Atia know it'd been his hometown and where to look for him? Tolo likely has relatives there now, probably not grandparents, but surely cousins, uncles or aunts. The Peeters wouldn't reject Tolo because he's illegitimate.*

An idea occurred to Gail and she rushed to the library. When she returned home four hours later, she called Adie. "He had to be returned for the Manhattan Project, as a scientist and physicist what else could it be? But I've searched through every related book and can't find a single mention of Six. It doesn't add up. If he was important enough to rescue and return to the States, and have officials travel to Italy to tell some Italian what happened, his family should have been told and his name should be listed somewhere!"

Reluctantly, Gail contacted Ralph Peeters, Six's older brother who still lived in Kenosha. She shared what she knew and he was dumbfounded, the family knew none of it. Ralph said he was on good terms with his Congressman, and he'd see what he could find out. He agreed to protect her confidences, but he wanted to meet his newfound nephew as soon as possible.

———

Tolo was born in September, 1944, in Amantea, his mother's hometown village in Cosenza Province. She'd returned there only after being certain Italy's liberation was at hand; otherwise she would have battled throughout her pregnancy, since Atia Rivitolo was herself liberated long before it became fashionable.

Atia was raised in a commune by passionate parents who'd abandoned conventional lives as a priest and English teacher to fight fascism and every manner of social injustice. The struggle took them to Spain where they joined the International Brigade fighting the Fascists during its notorious Civil War. Their only child, Atia, also did her part in that conflict by evacuating Basque children from the war zone and carrying messages. But the war left her an orphan at the age of sixteen.

Upon returning to Italy, Atia continued the fight, then against Mussolini, by linking up with partisans in the Apennines, the mountain chain forming the backbone of Italy. There they utilized a network of ancient sheep trails to disrupt the fascist government strongholds. She progressed from guard to messenger, from messenger to spy, and then on to group leader, proving herself as willing and able to kill as any man, and also a brilliant tactician. She placed women in key roles against stereotype, using them as spies while they cooked and cleaned, essentially invisible to men plotting around a dinner table. And she used them to carry contraband secreted under maternity clothing while feigning pregnancy. Yet, it was her foresight which most distinguished her: she possessed an uncanny ability to anticipate events and make perfect strategic decisions before enemy plans were known, and at times even before they'd been formulated.

Atia was tall, with flawless olive skin, thick and lustrous ebony hair, and deep brown, penetrating eyes that brightened when she smiled with her sensuous, full-lipped mouth. She carried herself with a forthright cockiness that made her even more irresistible to men. Combined with her fierceness, she earned the nickname *"Il Guerriero Splendida," the gorgeous warrior.*

In 1942, she worked with the OSS, the United States wartime intelligence agency, in improving the partisan communications grid to assist in the Allied invasion. Alongside a spy nicknamed "Capri Boy," they added seventeen radio relay points in two months. After Capri Boy died after a betrayal a year later, the OSS chose her as his replacement and the Gorgeous Warrior took on the ironic additional name of Capri Boy.

As the Allied invasion of mainland Italy was being readied, the OSS asked her to undertake the assignment which would fulfill her life. "Why do you want me on this now?" she'd asked, "I have others to handle retrievals. Shouldn't I be focusing on the invasion?"

"Actually, this is top priority and with Montenegro imploding it's time-critical. We have nothing in that sector other than your contacts and field experience."

"What's the time frame?"

"ASAP in retrieving him, Montenegro's becoming less stable every day. But we need him back in good condition, so take the time you need for a safe delivery. We know the zone will be hot."

"Does the package have a name?"

"Lieutenant Sixtus Peeters, a navigator shot down while returning from the raid on Ploesti."

"Doesn't sound important," she'd responded, even as a notable and unexpected warmth coursed through her.

"I just follow orders, but it originated far beyond my guy. It's a whole war, not just European, matter, so I can't have it f'd up. Our best shot is you."

She understood the importance of the matter, and her instincts also screamed out that her personal interests required her to accept. "So, all I have to do is avoid being caught while crossing the Adriatic twice, likely mid-invasion. No problem, Hopkins, you prick! If I make it back you'll owe me big time."

"It's a deal, thanks . . . Capri Boy." They both laughed at that.

———

After bombing the oilfields in Ploesti, Romania in July, 1943, *The Maid in America* was forced to attempt a crash-landing in a narrow, rock-strewn valley. Seven remaining crewmembers braced themselves for impact, understanding their chances of survival were slim. Their assessment proved accurate, and five died quickly when the port wing and belly struck the ground at one hundred thirty-five miles per hour. The angle and force of impact split the aircraft near the center of the fuselage, tossing the plane's ass end forward and upside down as if shot from a sling. It landed in pieces as far as two hundred yards away in front of the demolished flight deck, while the half deck that flew forward miraculously remained intact, protecting the radio operator, Earl Graham, and the navigator, Six Peeters, who were in it braced against the bulwark.

Battered and disoriented, the two remained dazed for a time after the crash, but they eventually crawled into the shelter of the surrounding forest. Six applied a sling to his crewmate's broken collarbone, extracted metal shards from his thigh and fashioned a makeshift tourniquet. They huddled together and slept until daybreak, awakening in an isolated, mountainous area in the middle of a thunderstorm without a clue as to where to find safety.

They were in a valley in the Prokletije, or Albanian Alps, a mountain range of the Balkans in the Kosovo region of Serbia, west of the city of Pec. They'd crashed at a desperate time in Serbia, but in a fortuitous location.

Supported by their fascist occupiers, Albanian nationalists were cleansing Serbia of its minority Christians. Prodded by Haj Amin el Husseini, the Grand Mufti of Jerusalem, the Muslims had begun taking drastic action as part of their religious duties. So by the time of the crash, Serbia had been ceded to Albania, forty thousand Christians had been slaughtered, and thousands more had been driven from their destroyed settlements. Fortunately for Six, many Christians fled into the Prokletije, a rugged, roadless area of scattered small villages near the border of Christian Montenegro.

On their second day of hobbled westward wandering, the airmen found themselves on the same narrow mountain ridge as Father Miroslav Porconi. An orthodox monk, Porconi had lived with other hermits in a monastery at the entry to the Rugova Gorge until persecution drove them into hiding in isolated caves and communities throughout the region. Father Miroslav had little interest in the troubles of the outside world, but recognizing the two men as Americans, known opponents of the genocide, he felt compelled to give them shelter.

For six weeks they remained in the comfortable and safe, prayerful fellowship of ten monks. Six mended fully, but Graham's badly infected leg had to be amputated, prolonging his recovery.

In mid-September, two Montenegrins arrived in response to messages sent by the hermits to the OSS. They'd been dispatched to help both men, but most especially Peeters, make their way to a safehouse until they might cross the Adriatic. The Allies were fighting in Italy near Salerno, but regardless, they would be safer on Italian soil than on the heavily fortified, restless east side of the Adriatic. Graham's condition forced Six to leave him behind, but optimistic about the inevitability of victory in Europe, they expressed hope of meeting again in happier times to toast their fallen comrades.

Six's love of mountains was tested during the first week of up and down climbing while he and his companions travelled from the Prokletije to the Tara River Gorge of Montenegro. They rested there for two nights, recouping their strength by feasting on marble trout, while avoiding the bears and wild boar that were far more prevalent than the enemy. Marko and Lazar were affable companions, impressed by his ability to keep up with the two lifetime climbers. Their limited English included, "Look," used to express pride in the singular beauty of the cascades, rocky beaches, and soaring cliffs of the Gorge, and "Danger," an expression which really meant "hide."

Unfamiliar places, faces, and names blurred together as the men zigzagged across Montenegro, hiding in wine cellars, farmhouses, a church at Korita, and a primary school. They skirted the populated areas and travelled at night across the Zeta Plain and the rugged foothills near the border. They moved through what would soon become an impossible passage, after the Germans designated it as their eastern front. On September 25, 1943, Six waited, safely ensconced in a cellar under the home of his newest friend, Goche Burzan.

"I have bad and good news, Six," said Burzan, offering him a glass of copper-hued liqueur poured lovingly into a crystal glass. "Which would you like first?"

"Your twinkle gives you away, Goche—it's time for a last drink, right?"

"You're a bright man, *moj prijatelj*. Your guide will arrive soon, then after a few hours rest, you'll leave at daybreak. I'll miss your company. I've enjoyed refreshing my English and philosophy these past few nights. *Zivjeli*, to better days ahead!"

"*Zivjeli!* It's delicious."

"It's Amaro Montenegro, Italian actually, but I keep some on hand for special times since it's dedicated to Princess Elena, my wife's namesake."

"You're a romantic, Goche, I'm sorry I missed meeting her."

"After the war, my friend, when everything is right side up we'll meet up with our loved ones, me in Switzerland and you in America, perhaps we'll even meet back here in Rijeka Crnojevica."

"Amen to that . . . do you know who's fetching me?"

"Of course, it's Capri Boy. But she'll decide what name you'll know her by."

"Her, really, Capri Boy is a woman?"

"Yes, interesting, eh? She won't be alone, but she'll be the most formidable. You'll see."

Late that evening, the trap door opened and three figures descended the stairs. Six rose from his cot and stood waiting as the smallest of the dark-clothed figures moved toward him, stopped, tossed hood and cloak aside, and undid and unruffled her long hair. She shook her head vigorously a final time, raised her eyes, moved to him and reached out her hand. In perfect English she said, "Hello, Lieutenant Peeters, I-I-I'm . . . Atia Rivitolo . . . " As her eyes adjusted to the dim light, she saw something in him that unexpectedly made her use her actual name.

Six held her hand and looked back, equally surprised. The name "Atia" had been part of a childhood game he and his brother had played when he'd dreamt of having lived in ancient Rome, of having loved and lost a wife with that name. He'd told his brother, largely in jest, or so he'd thought, that they'd surely be reunited one day. After that, whenever seeing an especially beautiful girl they'd joked, "She's pretty, but she's no Atia!"

This woman, this Atia, was the same familiar woman he'd dreamt of walking hand in hand with while surveying a vineyard in the foothills of a mountain in an ancient time. Her voice had the same soothing and melodic tone. He acutely sensed the exquisite feel of her legs and breasts pressed against him, the smoothness of her skin and the fine and silky texture of her hair sliding between his fingers. He even recognized her sweet scent. They stared at each other, holding a charged handshake until one of her companions said in easily understood Italian, *"Che cosa sta succedendo qui. C'e un problema?"*

Six answered without averting his eyes from her, "There's no problem. I'm just very glad to see . . . all of you, and looking forward to being reunited with . . . my comrades."

She calmed her companion. *"Non e' un problema Roberto, mi ha appena ricordato di qualcuno che conoscevo prima della guerra."* *He reminds me of someone I knew before the war.* She ordered Roberto and Aldo to get some sleep and told Six, "We have four hours before we leave, so we need some rest. But first, come sit with me, Lieutenant, you need to know what to expect."

She sat and patted the space beside her. Six sat down and they began discussing what lay ahead of them. But very soon their legs were pressed together and the conversation moved on to the wondrous destiny which caused them to be together again at such an interesting moment in time.

———

Gio Conforti was busy clipping his fingernails at his desk when Elise passed the call through. "It's Frank from D.C. on line three."

"I thought you died."

"Vietnam screwed everything up, but my man's back and I've got some answers. Can you be here Friday?"

"Drop everything?"

"You won't be sorry, but dinner's on you, and no house wine. Check in and wait for my call."

On June 30, 1968, Conforti flew back to Chicago after a memorable dinner with Frank at San Souci. He met Redford in the Hilton airport lounge. Entering, John spotted Conforti on a sofa with a wide grin, a martini, and a half-empty bowl of cashews.

"Bingo, Johnny boy, we've got the connection. Have a drink and I"ll . . . "

"Gio, please, I've been waiting so long! Bottom line, please!"

"Did you ever realize how people in wheelchairs are so often overlooked? Take another look at this CIA '59 photo."

Gio handed it to John. It showed Eisenhower shaking hands with a skeletal, sickly-looking man as a group of twenty-four suits surrounded them, most with their hands mid-applause. Part of a wheelchair could be seen, but its user was obscured by an overweight man. "I can't see his face and I don't know anyone who uses a wheelchair."

"It's Daniel Stegger, name sound familiar?"

John remembered Stegger, a guy from Fermi's team involved with plutonium. He'd never worked with him directly, but they'd ridden together when delivering the core elements for Trinity. He remembered part of their conversation, Stegger speaking of his wife's pregnancy and expecting twins. He hadn't cared for the self-absorbed and arrogant scientist who seemed to have a chip on his shoulder. He'd warranted a footnote in Groves's book, and John had listed him as a potential future contact. He didn't recall seeing him after he left for Japan. But he remembered him as being vigorous, not confined to a wheelchair.

"Are you sure?"

"Certain. He was injured in an accident after leaving the Company. The honoree is Brant Frey, name ring a bell?"

"Ya, but I never met him. Groves talked with him on the QT a few times. He was army, maybe a Colonel."

"On the QT is right. He was high up in Army Intel and after Manhattan he and Stegger joined the CIA. They were thick as thieves, obviously with enough clout to get the ops directors together for this reception, to give Frey his due before he died.

Stegger had to know you in Los Alamos, and why you were passed off as John Redford."

"Where's Stegger now?"

"He's a Howard Hughes type, rarely seen and very wealthy. I've heard rumors he settled in Switzerland. His son's a lawyer in D.C. and close to Frey's kid, an up-and-comer in the Company. I'm checking them both out. But meanwhile, I heard Stegger went to the University of Chicago and a little bird found his application for me. So, lucky me, I'm off to Milwaukee. It's his hometown and his parents will be in their early sixties if they're still alive. They'll know where to find him."

"What can I do?"

"Nothing, just hang tight; but fire up man, we're getting close! Stegger's the key."

As he left Green Oaks Cemetery in Milwaukee, Conforti couldn't help but admire the genius of Daniel Stegger. He'd visited the graves of Stegger's supposed parents who had died childless in 1926, in their early twenties, after he learned Stegger had never graduated from South Division High School in 1937. He found it remarkable that a seventeen year old had had the moxie to forge a transcript for college admission to a prestigious school like Chicago, all the while hiding his real background. It begged the question of what he'd had in mind by covering his tracks back then.

Thinking about the automobile mishap that killed Stegger's supposed parents, Gio realized he'd overlooked an important clue.

In the twenties, accidents were considered just a regrettable part of life, but by the time of Stegger's accident, voracious tort lawyers, Melvin Belli types, earned large fees representing clients looking for money to compensate them after accidents—they only needed a deep pocket to blame. He called Frank and learned that Stegger's accident took place in Chicago, and the city was responsible. Conforti knew of few with pockets as deep as a city's, so he made one more call.

"Cook County Clerk of Courts," a woman answered.

"I need Al Bella. Tell him it's Gio Conforti and it's urgent."

Bella picked up. "Hey, Gio, what's new with Dick Tracy?"

"You're a riot, Al. I need a quick favor, same terms as usual, fellow named Stegger." He spelled it out, "Daniel R., had an accident between 1952 and 1959 in the City and I'm betting there was a lawsuit. I need you to dig it out, get addresses, depositions, whatever helps me locate the plaintiff. I'll be in my office tomorrow morning if you can get it to me then. I'll return it intact. Let Elise know either way."

"Did you check out the real estate records?"

"No, take a look if you have time, but I doubt there's anything. His property would be held in a blind trust, he's not someone looking to be found."

The following morning Conforti reviewed a 1959 file entitled *Daniel R. Stegger v. the City of Chicago, et al.* The case settled for an undisclosed sum within ten months of filing. Breaking the seal on Stegger's deposition, Conforti discovered Stegger had two attorneys, including one Arlen Christensen from Racine, then of Miami. After his lawyer's unusual objections, and after securing an agreement and order sealing the answer, Stegger had given up his Chicago address, and he'd also repeated the bullshit story of a childhood spent in Milwaukee. Conforti learned his home address was a Gold Coast brownstone only a few blocks from his own Lakeshore Drive home.

Within two days, Conforti had determined that an attractive black woman lived in Stegger's mansion as a caretaker. On the evening of July 4, after she left with friends to watch the fireworks from Navy Pier, he disarmed the security system, entered the home, and poked through Stegger's things. He found some helpful items and left unnoticed before the fireworks ended.

Conforti found a phone number and address for Christensen in Miami, and a hand-written letter with instructions on letterhead reading "From the desk of Daniel R. Stegger." The letter was dated two weeks earlier and poked half-way out an envelope postmarked Grand Lake, Colorado. He took notes from an ancestral chart inside a family bible hidden in the library. The bible was stuck inside a fake book cover, *The Entire Works of William Shakespeare*. Conforti laughed, having seen the fake book so often it always called out to him "Look Here!" Few people read Shakespeare, but for fifteen bucks that fake cover had been available for hiding things for years.

Looking to find Stegger, presumably near Grand Lake, Colorado, Conforti headed to Wisconsin. The ancestral chart indicated his real grandparents came from Denmark and settled and raised a family in Racine. His actual parents, Lars and Katherine Stegger, should know where he could be found.

After two days in Racine, Conforti felt he knew Daniel R. Stegger, a local legend, quite well. Supposedly preparing to return from Chicago to help run his grandfather's successful business, instead, he'd returned just long enough to bury Grandpa Hans, close out his estate, and sell off his businesses, pocketing most of the proceeds and screwing his family in the process. The gambit explained why Stegger didn't care to be found. As icing on the cake, he'd worked on the Manhattan Project and in the CIA, positions assuring he'd remain outside his family's reach.

At the Racine Circuit Court, Conforti reviewed the probate documents which transferred control of the family businesses to Daniel. All were prepared by Christensen, the Racine lawyer who immediately thereafter left town and finished handling the estate affairs from Miami. *How perfect, give the son of a bitch the business on a silver platter, retire to Florida, and continue working with him years later—seems like something WAS rotten in Denmark.*

He'd go to Racine and Miami if necessary. No doubt Christensen knew Stegger's whereabouts, and he wouldn't be the first lawyer Conforti had had to shake down.

Weeping throughout her interview, it turned out Stegger's mother didn't know of either her son's paralysis or his current whereabouts. "Serbs da liddle besterd rite, and I'm glad fer it," spat Uncle

Gunther, seventy-five years old and still incensed when thinking of his nephew twenty-five years after he stole their birthright.

Skies threatened as Conforti drove west from Gunther's toward the interstate, and a summer storm broke with such fury his wipers couldn't keep up. He decided to wait it out over dinner at Kilbourn Gardens, a local landmark right off I-94 and a straight shot back to Chicago. He drank a Bourbon Manhattan at the bar and ordered, phoning his client with the good news before heading to his table. "I'm certain Stegger's in Colorado and I'll have his address soon. We're looking good, payday soon!"

Conforti drank far too much at dinner, but he'd driven in worse shape many times. The rain pummeled him as he pulled his hat down and ran to his Lincoln Town Car. Fumbling with his keys, he dropped them for just a moment before being grabbed from behind and tossed into his rear seat. He came up sputtering and angry just before a fist slammed into his mouth. He leaned back against the seat, dazed and wondering what in the hell had just happened and where his glasses were.

In the light of the restaurant's marquee, sitting in rain in the back of his car in a nearly empty lot, Conforti squinted to make out the man across from him. *It's James Dean,* he thought, *just older, but isn't he dead? Still, he has the same long, thin face with large lips and pouty mouth, thick eyebrows and . . . No, the hair is wrong, not thick and high-piled like the famous actor, but long and tangled and in desperate need of washing.*

"Who are you working for, man?" asked the faux James Dean, "and where is that cock-sucker Daniel?"

Conforti's head began clearing and he thought: *I have to take control of this situation.* What he said, just before a blow loosened an upper bicuspid, was, "Just who in the hell are you is the question here!"

"You're the answer man, hot shot. You told Gunther you had a good idea where to find Daniel, well, you've got one minute to tell me where he is."

"Look, I didn't . . . " he began, but he stopped, realizing he *had* told Gunther he thought he knew where to find Daniel. He realized this had to be his son Hans, the bad seed and longtime prison inmate, someone not anxious to revisit the joint.

In his most authoritative tone, Conforti managed to say, "I know who you are, Hans, but that'll remain between us. I'm a licensed private investigator on a formal retainer and I'm investigating a matter affecting interstate commerce. Assaulting me is a felony that could earn you a long prison stay. But I'll forget it and we can go our separate ways, live and let live, like this never happened. What do you say?" When he held his hand out to shake, Hans grabbed it and yanked down, fracturing his small phalanges with a crack that could be heard over the rainfall. Conforti screamed and rattled the car, and Hans punched him again.

Hans pressed a knife to his throat, said, "Tell me. I'm not fucking around."

In excruciating pain and very frightened, Conforti decided to change tactics. "He-he-he's in Colorado, my briefcase in the trunk has all my notes on him. It'll tell you where to find a lawyer in Miami, a man named Christensen, who knows where Daniel lives. Please, take my briefcase and just leave me alone. I promise I won't say anything about this to anyone."

Among Gio Conforti's last thoughts ever was, *Shit, the briefcase also contains a thousand dollars in cash and my Smith and Wesson .38 special!*

10.

Elementary, My Dear Watson

Kenosha, Wisconsin, 1968

Slick Retzling looked in the mirror and ran a comb through his hair. Bag packed and bored, what with the Motors shut down for summer break and his drinking buds away up north, he couldn't wait. Where didn't matter, just being with Hans guaranteed it'd be exciting.

Hearing the horn he ran out. "Florida," Hans told him, but Slick had only the faintest idea what that really meant. In forty-seven years, he'd rarely left Wisconsin, not counting forays into Illinois for oleo and cheap booze. Still, he didn't have much wanderlust and the only place he regretted not visiting was Yankee Stadium, hallowed in his mind and he thought just across Lake Michigan. He didn't own a car or know how to plan a trip or read a map. But now, knowing they were going somewhere so exotic sounding made him feel worldly, like he'd felt when he first got laid by a hooker in Zion. He vowed to be worthy of Hans's invitation.

In Tennessee, Slick snoozed sticky-sweaty against his window when a road bump woke him. He looked over at Hans, mellow and relaxed, his arm resting on the window ledge challenging the heat. The epitome of cool, Hans bobbed in sync with the songs spun by Dick Biondi "the Wild I-tralian." It amazed him they could still hear WCFL in Chicago even nine hours away. *This Malibu must have one hell of a radio*, he thought, *at home I lose the signal on my piece of shit tabletop every night.*

"About time you woke up, Slick. Let's call it a day, get high and get screwed, I mean, what the fuck, it's a road trip, right?"

"Damn straight, man."

Slick spotted a sign for Bubba's BBQ and Dance Joint which sounded about perfect. By midnight, after ribs, a few brews, and a joint, they were ready to get it on. Sadie's place smelled sour and had a motorcycle leaking oil parked inside, but it had a small couch on the porch where Slick could screw in relative privacy. Hans's flavor of the night, hot-as-hell Sadie, had long legs and a sweet ass pushing against tight denim cut-offs just enough to show off the right amount of butt fat, and her perky tits bounced in sync with her ponytail when she danced, arms held high, swaying and thrusting her hips invitingly. So, as usual, Hans would get it on with hot Sadie in the bedroom while he banged the ugly one on the couch. *Rebel might be average-looking if she invested in a tube of Clearasil Max,* thought Slick. *Still, I can't complain. I could be in K-town pounding my pud.*

"Grits, what the hell!" laughed Hans as they drove south after breakfast the following morning. "How does anyone eat that shit? Must be an aphrodisiac like Spanish fly though, these Tennessee women are hot, hot, hot!"

Slick didn't know about any aphro thing, but he understood hot. He'd had his pipes cleaned. Rebel might've been ugly, but she'd been a machine, showing him moves he wouldn't soon forget. It made him think, *maybe I'll stop chasing Hans's leftovers and target just the uglies.* He'd wanted to party another night with the skanks, but Hans said they needed to get on with their important mission.

Hans talked non-stop about his asshole cousin Daniel, and if half his ramblings were true Slick thought he deserved whatever Hans dished out once they found him.

Slick thought they had to be close to Miami when they passed a sign with a giant orange that Hans said read, "Welcome to Florida, the Sunshine State." But he soon realized Florida had to be a huge damn place, since they drove for hours afterwards. They pulled into a Howard Johnson's outside of Miami at ten p.m. on July 9, 1968, and splurged on an awesome twenty-dollar room. The beds rocked when you put quarters in a slot, and it had the cleanest bathroom he'd ever seen, with little bars of soap wrapped in paper, tiny bottles of shampoo which they could keep, plastic cups sealed in paper, and *holy shit, a strip of paper across the toilet seat.* Hans said it proved the can was clean. Slick had never seen anything like it and once again admired Hans's sophistication.

Hans explained the caper and said, "just follow my lead." They agreed that shaking down some old-ass lawyer for some info and robbing him seemed so small-timey it shouldn't even be a crime. The old fart wouldn't know them and they'd be out of Dodge before he had any idea what happened. They'd obey the speed limits and stay off drugs at least until leaving Florida, and whammo, perfect caper complete, they'd move on to the big-time score that would carry them to easy street.

Slick had brought his favorite baseball bat along, a 33-inch Tony Kubek model named after his favorite Yankee, a rookie of the year from Milwaukee. Hans had laughed, when Slick carried his weapon of choice out to the car, but he'd said "Sure, bring it with, tough guy."

Then in Miami, Slick asked, "Should I bring my bat tonight? It's good for busting kneecaps."

"Another time, Slugger, leave it in the car. Tonight we roll a tad different, not like a street brawl."

Once they'd moved to Florida and he'd stopped lawyering, Arlen Christensen had felt reborn. His sullenness disappeared since he finally was able to do only whatever he and his wife Mariana enjoyed. During the war she'd helped out in a Miami canteen comforting lonely soldiers, while he'd drafted wills for candidates at the Training Command. After VJ day they discovered their love of the outdoors, waking at daybreak and going to bed early, usually golfing when not on their boat. With that, early-bird dinners, bridge, and cocktails with friends on their lanai, twenty-five years passed quickly in generally indistinguishable days. By 1968, approaching seventy-three, memories of Racine seemed as if a lifetime away, and Arlen's sole regret was not having moved down to Florida sooner.

Other thoughts preoccupied Arlen the evening his past came crashing in: *sleeping alone sucks, but Mari can't take my snoring; the neighborhood is too quiet and our routine is getting boring what with our snow bird friends up north; the damned air conditioner sounds like it might be going on the fritz again, loud as hell even with my half-assed hearing; and it's eleven, I've only been in bed two hours, but I need to piss like a racehorse, although I'll be lucky to pass a thimble full, damned prostate.*

He rubbed his eyes, stumbled from his room, and headed for the bathroom, thought he saw a shadow, *what could* . . . Suddenly, he was lifted off his feet and a large hand covered his mouth. He pissed himself while being carried down the hallway into the attached garage, his assailant's strength making any resistance futile. *How the hell can this be happening in our peaceful, bungalow neighborhood? This isn't goddamned Chicago!*

The strong man placed him in a lawn chair alongside their Rambler Classic, next to a dull-looking man with greasy, swept-back grayish hair holding a finger to his lips and motioning for him to be quiet. *Absurd, he thought, let go of my mouth and I'll tell you bastards off!* But then he thought of Mari, nightly Xanex down the hatch and sleeping soundly. For her sake he nodded up and down, slowly at first, but very rapidly when he spotted the gun held by the dull-looking man. They tied his hands and he found himself staring into a long and hard face.

He whispered, "Please, just tell me what you want, you can have anything! If you need money I'll even write you a check!"

"Is anyone here but you and the old lady?"

"No, sir, it's just us. Please, please, don't hurt Mari. She's nearly seventy and very frail. She took her sleeping pills and won't wake up. She's no threat to you at all!"

Slick smiled. *Cool, the lawyer called Hans "sir" for Christ's sake, plus he wet his pants. Not at all like the joint, now we're the man!*

"We want contact information for one of your clients, your biggest asshole client, Daniel Stegger."

Of course. Daniel, the chickens come home to roost. "Who's that?" the lawyer responded, buying time.

In 1939, Christensen had reasoned that caving in to Daniel made little practical difference since his grandfather wanted him to be his successor anyway. But he hadn't discussed the idea with his client. Instead he'd ignored ethics and changed the trust to give Daniel virtually unlimited powers in return for his own payoff. He knew his client would never have approved. He'd always paid lawyers reluctantly, no matter the value of their work. But he'd known Hans would be dead and gone when the payments began and with the money Daniel promised he and Mari could retire to Florida. He'd felt a bit guilty when he died so suddenly—very convenient for Daniel—but he'd convinced himself Gramp's death had to be a natural one. Then he'd watched idly while Daniel cheated the entire family.

The letter he'd received from Lars, Daniel's father, made for a painful read. It recounted the meeting when attorney O'Neill told the family Daniel had them by the balls so they'd take what he offered or get nothing. Christensen had recommended O'Neill to

Daniel, but he thought for tough negotiations, not for such a harsh cram down. It bothered him to know that even Lars suspected he'd betrayed his client.

Lars had asked if they could still get a fair share somehow. But although Arlen knew they could challenge Daniel, as well as his own unlawful conduct, he'd lied, telling them nothing could be done and pretending Hans had understood everything. It might have gotten messy and his comfortable life disrupted otherwise. Which family member tracked him down didn't matter. He deserved the confrontation.

Christensen had maintained contact with Daniel, visiting him in Colorado and becoming an informal advisor and sounding board. He sympathized over Daniel's paralysis, and knew that apart from Frey and Nathaniel, he had few others to confide in. Still, he'd give Daniel up in a heartbeat to save himself and Mari.

Hans smiled and drew his face close. "That's bullshit, attorney C, and we both know it. Don't be a wise guy. Really, how smart are you? You don't even lock your doors at night when crazy motherfuckers like us are lurking about.

I'll say this only once: you have my word I won't kill you or the old lady unless you lie to me; but if you do lie, I guarantee that both you and the princess will die tonight, slowly and very painfully, her first while you watch. Got it?"

Christensen got it. He believed the scary man and nodded in agreement.

"Tell me where to find Daniel."

"He has a home in Chicago and another near Grand Lake, Colorado, but he's nearly always in Colorado . . . I'm sure he's there now. There's an address book in the kitchen, in the top drawer on the right side of the oven. Bring it here and I'll show you."

"Slick, check it out. Be quiet, but make sure the old lady is sleeping.

He really fucked us over, counselor, took the meat and left us the drippings," mused Hans. "Lars didn't deserve a son like Daniel—he did everything for that prick. Lars killed himself since he couldn't face the family anymore."

Christensen gasped. He hadn't known about the suicide. Whenever he'd asked, Daniel told him his family was doing fine.

"He paid you off, didn't he?"

"No-no, I . . . " Arlen stammered, and then he thought of Mari. He only needed to tell the truth. "Y-Yes, we made an arrangement that kept me on retainer for . . . a long time. But I had no idea . . . I trusted Daniel, like your grandfather did. He told me he would make sure the whole family was taken care of."

"That he did, counselor, he took care of us . . . big-time. Who lives with him?"

"He keeps a small staff, a valet named James Jackson, a cook, and a maid."

Slick returned, gave a thumbs-up and handed him a thick black address book. Daniel's information was all in it and his wife remained asleep and unaware. Christensen gave them precise directions to Daniel's place, even explaining how to locate the remote access road from the National Park.

"You're a stand-up guy, Mr. C," said Hans, "and I'm a man of my word. I'm not going to kill you. But here's the thing: you know I'm going after Daniel, and you could warn him if I left you alone. I've thought about it long and hard and decided you have two choices, let's call them A and B."

"I won't warn him, really, I promise! You have what you want, I even drew a map to help, you can just leave us . . . "

"No, no, I can't. You'd be on the horn to Daniel or the cops the minute we left. We both know that, so no bullshit, okay? Like I started to say, you have two choices: A, princess Mari comes with us, insurance that you'll stay quiet until we're finished with Daniel. It creates logistical issues, but we can work those out and she'll get back to you eventually."

"No, no, you can't take her! She hasn't done anything. Leave her out of this, please! She needs to be close to her doctor, she's not well! She means everything to me. I'm begging you, please, take me instead!"

"Nah, we couldn't just take you. She'd call the cops when she saw you were missing and they'd start looking around for you, asking who'd been seen in the neighborhood, blah, blah. See what I mean? It would create even more difficult problems. But, if she really means everything to you, we can go with choice B, it's much easier." Hans grabbed a towel from a bucket near the workbench next to the spotless car. "You keep your wheels clean," he said. Then he gagged Christensen. "I don't think you'll like choice B too much either.

You see, if you're dead, our problem's solved, and your old lady can move on without a scratch. But I promised not to kill you, so you'd have to help us out, killing yourself that is, right here and right now. It's not what you expected, but you can think of it as poetic justice, like payback for Lars who had only bad choices left too . . . So, how much do you really love her, counselor?"

Arlen gasped, sputtered, and struggled with his bindings. "Stop and think before you get all bent out of shape, counselor. Life has tough moments. This is just one of them."

Arlen felt an unexpected calm descend upon him. He realized his life was about to end soon either way. If they took Mari, she'd likely die for his mistakes, and if that happened he'd want to die, too. Mari had been his "Georgia peach" since they met, a day which seemed part of a misty, long-ago past when life stretched out before them, when it seemed they had all the time in the world. They must have been children, so young. He'd always lived to please her, sold out to move her south to spend their sunset years together in paradise. They'd had a good run, but he didn't possess her internal strength. She could move on after this, but he could never live without her. This cold, hard man spoke the truth: it *would* be poetic justice, atonement for the pain he'd caused so many others by betraying his client and his ethics. He sighed deeply, and then he nodded, yes.

Slick and Hans crossed into Alabama near Pensacola after driving straight through from Miami. They were tired and subdued along the way, but after crossing the state line Hans opened up. "The son of a bitch had stones. I'll give him that, even asking me to help him!"

"Like a movie, all that 'I'm sorry' and 'give me a moment' shit. I saw her picture in their hallway and she looked like any other old lady, go figure. I would have fought. I'd never be such a pussy."

"He wasn't a pussy, Slick, dude was a class act. He sacrificed himself, man! As long as he knew she'd be OK he accepted his sentence. He couldn't fight us, so he took his medicine like a man, even apologizing, very classy."

"Ya, maybe he did the smart thing, but it was ugly and it sure looked like he changed his mind when he started kicking."

"Don't be an idiot, Slick! That's a reflex thing he couldn't control, like when the doctor hits your knee with that little hammer. His lungs made his legs kick when his brain said, 'you're not getting any air, man.'"

"Where'd you get the idea?"

"Snuffed a guy that way once using his own laundry bag, but it took nearly twice as long. Next time, no clear plastic though, I didn't like seeing his eyes bug out."

"Why'd you take the gag off and untie him afterwards?"

"Duh, it's supposed to be suicide. People don't tie their hands behind their backs and gag themselves after putting a plastic bag on their head."

"I wonder what his old lady thought. Probably screaming and all, I'll bet she even threw up."

"It's the price of sin, my man."

"Huh?"

"She'll never know why he offed himself, you dumb shit. But she used the money too, knew it came from somewhere odd, so it's fair she suffers too. The beauty of it all is that there's no one to suspect, so we're good as gold. It'll be different in Colorado, but they'll have no idea who offed him either. And then we'll leave with so much cash the PI's thousand bucks will seem like chicken feed. We won't take any chances with that tricky bastard though, crippled or not we'll use firepower instead of a plastic bag."

"How long until we get there?"

"We'll stop in an hour and get to Colorado tomorrow. We'll case it out then, you know, plan while making sure we're not seen hanging around. We'll act like tourists, stay somewhere away from his place and do the call and hang up thing to make sure he's home. I'm planning on surprising cousin shithead late Friday night, so circle July 18 on your calendar. That'll be the last day that asshole enjoys what he stole from my family."

———

John Redford knocked his coffee cup to the floor. The banner headline screamed, "Chicago PI Found Slain in Wisconsin."

Apparently, it happened soon after he spoke with Conforti. He phoned his office, but couldn't reach Elise. He thought she would realize his death concerned his case, and if the police connected the dots what would he say about hiring Conforti? Maybe he'd violated the court orders. He wondered, too, if Stegger had anything to do with Conforti's death. He didn't know why he hadn't told Rose about the PI. *Maybe,* he thought, *because it seemed unsavory and I didn't want to worry her.* Everything was becoming complicated even when the answers finally seemed close at hand.

Elise, weak-voiced, called and said she'd been calling all Conforti's clients. "Gio thought PI's had a bad reputation, so he insisted we treat his clients' matters confidentially. Even though we were . . . close, he never shared any details with me. So if the cops ever called and asked what he'd been working on, I could always give the same truthful answer, 'I don't know.' And while he always called in, I had no idea from where or doing what. He made me promise I'd return all his files to the clients if anything happened to him and I won't ignore his wishes. He was too good to me, much more than a boss."

The police never interviewed John, and they came to believe Conforti's murder had been random violence. They surmised he'd been killed in an armed robbery, likely by Milwaukee gangbangers. No one came forward with any information, and the waiter who'd received a lavish tip and admitted Conforti had been drunk was fingerprinted and detained, but soon cleared as a suspect.

In Conforti's file, John found what he'd given him or already learned, along with notes of meetings with contacts identified only by initials and dates. The sole helpful item was a note reading "Stegger letter from desk postmarked Grand Lake, Colorado." John located the place in an atlas, saw it was a day's drive from Chicago, and decided he'd go and find Stegger himself.

A few months earlier, John had finished concocting a compound he believed would act as a memory booster. Although it required more testing, he reconsidered his timing, knowing a small nudge might be all he needed to help him remember more about Stegger. He decided to try it before going to Colorado.

He'd begun studying memory enhancement when his visions reappeared in 1956, and the compound was formulated based on hard data, solid assumptions, and educated speculation. He knew brain neurons communicated by releasing neurotransmitters, like acetylcholine, which linked gaps in the brain called synapses, and the quicker a link the greater the recall. These made him suspect his memory problems were attributable to suppression of the process by an excess of AChE, the enzyme likely used in programming him as Redford. Galantamine, a tertiary alkaloid obtained from flowers, inhibited AChE, so he used it as a key ingredient. But since his subconscious had created false memories, he needed to find a way to separate his real memories from false recollections.

Knowing barbiturates were useful in interrogations because they promoted involuntary subconscious release, John thought the right combination of barbiturates could allow accurate memories to emerge. The key was finding the correct dosage, since too much of such sedative-hypnotic drugs caused unconsciousness or death—the barbiturates would eventually be used for capital punishment.

It took three years for John to determine the combination he thought would work while remaining harmless. As he envisioned it, the compound would increase his recall to the point where mental concentration allowed him to cross the final hurdle. He thought of it as operating like muscle memory: similar to the way an athlete reached optimum exertion, and then used intangible desire and focus to elevate a merely excellent performance into world class status.

He shared his idea with Rose in detail, confidently downplaying the dangers, stressing his experimentation on rats which left them unharmed and healthy. She reluctantly agreed to cooperate when told this would be his final effort, successful or not. She knew he was a skillful chemist, but also that arguing about something he'd thought about for so long would be futile. By remaining involved and cooperative, she could at least monitor the effort and summon help if necessary. Knowing John, she also thought it might work.

On July 10, he kissed Rose good night and drank the first of five concoctions intended to be taken over five consecutive nights. She watched anxiously, but he slept peacefully through the first four nights, with no distress, discomfort, or side effects, except for an odd garlicky aftertaste and an unusually hearty appetite. After the final dose, he awoke fully energized and without any adverse impact, but also without any new memories. "Apparently I was wrong, Rosie, but I took my best shot and now it's time to move on."

Still, John wasn't being entirely truthful. On July 15 he packed for a trip to Colorado. "You're sure you don't want me to come along?" asked Rose. "I can shop while you boys reminisce. Since we cancelled San Francisco, my calendar's clear."

"I"m sorry about our trip, Rose, but when I heard about the reunion I had to go, I mean twenty–five years since Los Alamos and all, and it'll just be us men . . . I mean . . . "

"John, I'm sorry, it wasn't fair to bring it up. I agreed you should go. Your work there was so important you deserve to enjoy celebrating those times, and who knows what you might learn."

John hated lying to her, but it couldn't be helped. He couldn't tell her he was going to Colorado to confront Stegger and he was driving because he needed to bring a gun and all the rest along. He didn't want her to know the lengths he was prepared to go to get answers.

"I won't drive straight through if I get tired. I'll relax and just enjoy the radio. I'll call to let you know how it goes."

John crossed the Mississippi River near Davenport and decided that if his search failed he'd surprise Rose and fly her out to San Francisco first class. Then he could join her for an early anniversary celebration and put all this nonsense behind him. The mere thought of ending his marathon search refreshed him.

The night before leaving, John reread two of his favorite Sherlock Holmes stories. It made him wonder what made Sherlock so insightful and able to predict others' behavior. Somehow Sherlock had always . . . then it struck him, *no one ever called Holmes "Sherlock."* He couldn't remember him ever being addressed by his given name. In the English tradition, Holmes had always been just that, Watson was always Watson, and Lestrade always Lestrade. Women and servants were referred to by given names, but gentlemen were typically referred to by their surname or by title. When in England he'd been addressed as Redford or Professor, and the Brits spoke of Barnes and Merrill and Williams and the rest, always by surnames. *Did Williams really remember a man called "Peter?" Isn't it possible he was confused and the picture more likely showed someone he'd known as "blank Peter," no, that doesn't sound right, rather "blank Peters?" So, all the effort to find an officer with a given name starting with "P" most likely has been wasted. We probably should have been searching for a man with the surname of Peters.*

He cursed his stupidity, recalling what Holmes always said, "Elementary, my dear Watson." *God, how dumb could I be! And, not only the name! It's obvious one doesn't just fall off a tree and end up working on the Manhattan Project, and nearly all Air Corps officers were college graduates. So, as an officer and technical assistant to Groves in Los Alamos, I had to be a college grad with a strong science background, likely in physics. There aren't more than two dozen universities with strong physics departments, places like Chicago, Columbia, and Cal Berkley, and they all have alumni lists.* He realized he should have been checking a list of physics graduates of twenty-some schools over a two or three year prewar period to find a "blank" Peters. So, if he didn't get what he needed from Stegger, that's where he'd look next.

Thinking of Stegger, John focused on his image: *a good-looking, athletic guy, but his eyes, something about them . . . what was it about his eyes?* John's mind leapt as if blinded by a flashbulb as he saw . . . The honk of a horn startled him, and he jerked his car back from the left lane, enduring the glare and raised middle finger of an enraged teenager.

He pulled over at a rest stop west of Des Moines and locked the doors, stretching across the front seat with his head up against one. Closing his eyes, he concentrated on recalling Stegger, and as his compound belatedly kicked in he felt transported, imagined himself on the hard bench of a truck and in a somber mood, aware that Groves remained committed to the bombing of Japan regardless of its necessity. He pictured them approaching the control center with Stegger across from him, eyes aglow. Then he saw himself on the ground, shaken by the spectacular light show that had been Trinity, and looking over at Stegger, eyes ablaze and mouth drawn into a maniacal grin. Stegger delighted in watching the mushroom cloud of superheated gases soar upward, even knowing it would soon be sucking up incinerated and shredded human beings rather than dirt, debris, and desert air.

Now, a quarter of a century later, John once again heard the words of a disemboweled flight engineer while flying in combat over Romania, words first recalled by him at Trinity and so fitting for Stegger and his ilk: "You don't know any limits, goddamnit! We're here because none of you know when to stop. How many have to die?"

The obscenity of the Hiroshima bombing returned to him, and he remembered anticipating Groves's grilling for his refusal to fly to Nagasaki, remembered making a list . . . They took it, they questioned him about it as he lay strapped to a gurney. They called him a traitor for not going . . . No, not only for that, but because they knew his real name wasn't Redford. They said they could prove it, but then how . . . He again pictured Stegger's eyes glaring with hatred as he rambled on about chemistry controlling men's minds, just before a man injected something into him, and then there was nothing until he came to in a hospital and began suffering the chemical punishment.

He sat up, drenched in sweat and stunned. Stegger and another man, undoubtedly Frey, did this to him. There wasn't any failed experiment, he'd been accused, abused, and made to believe he was Redford. Anger born of years of suffering infused him, and although he couldn't recall ever hurting anyone out of anger, he felt that would soon change. Stegger hurt him, hurt Rose and his family, likely killed Conforti and God knew who else. He started the car and burned rubber leaving the rest area. He'd turn over every rock to find that son of a bitch and get his answers, and then he'd make Stegger pay for all his years of misery, all his lost years.

John left his car at the airport in Denver and used a fake ID and cash to rent a car from Hertz. He changed into a new suit, shirt, tie, and dress shoes, hardly hiking gear, and headed up into the mountains. Briefcase in hand and purposefully conspicuous as "Charles Smith," attorney at law from Seattle, he made inquiries regarding the whereabouts of Daniel R. Stegger, a reclusive rich man in a wheelchair. He said he was dispatched by a Washington State Probate Court to find him and deliver the good news that he'd been named sole beneficiary of a massive estate left by a wealthy relative in Seattle. The gambit paid off and he was directed to the bastard's home.

On Thursday, July 17, 1968, John fell asleep in a nondescript motel, preparations complete. That night he experienced vivid and sensual dreams full of rapidly shifting sensations. They were heartfelt and intense, and knowing they included images of Rose, he woke feeling certain every image reflected events from his actual past.

In one dream, he envisioned himself on the edge of a pond watching water roll down the long, thin back of a naked woman as she swept her dripping hair back with one fluid toss of her head. She turned to face him, smiling, arms to her sides, laughing softly in a clear and welcoming way. He moved to embrace her and his hardness pushed against her as he nuzzled her neck. He whispered something indistinct in his passion, but then he moved on.

A woman sat bent over, swaying slowly from side to side, her long hair obscuring her face. She looked up and pushed her hair aside and he recognized her tear-streaked face. It was the same, thin, delicate, angelic face with high cheekbones and wide, dark eyes he'd long since known, the face of . . . of, no, it seemed all wrong.

She'd always been the one to comfort him, so why was she weeping? He remembered her waking him, or had she been pleading to live, or was she only an image in a painting? He saw her rise and gesture expansively, then she pointed upward saying something . . . He understood her saying something about being worthy, and stars, but then she moved on.

Stars . . . he was on a train gazing at a blanket of stars in the sky above, feeling content, relaxed and at peace with the world, a woman's head resting on his shoulder. He held and caressed her, feeling more satisfied than he'd ever been, but when he tried to look into her face he saw nothing, only an unrecognizable void where her features should have been, and then he moved on.

He saw her just ahead of him, wearing a silky white gown that left the lovely bareness of one shoulder and her back exposed. She had flawless olive skin and thick, lustrous ebony hair. Her deep brown and sparkling eyes brightened with her smile, weakening him and emphasizing her sensuous, enticing mouth. "Salve," she sighed, as he enfolded her in his arms and felt her warm breath on his neck. He began stroking her silky skin with his fingertips, but then she was gone . . . no, not gone, different somehow, but looking at him and smiling with recognition, speaking of visions and reunion and the certainty that their child would survive and fulfill them, but then he moved on.

He was with his wife, Rose, distracted while thinking of a young angelic girl just become a woman, even as he watched Rose move atop him, uninhibited, breasts heaving, hands entwined in her hair.

In a comfortable and familiar rhythm she told him nothing could be better than the moment, nothing better than knowing they were creating their child. He pulled her face down and opened his mouth, touching his tongue to hers, sucking in her intoxicating heat at the very instant of release. It seemed a moment always meant to be, but it merged into the sensuality of every dream experience, from first on the edge of a pond, to a more recent time with a woman he'd known for ages, one who'd reveled in their intimacy and the ecstasy of their reunion.

John woke, wondering when he'd last had a wet dream, and then remembered. He'd been much younger then, in a tent on an early desert morning in "Libya," a remembered word which now made sense once again.

The women of his dreams all fit into his life and each had touched his heart in a singular and profound way. But the rich satisfaction of those memories had been stripped out of his conscious thought and recast as mystery rather as an essential part of the majesty of life, had diminished, even vanished for a time and all because of Stegger. He willed away his sense of weariness and loss and replaced it with resolve and intense anger. Stegger had best enjoy the newborn day since it surely would be his last.

———

On July 19, 1968, James Jackson, long-time manservant to Daniel Stegger, drove past the no trespassing sign, exited the truck, and pushed open the gate to the road leading to his master's retreat. The sun hadn't yet penetrated the dense forest and Jackson rubbed his hands up and down along his arms to dull the morning chill. He noted fresh tire tracks near the gate, surmised druggies or lovers had parked there to do their thing. He didn't recall strangers ever driving in all the way to the house. If they had and disturbed the "Crip," he'd receive a full ration of shit. He should have locked the gate, but often he didn't bother when leaving in a hurry.

James whistled as he drove, feeling good. Tammy, their new cook, was plain-looking, but his instincts had served him well. They'd enjoyed drinks, dinner and dancing before moving on to a marathon sexual escapade—Her performance catapulted her into the top ten of his all-time list, and since the Crip didn't bang the help anymore, he wouldn't have to share her. James filled Stegger's diminished needs by importing hookers biweekly. A blonde was scheduled for that very evening, since Saturdays were blondes only.

James thought, *I'll need a few z's today to recover, but no sweat, life's a lot easier now that the Crip's beginning to act like an old fart.* Life had improved dramatically as Stegger aged, and his duties took increasingly less time. He'd adopted a predictable, less demanding routine: no one visited except his son and hookers; he rarely left the place; and most days he only exercised, spoke by phone to keep tabs on his businesses, and read business, science, and political journals. Recently he'd become obsessed with videocassettes of new movies played on a prototype player from Japan slated for marketing by one of his subsidiaries.

Approaching the home, James noticed the kitchen shades were still drawn although Maggie should have already served breakfast since Stegger rarely slept past seven. He noticed wires dangling near the roof and shattered glass aside a towel on the deck with the entryway doors wide open. "Shit!" he exclaimed aloud. He ran to the truck, grabbed his shotgun, released the safety, and settled a round. He walked cautiously around the house and entered through the unlocked door leading to the staff quarters. He noticed immediately that the inside of the home smelled like a meat locker.

Emerging from a short hallway, James saw the maid splayed out on the floor. Maggie rested on her left side with her right hip thrust upward and her negligee pulled mid-thigh above oddly bent legs. Her stiff feet were raised just off the ground and her bare toes pointed awkwardly forward. Her right arm crossed her chest, its stiff fingers reaching down toward the floor as if preparing to play the piano. Her bare arms and legs were pallid and dull, and as he crouched down to look at her face, he noted her hazy eyes staring blankly, not surprising given the gaping wound across her neck. It quickly occurred to him that he was kneeling in a copious amount of blood pooling up from the soaked carpet. He jumped up and added his breakfast to the surrounding splatter.

He pointed his shotgun and whirled around calling out, "Is anyone there?" Hearing only deathly silence, he grabbed a phone, found the line dead, dropped it and hurried to Stegger's suite. It was in total disarray, but most especially his office where the safe had been ransacked. Splattered blood appeared here and there on the white walls, looking to have been artfully flicked from a brush to create a modern work of art, except for a smudged hand print which seemed out of place in the tableau. James approached the bedroom, noting a bloody footprint on the floor near the closed door. He knocked from habit before entering with his gun pointed forward.

With nothing left to vomit, James only gagged at the sight of Daniel Stegger's corpse looking up toward the ceiling from the blood-soaked white bedspread. His arms were stretched out to each side and his useless legs pressed together forming a letter T, with "JUSTICE" written in his blood in block letters on a pillow above his head. Despite the unmistakable reference, Stegger hadn't been crucified—he had died from a gunshot wound to the middle of his head above the eyes, execution style.

James ran out and drove to the nearest payphone, following Stegger's long-standing directive: "If anything ever happens to me, call Nathaniel. The most important matter then will be the contents of my safe, and he'll know what needs to be done."

James reached Nathaniel at 12:15 p.m. Washington D.C. time on July 19, and followed his instructions to the letter. One month later, he received three hundred thousand dollars in cash and returned to Chicago. Nathaniel needed nothing further from him but his adherence to the script.

After surveying the materials taken out of the home by James, Nathaniel knew it hadn't been an inside hit. Many household artifacts of great value remained in place, and a side compartment of the safe holding diamonds worth over four hundred thousand dollars remained intact. The killer had removed only two things: five hundred thousand dollars in cash, the enormous, precise sum Daniel kept handy in case a rare opportunity arose, and one of his treasured files—having ransacked the safe, the murderer hoisted only one file and the recordings accompanying it—the file labeled "Sixtus Peeters."

Nathaniel added it up at once. The bastard who'd seduced his mother in Los Alamos found and murdered his father and removed the single file that could identify him and betray his motive. Somehow, he'd learned what Daniel did to punish him and he'd taken his revenge. Well, two could play that game, and there was no question what he needed to do, no question at all about the duty a loyal son owed his slain father.

11.

Azume

Northern Massif Central, Europe 9,827 BP

Inside her home, a chamber off a passage leading to the central gathering hall, Azume gazed down at the underground stream below. The slow-flowing tributary provided crystal-clear, sweet water for drinking, cooking and bathing, and once a year it teemed with colorless, blind crustaceans, a shrimp-like delicacy devoured with gusto during the eagerly anticipated feast of Estaba. Deep in thought, cast in the amber glow of the oil lamp, (an obvious sign of her hearth family's elevated status), Azume fidgeted with the saber-tooth necklace marking her as a Council Daughter. But obligations also accompanied privilege, so nearing her eleventh birthday and on the cusp of womanhood, Azume faced the prospect of submitting herself to an evil man.

The mating of a Council Daughter followed an ancient edict, and the choice of the Clan Council was pronounced after they met in secret session. The divinely inspired choice required compliance upon pain of death, and none of the Daughters ever had a say in the matter. Because Azume had always been treated with deference, she found her helplessness in such a significant matter disconcerting.

Azume had a singularly compelling aura and bearing. Even during the awkward stage besetting girls before the beginnings of puberty, she'd remained as attractive as at birth. Then, her stern and usually impervious father, Oto, had stroked his rough fingers over the cheek of his infant daughter at first sight, overlooking his profound disappointment with her gender. Yet, it was difficult to pin-point what made Azume so alluring, since she had none of the qualities associated with the most desirable females—no long legs, no fair skin, no full and sensuous mouth, no sparkling eyes or glimmering hair. What she did have was copper-hued skin matching the color of her wide eyes, a thin and delicate face with high cheekbones and a cupid's mouth, and thick and long auburn hair which flowed down to rest gently upon her shoulders. Her arms, her slim and delicate neck, and usually a single breast were customarily fashionably exposed, and she typically wore a long fur draped over one shoulder, belted around her waist and otherwise covering her body to mid-thigh. Her appeal seemed due to the unique combination of her features and an unusual grace and bearing; her entirety, despite its quite ordinary components, caused males to become restless in her company, and she fueled many lustful fantasies.

Entering quietly and observing Azume sitting in the flickering, shadowy light of their subterranean home, her mother, Rena, was once again reminded of a spirit. Since Azume's birth, she'd harbored a disquieting sense that this child whom she loved above all others was too unique and precious to remain in their world. She couldn't help feeling that one day Azume would vanish like the morning mist in the face of the sun. She had to fight against revealing the premonition, understanding it intruded into the Shaman's realm and could be mortally dangerous. She hoped her sense of foreboding sprung only from foolish, unbounded motherly love, and that treating her beloved child dispassionately might help dispel it.

Azume rose and greeted her Hearth Mother with a smile. Rena asked, "Why are you here alone, my daughter?"

"I am trying to discern, esteemed Mother, what the gods intend for me when I become a woman. The Council's choice greatly concerns me."

"Remain silent and be patient. Soon after you learn to bleed, all will be known. Keep your faith. Our wise Council will ascertain the will of the gods. Always remember, my strong-willed child, your desire is of no account. All we have has been given us in exchange for our obedience to the gods' demands."

Above ground, less than a hundred yards away, Oto, father of Azume, Clan Lord, and one of the most powerful men on earth, reclined on a lush carpet of woodland groundcover, his head leaning against a fallen tree and his lithe frame nestled on a bed of ferns and moss. From his vantage point, high near the uppermost entrance to his home, he enjoyed an excellent view of his domain and could study its dominant point, the sacred mountain of Amar. Shaped like the back half of a sail, Amar sloped gradually downward for three miles from the sharp, startlingly high precipice on its westernmost side, until it transitioned into a series of gently rolling, low-lying hills to the east. Surrounded by lower land, Amar captured the attention of anyone approaching within miles from any direction.

As Oto looked toward Amar, the copper glow of the setting sun appeared to set its limestone tip ablaze. The splendid and frequent sight reinforced his belief that it was indeed one of the homes of the gods, and, as such, the basis for his profound responsibilities.

Oto learned from the wise Shaman that as Lord of the Colya, just as his father and his father's father before him, he bore an awesome responsibility as the primary human caretaker of Amar, one of only six such homes placed by the gods upon all of the land inhabited by men. It fell upon him to see that men revered and protected the forbidden place, and that the bidding of its divine inhabitants be done in all things without question. After all, without the guidance of the gods who possessed all wisdom, the Colya were likely to misinterpret the mysteries of the world and suffer such extreme misfortune and hardship that the entire clan would be extinguished.

The gods moved invisibly between their dwellings and monitored human conduct to assure they were given the homage they deserved as the source of all life, the sun, the moon, the earth and sky. Any clan failing to venerate them would be deemed unworthy and be doomed. There was precedent for the infliction of such punishment: near their home were vestiges of a race that once occupied their caverns, an enormous society of non-humans the gods found wanting and made extinct.

The extinct non-humans were a pale-skinned, red-haired lot that paraded about naked year round. Having examined their skulls and bones, Shamans determined they were similar to humans, but a head shorter than most of Oto's people, and of much thicker build, with large thighs and buttocks, and flaring ribcages supporting massive muscles. They had thick brow ridges over their eye orbits which continued across their entire faces; their foreheads were concave; and they were chinless, with large noses and nasal passages, the combination of features making their faces appear inflated. Male and female alike were exceptionally strong, and such skillful hunters that they were unafraid of the bears and saber-toothed cats which stalked nearby still and terrified Oto's people.

The extinct had ruled a territory large beyond imagination, one encompassing waters, forests, mountains, plains and grasslands, and all the other homes of the gods. Their daily implements, intricate weapons, and cave drawings, all bore testament to their cleverness and creativity, so clearly, they'd once enjoyed divine favor. But the gods abandoned them after they'd attained such mastery that they stopped paying homage to them, overlooking the very source of their power and well-being. Their lack of spirituality and disrespect was evidenced by the awful truth that they ate their own kind. What could be more offensive to the gods than beings who devoured creations in their divine image?

Oto saw evidence of the cannibalism in a cavern gallery just beyond the entry place of the underground river, a taboo location where remnants of the extinct were maintained by the Shamans. Upon his elevation to Lord, he'd been shown an ancient hearth below a cave shelf upon which rested a macabre altar composed of skulls and bone fragments of the extinct, alongside tools similar to those the Colya used when butchering animals. He saw jagged fracture lines on fragments of their skulls, on femurs and tibias and a single humerus; all readily matched the tools used to scrape deeper into bones while seeking flecks of flesh, or for digging to extract the soft, edible brains, or when probing into long bones in search of tasty marrow—the same methods the Colya used when eating beasts.

He'd seen definitive proof of their atrocity behind the hearth: When the Shaman lifted his lamp, it revealed a pit containing the discarded bone fragments of many skeletons, and graphically visible on the adjacent cavern wall, a disgusting three foot high drawing depicting a short, red-haired and well-muscled male gnawing on a detached, bloody forearm while holding it by the wrist.

Oto was sickened by the idea, and he believed any race which practiced cannibalism deserved such a fate. Still, he tried putting it into perspective: He ruled an area so large that it took five days of walking to reach its end, and he knew that other clans lived outside his realm. Extrapolating from the fact that there were six homes of the gods on all the earth, and 139 Colya, the total number of humans alive on all of the land had to be nearly 900. He knew the pain and sorrow expressed over the loss of one Colya, so the thought of so many lives being extinguished nearly at once was stupefying.

A complex but straightforward man, Oto obeyed the gods in all things while coolly judging the entreaties of all others. As sole possessor of the power to terminate the life of any clan member but for the Shaman, he couldn't appear weak-willed or malleable. It helped greatly that at twenty-six he was an extraordinary human specimen at the peak of his physical and mental powers. He stood an unusually tall six feet four inches, was slender but well-muscled and broad-shouldered, and had a pleasing face with a strong chin dusted by a thin beard. He wore his sandy brown hair pulled back into a ponytail, and his large and angular head was usually topped by a bejeweled leather headband signifying his majesty. He spoke slowly, without hesitation or stutter, in a deep and thunderous baritone. He was well-coordinated and especially fond of dancing, often punctuating his displays of joy with athletic leaps across a fire, a sight which always drew delighted yelps from his people.

He'd proven his courage in the five battles of his reign, killing four enemy tribesmen in hand-to-hand combat without showing the slightest fear. He proved particularly adept at dodging spears, and his towering presence caused enemies to flee in terror when he charged, bellowing, "Amar Destroys!"

Oto possessed exceptional intelligence. He'd quickly mastered the science of pressure flaking with an antler bone, and instructed others on its use in fabricating the sharp and intricate tools and spearheads which the science enabled. He also designed a system of perimeter defense using smoke and fire for more rapid warning.

As a child, Oto listened to the Bard's stories of preceding Lords, and he'd concluded that their unique leadership skills, as well as his own attributes, weren't accidental. He credited the Clan's divinely inspired breeding practices for producing the finest Lords.

There was little privacy available and copulation was commonly observed. Children mimicked adults to the point of simulating intercourse, beginning while still very young, with boys signaling their partner to assume the customary, face-down, haunches-up position. Penetration and pregnancy were rare, but because they did occur at times, Hearth Law decreed that any girl so impregnated would remain under the protection of her Hearth Mother rather than speculate about the identity of the responsible party. Because of this possibility, the Council Daughters (the daughters of the Lord, the Shaman, the War Chieftain, the Bard and the Chief Huntsman) were forbidden to engage in simulation and required to remain virgins until their formal mating. The taboo insured that every ruling Lord would be the offspring of a Council Daughter mated to a man carefully selected by the Council.

Twenty-five years earlier, Oto's father mated with Tava, daughter of the War Chieftain, and he was the product. After passing his four-year-old exam, Oto was designated as a potential future Lord, along with three others. He was selected as a Sub-Lord in Waiting at twelve, and selected as Lord when his father died eight years later at the respectable old age of thirty-six.

Despite the Bard's talented recounting of the past, none of the Colya had anything but a rudimentary concept of time. They believed their people had inhabited the land near Amar since time's beginning, which they envisioned as the passage of several generations before Oto's birth. But their origins would one day be traced back to a time, so long after time began, that it still remains difficult to comprehend in a meaningful way.

The Colya were descended from a group of twelve Africans who tired of nomadic life and began searching for a permanent home in

11,550 BP, nearly 2,500 years before Oto's birth. Their progeny ended up settling near Amar after a warming trend swept the continent, ending the Ice Age and producing a moderate climate in their new homeland, which would be known in modern times as the Bourgogne region of France, one of the most fertile places on earth.

Oto's forebears arrived from the west, drawn by the majesty of Amar. While moving toward it, they were intrigued by how the nearby terrain rose gradually across the flat and grassy plain until abruptly ending at a half-moon shaped limestone wall capped with brush and shrubbery, with roughly symmetrical and rising, heavily forested hills running north and south from each side of the limestone wall center. The entire formation covered six miles end to end at an average height of about three hundred feet.

Knowing such rock often contained fractures, crevices and cavities large enough to provide shelter for humans and animals alike, they approached the formation cautiously, spears drawn to the ready. After four hours of crisscrossing and probing the western side of the formation, they were unable to locate any entry points. Upon climbing to the summit of the wall and looking downward to the east, they realized that they'd discovered the mother lode of all settlements.

The eastern side of the formation revealed openings to an extensive interlinked network of caves, including running water in the form of an interior underground river. Over time, the Colya would modify and improve the nearly ideal site, retaining eight discreet and heavily fortified access points, all connecting with a central communal gathering hall large enough to hold half of the clan. They identified areas which were used exclusively for cooking, storage, Council meetings, and religious ceremonies. They also designated a number of distinct sleeping areas. Five of the largest, complete with adjacent nooks and crannies, were used as semi-private hearths by Oto and the other four Council members. Every sleeping area had hearths serving as the inviolate domain of a "family," although they could only be lit with the Lord's permission—Oto had implemented use of a single, well-ventilated cooking area for the entire clan, thereby reducing much of the past discomfort caused by acrid smoke constantly wafting through their home.

Azume first menstruated on a summer morning during her eleventh year, one month after she and her Hearth Mother had their earnest discussion, and two weeks after Estaba. The day after the appearance of the next full moon, the Council would announce its selection for her mate.

The choice for any Council Daughter was a keen topic of gossip, especially with such as Azume, daughter of the current Lord. If she birthed a healthy son he would surely be a future candidate for Lordship.

In assessing the candidates, the Clan members proceeded under the assumption that an apple never falls far from the tree. So, an obvious candidate was Shaur who shared the Bard's hearth and appeared likely to be his birth son. They shared the same stocky, thickly-muscled build, and curly and unruly black hair that appeared gnarled even the day after a thorough cleansing and combing. He and the Bard also shared the distracting mannerism of appearing disengaged and uninterested while absorbing every single nuance of conversation anywhere nearby. He had a tremendous memory, and he shared the Bard's enthusiasm for recounting clan lore, could recite a detailed history going back ten Lordships. Well-regarded, he was favored at least to be the next Bard.

Azume felt little emotion over the prospect of mating with Shaur. She found him inoffensive, but boring and tedious. Yet she doubted his selection. He seemed unable to father a child with the personality and force required to direct the clan in difficult times. His offspring would be thoughtful, kind, gentle, and inoffensive, but ponderous and slow to act, weak and uninspiring, more eager to talk than act, hardly the attributes of an effective Lord.

A most formidable contender was fifteen-year-old Nambe, the son of the Shaman. Parentage alone would have put him in the running unless he'd been a complete dolt, and Nambe was anything but. He had a razor-sharp, quick-witted mind and stood nearly six feet tall, and he was strong and athletic and blessed with the best vision in the clan. Cutting a handsome figure, with a well-chiseled face, full lips and high cheekbones, and with piercing hazel-colored eyes, he intimidated most men in the tribe regardless of age. He spoke convincingly and rapidly, with a commanding bearing leaving no doubt of his talent and leadership. But he had an attitude that diluted his many qualities: egocentric and cold to the point of detachment, he had an arrogance born of the belief that his father's achievements credited his own ledger. There was unfortunate truth to his belief in entitlement, but unlike more effective, privileged children, Nambe made no attempt to mask the unpleasant fact.

Nambe's father, the Shaman, had long been revered because of his position and accomplishments. During his tenure, the clan had prospered as he proved his understanding of the gods' demands time and again. His incantations and sacrifices brought warm weather, stopped the spread of fires, cured many illnesses, eased the pain of giving birth, and helped repulse invaders.

Most dramatically, the Shaman once had conveyed unwelcome and unprecedented news when the gods demanded a blood sacrifice, the painful deaths by fire of a dull young man and a maiden caught fornicating in the forest one moonlit evening. The Shaman charged that they'd offended the gods by seeking their pleasure when the gods had already provided a spectacular full moon for enjoyment—it was like biting the hand that fed them, implying the god's hadn't provided enough. The hearth members of the transgressors were shaken by the Shaman's inability to find a viable alternative, but they came to accept the sentence and eventually joined the others at the executions imploring, "Gods of Amar, accept our sacrifice!" The sacrifice and entreaty turned out quite well, since during the following two years not a single clansman died, the winters were mild, every clan birth was successful, and the Chief Huntsman conceived of a trap allowing the slaughter of a massive, pregnant mastodon, leaving the clan with a three-month supply of unusually hearty sustenance and oil.

Azume despised Nambe. She saw the ugly inner self behind his looks, knew the insincerity of his utterances, saw self-interest in his every gesture, and was revolted by the display he made of leering at her while running his tongue around his lips, as if preparing to consume her. He'd told her he intended to have her, "yum, yum," which she found disgusting.

Her hatred of Nambe began with an incident she thought she'd observed in her sixth year. Being so young, she later wondered if she might have only imagined it. *Still*, she thought, *how could such ugliness spring into my childish mind from out of nowhere?*

She saw the loathsome side of Nambe displayed on a fall day after the leaves dropped, when the secrets of the forest were revealed. Out alone before nightfall, Azume was strolling a few hundred yards from her dwelling entry, along one of the spider-webbed paths on the hillside, when she spotted Nambe and a hearth mate. They looked to be field dressing a deer, but as she moved closer she saw the doe had been hung head down with its mouth tied shut and its legs secured, and the two were laughing as they jumped to and fro, knives in hand, close to and then back away from the animal. Azume instinctively went to the ground and crept closer. She saw that the animal was wounded and punctured, but it still remained alive. It could only thrash about hopelessly while being sliced and stabbed for the maximum infliction of pain without the bittersweet release of death. She watched, mystified, as ten-year-old Nambe danced around with delight, and she watched, repulsed, when the two boys stood aside the dying doe, flicking at its genitalia with their knives and laughing hysterically as it moved through its death throes.

When the scene reoccurred to her in nightmares, she would wake up crying, remembering the look of terror in the bulging eyes of the animal. She felt she had read its mind: *What have I done to warrant this abuse? The gods gave them the right to kill, but not to torment and abuse me. I wasn't created for such as this.*

Watching the atrocity had reminded Azume of the wise old Shaman speaking of the sacredness of living things and the need to be in harmony with creation as the gods intended. Yet, she'd been afraid to disclose what she'd seen, felt she wouldn't be believed, and she sensed that leveling the charge would turn the Shaman against her despite his son's sadism. "A gift from the gods," Nambe had said hypocritically, upon delivering the belatedly dressed deer to the Lord that evening, betraying nothing of its torturous path to the communal pot. Instead, Nambe portrayed himself as a heroic provider, proving his duplicity. Azume ate none of the meat, would never put venison to her lips again.

How could she submit to such a man? What cruelty would he inflict upon her when she presented herself on command? Better to be consumed at once by a beast than dismembered night after night by a man-thing masquerading as a human and a Colya. Nambe was a monster, certain to cause suffering when unloosed in the darkness of his hearth. The prospect of his selection would make suicide a welcome option.

There were several other candidates, but none likely to muster such support as the Bard or Shaman could bring to bear for their own. Azume had her favorite, of course, and while she scarcely dared hope he might prevail, its possibility and the certainty he would be considered made her knees weak and her heart soar. She tried to restrain her optimism, although she believed Lord Oto was thoughtful and held the most sway in the Council. Wouldn't he select the best possible mate for his daughter? Wouldn't the gods enlighten him to see there was no better choice than Takla?

Azume had always felt close to Takla. He'd been part of her life and nearby from the time she'd first ventured beyond her parents and hearth mates. He'd been one of the older children, four years older than she when she'd first walked well enough to begin playing with others. He'd listened patiently to her babbling, was generous with his time and anxious to instruct her. Even in childhood he spoke to her as if they were age mates, listening patiently and treating her like a friend. Takla always showed his concern for her, and he was one of the few potential mates she couldn't intimidate.

Takla had a leaner and smaller carriage than most Colya men, but he compensated with strength and agility, and moved so smoothly that even when running he seemed to exert little effort. His speed and endurance allowed him to run faster, further, and longer than all but one warrior, a man twice his own fourteen years. Once, when communications had been disrupted before a battle during his twelfth year, he'd gone back eighteen miles for reinforcements, and remarkably covered the distance in only two hours. He'd helped secure victory against a daunting foe with only two lives lost, and his extraordinary feat would have been the object of a celebration if not for the low status of his Hearth Father.

Takla's father would have been of great value to the clan had he been more ambitious, but he preferred quiet evenings at his hearth to the meetings, intrigue, and alliance-forming required for leadership. He was content managing and safeguarding the clan's stock of harvested seeds, berries, grains, and nuts. Takla watched his father work, and even as a child decided he'd be a warrior instead—he could never do anything so mind-numbing.

Once apprenticed, his ingenuity and strategic sense impressed the War Chieftain. Mechanically adept and creative, Takla conceived of and fabricated an atlatl, a weapon carved from black walnut, consisting of an integrated shaft that fit a fletched two-foot-long, dart-like arrow-tipped projectile. Using the principle of leverage, his invention allowed a dart to be thrown by the upper arm and wrist with an angular momentum, causing it to travel a far greater distance than one thrown conventionally, and with greater, deadly accuracy, at speeds of up to one hundred miles per hour. The adoption of Takla's weapon by twenty warriors and hunters greatly increased the clan's killing range for prey and enemies alike, helping secure relative prosperity and peace. Coupled with his friendly, easygoing, confident and selfless manner and his attractive looks, Takla was a popular choice to mate with Azume.

Like lightning illuminating the sky, it had occurred to Azume early in the morning after the raucous celebration of Estaba, that Takla meant far more to her than his pet name, "Big Brother," implied, and she meant to take the initiative. In the onset of puberty, with her breasts past budding, her nipples and areolas darkening and traces of wispy pubic hair evident, her emotions had begun to rage, foremost with a fear that Takla might soon be part of her past. She lamented the loss of their childhood flirtation, when they'd openly and casually displayed affection, like so many other youngsters delighting in the company of the opposite sex before hit by the full force of raging hormones. It had been a wondrous time for hoping, and for teasing with adult words and innuendo. Life seemed precious as they'd kissed in jest, pushed and pulled and wrestled, and swam, carefree and joyful. They'd experienced everything available to most other clan children, except simulated intercourse—they knew from the deaths of the couple fornicating in the moonlight that breaking clan taboos could prove fatal.

Recently, Azume felt a barrier had come between them. Takla came around far less often, hadn't joined her to swim for weeks, and seemed so serious, almost unfriendly, when she ran up to tussle his hair or tried to engage him, hoping for no more than a returned touch. During that night's celebration, even disarmed by drinking too much mead, he'd ignored her when she'd pulled on his arm for attention. It was unbearable. She suspected he might have been intimate with other clan girls, feared he might have moved beyond simulation to commanding his way as a man could. It seemed unfair and foreign to their longtime bond.

Pleasantly full from the shrimp, her own inhibitions diminished from mead, Azume was determined to recapture their flirtatious relationship. She moved quietly through a room full of snoring revelers and found Takla lying in a corner. Rousing him, she persisted until he went with her from among the sleeping, sprawled bodies in the Gathering Hall.

"Where to, Zumy?" he asked in a deep and groggy voice that came with a yawn.

"Time for a swim, Big Brother. We'll have the pond to ourselves until sunrise."

"I"m not sure that's a good idea. I'm really not your brother, and sometimes I feel . . . "

"You're my best friend, Big Brother! We need a chance to catch up. Come on, like old times." He relented, laughed, and messed her hair, holding her hand as they went to the pond.

The pond was outside the caverns, in the approximate center of the limestone formation and within fifty yards of two adjacent entryways. Roughly the shape of a circle, it had a diameter of seventy-five feet, and a uniform depth of crystal clear water sloping down from three feet on the perimeter to twelve feet in the middle, where a flat rock served as a platform. Completely open on the east side, its closed north and south sides were formed from towering rock covered with vines and grasses running from the hilltop down to the water's edge.

The source of the pond's water was the underground river. It exited the caves in a slow but steady flow from a man-sized spout leading into a moss-covered gathering pool fifteen feet above the pond. After filtering through many years worth of green moss, the water overflowed into the pool at a steady rate, streaming down in a soothing waterfall. The pond water discharged through an ingenious series of rock dams, which allowed maintenance of a consistent discharge rate and pond depth, as the water dispersed into a stream which later joined with another before ultimately leading into a river which also carried off the downfall rain from Amar.

Predators avoided the pond because of human presence, and the clan treasured it for bathing, swimming, and relaxation. It was open for use at any time for anyone, except menstruating women. No one would have thought of using it clothed, and in summer months it was crowded with unashamed and clamoring naked men, women, and children.

Azume and Takla undressed and entered the water hand in hand, three hours before dawn. They swam off in different directions, cooling down and coming alive, wondering what they were about. It was difficult to see with only the light of a partial moon, but Takla watched closely as Azume emerged and stood on the edge of the pond, water running down her hair and across her smooth and unblemished shoulders. As she turned around, he watched as the water traced slowly down her long, thin back onto her ass. She smiled, looking back as he stared at her with his mouth agape, and she laughed aloud, in a voice that seemed lower and throatier than the one he'd long known. She saw the passion in his face as he feasted on the sight of her emerging breasts, the slight widening at her hips, and the wispy downy triangle between her thighs. She enjoyed the power of her effect on him, certain of his arousal as he continued to stare and imagine.

Azume felt her body respond, and motioned him to come to her. Takla emerged from the water, crossed the distance between them, and embraced her in a single smooth motion. She felt his flesh against her belly as his hands rubbed her shoulders and he nuzzled her neck. In one electrifying moment, she fully understood why women often squealed in what she'd once thought had to be pain when they bent over and men entered them on command.

Twenty yards away, low brush concealed the hazel-eyed young man with the best vision in the clan. Nambe could see everything clearly, and he smirked at the delicious irony: if Takla had Azume now, it would guarantee Nambe would soon possess her. Then he could consume a small bite of her sweet essence each and every night until he'd devoured her and his appetite was fully satisfied.

12.

Angels and Demons among Us

Grand Lake, Colorado, 1968

Sheriff C. Tom Wood plucked at his chin when troubled, and his fingertips worked overtime as he surveyed the worst crime scene he'd seen in ten years of service to Grand County. He considered his folks the law-abiding sort, except maybe once in a blue moon, when some fool got liquored up and lost it, not like the animals in the cities who attacked each other at the slightest provocation. He was a God-fearing man, and the symbolic crucifixion especially troubled him. In over his head, he took a statement from the servant, secured the area, and called in the boys from State. He longed to go home, ease into his hot tub and soothe away the stench—these two died hard, and the man disabled to boot.

Released ten days later, the coroner's report concluded that Margaret O'Malley suffered "a profound incised wound of the neck which transected the left common carotid artery and internal jugular vein as well as the thyrohyoid membrane, epiglottis, and hypopharynx, with her larynx visible through the gaping wound." In other words, her neck had been slashed from right to left, her head nearly decapitated. The angle of the wound indicated the perpetrator had been facing her at the time, and blood patterns, pooling, the lack of defensive wounds, and contusions on her wrists suggested she'd been murdered while under restraint.

Stegger's injuries were numerous. In plain terms, his left hand, nose, and two teeth were broken, and his right hand cut deeply. He had a penetrating wound in his left thigh and a gunshot wound in his right shoulder. The cause of death was massive hemorrhage, caused by a bullet which penetrated his forehead, scattering scraps of lead and pieces of skull throughout his brain. The skin around the entry point was powder-seared, indicating the fatal shot had come at point-blank range. The weapon was on his bed near his body: a Ruger Bearcat, a small, twenty-two caliber firearm used mostly by trail riders to shoot varmints and poisonous snakes.

Residue on Stegger's hand indicated he'd fired a weapon shortly before his death, and a Browning Hi-Power, single-action, semi-automatic handgun registered in his name was found at the scene. Two spent rounds from his firearm were found lodged in the door frame at the entry to his room.

Stegger wore blood-soaked red silk pajamas, and his body had been positioned post mortem to simulate crucifixion, with "JUSTICE" written in his blood on a pillow placed just above his head. There were latent fingerprints on the murder weapon and in three places within the home, but the only useful one failed to match any database. The forensics team also found a bloody footprint from a size 10, square-toe, "Beatle Buckle" Quinlan Brother's shoe, a common style.

The state initially had no leads, even though the decedent had been a provocative man engaged in frequent business disputes. His son, Nathaniel, a government attorney, arrived in Colorado on July

20. He reported that his twin sister, Alexandra, was Stegger's only other blood relative, and she lived in Lake Forest, Illinois, with Stegger's ex-wife, Abigail. Estranged since her parents' divorce, the daughter had never been to the Colorado home, would receive no inheritance, and had no apparent motive.

The large safe was reportedly used primarily for safe-guarding business records, but it had been culled a few weeks earlier by the decedent's business manager, Henry Stanich of Denver. They confirmed an alibi for Stanich at the time of the crime, and Stanich supported the fictional narrative, explaining that outdated records were periodically removed and destroyed. The safe had been ransacked, but still contained some recent correspondence, deeds and stock certificates all scattered about, and a number of hand guns, rifles and ammunition. An indeterminable, large amount of cash always kept on hand was said to be stolen.

Responding to the shocking news accounts, a local young woman came forward and gave a statement: "My name is Michelle L. Healy. My date of birth is April 30, 1948. I'm 20 years old. I have been a waitress at Larry's Coffee Pot since 1966. I worked from 7:00 a.m. until 3:00 p.m. every day except Sunday during the week of July 12. It was a busy week, with a large number of tourists stopping for meals, asking directions, and using our restrooms. A gentleman came in before lunchtime, I believe on Wednesday, July 15. He stood out because he was wearing a suit and carrying a briefcase. He was friendly and I said something like, 'Hi cowboy, dressed pretty fancy for these parts,' and he replied something like, 'goes with the territory ma'am, these are lawyer duds.' I laughed and said, 'Not many of you fellas come in here,' and he grinned and said, 'I'd count you folks lucky for that.'

I saw him studying a county map while eating his eggs benedict and drinking iced tea. He gave me a large tip ($10) and I said, 'You should come here more often.' He said 'I'd like that, maybe after my work is finished.' He said he was looking to find a man to give him some good news regarding an inheritance. I told him I know most folks in these parts so maybe I could help, and we ended up outside Larry's, with me pointing to the road leading to the Stegger place above Grand Lake. I said, that's where you'll find Daniel Stegger, our local wealthy recluse. Then I said something about the rich getting richer and he replied, 'The Lord works in mysterious ways.' I remember those exact words because they struck me as odd. He gave me his business card and said, 'Chuck Smith is indebted to you, ma'am,' then he winked and said he'd return to thank me properly. I didn't think much about it because older guys like him flirt with me all the time, and everyone knows the Stegger place, which locals call 'The Castle.' I never saw him again after that and didn't see what he'd been driving. When I heard about the murders I called Sheriff Wood.

I would say he's handsome, about forty years old with hazel-colored eyes, thick eyebrows and wavy, sandy-colored hair, with a touch of gray. He's thin and athletic-looking, probably about five inches taller than me, or about five feet ten, and I'd guess his weight at about 150 pounds. He had what looked a little like a scar, but it might have been a noticeable cleft in his chin. He wore a dark blue suit, white shirt, and a tie with gold and blue stripes. I believe I would recognize him if I saw him again.

I have given this statement voluntarily and asked the officer signing below to write it down exactly as I have told it. I have reviewed it and initialed the bottom of each page, and believe it is accurate. I am signing voluntarily under penalty of perjury. Michelle L. Healy, July 22, 1968."

Inquiries revealed that a man fitting the waitress's description presented a Washington State driver's license identifying him as Charles Smith of Seattle when he rented an Oldsmobile from Hertz at the Denver Airport on July 14. He made a cash deposit and Hertz recorded the license information, but didn't make a photocopy. The man returned the car to the agency on the morning of July 19, and a man going by the name of Charles Smith flew on United Airlines to Seattle early that afternoon. They determined he'd taken a room at the Littletree Inn outside of Granby, checking in on July 15, and out on July 18. Tire tracks at the entrance to the Stegger property had been obscured by various official vehicles and weren't useful for matching the tires of the rental vehicle.

Although the numbers on the license presented to Hertz were different, an authentic Washington State driver's license belonged to attorney Charles E. Smith, who practiced law in Seattle. So, on July 24, authorities swarmed into his law office and encountered a befuddled, bald-headed sixty-three-year-old who'd attended a family picnic on July 19 and served as a lector for church services on

July 20. He claimed to have no idea who would have used his name in Colorado, a state he'd never visited, to locate a victim he'd never otherwise heard of.

Authorities questioned numerous locals, the household staff, and the business manager, and pressed Nathaniel for more information. But by the time they'd determined that Stegger's daughter and ex-wife were preparing for her wedding in Illinois at the time of the murders, despite a big-deal victim and a hot-shot lawyer son, they had zero leads and only a slim hope that a nationwide alert would prove fruitful.

Nathaniel Stegger misled the police. He believed he knew the killer's name, at least his real one. There appeared no other possible explanation for the single missing file. Somehow Sixtus Peeters had located his father, tortured him, learned his true identity, killed him, and then removed the file and recordings to cover up his involvement in the murders.

Nathaniel clearly remembered the file his father had painstakingly described. It consisted of both official and unofficial versions. The official CIA version was CYA ("Cover Your Ass") bullshit which reported that its subject was an unnamed scientist designated in government studies first as "Chatter 5" then later as "MKULTRA 5;" he'd worked previously for the government on a variety of secret, war-related matters and been treated for brain injuries suffered in a mishap during a top-secret experiment; he'd been "successfully treated and reintegrated into society in mid-year

1949, subject to additional treatment upon request." The official version didn't cite his alleged name or indicate he'd been a spy, and Nathaniel knew the omission was intentional. It was a matter of cover, since without verifiable identification, the government couldn't be held accountable if the report surfaced unless some knowledgeable agent broke rank and testified—otherwise one needed access to the ultra-classified Chatter or MKULTRA indexes to find the actual name of the subject identified only as "Five."

The private version consisted of seven separate memos from Frey. In summary, they revealed that the subject had been Sixtus Peeters, an airman from the Midwest reported killed in the war before being inserted into the Manhattan Project as an OSS spy under a false identity. It listed various mind-altering drugs and chemicals administered to him which caused his amnesia, given under the pretense of attempting to discover his true identity and to help provide "benchmarks for mind-control studies" at Stegger's direction. The file recounted efforts by a psychiatrist named Edmund Wright to return him to normalcy. Sarcastically, it referred to a time during which he reportedly spoke Latin and claimed to be an ancient Roman, and it noted that Wright had collaborated with a psychiatrist named Graham Cowell who'd attempted to treat him through hypnosis. This was said to have resulted in unacceptable security risks "dealt with accordingly" and Wright's "misguided allegations of Company misconduct" had required him to be neutralized as well.

Frey had concluded that terminating Peeters wasn't an acceptable risk due to MKULTRA oversight, so Wright had been "persuaded" to utilize the Ludlow Technique to substitute false memories into the subject's consciousness before releasing him without further incident. A handwritten notation indicated Frey was unconcerned about any possible repercussions. He believed it all would remain hidden within MKULTRA, and there were no other records to compromise them.

Since Peeters's Manhattan name had been well known to both Frey and Stegger, neither it nor his discharge identity had been referenced in the private file which only deemed him "the subject." Knowing his new identity would have helped Nathaniel locate him, but he was aware the subject became a professor at Columbia in 1950, and Bradford Frey could track him down from there.

For a millisecond Nathaniel thought of calling his mother to tell her of Daniel's death. *Screw that*, he concluded, *James can tell the bitches. Father remains more alive to me than they'll ever be. With all the money I have now, I'll buy a family if I need one.*

It's personal now, he thought, *down to me and this Peeters bastard. "JUSTICE" indeed, I'll dispense my own brand to the man who killed my father after screwing my mother. I'll honor Father by doing it in an extremely creative and severe way. Let the son of a bitch relax and think he's safe, I'll hit him when his guard is down. I'll concoct a foolproof plan before swatting him. Waiting is better. Father always said revenge is a dish best served cold.*

———

John Redford executed his escape plan flawlessly. While it made little logical sense, following the script made him feel he was doing *something* while buying time to sort out the confusing recent events and revelations. He flew to Seattle as Charles Smith, and back to Denver on the next flight back as Redford, sporting a new shirt, a Dodger's cap and aviator sunglasses. He picked up his car at the airport and began driving back to Chicago. He reflected on how stupid he'd been, acting recklessly and becoming a criminal. It had satisfied him to take a small measure of revenge, but it had been at the cost of betraying his essential nature, and he still hadn't learned his identity. *How dumb,* when he'd already realized he could likely find his identity by simply surveying alumni records at a few American universities.

He ached all over, dog-tired and with a cut and bruised hand. He'd covered his tracks, but why? They'd find him. He couldn't just disappear without his family. His only hope was that they'd sympathize once they knew what Stegger and Frey had done. Ironically, once he was arrested the truth would come out, national security or not.

He'd fess up with Rose about the PI and why he'd really gone to Colorado. They'd fought through so much together that she deserved to know everything. He knew she'd be angry, and would surely force him to see a shrink for being so unhinged, at least. How he told her was crucial, so he kept the radio off, concentrating instead on how to relate his sad tale.

Tolo had to prod Alexie to leave their reception, even after midnight. But he realized, conscientiously, that they had an early morning flight. "I love you Mom, it was beyond perfect!" Alexie gushed as they left to their guests' applause, "Call you from Italy!"

Flush with excitement, Gail slept little that night. Mid-morning she sat at her dining room table with family and friends, sipping red wine and eating chocolates, chatting about the wedding while opening cards and surveying gifts. Gail handed Katya a card with a picture of a lovely bride on it, saying, "This looks like Rachel."

Katya handed the card to Rachel. "Give you any ideas?" she asked. "You're already twenty-four, not getting any younger!"

Rachel Hoffman Weber didn't resemble the lovely bride pictured on the card at all. As a child, her thin, delicate face, high cheekbones and cupid's mouth had been offset by shimmering auburn hair and wide and soulful dark eyes, creating an alluring vision of youthful loveliness. But time lengthened her face, compressed her mouth, and darkened her hair, so she no longer had the exquisite look of her youth. She appeared now as a bit stern and joyless, nearly six feet tall, small-busted, thin and angular. She reminded others of an asylum matron, a regular Nurse Ratched. Yet, that initial impression conveyed only a tiny measure of truth. Her appearance *was* authoritative, but her voice was soft and gentle, and when she flashed her engaging smile she lit up a room. And she was impossible to ignore when voicing her highly respected opinions.

Rachel took the marriage remarks in stride. Men found her attractive, and she'd dated seriously for a time. Yet she remained a virgin and doubted she'd ever marry. In her vision of life, she saw far many more interesting things to explore.

Her bearing and accomplishments made Rachel seem older than her actual years. As a high school senior in Milwaukee, she'd submitted college applications to Yale, Harvard, and Princeton, knowing her credentials were impeccable, but aware that none of the Ivies admitted women. She'd responded to their rejections with data showing the demographic equality of women and their comparable intellectual prowess, and she castigated them for maintaining single-gender student bodies in a co-existent world. They'd responded politely, citing tradition and their largesse in creating classes for women from sister schools such as Radcliffe and Vassar. This led to a flurry of correspondence ending with an abrupt, uniform response from Rachel: "I will be attending the University of Wisconsin, an institution with a one-hundred-year 'tradition' of admitting human beings on a gender-neutral basis. Unfortunately, your parochial views conflict with the equality we savages in the heartland see as a core American value. Shame on you! I recommend you 'gentlemen' search your consciences and reevaluate your mission before you are on the outside looking in, lacking in relevance as you now lack in enlightenment."

Intending to follow Adie's lead, and enrolled in pre-med as a freshman, Rachel still found time to write her first book. It included her correspondence with the three schools, expanded to analyze the impact of their exclusionary policies. Entitled *Elite and Obtuse Institutions of Learning*, the book placed Rachel in the center of a national dialogue and was featured in *Time Magazine*. When she followed up with a second book detailing womens' contributions and urging support for the Equal Rights Amendment, she gained even more notoriety. Nonetheless, she resisted being labeled a "feminist," and preferred to be known as a humanist. In that vein, she refused to join Betty Friedan in founding what would later become the National Organization for Women. Rachel insisted that she had no interest in obsessively advocating one single thing, rather she aspired to advocate every correct thing.

She thought that true believers, like many members of NOW, focused on singular goals, sacrificing their objectivity and diluting their effectiveness. She believed deceit, hypocrisy, intolerance, and immorality inevitably resulted when noble efforts morphed into fanaticism, their advocates blinded by obsession, and ignoring reasonable constraint. She thought this accounted for the moral corruption Bea and Katya had encountered in Nazi Germany, as well as the American ambivalence toward the unnecessary atomic bombing of Japan. She preferred to highlight matters which were wrong, and inspire others to address them. On a personal level, she sought, to do good deeds which touched others, seeing them as small acts of kindness, which acted like ripples in a pond, ultimately begetting overwhelming waves.

She was the birth child of Beatrice Hoffman, who died in Sweden during the war, and Katya saw much of Bea in Rachel. But she possessed a bearing and self-sufficiency Bea had lacked. Her unknown, Nazi storm trooper father evidently transmitted those traits when raping Bea, mercifully imparting little else of himself. Still, Rachel had a warrior's fierceness masking an outward calm and grace that drew others to her for comfort and solace. But unlike her mother, who'd used sexual wiles and manipulation to escape the Nazis, Rachel would never compromise to reach a goal, no matter how compelling, since she was incapable of being anything but true to herself.

Rachel's absence of guile had nothing to do with a lack of intelligence, which she possessed in ample supply. Rather, it was part of her essential nature: unswayable and unaffected, stalwartly consistent and guided by timeless truth, spiritual and ethereal in a way that, for want of a better term, seemed angelic.

Rachel's qualities made her an ideal arbiter for disputes and misunderstandings, large or small, within and outside of the family. "Ask Rachel," was a common refrain as her reputation grew and she became a source of reasoned understanding, stability, strength and guidance.

Before she turned twenty-two, Rachel had earned a degree in biology from Wisconsin and a Master's Degree in Psychology from Columbia and she'd completed a year of legal studies. A licensed psychologist, she ran a clinic in Chicago and attracted far more patients than she could reasonably hope to treat.

———

Stunned, Gail dropped the phone and reached for a chair. Taking the call from James, she'd thought Daniel had learned of the wedding somehow. But this . . . his murder, took her breath away. James explained it in a succinct monotone. He said Nathaniel had asked him to call because it would be in the news, and the police would consider it odd if she and Alexandra didn't hear from him first. Daniel would be buried in Colorado, the funeral would be private, and they weren't invited.

"Is there anything I can do . . . perhaps . . . ?"

"No, Madame, Mr. Nathaniel was very clear. He anticipated your offer, and I'm sorry, but he directed me to say precisely, 'No, you've already done enough.' Madame, I won't be working for Nathaniel any longer, so this will be our final conversation. Best wishes to you and Alexie. I always felt you deserved better from Mr. Daniel. Goodbye."

Daniel had been unlovable and evil, but Gail still regretted his terrible passing. She'd wait until Alexie came home to tell her. She and Tolo should enjoy Italy unburdened. *Italy, Sixtus, God, he still fills my thoughts. Even now I long to feel him holding me. Yet, not a single letter even though he didn't die in combat. Why did another woman have his child? I need closure. I need to believe my life was meant to be more than just a series of bad endings.*

———

Rose lay with her head on John's chest, her finger tracing the familiar cleft in his chin. He moved his hand lovingly up and down her spine, admiring the sheen of moisture covering it. "Ahhhhh . . . " she sighed. "If I didn't know better I'd think you were trying to hurt me. If that's what pain, is you're the master, so much beyond the Marquis de Sade."

"I missed you, as always. I think you could tell."

"I had a clue when you tossed the robe at me and pointed toward the shower. Did I look dirty?"

"I didn't want to waste any time!"

They were in suite 1612 at the Drake Hotel in downtown Chicago, their regular place for the dates they indulged in whenever the daily grind became too pressing and they felt the need to reconnect. John had called Rose from a rest stop in Iowa. "A night at the Drake and brunch in the Cape Cod Room," he'd suggested. The kids were covered, so why not?

John had been unusually intense and passionate during their lovemaking, as if it might be the last time. He stroked her twice when once would do, until she told him, giggling like a schoolgirl, "Stop, oh my God, you're killing me! You weren't practicing out there in Colorado with someone else, were you?"

A cloud passed over his face and he responded lamely. "Hardly, we're just pretty good at this after eighteen years." John leaned back and pulled his upper lip through his teeth.

"You're worried. You're doing that lip thing."

Ten minutes later, they faced each other on a sofa in their suite, the glow from the setting sun streaming in as John began telling his story.

"I lied to you, Rose, and I'm sorry. But I know you already think I'm over the edge on this identity chase. Well, the thing is, I hired a private investigator who found this lead in Colorado, and I went looking for a man from Los Alamos who knows my real identity, not for a reunion."

"Why didn't you tell me? What about our agreement? Why did you feel you . . . ?"

He held his hand up palm forward and gestured. "Rose, there's a lot you need to know and I want you to hear it all. When I'm finished I'll answer every question, but this is difficult, let me tell you everything first."

"Okay, it's your show."

"Everything pointed to a man in Grand Lake, Colorado by the name of Daniel Stegger, a scientist I knew in Los Alamos. Once I knew he'd been the . . . " John stopped in mid-sentence, seeing that Rose had clasped her hands over her mouth and was trembling with emotion. "Rose, honey, what is it?"

"M-m-my God, John, God in heaven, d-d-don't tell me . . . It was all over the news! Please, please, don't tell me you were the one who killed him!"

John appeared shocked when told of the brutal murders. He claimed he hadn't heard anything of what had happened since leaving Stegger's home. "I didn't kill him! I swear to God! I broke in and assaulted him—I hit him and broke his nose—but I didn't kill him. I wanted to, but I stopped. I'm certain of it. I remember dropping the gun. S-s-something made me stop! Don't look at me like that, Rose, I'm not crazy!"

———

Slick began to giggle, tried unsuccessfully to stifle it, then gave in and laughed aloud, releasing his pent-up tension. He woke Hans, who was scrunched up against the door, sleeping in the passenger seat. Opening his eyes, Hans squinted across at Slick, trying to copy the look of Steve McQueen in *The Cincinnati Kid*, one of his all-time favorites. "What's with you, numb nuts?"

"Think about it . . . We're driving a 1966 Rambler American station wagon! Two cool guys, cash up the ass on their way to Las Vegas, and riding in a goddamned green, four-door station wagon, not exactly a chick magnet!"

"My friend, that's why you need Hansie, I mean 'Tommy,' to do your thinking for you, 'Arthur.' We'll have time for hot wheels in Vegas. No one will notice us there."

Slick knew, as usual, that Hans was right. The man was clever, maybe close in smarts to even his old pal Six. All of the plan made sense to him then: from the time they'd checked into a rundown motel in Pueblo, Colorado, far from Grand Lake, a dump where no one gave a shit about them and they had come and gone as they pleased, unnoticed. They'd gone back there to clean up afterwards, before shoving everything they'd worn into garbage bags and tossing them down in a canyon somewhere in New Mexico. Slick had hated to lose his Beatle Buckles shoes though—nicest pair he'd ever owned.

They'd driven back north to Denver late Saturday morning, and Slick had waited until Hans came back with the shitbox car. They'd switched everything from his car into it, and he'd parked the Camaro in a ghetto with the keys dangling in place to guarantee it would be stolen and later sold off in small pieces. They had fake driver's licenses with the real names of old farts that never drove anymore, which Hans (now known as "Tommy Troha") had procured a year earlier from an old prison bud, so he and Slick (now "Arthur Moriarty") could ride off into the sunset. After that, all Slick had needed to do was avoid speeding. He'd re-looked at the speedometer hundreds of times, knowing Hans would kill him if he screwed it up.

It had gotten very strange and weird and ugly, but it had hyped Slick too, making him feel alive and confident in a new way, like for once in his life there was nothing he couldn't do. *So here we are,* thought Slick, *two unknown dudes with no parole assholes to meet every month, cruising to "sin city." Hans says Vegas has all the booze and drugs and gambling and easy women we could ever want, and us with a ton of cash, far more than I ever thought I'd see in my whole goddamn life. All thanks to Daniel Stegger, late of Grand Lake, Colorado. Prick got what he deserved, the girl maybe not so much. But bad things like that can happen if you just find yourself in the wrong place at the wrong time.*

When Slick had spotted the file and recordings in the safe he'd thought, *Holy Shit!* He'd been compelled to grab them. *Go figure, he'd thought, a file with the only name I know as well as my own, Sixtus Peeters. I can't believe it, it's like a dream.* Later, he'd asked Hans to tell him what the file said about Six.

"But if he didn't die in the war . . . I mean, how could that be? They had a funeral and all. What'd they put in the casket? Maybe I could find him . . . we were . . . his old man . . . God, the things I remember. Hans, tell me what's in it again."

Hans related a succinct version of what he'd gleaned from the file. It, and probably the recordings as well, told of Sixtus Peeters being reportedly killed in combat although he was still alive, so he could become a spy on the atomic bomb project, only God knew why. He'd been screwed over by the Army, brain-fried with drugs and let out years later as some different dude, and so confused he didn't even know his name. He'd even thought he was some kind of ancient dude (Slick knew that meant it had to be Six because he'd loved that Roman stuff).

"Do you think I could ever find him?"

"I don't know, man, but it shows we weren't the only ones Daniel screwed. It may be worth looking into some time, maybe we could shake down this Six guy for some coin. He'd probably pay a bundle to find out who he is. The Army sure pegged him for a sucker!"

You asshole, thought Slick, *you don't understand.*

They ditched the Rambler in St. George, Utah, and took a Greyhound into Vegas. There Hans bought a car more to Slick's liking. "Fuckin A man," he shouted as they drove down the strip in a 383 four-speed Roadrunner with mag wheels! "Oh yeah, we're riding now! Like that Wiley E. Coyote! Beep, beep!" Without question, the Bahamian yellow muscle car would stand out anywhere, although least of all in Vegas. "You were smooth," said Slick, "dealing on the spot and whipping out three grand like it was just ten bucks."

"That's Vegas, Slick my friend. Here we can flash the cash."

Later, ensconced in a suite in the International Hotel, they drank beer and toasted their good fortune. They spread the remaining $497,000 out on a bed and stared at the forty-nine neatly-banded packs of ten thousand dollars each, then tossed seven thousand dollars in loose bills around as if it was chicken feed. They roared with laughter, looking over the enormous amount covering the bed.

"Finally, it's all mine, a goddamn fortune, even if it's only part of the blood money Daniel stole. You're a good guy and my best asshole buddy, Slick, so I want to give you thirty thousand. So go ahead and take any three fucking chunks you like!"

Slick hesitated. It was more than he'd ever expected to hold at one time, but miniscule compared to the haul. When he wavered, he saw a mean look flash across Hans's face, so he replied quickly with as much relish as he could muster, "Thanks, Hans, you're one hell of a pal!" He smiled and made a big show of shuffling through his three banded shares, time and again. But he felt shit on, and a throbbing pain rose in his temples, spread down onto his neck and across his shoulders. *All his. Where do we go from here?*

They drove from Vegas to a whore ranch that night, and Hans convinced him to try an Asian girl, making a big deal of picking up the tab. He liked it well enough, especially the blowjob, but she wasn't much different from the skanks back home, and Mai Ling seemed bored throughout, which really pissed him off. Plus, everything Hans did had begun to irritate him, and the throbbing pain in his head wouldn't go away.

They bought some weed and acid at the ranch and cruised through the desert for an hour getting high. Slick drove and Hans kept telling him to go faster, faster, like a demanding pain in the ass, more like a prison guard than a bud. Hans was wasted, barely able to walk and in rare form, sticking his head out of the window and squealing away like a pig. Slick's head began to throb even more when Hans told him to shut the fuck up and be careful driving, even while he continued yelling out the window like a banshee.

Slick didn't like two sets of rules. He'd done everything Hans had asked, thinking the score would change his life and he could stop settling for leftovers. Next time in Tennessee, he wanted to be the one who got the hot woman in the bedroom.

"Pull over, Slick my man, Hansie needs to drain the monster."

Hans jumped out when Slick pulled off the road, and he stumbled over to an enormous saguaro cactus with a middle stem and four surrounding branches reaching up toward the moonlit sky. Its shape reminded Slick of the towering elm in Union Park in Kenosha, and the simpler times he'd spent there as a child with Six, a genuine pal.

Hans howled like a coyote in heat, eyes shut, streaming his piss up and down the cactus, swaying with his head tilted back, singing a final song into the dark and endless sky.

Hans's skull exploded when the Louisville Slugger trademark on the baseball bat met his right temple, as Slick rolled his wrists and focused on following through, just like Tony Kubek when he sent the ball deep into left field.

Even while dragging his corpse into the bottom of an arroyo, where it would make fine dining for the coyotes, Slick remained grateful for everything Hans had taught him. He'd never have his eye of the tiger or become such a hardnosed killer, but now he could read a map, buy a car, get a hotel room, use a fake ID, and make his way anywhere across the country. He even knew how to break in and kill a lawyer. He'd clean himself up, buy some fancy duds, and continue on to California, following the script Hans had outlined, with all the money he'd ever need. He knew he'd be just fine. And if he felt lonely, he'd find himself a bud who'd be glad to be *his* second fiddle.

The following afternoon, Slick cruised across the desert on Route Ninety-One, headed for the City of Angels in a brand new Black Chevelle SS purchased in his new name, Arthur Moriarty. He said it over and over again, tried "Art," "Arthur," and even "Mr. Moriarty." Damn, but they all sounded good, so very classy. Spruced up and humming in sync with the radio, he laughed aloud now and then, feeling good in his hot car, feeling smooth, able to listen to any station he wanted. As he swayed his head to the sound of *California*

Dreamin' he thought, *nothing could be more perfect.* He easily picked out the voice of Momma Cass. *She knows I'm the man and she's singing her heart out just for me. Sweet!*

Arthur Moriarty would drive however he liked and not take shit from anyone. A new life was opening up, he had more cash than God, and his headache had disappeared completely.

13.

Painful Recollections

Chicago, Illinois, 1968

Rose had once thought John incapable of deceit. Upon learning he'd lied about Colorado, and had failed to tell her he'd hired an investigator, she wondered why she should believe him at all. What were the odds that someone else had killed Stegger on the only evening John had ever been at his home? It seemed far more likely he'd lost his mind, maybe from his homemade memory booster.

"Tell me again why you used fake identification."

"I needed an enticing story to locate him, and I wanted to keep the focus far away from Chicago. I was being cautious . . . "

"In case you killed him."

"No, because of Conforti's death. It wasn't until my concoction kicked in and I realized what he'd done that I thought, yes, I might kill him. But apparently it isn't in my nature."

"What about the girl?"

"I never saw her. But she couldn't have slept through our confrontation. She was either hiding or came in later, I don't know, but seriously, do you think I could kill some young w-w-woman in cold blood? Oh God, help me . . . " He buried his head in his hands as he remembered once using them to strangle a young woman.

"Walk me through it again."

He reached out for her hand, but she rejected it and folded her arms together, waiting.

"Okay, well, I parked in a campground and walked about a mile to his private road. I saw car lights coming from the house and ducked into the brush, afraid he was leaving. But I saw it was a colored man with a young woman, obviously in a hurry—he opened the gate and left without locking it—I assumed they were staff leaving for the night.

I walked another five minutes to the house, circled it, and saw the lights were on in only one room. I snuck close enough to see it was him, sitting up in bed, reading. I disabled the alarm and cut the telephone line. The porch doors were unlocked, so I went in quietly, heading for the light."

"They reported that the killer broke in through the door."

"Maybe somebody locked it after I left, and the killer broke it to get in. I don't know, can't explain it."

"Go on."

"I found his room and burst in loudly, gun drawn, expecting to frighten him."

"Did you worry about fingerprints?"

"I brought gloves, but never wore them. It seemed pointless since he already knew me."

"But if you murdered him . . . "

"I suppose I already knew I wouldn't, even as much as I hated him. But to be honest, I'm not sure my prints are on file anywhere, maybe in Los Alamos, but probably not in any criminal database."

"Go on."

"I couldn't believe it, but he barely acted alarmed. He sat there cool as could be, almost as if he'd been expecting me, as if the gun meant nothing! First thing he said was, 'Well, if it isn't my old pal, Asshole Jack.'

I replied 'Hello, Stegger, what I am is your worst nightmare.' He laughed, said I didn't have the balls to play the tough guy and he said something snide about small men carrying little pieces. I asked him straight out why he tortured me and what he'd learned, but he wouldn't answer except to say he found out I was 'a boy scout sap, a dipshit loser from the Midwest.' He said it in a very matter of fact, and condescending way.

It made my blood boil. Then he said 'start guessing,' like it was a game, like my problems had nothing to do with him. He actually said I wouldn't be in such a 'sorry-ass position' if I hadn't been such a weakling! I was incensed, and I moved closer, aiming the gun toward his head and telling him he had one last chance to fess up. He said I didn't have the guts to fire 'that antique,' and then he grabbed for it. I smashed it down on his hand and broke it. He screamed, and then I hit him in the face with the gun butt and broke his nose. It all happened very quickly and it's all still a little confusing. I do remember thinking how strong he seemed for an invalid. I hurt my hand, maybe he bit it, I'm not sure. I can picture the blood spurting from his nose while he cursed me out.

I looked over at the wheelchair next to his bed and then at him holding the bed clothes up against his bloody nose, and I thought, what the hell am I doing here? I felt stupid and ashamed that I'd lost control. I tried to reason with him, tried telling him all the problems I'd had. I asked him to think about what I'd been going through. He responded by giving me the finger and saying 'Fuck you, loser,' over and over. He spat blood at me and said, 'Who do you think you're talking to, loser?' Ya, he was right, I thought I was talking to a human being who'd show some compassion, or at least some fear, but not that heartless bastard! Last thing he said before I left was that he'd have my ass for what I did. He said he'd get me no matter where I hid because 'Daniel R. Stegger always gets his man.'

That's about it, Rose. I ran away and didn't see anyone, just made my way back to my car and worked through my escape plan as if he couldn't just contact the police. I was confused and afraid and upset with myself. I realized I'd entered his home unlawfully and assaulted him, so I suppose I wanted to confuse the facts somehow. I wasn't thinking clearly, although I do remember thinking that being arrested might not be so bad, at least the truth would come out. I had no idea he'd been murdered after I left until you told me!

You need to believe me. I didn't kill him! I left the gun there, but I never fired it. I swear I didn't. I swear it on our children's lives, Rose! It's the God-awful truth."

Rose wondered and worried, but in the end she found it impossible to reconcile the crucifixion reference with his character. He would never have done anything so sacrilegious, so she chose to believe he'd given her a truthful if incredible account, rather than believe him schizophrenic and delusional.

They spoke of options, as if discussing how to avoid arrest for murder was rational post-coital conversation. They concluded they could only wait it out. The antique gun had been purchased by Abe at a gun fair and couldn't be traced, and if John had done his fake Charles Smith routine as well as it seemed, he couldn't be placed at the murder scene unless Stegger had reported the assault before being murdered, unlikely with the phone line cut. They'd know they were wrong if the police showed up with a warrant for his arrest.

Rose forgave John, but enforced their contract and made him see a psychiatrist. After four sessions and a battery of tests, the shrink concluded John manifested just one of one hundred and eighty-two possible disorders listed in the Diagnostic and Statistical Manual of Mental Disorders: damage to the medial temporal lobe of his brain manifested by retrograde amnesia. Unlike most such patients, his was a long-term affliction, and something had altered his hippocampus to replace memories of the time prior to his onset of amnesia with others that were false. The shrink knew of no cure, but said such amnesia sometimes resolved itself spontaneously. He suggested, not really intending to be humorous, that "more knowledge of his past" could help expedite his recall.

The authorities didn't call, and the Redfords resumed their normal lives. They felt uncharitably satisfied that Frey and Stegger and all those involved with John's condition appeared to be dead. Encouraged by the shrink, John returned to his "hobby" of trying to find his real identity.

Eight months after Stegger's death, John drove into Kenosha, Wisconsin looking for the Peeters's home. A gas station attendant on Washington Road directed him to an address furnished by the Registrar in Madison—a home across the street from some Catholic church. As he drew nearer his excitement mounted, even though nothing looked at all familiar.

John had discovered that two men with the surname of Peters had graduated with appropriate degrees from distinguished American universities just before the war, Stanley R. Peters from Cal Berkeley, and Louis L. Peters from the University of Chicago. Then he found a third and last, a man with the unusual spelling of "Peeters," who'd graduated from the University of Wisconsin in 1943, with highest honors and a degree in physics. This man had been in the Air Corps and reportedly killed in Europe, although his body had never been recovered. The clincher came with John's memory of the note McFarland had affixed to the pictures. He'd assumed it referred to six pictures, but then he realized it'd been a nickname for Sixtus Peeters, him, "Six," the loser from the Midwest.

He found the home two blocks from Union Park, and across the street from St. George Parish. *No doubt*, he thought as he recognized it from the McFarland photo and his Yankee Stadium vision, right down to the rocker in the corner of the porch. The curtains were drawn and the home reeked of vacancy otherwise, but a faded gold star hung in the front window, and there was a note on the door with a number. John scribbled it down, called and waited.

Ralph Peeters felt like a child on Christmas Eve as he sped toward their childhood home. He'd decided to maintain it after his mother passed away in 1957, as if having foreseen this bizarre possibility. He hadn't heard from Congressman Schadeberg, but the confusion over Six's supposed death no longer mattered—the man himself could explain it now. Two unanticipated calls, and both had been life-changers: first, when Gail told him his brother hadn't died in combat but had fathered a child in Italy, and now, a call from the voice he knew like his own. "Hi, Ralph, I was at your home on Eighth Avenue and saw the note. Could you meet me? I'm known as John Redford, but I think I'm actually your brother."

Ralph pulled up to the curb as Six waved, right hand held close to his chest in a familiar gesture. He looked much older, but the wave, half-smile, and effortless stride left no doubt. Like a miracle, twenty-five years after his funeral, Sixtus Peeters had finally returned home.

Ralph launched himself into his brother's arms, holding him like a precious treasure as he wept with joy. "Oh my God, Six, I can't believe it, can't believe it!" But when he held Six back by the shoulders to look into his eyes, he froze. He was met with the same friendly, open, and confident smile as always, but Six was emotionless, except for the obvious awkwardness one feels when confronted by an overly demonstrative stranger. Ralph dropped his arms to his side as Six splayed his fingers outward in apology. "You don't recognize me!" Ralph sputtered.

"No, Ralph, sorry, not at all."

"My God, Six, what have they done to you?"

They sat in the parlor of their childhood home, surrounded by family artifacts, looking through photos and working through years of information. Ralph spoke passionately about their family, Six's education and ambitions, his enlistment and military service, even his "burial." He gently disclosed the passing of their parents and three siblings, but felt affronted when Six only responded politely, curious but apparently unaffected. Siblings he could understood somewhat; they'd been older and not particularly close, but how could he be so unaffected by the deaths of Momma and Pop? Ralph fought the feeling that it might have been better if Six hadn't returned.

Six recounted what he could of his life from Los Alamos, and he spoke candidly of the inexplicable dreams and visions which spurred his search. He also apologized for seeming aloof.

"I'm sorry, I can't imagine how you must feel. It sounds like you and your . . . like we were very close. I'm disappointed, too. After all it took to get here I assumed I'd be jubilant, but still, I don't remember anything. Of course everything you're telling me is true, but I don't feel any emotional component. It's horribly frustrating, especially as a scientist used to definitive answers, and now . . ."

"Look, Six, I didn't mean to . . . "

"It's okay. We need to be candid and stay close to each other, Ralph. The more I learn, the more likely my memories will return. As brothers, we should be able to work together to understand what happened and what needs to be done."

"Agreed."

"Bottom line is finding out how I ended up as Redford and why the government helped with the cover up."

"Tell me the clues."

"Well, there's this odd refrain that popped up—I kept hearing repeated words: 'George, Libya, Atia, azume, the maid.' I think it has something to do with dragons, of all things, and the church across the street has to be the George part. There's also some mysterious trust that pays my . . . that, well . . . do you have any idea why I have so much money available to me?" He gestured around the house, "Obviously we weren't well-heeled."

Laughing, Ralph used a phrase Rose favored. "God works in mysterious ways. Actually, we owe it all to Pop." Then Ralph told the remarkable story of John the Bum, a Kenosha legend who'd been presumed homeless, but had in actuality been much more than a friendly bum wandering the County. He'd been sole heir of one of the wealthiest shareholders in Standard Oil. He'd been grateful for their father's friendship and help in managing his affairs, allowing him to live unconventionally. Upon his death he'd established a large trust fund to benefit each of Alexander's surviving children.

"The money came with two conditions: no more would be made available after two generations, so we'd be comfortable and secure, but our heirs would need to be productive to maintain their inherited lifestyle. We couldn't divulge the source of our money either, since he wanted us to avoid the stigma of having unearned wealth."

"My attorneys couldn't find those details. Two courts said it had to be safeguarded for national security purposes."

"Hardly. It's just powerful men who don't want you to get here and begin unraveling what they've done."

"Do those words I mentioned mean anything to you?"

"I'm batting eight hundred, four for five! George is obviously for St. George, the name of the parish across the way. A very big part of your life growing up. You're right about the dragon, too. You were fascinated by the statue of it being killed by the saint. It's gone now, replaced by a vanilla painting of some sissy-looking saint . . . the original statue was too graphic for the new church, apparently, don't get me started on that!

The 'maid' has to be *The Maid in America*, the plane you flew in when you left 'Libya' to bomb Ploesti, when you were allegedly killed." Six only remembered having flown to Tinian Island and Hiroshima, but he'd dreamt of the smell of dying men and moving forward rapidly toward imminent disaster, as if in a plane crash.

"I'm not surprised you came up with the name 'Atia' either. We used to rate girls, and we liked to say, 'she's pretty, but she's no Atia!' You really don't remember?" He didn't.

"When we were kids you went through an all-things-Roman period, including tall tales of ancestors in ancient Rome. Pop encouraged you, and you claimed you dreamt about a past when you'd lived near Vesuvius with the most beautiful woman in Italy, one named . . . oh, goodness."

"What is it?"

"Let's take a break and have a drink."

"What do you know, Ralph?" John asked, seeing through him immediately.

"Y-You had a son with a woman in Italy . . . His mother's name was Atia!"

They had two drinks after that, and exchanged expressions of astonishment: Ralph was stunned to learn John already knew Tolo, and had helped him come to Northwestern; and John realized why he'd felt such affinity for the young man from Italy. They spoke well into the morning, pushing around pieces of the puzzle until they were too tired to continue. John was exhausted and depressed, wondering how many of his relationships had been spoiled by the government cover-up.

The most befuddling disclosure was the final one: Gail's husband and Alexie's father was Daniel Stegger, of all people. *God Almighty, how does that play to Stegger in hell?*

At four a.m. they stood and hugged. Ralph said, "I'm overcome. I need time to digest all of this."

"I feel the same, and don't know what to tell my family . . . It's asking a lot from you, but I need to remain John Redford until we sort this out. I have to figure out where one life ends and the other begins, and we need to assess the danger. The government went to great lengths to hide this, so we need to tread lightly."

Ralph agreed. He'd ask his close friend, the congressman, to hold off on asking around for the time being. He squeezed John's arm. "We'll get on the same page eventually. Some things last forever."

John told Rose all he'd learned, and they agreed that little would be gained by resuming his true identity, and other lives would be disrupted, perhaps jeopardized, if he did so. They would have to wait until they knew enough to control the outcome.

———

Vegas had been a magical place of bright lights and easy money, but L.A. was unlike anything Slick had imagined. Its sunshine and beaches, freeways and cool cars, and rapid pulse of motion were exhilarating. With the hot Chevy and ample cash to flash, Slick felt welcome from the start most anywhere except for Watts, which he knew to avoid—there weren't any coloreds back in Kenosha and they frightened him.

The girls on the beach had amazing, tanned bodies and all seemed unusually hot, but they were so young not even his his hair impressed them. But he fit in with the older crowds in the clubs near the Strip, and he became a regular at the Whiskey a Go-Go. Although a tad older than most dudes, by dyeing his hair, growing a stache and dressing young (he took to wearing vests and scarfs, headbands and bell bottoms), he fit in, and the older guys showed him that almost anything in L.A. could be had for cash, especially the ladies. He had an awesome, self-indulgent time until he met Sally Ann Duncan.

Slick never knew whether he'd bought Sally Ann, but it didn't matter, they'd clicked from their first shared joint on Huntington Beach. No woman had ever responded to him like her. She laughed at his jokes, was generous with her body, and seemed crazy about him and his hair. She'd been down on her luck and needed a place to crash, so what the hey, he'd thought, he really liked her smile, her long, dark hair and pouty lips, and the way her breasts seemed about to pop out of her trademark high-waisted, short, tie-dyed frocks. Sure, he'd said quickly, and they began living together in his pad in Venice Beach.

"Artie," didn't need to work, so worldly Sally Ann (a drop-out, thirty year old bookkeeper from Albuquerque), taught him how to max out his nearly $490,000 stash, how to barter, how to use credit, and how to wash cash through different banks. Slick became less outgoing but happily homebound as they settled into a routine of mornings on the beach, sex in the afternoons, and dope and drinking every night after dinner. After four months of intimate comfort they went to City Hall in L.A. and became Mr. and Mrs. Arthur Moriarty.

Not long after his marriage, Slick thought to put his past behind him, and he asked Sally Ann to help him write a letter and mail a package, a task he'd planned but put off since making his discovery at Stegger's home. He had her write and patiently rewrite twelve drafts until he thought his note sounded adequately clever and intelligent.

His letter to his childhood friend read: "Dear Six, if this gets to you I want to say, 'Hey man, how ya doing?' I mean, it's been like forever and here we are, forty-seven-year-old farts, ha, ha! If this doesn't get to you, whoever is reading this should stop reading right now and give the enclosed money to charity. Anyway, if you're Six and still reading, I want you to have these files and recordings because they have something to do with the Army and all messing up your mind so you didn't know who you were, but if you have this now you must have found out. I never listened to the recordings because they're old-fashioned wire thingies and I don't know how to play them, but you will because you were always smart about science and technical sort of stuff and I'm sure you still are even after having been brain-fried. I can't tell you how I got all this stuff, just that it wasn't pretty. It was all strange and mysterious, something your old man really would have loved to talk about. The guy who had them was a class A prick, but you probably know that already. Like you told me once, 'what goes around comes around,' and Daniel Pricko got his come around big time. I learned a lot from you and your Pop, and I want to tell you that you were the best friend I ever had and I wish as much as anything that we could start over again, but still, now I'm happy here, happy as can be with a beautiful woman who's the love of my life and my wife. Can you believe that? I wish you could meet Sally Ann, but I'll never return to K-Town again so this is it for us unless you come out to California and see my picture in a post office, ha, ha. I was right when I kept telling you, since I've sure seen a real lot of it since we were kids and I know you have too, 'Who knows what evil lurks in the hearts of men?' The Shadow knows! It's a lot of evil for sure! Your old buddy, 'Artie' (think slick, like cool hair! It's a long story I wish I could tell it all to you!) P.S., If any of your family is still alive be sure to say hi but don't tell them it's from me since I broke parole in Wisconsin. But you always could keep a secret. P.S. 2, I know my brother deserved what he got. P.S. 3, Use the enclosed two thousand dollars to buy something special for yourself as small thanks from your old pal."

Slick mailed the letter with the file and recordings to the Peeters's home, one of a few addresses he could never forget.

In August, Slick hurried home with roses. Sally Ann was pregnant and he was thrilled about becoming a father. Coming through the door, he saw her leaning against a corner of the couch, transfixed by television, and looking distressed. She ran to him and threw her arms around his neck, "It's so awful, Artie, so unbelievable; I don't know how we can bring a baby into a world like this!"

"What is it, sweetie? I don't . . . "

"It's all over the news! Hippies massacred some people in the Hills and riots are coming and we should stay inside. It's . . . "

"Whoa, sweetheart, slow down and fill me in."

She was distressed about the reports of the horrific murders of a pregnant movie star and her entourage at a home in the Hollywood Hills, and the murders the following day of a couple on Waverly Drive. "My God, Artie, they cut the baby out of her and wrote 'Death to Pigs' in her blood and in the couple's blood too. They carved them up like animals! You love it here, but maybe, for the baby's sake, we should move away!"

Slick did his best to reassure her, and the moment, which reawakened his memories of two other especially familiar violent deaths, passed quickly. But the idea of writing with a victim's blood hung in his mind. Several weeks later, stoned and listening to Sally Ann recount the news of the captured killers and their bizarre leader, a guy named Charlie, Slick began a rambling, disjointed discourse.

"Sometimes bad things happen for good reasons," Slick began, apropos of nothing. "I mean, like going out with a good bud cuz he's a magneto type guy. I'll bet this Charlie has the eye of the tiger, is wired and talks like Hitler or Hans, real smooth and quick. Kids play 'follow the leader,' you know, and that's cool, right? And like so what if there's some collateral pain now and then, I mean really, there's not much chance of someone random being cut up by his guys so it's just like fate, like some people have really bad luck, like someone getting hit by lightning. Who knows, maybe even sometimes it's deserved, like with that Daniel prick."

"What do you mean, Artie? Who's Daniel?"

Slick took a deep hit and held it, exhaled, and took a shot of Jack to top it off. He offered the joint to Sally Ann.

"Honey, not so much, okay? I'd join you, but with the baby . . . I hope it comes early, nine months is a long time."

He reached over and pulled his wife's head down until they lay slouched along the couch with her head resting against him. Feeling pregnant and drowsy, she closed her eyes and caught about every fifth word as Slick rambled on. She called him "motor mouth" whenever he got into these moods, but she meant it affectionately. She found comfort in the soothing sound of his deep and familiar voice, as he spoke on a variety of topics simultaneously.

"She came running out of the room and would have run right into me, getting help I guess, I mean the dude couldn't walk, the phone lines were down and he was broken up and bloody already. It's a reflex thing, not something you think about, like when the doc hits your knee with a little hammer, you know, so The Man says 'do it' and you grab her by the arms and he has a knife and all . . . Like with this Charlie or Hitler, or Hans, you're not afraid or mad even, but he's The Man and you have to follow the leader, you know, he's even kind of your hero and there's an excitement you can't resist so you hold tight and close your eyes and listen to the swish of the knife a few times, then the screaming stops and there's just a little gurgling, real calm and quiet like water bubbling in a brook. Blood's everywhere, but you're so amped you don't even notice it, don't feel anything—the bad karma only comes later, after the rush and the high wear off."

"Who are you talking about? Who are these people?"

"So, like, the dude has a piece, which you find out when you follow the light to his room, and then he's shooting at you, trying to kill your ass. I mean, you're not even introduced and he wants to take you out. Hans was pissed, even more than knowing they fucked his family over, him and the Miami lawyer, Arlen something, the old classy dude. He gets off a couple rounds and almost kills your ass in the doorway, but Hans, silky smooth as ever, clips him in the shoulder. It moved real fast after that, you know, like when you're driving down a highway watching the signs go by so fast you can't understand them when they blur and you turn to look back at the one you passed and miss the next one ahead, know what I mean? Just like Burma Shave."

"You're losing me and scaring me honey, please, stop, get some coffee or go for a walk or . . ."

"Knife stuck in his leg, bleeding and all, dude says, 'call an ambulance,' then soon he's begging, saying 'for the love of God,' I mean like, hello, you screwed my whole family! 'Who was here before?' asks The Man. But the dude just keeps asking for help, talking about his pain. He knows him though, knows he's a Hitler-type strong magneto, so like what was the point if you really know him? I mean, he had to know the girl was offed by then, so really, does he really think he'll call an ambulance? Hello?"

As if in a trance, Slick ignored Sally Ann's frightened crying and held her so tightly she couldn't rise. Nothing would stop him from regurgitating all of it.

"Dude was fading, The Man astride him, twisting and hitting and cutting this and that, maybe trying to find out who'd hit the dude first, maybe just for grins. He stopped screaming after a while and started moaning, in a rhythm almost like a melody, funny at the time. Hans says to him, 'Cry me a river,' like the old song."

"Tell me you weren't there, Artie; tell me it's just some wild story, please, you couldn't have been part of such . . . "

"Hans had a great imagination, plastic bags and all, and while he worked on the Daniel dude some more, I checked out this huge safe, found a shitload of money lined up on a shelf real neat, like pairs of socks in a drawer, so The Man knew he didn't need the dude anymore, could just give him his due for his family and get a stash of cash. So he took that old pistol, held it to his head and said, I'll never forget it, so cold, 'Night, night, cousin shithead, say hi to Satan for me.' Then, after blowing him away, he stretched his arms out so he looked like Jesus, then he writes 'Justice' in his own bright red blood on his satin white pillow. I have to say, I thought, cool, just like that thing above Jesus on the cross, which I didn't get entirely because I don't think either The Man or the dude were anything like Jesus, but blood writing sure seems the thing to do at murders these days.

That's when I found the file and recordings we sent to my old pal, some CIA connection Hans said, real spy shit. Can you believe it? Such a small world. We ran and I ditched a great pair of shoes and later I ditched Hans too cuz he really wasn't a bud, just a selfish prick, kind of like being a prick ran in his family, and I didn't need him, I just needed . . . I don't know, just . . . just . . . I'm really tired, Sally Ann . . . "

His head nodded and his rambling turned to snoring. Very slowly, she moved his arms aside, rose, packed a small bag, and closed the door quietly and left. She had no idea where to go, just knew she had to get away. It seemed her lovable husband had been a monster just like the cold-blooded, crazed killers in the Manson family. She should've learned more about him before she became pregnant, but she still had time to address that issue.

Slick looked for Sally Ann for days afterwards, asked all around, but no one could help. No note, nothing, she'd just run out after he'd gotten good and buzzed and started running off at the mouth. He guessed he knew what he'd said, knew he'd been thinking a lot about his fucked up days with Hans. But that wasn't him anymore. Now he was a family man, less than six months from having a kid of his own. Why would he tell her what he never wanted to tell, the story of those murders? Maybe the nuns had been right. *The St. George dummy blew it again.* He felt lots worse than he did when he killed the girl while driving. Now he had something worth losing. He wasn't sure he wanted to live without her, so that night he did something unimaginable. He prayed.

Slick Retzling/Arthur Moriarty lay alone in bed on a hot night in September, thinking about two boys kneeling in the front pew at St. George Parish, dressed in white suits and shoes, about to take their first communion. He'd been a fervent believer when the communion host had first touched his tongue, trying to match Six who'd had an innate spirituality he lacked. Now, feeling utterly lost, he decided to again try to follow his friend's forty-year lead: *Dear God,* he thought, *I've been awful and done horrible things and have more than I deserve, but there's nothing I care about at all except Sally who I know once loved me. Is it too late to forgive me? What if I promised to do good things for the rest of my life? I promise, promise, promise!* Concentrating as hard as he might, but with no response or sense of hope, Slick fell asleep and dreamt that night of sticking a pistol's barrel into his mouth and blowing himself away. He awoke before dawn, thinking God had answered his pathetic prayer by suggesting suicide.

Sally Ann came home the following evening, noticeably larger. Slick ran to her, crying out with unabashed joy. She stopped him short with her raised hands. "I went to Albuquerque to think about us, Artie, and decided here's the thing: I know I love you for the man I think's inside, but I need to decide if we have a future, if I want you to help to raise our baby. So, tell me how you feel about the awful things you did with that Hans? Are you willing to leave L.A. and go anywhere I want? Do you promise to stop doping and drinking and live a good life with your family at the center of your world? Answer me truthfully!"

Every year thereafter, she asked Slick the same questions and received the same satisfactory answers: He felt awful about the things he'd done and he'd spend his whole life seeking redemption; he would go anywhere she wanted if she would only stand by him; and never drinking or using dope again was a small price to pay for sharing their lives together.

Almost exactly thirty-six years later, in October, 2005, Arthur Moriarty, respected citizen, three times Chairman of the United Way Campaign, and one-time Rotarian of the Year, passed away peacefully in his home in Manoa, on Oahu in the Hawaiian Islands. At the time of his death, Sally Ann, his long-time faithful and loving wife was sitting on the bed beside him, clutching his hand and praying for his eternal soul.

All three Moriarty children and two of their four grandchildren were nearby when "Poppa" passed. They all grieved the loss of the joyful bear of a man who'd remained youthful at heart into his eighties. Poppa never spoke of his past before meeting Momma in Los Angeles, although they all had known him to be a world-class storyteller. His best stories had always emerged as the family sat together on the lanai of their home after dinner, overlooking the lush green tropical valley as they discussed religion, ethics, and current local and worldwide events. The ritual had become so ingrained, important, and nurturing that after Poppa passed on, each of his children, Pamela, Terrence, and Sixtus, vowed to carry on the tradition within their own families.

———

On May 24, 1969, Ralph Peeters stopped by the Kenosha post office and picked up his mail, which included an oversized box from Los Angeles. Bold black, block printing on it warned, "IMPORTANT AND PERSONAL FOR SIXTUS PEETERS ONLY." Ralph called his brother's office at Northwestern University, and using a greeting that still caught in his throat, he said, "Hi . . . John, I received a package from L.A. addressed to 'Sixtus Peeters' at the old house and it looks important . . . No, I don't know . . . can't imagine either . . . Can you come up tonight? Great, make it five at the old place and we'll catch dinner at The Bartley House before you head back home."

By the time the package arrived, Ralph and John had been meeting frequently to exchange information and discuss how to address Six's mistreatment. The process was slow, deliberate, and confidential. They understood the information in their possession was explosive, revealing treachery and crime at the very highest levels of the government. If they went public without verification already in hand, any remaining records would be destroyed, and they'd be personally at risk.

They glanced through the contents of the mailed file, counted the seven spools of wire recordings, and read Slick's letter aloud. Ralph put it in context: "Two thousand dollars is unbelievable! He never had a pot to piss in, and the last I heard he was living above a bar on Fifty-Second street! He couldn't even have written this letter!"

"Probably his wife wrote it, but he knows what they did to me and that Stegger got what he deserved. These had to be in Stegger's possession . . . How the hell did he become involved with Stegger?"

"Maybe the files or recordings explain it."

"Ralph, I'm passing on dinner and heading back to my office. I don't get the Slick connection, but this is an answer to my prayers. I'll call after I review the files and find a way to play the recordings. I'm thrilled, I've been waiting forever for this!"

14.

Timing is everything

Oahu, Hawaii, 1969

Life invites speculation about the importance of seemingly random choices, and such was the case when two old friends arrived unbeknownst to each other at Honolulu International Airport on September 30, 1969.

After arrival from Los Angeles, Arthur Moriarty, aka Slick, decided he and his wife, Sally Ann, would stop at the E Komo Mai Lounge to toast their relocation to Hawaii. Otherwise, he would have exited the terminal at precisely 1:03 p.m. and been reunited with John Redford, aka Six, who entered then. Also, the two might have met in the concourse at 1:27 p.m., had John not stopped in a telephone booth to place a call which itself would alter the course of many lives.

As it happened, he wasn't there when Arthur and his wife passed by and wished good luck to Rose Redford and said, "God bless you for your service," to their son, Abe, who merely grunted in response. The Moriartys believed disabled soldiers deserved to know their sacrifice had been appreciated, despite the war's unpopularity.

Four months earlier, John had raced to his office, long sought answers at hand. But a note marked URGENT diverted him, and after a few words from Rose, his own problems seemed insignificant. A telegram delivered to their home read, "Lance Corporal Absalom J. Redford USMC was injured 19 May 1969 in the vicinity of Quang Tri Combat Base, Republic of Vietnam. His condition is critical and his prognosis guarded. We understand your concern and will send daily updates of his condition."

The Redfords weren't surprised when their eldest child enlisted in the Marine Corps. He'd been the one most affected by John's absences throughout his obsessive search, and he'd become the family contrarian. He underachieved, didn't believe in God or attend church services, and no longer had an interest in sports. He seemed uninterested in anything but cars, firearms, girls and rock music. He delighted in being provocative, and he outdid himself by enlisting because he claimed to support the Vietnam War.

On the eighth day of a ten-day battle in the rugged mountains of southernmost Vietnam, Abe was moving toward an enemy position when he became engulfed in the thick smoke of air support. A fragmentation grenade and three pieces of steel shrapnel struck him when he overlooked a trip wire, one embedding in his left calf, another grazing his right cheek, and one small fragment fracturing his skull.

A chopper ferried him off Hill 937 to the Da Nang medical facility. Surgeons there removed the shrapnel and skull fragments and filled him with antibiotics. He emerged from a coma after ten critical days, and was moved to an Army hospital in Yokohama, Japan for further treatment. His earliest post-explosion memory was waking up and finding his parents at his bedside, just before realizing he couldn't move his legs.

Based upon x-rays, scans, and the experience of treating eight thousand soldiers each month, Army physicians diagnosed his brain injury as moderately severe and expected it would leave him with emotional deficits for the rest of his life, manifested by depression and anger, inappropriate behavior, and social withdrawal. His cognitive skills were expected to remain unimpaired, and half the soldiers suffering suffering similar injuries eventually overcame their paralysis. A favorable outcome depended on his attitude, the effectiveness of rehabilitation, and fate.

John and Rose kept their faith while devouring daily telegrams from the DOD. They flew to Japan when Abe was evacuated from the war zone, full of faith and hope. But dealing with Abe's emotions required all their patience and understanding. It also required John to keep his true feelings stifled while others blithely praised his son's "brave sacrifice." He knew it'd been a waste, and the war a futile intrusion into an insignificant country's political affairs by leaders who were, to borrow a phrase from his past, sanctimonious pricks who didn't know when to stop. His son's hospitalization also triggered his sense of irony, as he recalled flying over Abe's current sanctuary to bomb Hiroshima seemingly not too much earlier. It galled him to realize his government continued to display the same disregard for innocent life as he'd seen firsthand in 1945.

John's attitude hardened further when he learned Abe had been injured in an effort to dislodge the enemy from a well-fortified position in a singularly unimportant location. It struck him that his son's commanders were pathetically immature, acting like children playing capture the flag. He discovered they'd abandoned the captured hill almost immediately because of its insignificance, and he joined many others by referring to the prize as "Hamburger Hill." In the desperate battle over the worthless land, men had been chewed up like ground beef.

Rose returned home while John remained in Japan with Abe, rejoining them after his transfer to Tripler Army Medical Center in Hawaii. They were headed home with their son facing an uncertain future on the day John nearly reunited with Slick.

Sparing no effort or expense, John hired professionals for Abe of the sort he'd long refused for himself. He'd been calling Chicago from Hawaii when he'd missed Arthur/Slick, confirming his son's appointment with the finest psychotherapist available. "Yes," Rachel Hoffman Weber had replied, the time remained open and she looked forward to meeting them.

Abe's injury gave John time to review the files sent by Slick. Between what he'd learned, a visit to Hiroshima, and Abe's injury, he was finally firmly grounded in the present. He'd postponed listening to the recordings since the files, together with what Ralph had uncovered, gave him enough knowledge of his past that the sense of urgency had passed.

He'd learned about his academic background, military service, recruitment by the OSS and meeting with President Roosevelt in Denver. He marveled at having been so naïve that he hadn't insisted upon written authorization before undertaking the unique, secret assignment.

He'd learned about his transfer to Libya, the Ploesti mission and the plane crash near Serbia. He knew he'd been rescued and taken to Italy by Atia. And no matter how implausible, he believed he'd known her far longer, at the very least when he'd first dreamt in his childhood of living with her in ancient Rome. Brant Frey had scoffed upon learning he'd spoken Latin and acted as if he were an ancient Roman, but John was convinced he was connected to Atia in a very real way.

He'd learned of being abused by Stegger and Frey, and of Doctor Wright's efforts to help. He also knew that during treatment he'd been hypnotized by a Doctor Cowell and had revealed what the CIA termed "wild and misguided allegations of Company misconduct and abuse," which actually had been an accurate recounting of his mistreatment. Finally, he also discovered he'd been reprogrammed by use of the so-called Ludlow Technique, to avert "threats to the national security," an obvious euphemism for maintaining the government cover-up.

He wasn't likely to learn much with Wright hidden away somewhere in Brazil, Cowell killed by Frey, and everyone responsible for his transformation from Peeters to Redford dead. He recognized the hand of the Company in Cowell's death and he thought they were likely complicit in the murders of both McFarland and Conforti, since both bore their dangerous trademark.

He hadn't heard of the Ludlow technique before, but it seemed a logical extension of the Nazi brainwashing documented in the

Nuremberg Trials. They'd shown amnesia could be induced and actual episodic and declarative memories eliminated, so obviously Ludlow had taken the next step; he'd found a way to couple retained abstract skills, like mathematical and scientific abilities, with newly-programmed false semantic memories—amazing, but depressingly true.

He had also discovered that Brant Frey had been unconcerned about their wrongdoings being uncovered, and it appeared he'd been correct: those responsible would never be held accountable for their actions. The files clearly documented governmental crimes, but John couldn't release them without incriminating himself in Stegger's murder—no one would believe they were sent to him by an old friend they'd never find, while he'd be identified easily as the man masquerading as a lawyer from Seattle, the prime suspect. Even if he could leak the files anonymously, he didn't know anyone who would pursue it when all verification would be destroyed by the CIA as soon as the allegations became public.

Frey's son, Brad, was top-level CIA and close to Stegger's son, Nathaniel, who was himself well-connected counsel to a Senate Committee. What witnesses would come forward to confront men so formidable? John also questioned the entire point of pursuing it further. He had most answers, and those responsible for his mistreatment were all dead. He might expose a corrupt system, but it wouldn't benefit him, and it could expose him to personal harm. Did he really want to chance more grief and possibly jeopardize his family? *Fool me twice, shame on me*, he thought.

John already had his hands full with Abe. How could he deal with the consequences of telling his tale to Tolo, Alexie, and his children as well? As idealists they were likely to charge off intent on righting wrongs, like youthful Don Quixotes, too inexperienced and naïve to understand they might become victims too, with their lives permanently altered. It had happened to him when he merely passively opposed using the bomb against Japan. He hadn't appreciated the lengths to which powerful men would go to prove their prowess and protect their interests.

John had learned the hard way that some truths were best left untold. He'd had enough of conflict. He'd continue doing his best to make a difference, but from now on he'd do it quietly. Being bold and self-sacrificing hadn't done much for either him or for Abe. He'd figure out how to play the old-time recordings, then close out that chapter of his life. He'd let others struggle for justice while he'd make easily manageable efforts to sway the battle, like building a Japanese pagoda in Illinois.

After a few months at home, only a faint line remained where the shrapnel had grazed Abe's cheek, and the wound in his calf left only a small scar. His head was covered by fashionably long hair, and with debridement, plaster retention and time, his skull wound was largely unnoticeable. But walking remained problematic, mostly due to invisible, emotional wounds remaining. Recovering at home, Abe gave hell to anyone coming near.

"Don't throw anything else, there's glass all over and it just makes more work. Try ringing the bell when you're upset!" In response, Abe threw the brass school bell at his father, who caught it in mid-air. "Come on Abe, nice catch, right?" he said engagingly.

"Screw you."

"Patience, son," he said. "It'll get better. Miss Rachel says it's only a matter of time till everything starts to make sense."

Few things made sense to Abe then, not with useless legs and four buddies dead, and the oldest not even twenty-one. *Semper fi my ass,* he thought, remembering the pride and glory and proud tradition bullshit he'd been fed throughout training. *I wonder how many guys could have enjoyed a full life if not wasted from the Halls of Montezuma to the Shores of Tripoli. I've got a drawer full of medals, including a Purple Heart, but none of them are worth a good shit.*

He'd set out to show his family he hadn't needed a degree or a conventional life to be successful. *I've shown them all right, shown them I'm so damn dumb I caught metal in my head fighting to take a hill no one gave a shit about. Grunts ground up like hamburger is the meat of it!* He hated himself for the role he'd played. His recklessness meant he'd spend the rest of his life trying to prove he really wasn't an idiot. He sniggered. *I'll ask Mom about that saint for hopeless causes, maybe she'll pray a damn novena or whatever they call it.*

Rose Redford had first met Rachel Hoffman Weber at the Knollwood Club in Lake Forest, at an event for special needs children. An enticement for attending had been the chance to meet the prominent psychologist who would be at her sister Adie's fundraiser.

Rose admired the persona of a woman daring enough to write a book challenging Ivy League schools at nineteen. She expected to meet a firebrand, but found Rachel charming and gracious, a soft-spoken conversationalist who managed to soothe even while being forthright and compelling. Even in a brief conversation it was apparent why she enjoyed her stellar reputation, so when Abe needed help, Rose sought her out. Rachel held injured soldiers in special regard, and she adjusted her schedule to take on Abe. But, even with her expertise and skill, it took more than three months of treatment before they addressed the fundamental issues stalling his recovery.

"Abe, cut it out, your anger is counterproductive. It taxes your system and prevents you from regaining your equilibrium and making an authentic effort to regain use of your legs. You may not succeed, but you'll never forgive yourself if you don't give it your best shot."

"It's not like I haven't been trying! I'm exhausted from trying, it just isn't happening! You think it's so damn easy . . . "

"Come on, I see in your eyes that you know better. Honestly, you've struggled with it for months now. Isn't it time to confront the elephant in the room with us?"

"I don't know . . . "

"Sure you do, you're far too bright to miss it."

"Tell me."

Rachel thought for a few moments, feeling herself on the brink with a patient for the first time ever. She felt unaccountably invested, fully aware far more than professionalism was at stake. Yet she understood, had really foreseen it was always meant to be personal, her and him.

"Let me tell you about someone else, a young girl who wanted to be special, a girl who wanted to live a relevant and helpful life, one of real substance and achievement. She didn't let anyone else see it, but deep inside she felt she never could, because she was odd, out of step, extraneous and different than everyone she knew. No matter that she'd been well-raised and loved, like a puppy taken from a litter too soon, she felt she lacked any sense of belonging. If she could have articulated it then, she'd have said she felt abandoned and hopelessly out of place in childhood, though she masked it.

Her mother died soon after her birth and she didn't have any other relatives. And she couldn't get past the embarrassment she felt not even knowing her own father's name—a stranger who'd raped and impregnated her mother. With those underpinnings, and feeling so out of step, she'd been sure she'd never really reach her goals, could never overcome her sense of emptiness and poor foundation. She was much like you."

"I don't see it. I have a mother and father who always, who well almost always . . . "

"You're *emotionally* paralyzed; your feelings of rejection and worthlessness are evident. They've weakened your foundation and are making you too fearful to even try to succeed."

"I was a goddamn Marine charging up a frickin hill when . . . "

"I'm not talking about physical courage. You showed that in spades trying to gain your father's attention. But you feel empty and abandoned, like the puppy out of the litter, and that's why you're spinning your wheels. You're still fixated on your father and the need and fear involved with attempting to prove you'll succeed in spite of him. But your physical issues are allowing your emotional fear to dominate and overwhelm you, so you find it easier to do nothing rather than face that fear."

"What is it I'm supposed to be so afraid of?"

"Come on, Abe, isn't it obvious?"

He sat still for a time, then tears filled his eyes and he let them roll down his face. He nodded, almost imperceptibly, knowing he'd always understood. Abe had been determined to show his father he'd be fine without him by being strikingly different. He'd made himself into the uneducated, redneck outcast, the atheist and gun lover, the one family member rejecting his father's many warnings about government and politics and men sent off to war. He'd even thrown it in his father's face, advocating a war he knew he hated while becoming the truest of believers, a Marine, ready to respond, "Yes, sir!" to any command with no obstacle too difficult to overcome. But he'd been proven wrong, had come to his sorry state for nothing. Politicians were falling over each other to quit the war, preparing bullshit excuses for flushing all the soldiers' sacrifices away. They'd failed him, and their blatant duplicity added to his plight by now showing up his judgment to go to war based on their hollow pronouncements. Coupled with his ailments, it all combined to rob him of his confidence and self-reliance.

He'd only gone through the motions in rehab because Rachel was right: he doubted he'd succeed. It had seemed an impossible, uphill climb due to the resurfaced, repressed feelings of emptiness, abandonment and isolation. The idea of yet another failure terrified him, because it would prove definitively that he'd never deserved the attention he so desperately wanted.

Rachel finished, "That isolated and frightened girl overcame her own emotional paralysis only because, despite everything else, she simply dared to try. I'm certain you know what she finally realized that let her make the attempt."

"Come on, Miss Rachel, haven't you beaten me up enough for one day?"

She smiled and gently placed her hand on his. "Not nearly enough. We're not through yet. We're too close. Take your time and tell me what she saw that gave her the incentive she needed." Some time later Abe would remember looking at Rachel at that very moment, watching her eyes sparkle as the hint of a smile appeared on her thin lips. He'd been amazed by how quickly the tall, thin and angular, decidedly average-looking woman transformed into a dazzling beauty. Six years older, famous, successful, and his psychologist, it was nonetheless at that moment that he realized he loved her.

He took his time with the answer, knowing she'd made it personal. In return, he wanted to please her more than anything. "It had nothing to do with her parentage or upbringing. All that mattered was what she," he smiled, "what *you* found inside of you, your character and spirit, your drive, attitude and determination, all those things, the only things that you can control. Even if you set your goals too high and failed, you'd be content knowing you gave it your all. The one I need to emulate is YOU . . . I'm right, aren't I?"

Rachel wanted to hug him, but she settled for clasping her hands together and shaking them back and forth rapidly in delight. "Yes, yes, of course it was, and in your case . . . "

"I need to confront my problems without thinking what my father who disappointed me might think. He has no idea how difficult it is for me, since no one else can judge what I have to overcome. It's apparent he'd do anything for me now. He must have struggled with something during my childhood that I couldn't appreciate. But he overcame his problem and now I need to work on mine. I need to know I gave it my all and look ahead rather than behind me, obsessing over a past that can't be changed."

Abe continued to have setbacks from time to time, but his outbursts lessened dramatically and his depression morphed into optimism. He returned from his therapy sessions energized, and began reaching out to his parents and siblings, looking for common ground rather than emphasizing their differences.

He began reading voraciously, and at Rachel's prompting began preparing for the SAT so he might start college as soon as possible. As his attitude improved, so did his rehabilitation. Within three months he'd begun walking, albeit with metal braces and the use of a cane. It seemed only a matter of time until he walked unassisted.

By May of 1970, Rachel knew she could no longer work with Abe, so she referred him to another psychotherapist. Katya Weber foresaw it coming, had noted a newfound attention to appearance and a distinct lightness in her daughter's bearing, an unfamiliar, uncharacteristic distracted air. She'd heard all about Abe by then, met him and understood why it made no sense, given his age and her daughter's long expressed disinterest in such mundane things, but when Rachel spoke openly to her Katya understood and said so. "You don't have to apologize or explain to me, sweetheart. Few things in life are as linear as we suppose. I'll support whatever choice you make and never doubt your judgment. Abe may only be twenty, but he's a fine man who brings you joy, and timing is everything in such matters. Once all logic is exhausted, the only remaining truth is that the heart wants what the heart wants."

On the evening of August 20, 1970, Rose Redford lifted a champagne flute to toast the engaged couple. "I'm unaccustomed to moments like this, but I need to express my delight. So much has happened ever since Abe enlisted that it's difficult . . . " Her voice quivered and then trailed off in an emotional outpouring very much unlike her. She'd always been the family's strength and glue, soft and passionate inside, but outwardly stalwart and rational, the necessary counterpart to a husband prone to self-reflection and withdrawal. "Forgive me for being sentimental, I don't cry very easily, but this is our first engagement party, after all!"

The small group laughed, and John smiled with appreciation for his rare wife. Only they could fully appreciate how much things had changed so quickly, for them as well as for Abe.

They'd been skeptical of accepting Abe and Rachel as a couple, concerned he wanted affection because of something like post-traumatic distress. They had also worried she might be a parental substitute, given their age difference, her dominant personality and authoritative position. Yet, the relationship positively transformed each of them.

With Abe, Rachel was softer, more gentle and down to earth, still forceful to be sure, but with an endearing new vulnerability as well as a satisfied glow. Defying his prognosis, Abe overcame his anger and regained his emotional stability. Moreover, Rachel ignited his intellectual curiosity and he began to show a compassion never shown before. He began exploring his spirituality and he spoke openly of his newfound desire to lead an exemplary life.

Rose's emotional display was also due to a profound change in her relationship with John. He'd finally listened to the wire recordings and discovered they were a missing link. Afterwards he shared them with her, primarily in order to verify his sanity, but by revealing his haunting story and trusting her with his innermost thoughts, they'd discovered a newfound intimacy of their own.

The revelations included his past relationship with Abigail Stegger, and they'd agreed she needed to know at least part of his story since she and John would meet inevitably—with Abe engaged to Rachel—and Gail would recognize him as Six. They asked his brother Ralph to break the news to her and the encounter went better than expected, providing yet another reason for Rose's heartfelt release.

Rose drew on her self-confidence to overcome the jealousy she fought when learning of John's encounters with other women. She managed, despite the intimate details, to be grateful for the peace it gave him. She wasn't sure just what she believed of every strange thing she'd heard on the recordings, but finally there was nothing she didn't know, no matter how supernatural or mysterious, and she also finally understood his reaction to the portrait of *Angel:* unaccountably, Mary Thayer looked exactly like a young woman he'd known as Azume, someone he claimed had been an angel nearby throughout his life.

Rose finished her toast. "I wondered why God let Abe suffer such such a frightful injury. Now, I know it was to allow this wonderful angel, Rachel, into our lives. God love you all! Now, Katya and I have to get to work. We only have a year to plan! Cheers!"

15.

A Good Day at the Office

Evanston, Illinois, 1969

The faculty offices were closed the day after Thanksgiving, and John went there to listen without interruption to the recordings sent by Slick. After a few days of tinkering, he'd managed to refurbish an obsolete wire recorder found at a home rummage sale, and he'd repaired the damaged spools as well as possible. But careless handling over two decades had entangled the hair-sized wires, and they had to be cut and trimmed to be played, losing portions in the process.

John began listening with limited expectations, anticipating he'd hear Frey dictating his notes. He started up the spool marked number one, and immediately heard, "Hi, I'm glad we can be alone and play together. My best friends call me Hammie. Do they really call you Five, like the number?"

Knowing he'd been hospitalized as subject number Five, John realized he was listening to a man speaking with him as if he'd been a child. He moved closer to the device and heard, "Once I stayed in my bed for two years and read books to pretend I was a different person doing things in places far, far away. That's one of my secrets . . ."

His spirits soared. He'd read Cowell's biography and realized he was listening to the voice of Graham "Hammie" Cowell, the celebrated psychiatrist who'd worked with him in 1946, a man bed-ridden for two years as a sickly child. Immediately he had the heart-pounding realization these could be the missing link: recordings of his lost memories recalled under hypnosis.

He listened to the psychiatrist attempt various means of gaining his trust, and after an hour of pleading, long pauses, and a rhyme about an itsy bitsy spider, Five opened up. But, just after he said the first secret he remembered showed he was bad, the spool ended.

The first portion of the second spool was corrupted. When it started up again, two men were speaking as adults rather than children, and Cowell was addressing him by an odd name.

"How old were you when this happened, Takla?"

"It was fifteen years ago, when I was a fourteen year old warrior ready to stake my claim to a hearth."

"I need to know more details of your life then. I don't understand what you mean using words like 'Amar' and 'hearth' and 'Estaba.' Tell me about those, and what your life was like before you . . . before you ended up alone with Azume in the valley."

"I belonged to the Colya, a clan of about a hundred and twenty members fairly evenly divided between men, women, and children. Our Lord's name was Oto, and we considered him a fine man and thoughtful leader. He exercised supreme power in nearly all things, although in such as the mating of a Council Daughter he made his decision in consultation with a ruling group called the Council."

"What's a Council Daughter?"

"They're the daughters of the rulers: the Lord, the Shaman, the War Chieftain, the Bard, and the Chief Huntsman."

"Where did your clan live?"

"We lived in interlinked caves near the sacred mountain of Amar, said to be one of six homes of the gods, the one the Colya were responsible for protecting. The nearby terrain consisted mainly of sparse grassland, but it also contained valleys, woodland, and lush meadows, where we irrigated and grew edible plants and fruits easily much of the year. Except for rare battles with enemy tribesmen, we lived peacefully and comfortably, well-protected from animals and seldom lacking for food."

"I can't imagine living in a cave. What's it like?"

"Most of the time very pleasant. The temperature is fairly constant, and we're kept secure and sheltered from storms and intemperate winters, animals and enemies, and entrances are easily guarded. We sleep on comfortable mats made from earth mixed with grass in small quarters, called hearths, which we share with eight or so related members. We have a constant source of water and a separate (unintelligible) area suitably apart from our hearths, storage and communal areas. We always are . . . " There ensued a sixteen minute gap before the recording resumed.

" . . . with my brother, and my hearth mate, Gros."

"You believed they would keep your confidence?"

"Yes, we were very close. But being powerless, all they could do was reassure me of what I already knew, that with or without Azume, I would continue to do well and advance within the clan. I could never become Lord because of my birth circumstances, but I was creative and well-respected by the War Chieftain, and it appeared likely I would succeed him. It never occurred to us how things would play out. We were all terribly naïve."

"When did the problems begin?"

"When Azume became a woman. You see, as a Council Daughter, and especially as the daughter of Lord Oto, the selection of her mate had great significance. If she produced a healthy son he would almost certainly be considered a possible Sub-Lord in Waiting."

"What's that?"

"At the age of four, the most precocious sons of the Daughters are selected for training, with the best of the lot becoming a Sub-Lord in Waiting upon reaching maturity. Usually there are several, and they succeed to clan leadership in order of seniority after a Lord's death. They live very privileged lives.

I was born a commoner while Azume was a Council Daughter, yet we'd been soulmates from childhood. We felt so connected we often communicated without speaking, as if able to read each other's minds. As we matured, our attraction became more physical, yet it never occurred to me until I became a warrior that someday we might be allowed to mate."

"You needed permission to . . . to mate?"

"Azume did, since Council Daughters were off limits to all but the man selected by the Council. The taboo was meant to assure the best leadership, and its violation warranted execution."

"Soon after I became a warrior, the Lord and every member of the Council began to praise and tout me as an example to others. It seemed apparent then that I would likely be selected as the mate for some Daughter, and as it happened the first one available was Azume. The thought of mating with her and keeping her in my hearth was exhilirating! Young and idealistic, I knew if the choice was made on merit I stood an excellent chance. Still, I thought no one could be certain what the gods might inspire, so I was prepared to accept the decision regardless of the outcome. When I realized the Council was corrupt I was ouraged and felt deceived!"

"What made you believe that?"

"Seven days before the full moon and announcement, I was summoned before the Council and accused of having fornicated with Azume. Outraged, I erupted in anger—against every instinct, I had foregone the opportunity, even when it might have been easily understood, even if not excused, when I was under the influence of mead after a feast. 'Please,' Zumy had pled, 'nothing could be more natural.' I don't know what restrained me, perhaps because the pleasure of merely holding her was so blissful it seemed enough, or maybe because I refused to put her at risk. Regardless, 'The charge isn't true!' I'd shouted in response.

'You had relations near the pool on the early morning after Estaba,' replied the Lord with confident certainty. 'Our informant is an unimpeachable source who spoke with an eyewitness.'

'Your source lies,' I'd exclaimed, 'I would confront this perjurer!'

Oto erupted with anger at my rebuttal and responded in his most authoritative tone. 'Calm down and think clearly, warrior. Don't make things worse! You know the penalty for perjury can . . .'

'Of course! And I swear by the Gods that I never knew her carnally!' I exclaimed with youthful foolishness.

A collective gasp escaped the Council, and the Lord glanced quickly at the Shaman, a small sign which I first understood only sometime later. Everyone knew the penalty for swearing falsehood was banishment or death, but what I didn't realize was that I'd put myself in an impossible position. I hadn't considered that the accuser would be the one with the most to gain, my chief rival, Nambe, the Shaman's son.

I disliked Nambe intensely. He was an arrogant, ruthless power-seeker who'd openly lusted after Azume. We laughed at him once, when he'd licked his lips with an exaggerated smirk and mouthed 'yum, yum,' while leering at her, even knowing she detested him. But then it was no longer humorous.

I was dismissed and ordered not to discuss the matter until the Council concluded their investigation and rendered a decision. Days later, Azume would tell me that after my confrontation with the Council, she'd been examined privately by the Shaman to determine if she was still physically intact. She was befuddled and intimidated by his painful probing of her privates, and after he finished she wasn't intact any longer—the Shaman made certain her condition matched his son's contention.

Despite being confined to quarters, Zumy managed to send a simple message: 'meet me tomorrow outside the cannibal cave three hours before daybreak.' By the time I received it, I too realized we faced an insurmountable problem."

"Couldn't she just speak to her father and . . . "

"A Lord's daughter wouldn't ever approach him without being summoned, and once I'd sworn my oath it no longer mattered. Nambe knew how Zumy and I felt, so the accusation had to originate with him. Obviously the Shaman was using his lie to tilt the selection. Presumably he intended to graciously sweep all the problems their gambit presented away by telling the Council sometime later that he'd prayed on it and the gods wanted our transgression forgiven for the clan's benefit. Then there would be no unseemly disruption, and except for Zumy and I being miserable, clan life could continue as before. But my outburst forced the Council to rule on the matter, the Shaman's examination supported Nambe, and no one would dare question whether the esteemed Shaman had ulterior motives."

"What exactly was the Shaman's role?"

"As the overseer of science, he was responsible for maintaining all Colya knowledge regarding the nature of things. So the clan relied on him to explain all otherwise unknowable phenomena, everything from the rising of the sun to the cause of droughts, from birth defects to death, and the nature of the spirit world. Considered as a conduit to the gods, they were said to repay his devotion by instilling in him a knowledge of these otherwise undiscoverable matters. So opposing the Shaman was unimaginable, tantamount to opposing the gods who created and controlled everything."

"Didn't the Lord have the power to overrule him?"

"In theory, but because the source of the Lord's strength and power was the gods, the two could never be in opposition without angering them. So they acted in concert, and the Council united behind their decisions on all but the most trivial matters. On this issue, as a practical matter, the Council would calculate that Nambe's strong arm and cunning compensated for the loss of my skills, so I would be reluctantly expendable. Sacrificing a pawn to maintain their incestuous power didn't trouble them, the truth of the matter meant nothing."

"But you might have survived and only been banished, right?"

"Banishment would never have been a viable option. I couldn't wander about alone for long and live, so with skills to trade, they knew I'd likely join the Marche, fierce Colya enemies who'd be delighted to use my knowledge against them.

I thought to be noble and insist Azume remain with the clan while I fled, but when we met her desperate appearance dispelled any such idea. She'd swum under the water of the tributary flowing through our cave and into the pool to escape. Few could have accomplished such a feat at all, and all I'd had to overcome was one sleepy guard. In the cold morning air, with water dripping off her small, shivering body, Zumy looked so young, so vulnerable and afraid. Then she eliminated any of my remaining doubt: 'If you leave me here alone, I want you to know I'll kill myself rather than submit to Nambe. I swear it, Big Brother! Your only choice is to take me with you and help us find a new life, together.' What could I do? Azume never said anything she didn't mean.

I could easily outrun the clan members, but Zumy couldn't, so I believed a sustained chase by Oto's men would be fatal. But I thought we might successfully hide in a remote area of the Colya land and move on later when their guard was down and the frenzy of the events and pursuit passed. Our choice for a hideout seemed easy—we'd secret ourselves on Amar. We no longer believed in the Shaman or his warnings of offending the gods by intruding into their realm, and we assumed the clan's reverence for Amar would prevent them from searching for us there.

Carrying Zumy, I ran for an hour to the foothills of Amar where I concealed her in a thicket of evergreens. Then I ran back to our starting point, obscuring all signs of our passage before heading off in the opposite direction leaving readily detectable signs, making it appear we'd fled recklessly at daybreak. I moved quickly enough to . . ."

Spool two ended and number three started up after a time, " . . . so intent on being followed that I misjudged their proximity, and a spear launched by an atlatl, ironically a device I'd invented, struck me on the inside of my bicep, one of the few parts of my body left exposed while I carried an animal carcass posing as Azume hanging down from my shoulders. I still carry the scar . . . look right there . . . it pierced the muscle and I was able to break the ends of the spear and extract it cleanly. As I resumed running it bled significantly, and I thought that might help us by leaving a trail away from Zumy."

"You must have been exhausted."

"I've always been an exceptional runner and had been in a runner's trance since leaving the caves. But the bleeding and throbbing pain of my wound made my stride awkward and my running became labored. Glancing down at the chalky remnants of bone and fur strewn about the plain, I recall wondering if my pursuers or some beast would soon reduce me to a comparable state. But unexpectedly, blessed relief washed across me from somewhere unknown, as if I'd been caught up in the breath of a watchful spirit disguised as the wind, and my pain lessened appreciably. I began to feel light as a bird, as if I could increase my stride and move up into the air, floating and with increased speed, and I covered a great distance so quickly that the fastest of Oto's charges remained hopelessly behind me and out of sight. When I reached a stream, I cleansed and treated my wound with plants before looping back around behind my pursuers. By nightfall, I could tell by their camp lights that they were more than half a day away while I was very near Azume. With any luck they would continue moving away, searching aimlessly while we hid atop Amar. When they eventually gave up we could cautiously slip away, leaving Colya territory for good.

I should have realized Nambe didn't respect Amar and would consider what he'd have done in our stead. We first knew he suspected our plan and had convinced the Shaman to allow a group of . . . " A twelve minute gap in the recording followed.

The playback resumed, " . . . or die together. We were confident, regardless, not because we believed the gods ordained it, but because we felt we were meant to be linked together forever, no matter what happened. When the shouts of the pursuers became louder we knew they would soon be in sight, so I hugged Zumy and told her I loved her, and holding hands we walked back ten feet before running off the edge of the cliff together and leaping out as far from the precipice as possible.

We trusted in our fate, reasoning that we might break our fall on the clumps of lush shrubbery and meandering vines framing the limestone face less than half way down. From there we could leap again, and then one final time until landing on the edge of the expansive valley far below and safely beyond the limestone face of the cliff. We were shaken when we picked ourselves out of the vines at the first level, and Azume had fractured her thumb, but once we'd gathered our wits we shared our exhilaration, knowing we only had to repeat . . . "

A seven minute gap in the spool followed. It resumed, " . . . to animals, and once to an enemy in battle, but those were impersonal experiences. When I realized she had suffered the same injury, I . . . even after all these years I still find it impossible to describe my feelings, other than being devastated and forlorn. For a long time afterwards I felt guilty, too, but that eventually passed. We'd discussed the risks and knew we might well die in our effort, but we weighed that against the certainty that we otherwise would die slowly and painfully by fire. They would have done whatever it took to keep us alive until a public execution, dramatically reinforcing the consequences of defying the Council.

When she landed on the ground, Azume screamed out in pain and fright, and by the time I made my way over to her she was whimpering and having difficulty breathing, could only barely, quietly whisper. The gravity of her condition was apparent: she couldn't move her limbs and her legs were twisted beneath her in a grotesquely impossible angle. I lay beside her and stroked her face with my fingertips, her loveliness obscured by my tears. Her intense pain soon turned into shocked numbness and I indulged myself in touching my lips to her forehead, her cheeks, and closed eyes. She opened them and whispered, 'I will love you forever,' and I knew she meant her words as a parting expression.

There was so much I might have said to ease her way, but time was short and the words wouldn't come. I was inadequate and overwhelmed by what needed be done. I leapt up and picked a beautiful yellow flower off a nearby bush, held it for her to see and smell. 'I'll always see your beauty in such as these,' I said. Then I placed the flower behind her ear, touched my lips to hers one last time and whispered, 'forever.' I rose up and straddled her lovely, naked body and paused, searing her image and my longing into my mind even as I steeled my nerves. I looked beyond her as if for some cue, so cowardly, and then I felt her tremble and gasp, 'I want to live . . . to stay with you.' Tears rolled across her cheeks and I nodded in agreement, if only it could be. I smiled at her one last time and then quickly did what will haunt me always, what surely will be the most difficult act of my life. I broke Zumy's neck with my hands, and the crack of her bones burst like a thunderclap in my head, tearing out my heart.

I've seen others die, but compared with her elegance in life, Azume's barren corpse was the most disturbing thing I've ever seen. What was lost with her wondrous spirit seemed so irreplaceable that I couldn't imagine loving gods allowing it.

I carried her to an ideal spot, and like a mad man I used my hands and branches and whatever else I could reach in a frantic effort to bury her and disguise her grave, to keep it secret from our pursuers and undisturbed by beasts. I situated it in the finest spot in the valley: near the looming shadow of Amar, where in the reflection of a moonlit sky the setting would be magnificent and unparalleled. I owed it to Zumy. I told her only the night before, under a glorious star-laden sky when we still dared hope our flight might end well, how remarkable she was, the only one I knew worthy of the miraculous display of stars above us.

When I left her gravesite I vowed I would return and tell her of our revenge. It took me nearly ten years and a miraculous vision before I understood how to accomplish it, but I repaid their injustice, personally sending the new Lord, the Shaman, and Nambe to the underworld, and uniting the best of the Colya with the Marche. I found a measure of satisfaction knowing the masters of the Colya would never again victimize anyone by disguising the will of the gods with lies. Unlike the night I slunk away from her resting place alone and uncertain, I returned to Amar with my head held high in the company of sixty loyal warriors who followed me readily, since by then I had . . ."

John turned off the recorder, suddenly aware he hadn't moved from the chair beside it for more than three hours. His back and neck ached from leaning over while listening and filling eight pages of a yellow legal pad with notes. It occurred to him that perhaps it marked his particular form of insanity, but he felt certain Azume and a life near Amar were an integral part of his existence, and that when he spoke as Takla he'd been reciting history. He splashed water on his face, looked at himself in the bathroom mirror, and splashed his face again, stood there dripping and laughed aloud. He felt better than at any time since his first aircraft flight, when he first learned how different earthbound things appear from the sky.

John filled his "World's Favorite Dad" cup with coffee, fished two chocolate chip cookies from a jar, and settled down to resume listening. The gap continued to the end of the spool, and toward the end of the next spool he listened to himself speaking as Jack Redford from Los Alamos and saying, "He promised to teach me a lesson, said he'd 'yank out everything stuck in my head.' Then my world went blank, until I realized I was in a hospital."

"What did Stegger mean?"

"He thought he could discover my real identity by treating me with chemicals. He thought I must be some kind of a spy."

"What do you mean by 'a spy,' and your 'real identity?' Weren't you Jack Redford?"

"It's a long story."

"Tell me, please. I've got lots of time."

He told Cowell his real name had been Sixtus Peeters and he'd been working as a spy for the OSS on the President's behalf in Los Alamos. As he listened to the recounting, John found it awakened memories of his family as they'd been in his youth, most especially his father, Alexander, and his brother, Ralph, but also of his friend, Slick. Still, many other aspects of his past remained misty and beyond recall, including his intense relationship with Gail. As he took notes, he frequently felt like a student listening to a lecture and preparing for an exam, but certain emotionally charged matters triggered present recall, including his regrets over his involvement in the Manhattan Project.

"Watching the mushroom cloud rise over that pitiful place, I felt an ache in my stomach, knowing I'd helped pervert the role of science. In rushing to replicate the power of nature, we'd overlooked our obvious limitations: we lacked the wisdom to recognize the responsibility inherent in our discovery, a need to respect its sublime beauty by using it only to benefit creation! Recklessly, we chose instead to incinerate human beings strolling along under the sunlight of a glorious morning. You have to wonder how men could be so incredibly capable and so ignorant at the same time. I realized later that she'd remained nearby so I would recognize the real essence of what we'd wrought."

"Who do you mean, *she*?"

An audible sigh followed a lengthy pause. As Six in the recording, he hadn't yet spoken of the mysterious young woman who had appeared to him in his early life. But as the session continued, he opened up and described her visits, his certainty that he'd murdered her in his youth, and his fear of discovery. He described her thin and delicate, angelic face, with high cheekbones and wide, dark eyes framed with thick auburn hair. The tension in Cowell's voice belied his effort to contain himself, knowing that Six was unwittingly recollecting the death of Azume at Takla's hands—a mercy killing, not a murder.

"What was her name, Six?"

"You mean, what *is* her name. I thought she died, but she continues to appear to me, most recently on our flight to Hiroshima, on our way over there to drop the bomb."

"How is that possible?"

"She's real and alive in a way I don't understand and find hard to describe . . . I never knew her name. I don't know who she is or where she came from."

"Does the name 'Azume' mean anything to you?"

"No, I've never heard it before."

Cowell had understood, and listening all those many years later John did as well. Takla had killed Azume, and the memory of it, or perhaps merely the memory of such a story had consumed Six as if *he'd* been Takla once, and remembered only enough to know he'd inexplicably killed someone he loved. The experience haunted him and made her a constant presence in his life.

"Why do you think she appears to you?"

"She's wise and knows where my life is heading. I think she wants to help me make the best choices, maybe as an example for others, maybe to atone for evil, maybe for some different reason altogether. I'm not sure."

"What evil would you need to atone for?"

"At first I thought the evil of killing her, but that's illogical. So I think it's all the unnatural evil that men cause throughout the world when they ignore moral barriers, whether exploiting innocents, bombing Japanese civilians, or destroying a man's essence out of jealousy."

"Why would this be your responsibility when you were victimized?"

"It isn't mine alone. Everyone's obligated to advance mankind's well-being since everyone acts in conjunction with others even if they fail to see it. But everyone's small acts combine to create worldwide trends. Whenever someone isnt helping push in the right direction they bear responsibility when men flounder."

"How do they flounder?"

"When they commit the seven blunders Gandhi spoke of and turn away from God, ignoring the ultimate truth."

"You speak of this mysterious young woman as if she's more of an angel than an actual person."

Maybe, thought John, as the vision of Thayer's *Angel* sprang into his mind. He turned off the recorder and sat totally still for a time, awash in revelation. He had much to mull over, but he felt a great

THE ANGEL OF AMAR

weight had been lifted away. Hearing the recording made him feel like Takla when he'd leapt into the air and began floating, increasing his stride and moving forward rapidly with his sights set on his final destination.

John left the building and circled the campus, stopping to skip stones into the Lake as if a child once again. Then he called Rose, told her he loved her and would soon be home with wonderful news.

Refreshed, John returned to his office to finish listening to his hypnotized younger self on the recordings. He felt his equilibrium return as the voice spoke easily of all the defining times from his past that he'd otherwise forgotten.

———

Bradford Frey looked out at the intense snowfall, pleased to be back in D.C. Of all the properties his old man had left him, he liked the Georgetown townhouse best. It had an elegant feel, and when he put his feet up near the blazing fire he felt transported back to simpler times, and simple had been a stranger for far too long. At the age of only thirty-five, he intended to continue to live an engaged life, but he had to consider working outside the Company since suddenly everything was becoming too hot for comfort.

Nathaniel entered, mellow, relaxed, and almost looking like himself again. Since his father's murder he'd worked full time at the Senate while running his father's mini-empire and the effort had taken its toll.

"Mr. Spy Man, how are you, sir?"

They shook. "One hundred percent, counsel, but I'm still trying to avoid an ass-kicking."

"I thought so when you called. Where's the fire?"

Bound together by their fathers' escapades, the two had worked together for four years, beginning under Daniel's tutelage while Nathaniel finished up law school. It had worked well, and Brad rose up in the CIA while learning Stegger-level nut crushing. But the problem they faced after Daniel's death was remaining ahead of the investigations. They'd begun to fear the thought of prosecution and the dreaded "C" word, confiscation.

Frey highlighted the problem. "Nixon took the next step, telling the Director that all Company intelligence reports need to go through Kissinger."

"So, he wants to do Johnson one better?"

"You got it. He wants us to look over his political opposition—so any heat on Nixon will hit Kissinger and implicate the Company."

"I thought he was smarter. Christ, so flush with victory that the dumb shit forgets the need for cover. Johnson used a boatload of buffers when dealing with us."

Frey and Stegger knew domestic spying on Americans for political reasons made for irresistible news, and would lead to investigations, subpoenas, and hearings, and sooner or later to the CIA's family jewels, MKULTRA and Chatter, their rogue programs focused on behavioral engineering, as well. The details included drug usage, torture, biological agents, regime change, suicides, and deaths, all irresistable fodder to the voracious media. Their fathers had been key players, and the jewels had helped secure insider contracts which had generated much of their initial wealth.

"My father thought everything was untraceable," said Brad, "but I don't think it's hidden well enough to withstand a full scale shit storm. If just a single traceable detail breaks loose . . . "

"I agree. It's time to move on, better safe than sorry! I'll handle the liquidations and transfer funds to the Caymans and BVI while you destroy the files. I've got Daniel's covered. Let's see who needs juice to make sure the right Committee member heads up any investigation. I'm guessing it'll be Church since he eats this crap up."

For sixteen months Frey and Stegger worked through their plan, and each retained a fortune, but the dismantling took much of the zest from their lives. It was especially disorienting for Nathaniel who'd emulated his father, and without schemes had little else that really interested him.

Their partnership concluded, Stegger moved out of Frey's orbit in 1971, and Frey could not have been more pleased. Like his father before him, he'd experienced a Stegger deterioration first-hand. Nathaniel had been a well-respected and effective Senate counsel as long as his ego remained in check, but once his business ceased he found it impossible to remain deferential to the formidable men he served. He'd resigned before being fired, insisting the problem was with the Senators who resented him for being "brighter, more significant, and far more capable" than any of them. In truth, he 'd precipitated his deterioration by relying on the most powerful central nervous stimulant found in nature, cocaine. He filled his life with the drug and his fixes fooled him into believing himself superhuman and invincible. In that frame of mind, he began planning his attack on his father's killer, a loose end he wanted resolved.

Brad Frey came through again on that, tracing Peeters to Northwestern and locating his Lake Forest home for Stegger. Frey's involvement would be wholly obscured and easily disavowed, but he'd set Stegger up with ex-CIA operatives who'd be ideal for the task, men who'd readily tortured and killed to keep the world safe for America. For financial rewards that were inconceivable when they'd been drummed out of the Company, they'd follow his instructions to the letter and use their expertise to visit horror upon John Redford, also known as Asshole Jack, and Sixtus Peeters, the bastard Nathaniel Stegger believed slaughtered his father.

———

The small engagement party for Rachel and Abe was held on a deck spanning the width of the rear of the Redford home. The deck overlooked a manicured lawn bordered with flowers backed by daylilies fronting a tangle of forest brush and towering hardwoods. But the impressive natural beauty was eclipsed when sunlight set ablaze the golden spire and tiled roofs of the imposing structure forty yards beyond the deck.

Visiting Hiroshima on the ground had inspired John to build what became known as "John's Dragon Pagoda." Such towers were often intended as monuments, and John intended his to honor the victims of the atomic bombings. It took six months of planning and four months of construction, but the final product was as authentic as any found in Japan. Incongruous behind an Illinois home, Rose disliked and admired it at the same time, but she considered it pure John.

The red, black and gold structure rose to thirty feet at the peak of the central spire. Each of its three stories included an overhanging gold tiled roof flowing down from the center column and curving upward at the edge, with each story progressively smaller from bottom to top. Each roof had five distinct sections of tiles, each section separated by five diagonal beams, known as tanuki, each representing one of the five essential elements: earth, fire, water, wind, and heaven.

The outside tip of each tanuki protruded a few feet beyond each roof, and each of the fifteen tanuki tips bore a design of John"s imagination: a decorative dragon with a neck curved upward like a cobra and its body tensed, with paws facing downward, and three long, sharp talons on each paw prepared to thrust into prey.

The pagoda was set upon a raised pedestal with teak benches surrounding the open center, the seating accessed by six wide steps at the end of a curved bluestone walkway. Hung near its top were lanterns outlining the structure and spotlighting a small teak plaque bearing gold Japanese kanji and kokuji characters which encircled a green dragon. These composed a message known only to John.

The pagoda was flanked by a fountain, and the sound of running water added to the contemplative setting. It had become his refuge of choice, a place for coffee in the morning and wine in the evening.

It'd been a long and convoluted journey, but by the summer of 1970, John/Six felt he'd finally found peace and contentment. God willing, he believed he had nearly three decades left in which to enjoy his life without being interrupted by his mysterious and long-indecipherable past.

16.

A Memorable Holiday

Lake Forest, Illinois, 1971

The wind shifted, torrential rain began to fall, and lightning struck nearby. It woke Rose, who looked out and started to worry. In three days her yard would be filled with guests celebrating the first of a series of events culminating in her son's wedding.

A few miles away, Adalia Marshall was also awake, pondering a disjointed dream in which her brother, Hanny, pointed his broom gun at her and repeated words foretelling his death. "Nurse Heller said we'd be together again soon to go to the special Jesus place, but I bet she meant here because nowhere could be nicer. I know you'll like her too, Adie—she's an angel, so sweet and pretty!" Adie wondered if her sister Rachel's kindness reminded her of the guardian Hanny imagined, and if that's what made her first think of Rachel as an angel years before.

Adie hadn't remembered her dreams for a long time, but as her daughters grew and her life became more settled, she'd begun recalling them again. Several times recently she'd re-experienced a dream in which Rachel jumped off a cliff and fell to her death before rising up and beginning a new life as Bea's baby. Now that she was marrying Abe and a happy ending seemed imminent for her, she planned to ask her sister about the psychological implications of the unusual dream.

Rose first gave a Fourth of July party in 1962. Her immigrant mother was so proud of their citizenship that they'd celebrated the Fourth as much as Christmas. After moving to Illinois, she'd wanted her children to experience the excitement she remembered growing up. They were aged three to twelve then, and her first few parties were modest affairs: Morning bicycle parades winding down the drive with parents cheering the kids along; prizes for the best decorated bikes; ice cream and red, white, and blue balloons for all. In the evening they'd gather for snacks, croquet, and water balloon fights, and end up eating popcorn on the beach watching fireworks.

As they became fixtures in the community, the guest list expanded and the affairs became more elaborate. Nighttime events began to include live music, drinks and a buffet dinner served under a large tent. The eagerly awaited annual event was cancelled only once, the year Abe was wounded in Vietnam.

This year her teenage kids had lobbied for a younger band to perform before "the old fogies" played the patriotic standards, and Mark had recommended his friend Don Paradise's group, *The Continentals*. "If you close your eyes you'll think its *Three Dog Night*," he'd insisted. Rose appeared clueless, so he sang *Joy to the World* and by the time he got to "fishes in the deep blue sea" she recognized it.

Why not liven it up, she thought, *it's our tenth year, we're touting Rachel and Abe, and everything's going so well I'll expand the guest list. We'll even call for costumes. It'll be a hoot to see the yard filled with Uncle Sams!*

Abigail Stegger gave her response a great deal of thought before accepting Rose and John's invitation to their annual affair. It came at a time she'd been likening herself to Job, kicked around by God now and then to prove her faithfulness. She wasn't certain she remained faithful or whether, at forty-eight, she had time left for any earthly rewards.

When Ralph had called she'd welcomed the chance to meet, always interested in news about Six. But he'd dumbfounded her. As a skilled labor negotiator, Ralph was good at making a point palatable, but this one made her stomach flip until she actually vomited. Afterwards, handkerchief to her mouth and Ralph's hand on her shoulder, she felt numb and confounded by the litany running through her mind: "Abby, I could talk to you forever; when this war's over; it's no mistake, he really was killed in action; he promised they'd marry after the war; he lost his life in an experiment and the bodies couldn't even be returned to their families." She thought, *All right, now just forget all that, he's really alive, but not just alive, he's been living nearby for ten years with his wife and family! Oh, and by the way, he's your son-in-law's mentor at Northwestern, as well as his father. Holy shit!*

Learning Redford was Six, abused and then reprogrammed, she'd been as stunned as if struck by lightning. She'd never heard the name while in Los Alamos, but she'd been disengaged much of that time, preoccupied with Daniel's abuse, their failing marriage and her pregnancy. She didn't ever know the name of the foe no one spoke of around Daniel, the one he'd berated as "Asshole Jack." It seemed odd they hadn't met in Illinois, although he wouldn't have remembered her, and she might not have recognized him, thinking him long dead.

Ralph explained it all generally, but he didn't disclose that her ex-husband, Daniel, had been responsible; he saw no reason to add that disagreeable fact to her burden. She responded reflexively by insisting he seek justice, but she soon saw it as he did after considering the possible repercussions. It would be even more tragic if he was confronted with more troubles now, particularly if they ensnared Tolo and Alexie. If Daniel's successors in the CIA were anything like him, they'd be unscrupulous, dangerous and vengeful.

She felt guilty, but Gail couldn't help wishing Rose ill. They'd met at Adie's fundraiser and she seemed a fine woman, but she occupied the role Gail coveted. Still, she realized if it hadn't been Rose, it might have been the Italian woman—although she was dead, *and if Rose were to die too*—she asked God to forgive her such ugly thoughts. Apparently she needed to be content knowing she'd placed third fighting for Six, and in a contest where she was the only aware competitor.

"Of course," said Ralph, "he wants to meet you, too. But realize that he won't remember you. Let me tell you, it's painful to find out he doesn't share your emotional bond."

He hadn't convinced Gail, who believed the chemistry between them had been so charged that nothing could alter it. She even felt a tinge of guilt, since thoughts of seduction lurked selfishly just under the surface. She primped for their meeting like a girl going to her first prom.

They shook hands upon being awkwardly reintroduced near Buckingham Fountain in Grant Park. Ralph discreetly moved away, and they faced oone another on a bench at high noon. Gail managed not to cry, and after exchanging personal information, as if total strangers, the conversation became more pointed.

"In some ways, I feel like I did the night we were on the Zephyr," Gail ventured.

"Except now you're with a man who carries fifteen extra, poorly distributed pounds, wears glasses, and has gray, thinning hair."

"I'm not so trivial. I'd have recognized you anywhere. The man I fell in love with isn't so easily disguised. After all, it's only been twenty-seven years, eleven months, and twenty-three days, but who's counting? My God, where has the time gone? You're still as attractive as ever . . . and I see I can still make you blush!"

"It must be the sun, old men don't embarrass so easily."

"Not too old, there's a lot of life ahead of us."

"You're lovely, Gail. It's obvious why I fell for you."

"But you don't remember it, do you . . . don't honestly remember our night on the train?"

He hesitated. The night before Stegger's murder he'd dreamt of being on a train under the stars, locked in her embrace. The exquisite feeling had been palpable then, and also as he listened to the recordings. He knew he would have married her but for the war and all the rest. Uncomfortable, he tried to lighten the mood. "Did the young man do anything indiscreet?"

She laughed. "No, unfortunately not, we were babies and didn't know any better." She sighed. "John, let me be serious. You have a wife and family and need to know where this is going.

I wanted to die when I thought you had. Then, for all the wrong reasons, I tried rebounding with a man who reminded me of you. But my judgment was awful. We divorced and eventually I dated some, but reluctantly, burned twice, Catholic and all of that. It wasn't that I still pined for you, only that our relationship set a standard I couldn't match, and after one disastrous marriage I wouldn't settle for less. So, I focused on my wonderful daughter. If she hadn't met your son I think my memories of you would have faded away over time, since I'd been reconciled to what I lost. Even hoping to regain it, I think I knew I was searching for something unattainable. I don't know if anyone can duplicate the intensity of their first real love.

Even here, now, it's far easier than I imagined because we're shadows of who we were then, nowhere as impressionable and passionate. We've been around the block, my God, you especially! But you were an optimistic philosopher and you've survived, and I guess I've learned something about survival, too."

She reached over, gently laid her hand atop his and squeezed. "I will never forget what you meant to me, but as I told you on that magical night, we'll be judged by whether we try doing the right thing as we see it. Well, I see where your life is, and I won't interfere. I'm strong enough to fight off the temptation.

I'm flattered you took me into your confidence and I won't betray it. I'll enjoy your company and look past our history. Over time, I hope we'll become good friends."

"God bless you . . . Abby."

"Thanks for that, and on balance He has, just not as I'd expected. But, I will need an indulgence from you, Professor Redford."

"Name it, young lady!"

"You need to promise to wink at me when our children have *our* grandchildren. Can I count on you?"

"I promise you can."

Gail vowed she'd keep his secret. Even if Adie noticed the resemblance between Tolo and John, she'd never disclose his real identity, not even to her best friend.

Gail called around to see what others were wearing to the Redford party. She wasn't feeling particularly proud of her country, so red, white, and blue were out. She decided to revert to her adolescent days and dress like an iconic Bobby Soxer, with a poodle skirt, scarf, and wig of red, bobbed Lucille-Ball-style hair, sunglasses, and tennis shoes. She'd look off-kilter for a fifty-year-old lady, but also anonymous. She couldn't be a Betsy Ross or Martha Washington. She thought those costumes only looked good on women who'd married well.

While Gail debated what to wear, three former CIA operatives waited for her son in a warehouse in North Chicago, Illinois, a dingy place only five miles but light years away from urbane Lake Forest. It was filled with strip clubs and bars catering to the sailors at Great Lakes, and tired homes, trailer parks, and metal buildings housing struggling enterprises.

"He's a sick fuck," said the operative called "Red." "White" and "Blue" both agreed.

White spoke to the bottom line. "There's nothing sick about what he's forking over. Simple jobs aren't worth a tenth of what we're getting. For this payday there aren't many people I wouldn't chop up, present company excepted!"

They'd been hired by Stegger for three hundred thousand dollars each; ten percent was already wired into Swiss accounts, forty percent would be paid when the targets were secured, and the balance after the last death. After this job, they'd never have to work again. Nathaniel Stegger would get his revenge and they'd return home and sleep like rich, untroubled babes while Redford and his kin would never, ever sleep easily again. Stegger might be a bit crazed, but he'd concocted a fate worse than death.

He'd thought it up after Frey tracked down Redford. He aspired to make the tribute to his father as brilliant as Daniel's own theft of Peeters's identity, and when he heard about the annual party, the plan came to him as if from the great beyond—on every one of his birthdays, Daniel repeated the mantra that the Fourth of July was intended to celebrate the "esteemed Daniel R. Stegger." So the time and place rather chose itself. It would be memorable and explosive, *God bless America and Happy Birthday, Daniel!*

The details came to him after an especially effective hit of cocaine. He'd thought, *There's four of us CIA guys and it'll be a goddamn huge costume party. How hard could it be to get in and steal away his bitch and a few of their brats? He'll be hanging out, distracted by the whole host thing, and before he knows it it'll be like, "where'd they go, man?" We'll snatch them out from under his nose, swoosh, we're gone, and hello heartbreak!*

He had to control his hits. Sometimes he felt overly anxious and paranoid after coming down from a high unless he stretched it out with smaller bumps. Then he could be mellow and at his finest, even though things sometimes appeared a little misty, and dim light often seemed too bright. But he was smart as hell and capable of maintaining his balance, and with a buzz on, he was sure no one could match his prowess *at anything.*

Killing Redford wouldn't be enough. He preferred punching him where it hurt the most, like kicking him in the nuts repeatedly and inflicting pain that never stopped. He wanted him to be tormented, to ask again and again why something so God-awful happened and what he might have done differently. So he'd attack his All-American family. They'd get his wife and a few of their kids on the boat and take them back to the warehouse in North Chicago. Then, when Redford couldn't comply with his impossible ransom demands, they'd send him body parts every few days so he'd obsess over the suffering of his loved ones, knowing it was all his fault. Of course they'd all be killed in the end, and when Redford found out he'd become a total lunatic or more likely off himself.

The money was irrelevant, the ransom demand a ruse diverting attention away from any wealthy suspect. He wanted the authorities focused on lowlife bad guys willing to do anything for some coin.

They knew the property layout from home plans stolen from the architect. There was an access hatch aside the deck at the rear of the home leading down to a fruit cellar, and a well-concealed pathway the kids made over the years through the woods along the south property line all the way to Lake Michigan, ending behind the porta pots. They'd take each victim to the rear of the home, immobilize them, and hold them in the cellar until most of the guests were gone. Then they'd make their way down the path to the dinghy and cruiser, and with a little luck be back in the van beside the North Chicago sewage treatment plant within thirty minutes. Five minutes later they'd be in the warehouse ready to start working on the captives.

Everyone would be costumed at the party, making it easier to blend in, although it could be harder to pick out the kids. It might be especially hard to separate Madame Hostess from her guests, but still, he knew she'd come running at once if she thought her kids were in trouble. There were five of them, but Abe, the oldest, was twenty and an ex-Marine. They were audacious but not stupid, and they planned to leave him alone, even if he was a little gimpy. They had pictures to identify the others: Mark, seventeen, Mary, fifteen, and the twins, Lizzy and Timmy, who were twelve. Mark's age made him iffy, but Nathaniel would be satisfied if they grabbed at least Rose and a couple of the younger brats.

Stegger swooped into the warehouse an hour late, high and pumped up. "How's the team doing today?"

They were all "awesome" and raring to go.

While planning, they'd cruised on the boat near the Redford property and selected a concealed landing spot between the barrier rocks protecting the adjacent property to the south. Blue could easily land the dinghy and filter in from there, while Red and Nathaniel entered the Redford's front gate with other latecomers. White would be part of the catering crew and be overlooked in the open, with full access throughout as one of a team of thirty-some temporary hires.

They'd studied the yard and set gathering and rendezvous points. They realized a few guests would wander toward the main staging area early on to glimpse the weird pagoda, but it would empty out by nightfall and was well-isolated from the main yard and beachfront activity centers.

They'd counted forty-five wide steps from the height of the yard at the top of the bluff down between the jumbled rocks to the beach. It had a handrail and could be descended easily, even with a target thrown over one shoulder. Plus the operatives were trained CIA bullshit artists, well able to blend in and lure their targets to the rear of the home at opportune times. Still, they'd been concerned how to restrain them, and had suggested to Nathaniel that the easiest thing would be to simply snap their necks and dump them in the woods.

"They have to be taken alive. I need fresh body parts and some audio of their suffering to make my point. If I wanted everyone simply killed at home I could have hired riffraff to do it for next to nothing."

He produced three syringes for each of the team. "Obviously, we need something faster than chloroform, so here's the ticket. Each of these holds our best immobilizer, a variant of C14. It's a fast acting anesthetic combined with a hypnotic agent and high potency benzodiazepine. It'll immobilize each target within thirty seconds and for at least forty minutes. But it has to be administered intravenously, so you'll probably need two men to inject it. The best spot is in the hand or arm near the wrist, but the jugular will work fine. If you need to choose, go with speed rather than technique since it won't matter if some skin gets torn up in the process."

The holiday evening weather was ideal, with clear skies and temperatures in the seventies. The twins, Lizzy and Timmy, welcomed their family's guests at the front gate dressed as bald eagles, complete with beaked hats and wings. They gave out name tags, encouraged the best disguised to scribble a question mark on theirs, and pointed the way to the food and beverage tent.

Most guests wore shorts and dresses, shirts, hats and such sporting an American Flag and a mélange of red, white, and blue. Others went all out: guests came as Uncle Sams with striped pants, top hats, wigs, and pointed white beards; Statues of Liberty with flowing gowns, spiked hats, and torches; bearded Abe Lincolns in morning coats and top hats; Colonial generals and admirals, soldiers, gents and ladies; roaring twenties flappers; patriotic cheerleaders; pilgrims; and one 1940's era Bobby Soxer. Betsy Ross, the Washingtons, Thomas Jefferson, and Ben Franklin were all represented, along with the Worthington's dog, Betsy, a huge Newfoundland sporting a striped hat and blue bow tie.

The twins judged the best costumes were those worn by several men and their brother, Mark, all appearing as Captain America: They wore blue jumpsuits with a large white star at mid-torso above red and white stripes, red gloves, shin high boots, a blue cap and goggles, and most held striped and starred round shields.

The twins wandered off after their friends about 6:45 p.m., deciding most guests had already arrived. The latecomers could help themselves to name tags and follow the noise to the festivities. *The Doors* lead singer was reported dead that morning in Paris, and they didn't want to miss the Jim Morrison tribute the band hastily added to their performance.

At 8:00, Rose Martha Washington and John George Washington took the stage. They apologized for being unable to greet everyone personally but thanked all for coming. The crowd of nearly two hundred applauded loudly when asked if they were enjoying themselves, clapped when the children were introduced, and cheered when John introduced the embarrassed, happy couple beside him, announcing that in a few months Wonder Woman and

Abraham Lincoln would be tying the knot. "Imagine their children!" he joked.

After dinner, Red and Blue slid out from the shadows and loitered on the fringes, wigged and hatted as two of several colonial soldiers. They didn't carry toy guns, but they had flashlights, syringes, and Colt pistols secreted beneath their vests. They steered clear of the owners, stayed away from the tent and lantern lights, frequented the porta pots, and stood unnoticed in the middle of a large group listening to a John Phillips Sousa medley. They only needed to introduce themselves a few times, and said they were first-time attendees and old friends Abe asked to stop by. White scurried about for an hour, unnoticed while carting food, helping tidy up, and scurrying about near the kitchen and guest tents with the other servers.

Captain America Stegger showed up near dusk with a beer in his hand and a name tag reading "Daniels." Circumventing the yard several times, he caught the eye of Alexie, who was startled by his familiar and arrogant gait. His stride reminded her of her twin brother, and she found it difficult to dispel the resemblance from her mind.

Some preferred to view the fireworks from the yard, including the prospective bride and groom, who perched together in the darkness. They remained away from the stairs and crowd, atop a large flat boulder in a corner of the yard above the beach. They were delighted to be alone after a day full of congratulations. Leaning back from between his outstretched legs, Rachel whispered, "It feels like this was actually our wedding day."

Abe responded by leaning over, nuzzling her neck, and reaching down to caress her thighs under her short blue and white starred skirt. "Hmm," she moaned, "You need to stop doing that sometime in the next hour or so." He nibbled at her ear as she pushed back against him. "I was right. I definitely am getting a married sort of feeling."

"No one's in the house and you know how slowly I walk. Maybe we should start back . . . like right now."

Rachel turned her face upward and gave Abe a lingering full-mouthed kiss as he trailed his fingers along her neck and across the skin above the bodice restraining her breasts. "It's a little weird, but Wonder Woman feels like lying down with our sixteenth President . . . Come on, we can make better fireworks alone!"

The two lovers passed the kitchen tent and entered the home on its north side, while Captain America walked along with fifteen year-old Mary Redford as she escorted him along the south side of the yard to the rear of her home. "Thanks, Mary. It'll only take a minute. I know the professor will love it, and I think your mom will, too!"

Mary was irritated at having been asked for the favor just as she'd been heading to the beach with friends, but there weren't any siblings around to enlist, and she'd been taught to be respectful to their guests. She felt especially obliged to help Mr. Daniels since he'd told her he was Daddy's graduate student and she knew how he felt about them. Besides, she was curious, hardly able to imagine what the man said took six months to build and five students to carry and her father needed to complement his pagoda.

Of course she knew where her parent's bedroom was, so she'd be able to show them where Daddy could see it from his window after they illuminated it. "The people in the kitchen tent were amazed," said Nathaniel, posing as the graduate student, "they'd never seen anything like it before. We're going to hang a banner on it that reads 'Thanks for Everything, Professor!' More than a hundred students and the entire faculty signed it. You must be so proud to be his daughter." Mary nodded, supposed it was true.

When they rounded the corner into the rear yard, Mary was confused. All she saw were two other men, one dressed as a colonial soldier and the other man one of the catering crew. Before she could react, Captain America reached out and abruptly pulled her toward him, smacking her with his hand as he clasped it around her mouth. She thrashed and kicked and let go a muffled scream as he lifted her off the ground and slammed her down hard on her back. In pain, frightened and trying to catch her wind, she felt her arm being yanked to the side, then something sharp was jabbed into it just beneath her hand, once, twice, and finally a third time. She tried to bite the hand with the needle but her jaw seemed floppy and useless, then all pain ceased and she lost all awareness.

"That's two," said White, after depositing Mary in the fruit cellar next to her unconscious sister, Lizzy, who'd been lured earlier.

"Fucking Timmy is running around with a big group and hasn't even taken time out for a piss. What about Mark?"

"He's been with some girl ever since we got here. He's got his arm around her and they're making out like there's no tomorrow. We can't grab him unless we take her too."

Captain America Stegger stomped over to the deck, pissed. *It took a lot of effort to sweet-talk this Mary bitch, and now after all my planning we only have two brats. It isn't fair. I wanted at least three! But how can we get close enough to grab another one now?*

His head ached as he peered around anxiously. Running to the south corner of the home, he looked out across the grounds. It was quiet, and no one was anywhere near the house. He heard the sound of fireworks and tried to relax, knowing most everyone would be absorbed in the display.

Initially they'd planned on moving through the woods down to the Lake about 10:15, soon after the fireworks ended. Everything would be cleaned up by then and the help would be gone, and the guests would be streaming toward the exit in a different direction. He drew some coke from his pocket, did his thing, and took a hit. Immediately he felt better. All he had to do was remain levelheaded.

This was proving more difficult than he'd planned. *Everyone is so damned friendly it's hard to blow them off without throwing out another bullshit line that might trip us up. Then there's my goddamned sister, just like in Casablanca: 'of all the gin joints in the world,' why in the hell is she here?* He hadn't seen her for three years, but even dressed as a pilgrim she looked so hot she'd caught his eye. She didn't seem to recognize him, but he still did all he could to avoid her. *Why is she here? Is Lake Forest such a small place? Last I heard she married a wop, some guy with a name like Ravioli.* It was one more thing to think about when he didn't feel much like concentrating.

He took another quick hit by pinching some up his nose, felt mellow and confident again. He thought, *Really, two brats are plenty. With two, at least one will last long enough to make my 'here's today's piece' point with a finger or an ear or whatever chunk seems right at the time. I'll forget about another kid and focus on the old lady—she's the grand prize anyway. I'm really looking forward to slicing her up. I think I'll nail her first and film it, even though she's old and hardly my type. But she's the love of Redford's shitty life. When he sees a Super Eight film of her being had by Captain America, he'll appreciate the irony of America screwing him once again. How sweet will that be?*

Stegger went back to reconnoiter and emerged from the woods near the porta pots. He leaned against a tree, goggles and cap off, taking a breather. He could see Rose and John Redford sitting on lawn chairs in a group viewing the fireworks from atop the bluff thirty yards away. He figured they'd split up when saying their goodbyes, she with the women and he with the men. He thought, *I'll stay right here until the perfect moment, while Red and Blue stay hidden behind me in the woods with the brats. Once I tell her Mary's been in an accident, she'll rush off with me. Then I'll grab her, and dash toward the dinghy and the others will . . .* Startled by a hand tapping his shoulder, he spun around and a familiar voice from his past asked flatly, "What are you doing here, Nathaniel?"

He stared at a red-haired Lucille Ball Bobby Soxer with white sunglasses atop her head and tried to think of the face and name that belonged to that voice. *Jesus Christ! It's the nagging voice of my pain in the ass mother. Am I hallucinating? Did I take acid by mistake? Why in the hell is she here? She cheated on her husband with this Redford bastard, so why would she be at his home now?*

"Yes, Nathaniel, it's your mother, and I demand to know what you're doing here!"

As a teenager, Daniel had insisted he perfect a karate chop which would compress the carotid arteries and the surrounding veins, instantly leaving the victim as unconscious as if sedated. Its use was limited since it could lead to brain damage and death, the very reason it hadn't been right for the night's snatching, but his father told him he needed it in his arsenal and Dad had been right once again.

He struck his mother aside the neck with one single and solid blow from the side of his hand. He'd acted reflexively to the perceived threat, but still, it *was* his mother. Unsure about how to handle this complication, he rolled her onto her side and saw that she was still breathing. She soon regained consciousness. "Nathaniel, what . . . " was all he let her mutter, before covering her mouth and sedating her with the needle he'd intended to use on Rose Redford. He carried her some forty yards and concealed her behind a bush near the path through the woods. He wasn't prepared to kill her, but something had to be done since she'd surely link him to the kidnappings.

This new wrinkle complicated everything. Maybe they needed to accelerate their departure since she'd be out for less than an hour, and being larger than the kids, she'd be more difficult to restrain. He hurried back toward the staging area behind the house, his mind racing, desperate for more coke to help him think it through. Time was moving quickly and they needed to be fully prepared to move as soon as the fireworks ended.

17.

Liberty Leading Lives Past

Lake Forest, Illinois, 1971

The City fireworks were muted that year, with lengthy intervals between bursts and few noteworthy effects. They ended earlier than usual, and many remained in place still anticipating the grand finale. The low-key effort was designed for a citizenry questioning its patriotism, not wholly unexpected since the leaders who'd sent so many thousands to die in Vietnam had later reduced troop levels to a point which assured those lives were needlessly wasted. On the other hand, the Redford's guests were in a celebratory mood, festooned in costumes, responding to an invitation to "Celebrate the Best of America!"

Tolo and Alexie sat on the beach holding hands and enjoying the antics of the children scampering nearby, looking forward to having a child of their own soon. Alexie's day had been unpleasantly interrupted when she'd spotted a certain Captain America who eerily reminded her of Nathaniel. She was greatly relieved when her mother assured her he couldn't be her brother—too tall and well-built—and besides, nothing could be more improbable. Alexie was thrilled Gail had come to the party. She'd wanted her to feel the support of a large, extended family, and to begin enjoying life again.

Adie and Hal watched their daughters run around wildly with the other children. Her eldest was being bossy and aggressive, and Adie had to remind herself to enjoy this phase, too. Soon she'd be trying to capture the boys' attention rather than competing with them. Adie was also pleased her sister-in-law had been included. Gail and Rose were both fine women and generous supporters of her foundation, and she thought they could easily become good friends. She also hoped Gail would begin dating, thinking she'd finally overcome the memory of her lost love, Six. She'd tried to help by introducing her to two widowers from Northwestern that very evening, and Gail seemed vibrant and receptive. If she were to meet the right man at the party it would truly be a night to remember.

Reclining on a lawn chair near friends, Rose tweaked John's hand so he'd look over and she'd smile back to share the night's success. Perhaps the crowd had been a bit large, but she'd enjoyed meeting the newcomers and had been delighted with the costumes. Her children had made her proud, too, so helpful and mature. Abe and Rachel were especially cute. She'd watched them sneak off and it reminded her of when she and John wanted northing more than to be alone together; now, they were content to sit quietly on the bluff relaxing after the guests left, toasting their day. In the back of her mind, she'd been worried Gail would try to flirt with John—she was still so very attractive! *Silly me,* she mused, *Gail couldn't have been more appropriate. She spent almost all of the evening with her daughter and brother.*

John knew what happened when explosives were carried to an extreme, and he'd never cared for the holiday fireworks after Trinity. He only tolerated them now because they delighted the children. He'd seen Abe and Rachel sneak away and understood why, but he wondered if Abe also disliked explosives after his experience in Vietnam. He'd agreed to the costumes to please Rose, but they made it difficult to recognize guests and he secretly hated the idea. He took off his coat, hat, and wig as soon as they'd left the stage. After being someone else for so long, pretending to be another person wasn't his idea of a good time. He'd visited with Tolo and Gail and been pleased she seemed so at ease, as if his "resurrection" hadn't troubled her at all. He admired her resilience and strength. Still, she seemed to have had enough, since he saw her heading toward the exit about the time the fireworks began.

Every mother knows her child, but Gail pretended otherwise when she immediately recognized the strutting Captain America. His size was just like Daniel at the same age, but the real giveaway had been the oddly characteristic, arrogant upward cock of his head as he moved it stiffly from side to side while looking about. Gail couldn't imagine why he was there. The only connection she could think of was through Daniel's role in the CIA and its cover up of Six's abuse, *maybe some sort of concern that John might expose them someday?* But while she couldn't wrap her mind around the confusing pieces, neither could she imagine his presence was random or harmless. She intended to find out why he was there, but instinctively knew she had to keep Alexie out of it. "You're imagining things," she'd told her with false assurance when she'd spotted him. "This guy's too tall and stocky, don't think twice about it."

After the fireworks began, Gail left "to visit the loo" and circled the tent looking for her son. She saw him leaning against a tree with his cap and goggles off, dispelling any lingering doubt as to his identity. She made her way up behind him and tapped his shoulder. When he spun around and she looked into his face for the first time in ten years, she was alarmed. His eyelids were dark and swollen and his expression odd and a bit crazed, *like a drug addict,* she thought immediately. He looked surprised at first, but quickly his eyes came aglow with a wild intensity and hatred, a look she'd last seen on his own father's face just before he'd raped her in New Mexico. She started to question him, but instead of answering he knocked her unconscious.

After stashing his mother under a bush, Nathaniel rushed toward the house. His thoughts were mush on a plate, muddled and struggling for form, and churning in multiple directions. Before reaching the rear yard, he made two firm decisions: first, mother or not, she had to die. He should have killed her immediately since she'd otherwise finger him for the crimes—he'd been too surprised to think clearly; secondly, he needed to sit down and relax for a few minutes. He desperately needed another, larger hit of coke to pull this thing off. The timing had to be masterful and he needed to perform at his best to keep it all from unravelling. *She is such a bitch, adding to my problems again tonight like always. What in the hell is she doing here?*

The dimly lit rear yard remained quiet. Lanterns atop the pagoda outlined its tiered roofs and highlighted the dragon figures on the ends of the tanuki in an eerie light. Red and White signaled to Stegger and he went to where they waited, keyed-up and anxious. The fireworks would end in fifteen minutes and they had to be ready to move quickly. Captain America gestured they should stay put. "Look, Mister S," said Red, "I think you've had enough of that shit already, so . . . "

"Motherfucker, don't tell me!" hissed Stegger. "All *you* need to do is get the brats up here and I'll be ready to go. I've got the lay of the land and the players. I just need a few minutes to pull my thoughts together. Meanwhile, don't forget who's the brains running and bankrolling this mission!"

His men retreated into the cellar to retrieve the captives and Stegger raced to the pagoda. He knelt down inside its open center, racked three rails of cocaine on the teak bench, and snorted each in turn through a rolled up bank note. More juice than usual, but confronting his mother had left him with a pounding headache that needed squelching, and he reckoned the dose would let him peak about the time they shoved off in the dinghy. He sat down on the bench and rocked from side to side, feeling mellow. Too soon he felt Red shaking him, but he put his brain into overdrive. "Fuckin A, it's time to rock and roll!"

As Stegger snorted his dope, Rachel traced her fingertips across Abe's lips up in a second floor bedroom. Their rush into the house had ended with an intense and short but satisfying romp after which he promptly fell asleep. She planned to tease him about it in the morning by telling him Wonder Woman had been prepared for a marathon. But she needed to return to her own room for the night. She didn't feel comfortable confirming what she knew everyone already suspected of the two lovers.

Rachel slipped from the bed and cloaked herself in his ample robe. She inhaled his familiar scent and luxuriated in the afterglow, enjoying the surprising turn of her life. She'd once believed sex and marriage and all that entailed too trivial, too common, and too distracting for her calling. But she'd been overwhelmed by her feelings as they worked together, and her sensual awakening craved expression. Against her preconceptions, their lovemaking had energized her, actually making her feel even more capable of assisting others.

Looking out Abe's window, Rachel saw that the caterers were gone and the fireworks had ended, and the crowd had begun filtering toward the gate. She walked down the hall toward her guest room at the rear of the home, and turned out of habit to glance outside at John's Dragon Pagoda. The pagoda moved her, especially when seen at night. Many others thought it hopelessly eccentric and out of place, but Rachel considered it a marvelous idea and knew how much it meant to John.

Although it was only thirty years after World War Two, Rachel had always felt she understood too little of it. She'd been taught largely perfunctory matters in school, such as dates, battles, and strategies, making it seem like some alien historical period rather than part of a continuum integral to the lives of many she knew so well, like her mother, her sister Adie, and John. As a psychologist, Rachel believed that a conflict's significance was best understood by examining the root causes, those often difficult choices made between good and evil which are obscured at the time by pride, love, justice, patriotism, self-interest, or any number of emotions clouding sound judgment. Yet such root causes had never been dissected for their war as part of any of her studies, even though the lessons learned might have prevented repetition of similar mistakes by following generations.

Katya and John developed a close friendship soon after meeting, even before their children's engagement, largely because they shared similar views. John didn't generally care to discuss his work on Manhattan or his role in the bombing of Hiroshima, and Katya was reluctant to provide details of her time in wartime Europe. But despite vastly different experiences, they appeared linked in some way by their participation and they spoke easily of those times to each other. Overhearing their discussions, Rachel gained valuable insight.

Katya spoke of her husband seeking security and comfort, of being a well-motivated provider for his family, but so blinded by his goals that his tolerance became a tacit approval overcoming all his good intentions. For herself, she questioned why she'd remained so restrained and inactive until provoked by the horrific slaughter of innocents in the Aktion program. It raised the haunting question of how many lives she might have saved otherwise.

John spoke of sacrifices he had made to benefit the collective good while being uncharacteristically naïve about the deceptive ways of powerful men. He regretted not understanding that so many others would remain passive and fail to see the impact of the use of the bomb. Now it seemed painfully evident that the calculated infliction of terrible suffering and death on the Japanese had set a precedent for future use of the weapon against those it had supposedly defended—you could win a war but squander all of humanity's promise by unleashing a weapon developed under the guise of noble service, but capable of destroying all life. Still, John expressed his belief that reckless and powerful men were best countered by acts of marginal defiance, like his pagoda, until lulled into complacency as public consensus built up to ultimately counter their excesses.

Katya had responded candidly. "John, my country's calamity was guaranteed when well-intentioned men relied on essentially passive opposition. I'd have hoped America would have learned from our mistakes—passivity is inadequate when opposing unprincipled men who are willing to use any methods, including altering laws, to attain their ends. Mankind has a long way to go before it begins following its angels."

Looking outside, Rachel spotted someone standing in the pagoda. Then she saw a caterer and a man costumed as a colonial soldier lead two smaller figures toward it. The two were moving very slowly and appeared tethered together with rope. One was dressed as a red, white, and blue cheerleader, in costumes much like those Mary and her friends wore, and the other was unmistakably Lizzy or Timmy, wearing the wings of a bald eagle. Her first thought was that the kids were playing some sort of a game, maybe after illicit drinking, since they were having such a hard time walking. But as they approached the pagoda, the cheerleader fell and the soldier yanked her to her feet by the hair. Realizing it was no game, Rachel raced down the hallway toward the stairs leading to the deck. Something was very wrong and she had no time to lose.

Rose and John were standing atop the bluff, saying goodbye to guests as they came up from the beach. As Rose thanked a friend for coming, two of her childrens' schoolmates stood by patiently waiting to ask if she'd seen either Lizzy or Mary.

"Weren't they on the beach with you?"

They hadn't been, and she knew they weren't the type to just wander away. "Don't worry, Rose," said John, "They probably ran to the house for something or hooked up with some other friends. I'll check it out."

After the grand finale, Blue scaled the rocks from the adjacent property and concealed himself in the woods. From his vantage point, he watched John leave Rose's side and head towards the tent, creating a perfect opportunity. Most of the guests were already approaching the gate, so if the others came along soon enough they could snatch the old lady and be at the boat in half a minute. He looked down the path toward the home, but instead of seeing a signal, he saw a woman dressed like a Bobby Soxer staggering along as if drunk, lurching forward a few feet at a time, then stopping periodically to rest against trees. As she passed nearby, he saw she was injured, but knew she hadn't been one of their targets.

After passing Blue, the woman turned toward the top of the bluff, along the same route he'd planned on using to get to Rose Redford. He had no idea who she was, but her timing was lousy. He began edging toward the rocks, knowing he could get to the dinghy quickly if need be. No way would he stick around if he risked being caught. He wasn't going to chance dying an old man in prison, not for all the money in the world .

Rose saw a figure staggering toward her from near the porta pots and shook her head in disgust. She could only recall one other time when someone had gotten so loaded at their party. They didn't serve hard liquor, and she wondered if the woman had brought her own flask along. "Oh, oh, my God," she exclaimed as she realized it was Gail. Running to her, she saw that the left side of her neck was purple and bruised and so swollen it pushed her head downward against her right shoulder. Her eyes darted about, but she was too dazed to speak.

Rose led her to her nearby lawn chair while a friend ran to call an ambulance. They made Gail as comfortable as possible, mopping her brow, applying ice to her neck, and giving her Seven-Up to drink as they waited for her to tell them what had happened. Then they heard a series of explosive bursts from somewhere near the house.

They didn't recognize the noises, but they didn't sound at all like firecrackers.

Blue heard the unmistakable sound of gunfire and immediately headed toward the rocks and scrambled down to the dinghy. *I'm out of here*, he thought.

John heard the distinct sound and dropped the beer he'd been drinking while enjoying a joke with a friend. He dashed from the tent, thinking, *Good God, there's gunfire in our backyard!*

Not long before the gunfire began, a maniacal, uncapped Captain America stood at the edge of the center of John's Dragon Pagoda, instructing Red and White who faced him with their backs to the house. Each held an end of an eight-foot long length of rope securing two gagged and lethargic Redford children. They wobbled in place, struggling to retain their balance. "Red, you hustle down the path and when you're past the garage signal Blue. But before you reach him, just west of the shitters, you'll see a single large weeping hemlock—you can't miss it, it's overgrowing the path. There's an unconscious lady under the bush in a red wig, wearing tennis shoes. You need to off her. Just snap her neck before you hook up with Blue. We'll be coming up behind you and . . . "

"Whoa, Mr. S, who is this lady?"

"Just some bitch that could present a problem, okay? It doesn't matter who she is, but I guarantee you don't know her . . . and look, I'll add another fifty large for your trouble, all right?"

There weren't many hits worth fifty k, so Red nodded in agreement. He thought, *in for a dime, in for a dollar.*

"We'll get the brats out to the boat soon enough even if we have to shoulder them. Keep an eye on old lady Redford. She'll most likely be hanging out on the bluff. When we get there you'll take the load to the dinghy with Blue while I-I . . . " He stuttered as his headache returned. *What the hell was I saying?* he wondered.

The three men were suddenly startled by the sound of a door banging against its frame. They froze in place and looked across the lawn toward the home where a long-haired woman was walking out to the center of the deck. She stopped and stood in place, sixty yards away, and stared out at them. She didn't appear to be a threat. She looked to be alone and was wearing only a bathrobe. "Stay here," said Stegger, stepping down from the pagoda and moving in front of the others. Colt revolver drawn and held behind his back, he started walking toward her while calling out, "Hi, how's it going?"

"Bring the children to me," the woman called back in a calm, flat voice in a matter-of-fact tone.

"There's no problem here," Stegger shouted as he began moving more quickly. "We're just . . . "

"Stop!" bellowed Rachel, in a voice so powerful and unexpected that it froze Stegger in place, leaving him wondering how she could have produced such a potent utterance. Then, adding to his amazement, she yanked her robe open, and clutching each side, she pulled upward until her outstretched arms and outline formed a shape like the letter V.

Stegger gaped at her, trying to make sense of it. *It's only one woman doing God knows what. Surely I only need to convince her . . .* Then he thought, *No, I'm wrong. It's much more than that.* It seemed to him that her robe fell off her shoulders and hung beneath her bare breasts, somehow held in place while encircling the lower half of her body like a flowing gown. *It makes no sense, and, what the hell, she seems to be holding a rifle of sorts, like an old-fashioned musket, in her left hand while her right arm is stretched out upward holding a goddamned flag, as if she's leading a fricken charge!* And he saw she wasn't alone anymore, at least three others stood aside her, all of them looking out toward him with angry expressions, and the deck she'd been standing on had somehow vanished and been replaced by a pile of corpses! It all looked so odd and out of place, yet at the same time it seemed somehow vaguely familiar.

Red and White implored Stegger to rush her. They saw only a woman standing alone on the deck, a woman inexplicably holding her robe wide open and exposing her naked body as if making room for something, *like maybe she thinks she's going to sprout fucking wings,* thought Red. He figured she had to be drunk, and regardless, she posed no serious threat. They just needed to take her out quickly.

Stegger shook his head, trying to clear it. He blinked his eyes repeatedly and struck his head with his hand. He tried in vain to dispel the fog that had settled in his mind and get a grip. But Red and White kept talking to each other, distracting him, saying things he barely heard and couldn't quite understand, except something like he should handle her and stop wasting time. *Why don't they just shut the fuck up so I can concentrate and think this through? Why are they chattering away and staring at me rather than her and her entourage? They're really pissing me off! Don't they understand this isn't handled so easily?*

Red dropped the rope. He came up to Stegger and repeatedly snapped his fingers in front of his face until Nathaniel started from his stupor and reacted by shouting, "Leave me alone and shut the hell up! I'm in control here."

"Fuck you," spat Red, "I've got this." He drew out his Colt and began jogging toward the woman.

Stegger thought that Red must be crazy running into all of that, but it also occurred to him that he might be confused. Maybe it all had to do with the costume thing and there wasn't that much to be concerned about, only a few guests they could take out easily before finishing their business. *Yeah, that has to be it. No woman here would be bare-breasted. It has to be some kind of a quirky costume.* Then he realized why it looked familiar: it looked like Lady Liberty in that French painting about leading the people. That made some sense to him, what with it being the Fourth of July and the lady dressed something like the one holding the torch for the Statue of Liberty and all.

He saw that the woman and her companions were moving ever closer toward them, flowing steadily forward almost as if carried along by a slow-moving stream. It became apparent, too, that the figures beside her weren't anything like those in the famous painting.

To the left of Lady Liberty, Stegger distinctly saw a lovely, full-figured, olive-skinned woman with thick, lustrous ebony hair and a sensuous and enticing mouth. She was holding a pistol in one hand and a knife in the other, and even from across the yard he could see her deep brown eyes boring into him. She was undoubtedly gorgeous and desirable, but at the same time aggressive and threatening, much more like a warrior charging into battle than an approaching goddess.

Behind the female warrior's right shoulder, he could make out a World War Two officer from the Nazi SS wearing a peaked cap with an eagle and swastika atop its crown. He held a Luger upright in his gloved hand and seemed to be staring him down with a look of disgust and disdain, if not outright hatred. Stegger may have been confused about a few things but he thought, *This guy's not wearing any costume you'd expect to see on the Fourth of July—he's a goddamned Sturmbannfuhrer!* The third figure made even less sense than the others: he was a large teenaged looking boy with a broad, nearly rectangular head and a lopsided smile spread across his entire face. *Retarded*, Stegger thought. The boy was holding his fists clenched tightly in front of him while jumping up and down alongside Lady Liberty, seemingly excited at the prospect of seeing him thrashed.

Perceiving imminent danger, Stegger assumed a firing crouch, kneeling and holding his pistol in his outstretched hands, aiming directly at the threat. He fired at least six rounds at Lady Liberty when she entered his range of deadly accuracy. Immediately after he stopped shooting, he heard a deafening noise behind him. He turned and looked back at White. Seeing what happened to him then, he felt bone-chilling fear for the first time in his entire life, felt he was being judged and about to be condemned for the kidnapping, and more, for everything he'd become since childhood. Panicking and forgetting all about their plan, he dropped his gun and raced off alone toward the pathway.

When Stegger's shots exploded, echoing off the inside of the pagoda, the children fell to the ground, terrified. White had been standing in place just underneath the outside edge of the pagoda roof, open-mouthed, stunned, and in disbelief as to what he saw. His stupor was short-lived, however, disrupted by the keen and distinctive sound of timber splintering above him, and he looked up toward the pagoda just in time to meet his destiny.

As John Redford ran as fast as he could toward his backyard, Nathaniel Stegger dashed from the opposite side of the home toward the lake. Stegger couldn't have said exactly how he felt at the time, but fear, anger, disgust and surprise all coursed through his confused mind. A sense of abject failure would also have been near the top of the list. Blowing the plan to avenge his idol was all the more devastating for a man who'd never failed at anything he'd ever attempted.

By the time he reached the porta pots, Stegger knew there was no hope of escape. His mother wasn't where he'd left her, and Blue had likely heard the gunfire and fled to save himself. For an instant, Stegger thought he might do the same, scramble down to the beach, swim a little ways, emerge somewhere safe and hide away. But even while considering it, he realized it was only wishful thinking. After his mother identified him he could never return to his old life, and it wasn't in his nature to be a fugitive hiding away somewhere off in the boondocks. He'd rather go out his own way, with a bang, doing something memorable, like offing the bitch. *I can still break that bastard's heart.*

He was in luck. Rose remained atop the bluff with a few other women. He took a few deep, calming breaths, pulled himself together as best he could, and ran a hand through his hair. Wearing his brightest smile, he jogged out of the woods, waving like an overjoyed, approaching friend. "I've got good news, ladies!" he shouted as they all turned expectantly toward him.

———

In the early morning hours of July 5, 1971, the Redford home was awash in artificial light of daytime proportions as responders from local police, the Lake County Sheriff's Department and the State of Illinois swarmed through the grounds, compiling evidence as they tried to piece together the unprecedented violence visited upon their community. The FBI would become involved and play a significant role in the investigation, and after one additional death, relying upon forensic evidence and the statements of key, reputable witnesses and two unchallengeable agents, they would release official findings concluding justice had been served, and a kidnapping attempt gone wrong had confirmed the old adage that crime doesn't pay.

Former government employee Frederick Mauser, dressed as a colonial soldier, had died instantly when shot in the back of the head while running with a pistol in hand toward psychologist Rachel Hoffman, who was crossing the rear yard of the Redford home in an attempt to rescue Lizzy and Mary Redford.

Former government employee Alfred Morrison, wearing the white uniform of a caterer, died within minutes of Mauser after three sharp talons from the paw of a decorative dragon on a backyard pagoda pierced his forehead and face as he looked upward toward the sound of a beam breaking. Experts concluded that a recent lightning strike combined with reverberating gunfire to splinter the wooden timber supporting the dragon as he stood beneath it, even as he held a rope securing the children he was attempting to kidnap.

A month later, former government employee Richard Oleniewski died from a gunshot wound to the back of the head inflicted by an FBI agent attempting to arrest him. He died at his home in Falls Church, Virginia, having been tracked down from a boat on Lake Michigan to a warehouse in North Chicago, Illinois, to stays in

Indianapolis and Columbus, and finally to his home in the Washington D.C. suburb.

Statements from key witnesses detailed the final violent acts of the late evening: "This man dressed like Captain America came out of the woods waving and shouting that he had good news. We'd been worried because we didn't know where the girls were, Gail appeared drugged and injured, and we'd heard explosions near the house. I didn't recognize him, but I guessed him to be in his thirties and remember thinking he must have been good-looking once, but his face was drawn and haggard with dark circles under his eyes. He was shaking and agitated. He said something very rapidly, like 'They're fine. Don't worry, they're really, really fine.' I asked, 'What happened?' He tried to say more but he stumbled over his words and began shaking and I realized something was very wrong with him.

I backed away, but he grabbed my arm and then my neck and he dragged me toward the rocks. I screamed and pounded my fists against him, but he barely seemed to notice. My friend, Lynn Wedell, screamed and started kicking at him, but he backhanded her while we were struggling and easily knocked her to the ground. I tried kicking him between the legs, but I lost my balance and fell down hard against a boulder, knocking the wind out of me.

Gail was on her feet by then, and she stood six or seven feet away, resting her hands on her hips and taking deep breaths. He stared at her with a stange, confused look and I thought he might be having second thoughts, but I was just being hopeful. She said his name,

'Nathaniel,' then 'Nate,' in a mournful way, and then I realized it was her estranged son. He stood there a moment, panting for breath, then he let out a bizarre, high-pitched wail that sounded like a wounded animal. His demeanor changed immediately after that and he drew himself up, pointed at Gail and said, 'You're next, bitch.' I remember thinking it was odd how her said it, not at all in a threatening tone, just like stating a matter of plain fact.

My throat hurt and I couldn't shout so I didn't call for help. But I heard people shouting nearby and knew help would arrive soon if I could hold on long enough.

He yanked me off the ground, said something to Gail that sounded like 'lover boy,' then tried putting his arm around my neck while pushing his hip into me, like he wanted flip me down onto the rocks or break my neck, I don't know which. But I knew he meant business and I fought as hard as I could. I thrashed about with my upper body and arms and kept moving my head away, all the while kicking at his legs, trying to make him let go. Somehow he got his hands tangled up in the shawl and head wrap of my costume and he began cursing, spitting out one vile word after another. When he managed to untangle his hands, he grabbed my blouse and held me at arm's length, straightening up, arching his back and raising his fist to hit me. I shut my eyes and started turning away to deflect the expected blow, but it never fell. The next thing I knew, both he and the front of my blouse were gone."

Lynn Wedell continued the story. "I was on the ground, next to where Gail had been sitting. I was crying from pain because I tore up my knee when he threw me down and couldn't stand at all. I saw he'd thrown Rose down, too. I saw him standing over her, just where the erosion rocks begin, trying to catch his breath. He was staring at Gail who'd moved closer to him. She said something I didn't hear and he paused as if considering her words. I could see a wildness in his eyes, and I heard him spit out the word 'bitch.' He looked back and forth from Rose to Gail, like deciding who to attack first. Then he gave out this freakish scream and a moment later he grabbed Rose.

She fought back and it looked like they were wrestling, with him trying to get ahold of her head and her kicking and striking back while moving her body frantically, fighting for her life. It was chaotic and it happened very quickly, but somehow it all seemed to suddenly slow down. I can't explain it, but I remember it happening like in slow motion. First they were tangled together, then he backed away from her, holding her by her blouse with one hand while raising the other, and at the same time I heard shouts behind me and knew help was at hand. I could see he was straining to put all his might into the blow and thought it alone would kill her, Gail and I would be saved, but help would come too late for Rose.

I thought Gail could hardly walk, and when she moved so swiftly it took me by surprise. It obviously surprised him too."

As her personal fog lifted, Gail recognized that her bad seed son had reemerged and the condescending, abusive words of an unpleasant teenager had been just a vile beginning, the first glimpse of an inner self now comfortably, almost casually exploding in words and blows of mortal intent. How and why didn't matter, nor would she spend another moment of her life wondering what she might have done to save him. A guilt trip wouldn't consume her, had become far beside the point. Her ultimate judgment would depend on how she responded, with no points for recrimination. God only knew what other harm he'd caused, but he surely intended to kill Rose, the competitor who'd accepted her in a way she never could have. Rose had already suffered because of Daniel's cruelty, and she deserved more, was a more worthy woman then her. Having given birth to Nathaniel, it now seemed it was also her responsibility to dispatch the animal he'd become.

She watched him as he grabbed Rose and fought with her atop the pile of glacial rocks forming the steep erosion barrier of the bluff. She waited for the precise moment. The drug had run its course and her mind was clear. She'd stumbled and continued acting listlessly to lull him, and then she managed to move within reach. She was strong, athletic, crouched and coiled, and she steeled her will. She had her tennis shoes on and thought of it like charging the net and slamming an overhead down the line.

The two struggling figures separated just enough, and Gail sprang forward with two quick steps, placing her left foot on the cleft in the top rock of the erosion barrier, and launching herself at Nathaniel with all her might. He turned toward her just as the linked fists at the end of her outstretched arms reached his chin. The force of their collision snapped his head backwards and he lost his footing. His grip on the flimsy front of Rose Redford's costume blouse tore a portion of it away, and it remained clutched in his hand as he tumbled twenty feet down the rocks. It didn't matter, so afterwards authorities never bothered to determine precisely which of the three rocks his head struck on his final short trip caused his brain-splattered death.

Gail's momentum made her bounce off of one boulder and strike two more, cracking vertebrae, fracturing her skull at its base and rupturing meninges tissue. Her survival appeared unlikely; still, rescue workers concerned with the risk of spinal nerve injury stabilized her as well as possible and called for additional help before attempting to extract her from the position in which she was wedged, between the massive boulders of the erosion barrier, rocks which had been carried into Lake Michigan eleven thousand years earlier, in the last throes of the North American Ice Age, at the very same time that Azume's forebears located their permanent home near a mountain named Amar.

Scrambling down to Gail, John was wracked with guilt over her frightful injuries, acutely aware of how much she'd endured in her life, and how much of it was due to him. "Gail . . . Abby, I-I, oh God."

She struggled to respond and he leaned over, ear close to her lips. All nearby were still, the deathly quiet broken only by approaching sirens and sobbing, all sorrowful and in disbelief. "I'm sorry . . . Rose almost . . . " she tried to say. He told her she had nothing to be sorry for, she was wonderful and brave and heroic. She'd been God's gift, Rose's savior. He said everyone had survived because of her and the bad guys were all . . . accounted for. He assured her that yes, of course, he'd always be there for Alexie and Tolo, be as much a father to them as she'd been a wonderful mother, but she shouldn't think that way, everything would be fine. Of course she would be in his prayers, always in his prayers, and forever in his heart, always lovingly in his heart. She needed to know that she'd encouraged him, had helped him be the best man he could ever hope to be.

Abigail Marshall Stegger felt the depth of his love and thought to die contentedly. She'd accomplished all she could with the cards dealt her, knew she'd remain in the hearts of those who mattered and she wouldn't be leaving any evil remnant behind. It wasn't the way of things to receive all one desired in life, and there was purpose in that. Her daughter wouldn't have been born had her life unfolded as she'd wanted, and Alexie's promise far eclipsed all of her heartaches. Her destiny had been fulfilled by raising such a child, and by acting selflessly to atone for some evil, perhaps to be worthy of finding greater love and fulfillment in another time, with a man such as Six had been for her on the very best night of her life.

Gail's paralysis added to John's torment, making him weep despite his attempt to remain strong for her sake. In comforting her, broken and paralyzed in his arms, he felt transported to his earliest beginnings. He wept and grieved for Abby to be sure, but he grieved for Azume as well, another woman he'd loved and comforted after she'd been broken in her own fateful fall off the slopes of Amar before he took her life in a time long before.

18.

Cosmic Justice

Lake Forest, Illinois, 1971

The media had a feeding frenzy covering the tragedy in Lake Forest, pursuing every detail and rumor, intrigued by the setting, the costumes, and the idea a mother would kill her son to protect a relative stranger. The story produced headlines ranging from "Night of Horror and Mystery" and "Mother Kills Crazed Child" to "Unexpected Fireworks." In a bizarre twist for even a gossip rag, *The Enquirer* attributed blame to the event itself, insinuating that tragedy should be expected when rich people party lavishly. The worst coverage came after excerpts from Rachel's statement were leaked, generating crude jokes about her body and prompting the headline "Nude Shrink Scares Kidnappers!"

Abe reacted ferociously, but Rachel disregarded the frenzy. She'd accounted herself well and given an accurate rendition of events, beyond that she didn't care what others might think. As she recounted while first being questioned by the authorities: "I was going to my room when I looked outside and saw the children were in trouble, so I raced down the stairs, threw open the door, and ran onto the deck. I couldn't tell exactly what was happening, but the idea of it being a kidnapping never occured to me . . . There wasn't time to wake Abe, look for a weapon, or call for assistance. The need appeared too urgent.

I could see the children were being led to the pagoda, but the captors were too far away to . . . Obviously you've measured the distance, why should I guess how far away? . . . My eyesight is perfectly normal, thank you. From their body language I could tell that the man dressed like Captain America was the leader. I was considering what to do when he came down from the pagoda and yelled out, 'Hi, how's it going,' in an attempt to project friendliness and ease my concerns as he began moving toward me . . . He saw me run onto the deck so my concern must have been apparent, don't you think?

I considered how to best handle the situation and knew that without a weapon my choices were limited. I had only the element of surprise and my authority to utilize.

I shouted out, 'Bring the children to me' knowing . . . I used those specific words because he needed to understand I intended to address the fundamental issue. Then I bellowed, 'stop,' which apparently worked since he halted in place to assess the threat, and the others also froze . . . No, I didn't hear him tell them to wait, but they were evidently following his lead.

Look, officer, this will go much better if you just let me tell my story through without interrupting me with these obtuse questions. You're recording this, so when we finish you can review it, discuss it with whomever you like, and I'll answer your follow-up questions, all right? . . . Thanks.

I knew the leader would surely be stronger than me and likely armed and I realized all I had to confront him with was my body—most men are startled by the unexpected sight of a naked woman—and I'm aware too that animals attempt to appear larger to be more intimidating to their challengers. So, I held my robe open, extending it out and upward to make myself seem as large as possible. After about thirty seconds of that, I stepped off the deck and began walking toward them at a steady but unhurried pace, as if out for a casual stroll while showing off my figure. It disoriented them for a time, but soon the man dressed as a colonial lifted his gun in the air and began running toward me.

He closed to within forty feet, but I kept staring at him as if unimpressed by his threat. Suddenly, he stopped running, dropped his shoulders in a gesture, in something like confusion or disbelief, and lowered his gun. I was about to tell him to give it up when he gestured with his palms held upward as if asking, 'What's going on?' Before I could respond, I heard the sound of a gunshot, the top of his head exploded out toward me, and he collapsed in a heap.

It was disturbing, but I didn't pause or react to it in any noticeable way. I just continued moving toward the pagoda, passing his body by, as if his death wasn't worth noting. By then, Stegger had lowered himself into a shooter's crouch and was holding his gun in both hands aimed directly at me. When I closed to within about thirty feet, I heard his gunshots echo off the pagoda and throughout the yard, and I heard bullets whizzing past me, but I didn't flinch or hesitate. I just continued moving toward the children.

After his shooting stopped, I glanced up at a dragon on the pagoda roof just as I heard the sound of wood splitting. Then its support gave way and the dragon smashed down on the third man's head. It seems a bit strange thinking about it now, but as the dragon started to fall down on him, I felt a real surge of relief, felt certain, somehow, that the children would be safe.

I passed within ten feet of Stegger, who only stared back at me with a wide-eyed and puzzled look. I saw him drop his gun and run off, but he never said another word. I hurried to the children and comforted them until John rushed up to us. Really, that's all there is to tell."

Forensics tests established that six rounds had been fired from Stegger's pistol, but only three could be accounted for, two found embedded in the home and the one which killed "Red."

John believed there was more to the story than Rachel revealed, but she shrugged when he asked, saying only, that "God works in mysterious ways."

Rachel knew more than she divulged. While she had abundant self-confidence, she knew few criminals would be stopped for long merely by the sight of a nude woman. Yet, she always believed righteousness could overcome evil if sincerely summoned and focused. She wasn't certain if prayers were answered, but found prayer to be a useful psychological tool; indeed, she believed it had helped her overcome her youthful misgivings over being the daughter of a Nazi, as well as her recent concerns about falling in love with a younger man who was her patient. Still, the episode near the pagoda hadn't been comparable to a subtle response to prayer. It seemed rather, a spontaneous and miraculous response to an evil threat.

As she'd stepped from the deck, Rachel had felt invincible, as if by choosing to directly confront the evil of Stegger, she'd summoned the force of righteousness, unmatched power compiled throughout time by the efforts of many others who'd lived before and nurtured virtue. Some such others seemed almost to be standing alongside her, aroused and infuriated by Stegger's evil presence and lending their support in the classic confrontation. So, if Rachel had answered John's question completely, she'd have said that in attempting to rescue the children, she'd wielded such power that she'd known Red and White would perish and Stegger would flee in terror. In full candor, she might also have admitted willing the dragon to fall and sink its talons into White. Precisely how it all occurred didn't concern her. It only mattered that she'd been an effective instrument in confronting and overcoming evil.

As the ambulance sped to the hospital, Gail began to seize as her brain swelled from the head injury. The physicians at Northwestern Medical Center felt her condition warranted inducing a coma to reduce inflammation and to facilitate the surgery needed to remove bone fragments from her spinal canal and to repair her vertebrae.

Alexie, Hal, Tolo, and Adie rotated visitations at her bedside so Gail was never left alone. But no one spent more time with her throughout her first three critical weeks than Rachel. Knowing Gail had risked her life to save Rose, Rachel considered it her duty to save Gail. She sat by her side, whispering encouragement, praying for her, and likewise encouraging everyone else who came into her presence, doing everything possible to generate a positive uplifting force. As she had when confronting Stegger, she again called upon virtue to save Gail.

Against the physicians's expectations, Gail was easily weaned from her coma and her brain adjusted, allowing her to regain of all her preexisting mental acuity. It also turned out that her paralysis was temporary, caused by compression of the spinal cord rather than by severing. After a period of physical therapy, Gail would be able to walk as well as before the incident.

The investigation proceeded apace throughout her treatment and recovery, and the incident seemed easily resolved as an attempted kidnapping of the children of a wealthy man orchestrated by a druggie working with greedy others known from their mutual government service. Stegger had recently liquidated his business interests and withdrawn a staggering amount of money from his many accounts, yet the proceeds couldn't be located except for sums wired to his partners in the crime. Authorities speculated he'd become cash-poor despite owning various homes and other hard assets of great value due to his drug addiction. The cocaine scattered throughout his numerous homes plausibly explained his deterioration, his resignation as Senate counsel, the missing money and the warped thought process leading to the crime.

Gail and Alexie tried to understand why Nathaniel had chosen the Redfords as his target, since neither believed it was random. When Alexie recounted her last conversation with Nathaniel, she remembered he'd said, "I know what he did to the bastard she screwed in New Mexico and believe me it wasn't pretty," and they realized it squared with the adultery charge Nathaniel had leveled against Gail many years earlier. Without a hint of truth, Daniel had somehow misled Nathaniel into believing she'd had an affair with John and he'd been targeted for revenge. Gail couldn't help but think that what had happened to Daniel Stegger hadn't been pretty either, so she decided to revisit his murder investigation and to see if it led where she feared it might.

John visited Gail in the hospital one week after she emerged from her coma. He expressed all the gratitude, sympathy, and regrets she anticipated, kissed her on the forehead in parting, and turned to leave when she called out, "Jack?"

He stopped with his back to her before turning around very slowly. "Yes, Gail?"

"They called you 'Jack' in Los Alamos, didn't they?"

"I guess they did."

"You knew Daniel there, didn't you?"

"Yes."

"He hated you, didn't he?"

"Yes, I believe he did."

"Did he refer to you as 'Asshole Jack'?"

"I wouldn't be at all surprised."

"Was Daniel involved in the abuse that caused your amnesia?"

John didn't respond.

"I read the description of the suspect who'd been trying to locate him in Colorado, the suspect posing as a lawyer from Washington state. It sounded like the witness might have been describing you, with a cleft chin, thick sandy hair and eyebrows, hazel eyes, the right height and all. Was she describing you, John?"

He said nothing.

"Please, tell me you weren't in Colorado when Daniel was murdered. Please, be honest with me."

He paused, struggling with his choice of words. "I-I was there, Gail, I'll admit it. I confronted him and I even struck him out of anger. But when I left the house he was alive and not seriously injured, angry, but certainly not dead. He was a terrible human being, far more hateful than he'd been in New Mexico, but I didn't kill him. I couldn't have!"

"John, my God, how could a man like you . . . "

"Abby, I swear to God I didn't."

She didn't believe him. Everything added up otherwise: Ralph knew Daniel had been involved in causing Six's amnesia but he had never told her. Apparently he was covering for his brother who'd tracked Daniel down and killed him for revenge; bloodthirsty, sick, even if nearly justifiable. She'd never have known about it except for Nathaniel's vengeful attack. Somehow Nathaniel had learned that he'd killed his father and he'd come to Lake Forest seeking his own twisted revenge. The murder had been brutal and sacrilegious, and so unlike Six, but who could say what had been running through his confused mind then? "Oh, my God," was all she could say in response.

"Abby, I-I . . . "

"John . . . you need to leave. Please, just leave me alone . . . I'm having a hard time processing all of this . . . I need to think what I-I . . . should do."

The local police loved closed cases, and this one tidied up nicely. After cross checks, interviews, and a thorough analysis of the evidence at the scene, the warehouse, and the perpetrators' homes, they soon believed they understood all that had transpired. They knew there were loose ends, like Nathaniel's choice of victims, but they didn't need to look at that or anything else outside their jurisdiction.

The FBI also considered the crime solved, but their newest agent on the case, Whitman Wilcox, remained curious how Stegger chose his intended victims. The connection between Daniel and John Redford in Los Alamos fascinated him. Either it was one hell of a coincidence, or a key to the case. After reviewing the unsolved murder of Daniel Stegger, *My, oh my, the description fits*, and he too believed it likely Nathaniel had targeted Redford to avenge his father's murder.

He explained his theory and was sent to interview Redford again, but this time accompanied by one of the agents who'd killed Blue while arresting him in Virginia. By then, the D.C. office wanted to maintain full control over the direction of the Redford affair.

On October 16, 1971, Wilcox called John. "We have a few more questions to ask before wrapping things up. Will tomorrow work?"

John met the agents in his library. After some preliminary chit chat they went right to the heart of it. "John, we believe you had more than a passing acquaintance with Stegger in Los Alamos. We know the two of you delivered plutonium for the Trinity Test together, isn't that right?"

Within fifteen minutes of beginning the conversation, John made a decision he'd been mulling over ever since the fiasco on the Fourth. He'd thought long and hard about Katya's warnings of the risks of passivity, such as had existed in prewar Germany, and he'd begun to think himself cowardly by not confronting those responsible for causing so much heartache. *Besides,* he thought, *how could it get any worse? My family has already been attacked by what had to be the CIA, with four "former government employees" involved.*

The agent asked him, "Was there anything contentious in your relationship with Daniel Stegger? Anything that would help explain his son's interest in your family?"

John had cautiously answered similar questions before by saying "Not that I know of," but he decided the time had come to stop being passive. He asked the agents to wait and went into his office to retrieve the two files kept hidden in his safe.

Holding the files close to him like treasure, John laboriously parceled them out, page by page, retrieving and replacing each after it was read before offering another. "These will show you what Stegger, Frey, and the CIA did to me. Tell me if it's contentious enough for you."

After several private and whispered conversations with his colleague, the lead agent said, "This is astonishing, and these certainly look authentic. How did you get your hands on them?"

"For now, the real question is where it goes from here. I'm obviously at risk because I know what was done to me. Can you contain the CIA and prosecute them before they seek retribution?"

"Our job is to investigate federal crimes, and this is far more serious than most. It'll receive the full attention of the Bureau. Once our investigation begins, the perpetrators will stay far away from you and your family. They're not *that* dumb. This looks like proof of government misconduct at a very high level . . . I'm surprised you didn't report it sooner. Who else knows about this?"

"Only Ralph Peeters and my wife, Rose."

"My God, man, why haven't you reported it?"

"I've been fearful, afraid that if I shared these . . . "

"That all changes now! It'll take all of our resources to investigate this thoroughly, but fortunately no one is more capable. We'll log the evidence into our crime laboratory and verify its authenticity, involve the division dealing with governmental misconduct and gather all available supporting material. Once that's done, we'll coordinate prosecution with the Department of Justice. Believe me, if the CIA really did what this seems to prove, we'll use all our means to hold them accountable!"

"This is my only copy . . . I'd like to . . . "

"We need to follow protocol to preserve the chain of evidence, otherwise defense attorneys will be able to argue that the prosecution is tainted because we lost control of the originals. Don't worry, we'll log these files into our system, distribute copies to selected agents and the DOJ, and then return the complete set to you. Your copies will also contain our log in data and notes so that you and your attorney can follow . . . You have an attorney, right?"

"No, I haven't spoken with one yet."

"You need to involve one ASAP. He'll guide you through the legalese of the process and we'll be able to keep him in the loop. He'll be able to reassure you it's being handled expeditiously—most non-lawyers have difficulty understanding the timelines we have to work under. Let us know when he's on board and we'll give him copies as well, and fill him in on our efforts to find supporting evidence. Here's my card. It has my office and private numbers so you can reach me anytime, day or night. Don't hesitate to call.

We'll schedule a follow-up meeting for further questions as we move forward to nail these bastards. Believe me, you did the right thing bringing this to our attention. We can't root out government corruption without the help of people like you. Meanwhile, don't discuss this with anyone except your lawyer. Leaks could lead to the destruction of supporting evidence."

John paused, apparently deep in thought, then he reluctantly handed his files over to the agent. He was reassured that no one had "more experience than the FBI in safeguarding such critical material."

———

As Nathaniel Stegger and Brad Frey had feared, the unpopularity of Vietnam and the political pressure put on President Nixon resulted in unprecedented heat on the CIA. The Congress requested all documents related to Chatter and MKULTRA, and learned that the CIA Director had ordered all files related to those projects destroyed. His order included files in the custody of friendly and aspiring accomplices at other agencies, including the FBI.

After more than a month passed without any word from the FBI, John retained counsel who called and wrote repeatedly, but never received a response. By the summer of 1972, it became clear the Bureau had no intention of responding or of returning copies of his files. They weren't investigating the CIA or working with the DOJ. So, once again, John found himself on the outside looking in. But determined not to remain a patsy, he hired bodyguards for his family and decided to launch his own attack.

John retained Walter J. Burroughs of Washington, D.C., a specialist at suing the government, who understood his family concerns and agreed to keep John's case as quiet as possible. Burroughs explained that as a sovereign entity the government couldn't be sued except by its consent, and it only consented to lawsuits based upon negligence. "So what you're saying is that if government employees *intended* to harm me, the government can't be held responsible. Is that right?"

"Exactly, you can only sue them if you were injured because they were reckless or careless; then again, you can always sue the employees themselves for their intentional misconduct."

"That would be difficult, seeing they're all dead."

"Admittedly, that's generally correct."

They filed claims against the CIA and the FBI, alleging that key employees had been "negligent in their supervision and control of other employees, in regards to the duty owed Jack Redford while in their custody, and in handling and processing evidence given up for investigation." The suit also alleged that he had not consented to being "treated" with experimental chemicals. When the claims were denied perfunctorily, they filed a lawsuit under the Federal Tort Claims Act in the District of Columbia. By agreement of the parties, the anticipated lawsuit would remain sealed until presented to a jury, to safeguard the sensitive national security information it included.

The government denied everything, and filed a staggering number of motions over the next two years, intent on having the case disposed of on technicalities, or delayed long enough for potential witnesses to die or until John ran out of money to pay his lawyers. But John's attorneys were aggressive and he remained stalwart, living day to day and putting the matter out of his mind while patiently awaiting the justice long denied him.

On August 5, 1975, the parties gathered in a conference room at the DOJ for the long delayed depositions of the FBI agents and Redford. The agents went first. Under oath and penalty of perjury, they all spouted a similar version of their meeting with John. Even young agent Wilcox had learned how the game was played.

"Yes, I remember the meeting with Professor Redford very well. We met in his library and told him our work was completed. We expressed our sympathy for what Nathaniel Stegger had attempted to do, and asked if there was anything he hadn't understood about the process or if we could be of further assistance. He said no, he was fine, pleased to move on and very thankful that Stegger's mother was recovering. He expressed his gratitude for our efforts.

Contrary to his claims in this lawsuit, he repeated that he'd had virtually no dealings with Daniel Stegger in Los Alamos and they had no feelings toward one another, let alone any conflict. He presumed he'd been targeted merely because of his wealth, possibly because Stegger's mother or sister had mentioned him or his annual party at some point, perhaps while James Jackson still worked for the family.

We have a duty to log in the evidence we receive on every potential case, and we take that responsibility very seriously. I have no idea why Redford made up his story, but he never told us of any files or materials related to alleged CIA misconduct. He never gave us the supposed files and we never said we'd contact him again unless he wanted help in some way. His account makes no sense. The idea that we would keep a complainant and his lawyer informed about an ongoing investigation is absurd. The letters his attorney sent demanding we return non-existent files were treated as self-serving nonsense. We never answer requests that don't deserve a response. As you can imagine, we receive many letters from deranged individuals, and I'm afraid I've come to question Professor Redford's mental competency.

I thought we left on very good terms. I remember telling him he'd been lucky and we were pleased for him. I also told him I didn't fully understand the pagoda he built in his yard, but I liked it!"

John's deposition followed. It was taken by a DOJ attorney named John L. Stern, who habitually asked unrelated questions in illogical sequence, trying to catch witnesses off guard. After eliciting his name, address, and personal data, Stern asked John if he'd been hospitalized for some time as a result of mental illness, treated at government expense, rehabilitated, and assisted in landing a "plum" position at Columbia.

John admitted it was all true.

Stern asked him to concede that the first time he filed a claim or told any third party about this "tale of abuse" was almost twenty-seven years after the alleged assault.

John admitted it was true.

Stern asked Redford if he was in Colorado on July 18, 1968.

John's attorney objected to the question as irrelevant and immaterial and outside the scope of discovery, and he directed his client not to answer. Stern said he'd raise the issue of his refusal to answer with the judge. Then he wound up to deliver a knockout blow. "Isn't it a fact, Professor Redford, that you don't have any documentary evidence, not a single writing or scrap of paper which in any way supports these wild and unfounded allegations of alleged mistreatment by government employees, Stegger and Frey, and God knows who else?"

"No, actually, that's not true."

"What?"

"It's not true. I have written proof."

"All right t-then, w-what do you have?"

"I have a duplicate copy of the files I gave to the FBI in my library on October 17, 1971."

"I t-thought you claimed the FBI destroyed them?"

"Yes, I believe they did, but I meant the originals. With my wife acting as a witness, I copied a complete set of the files the night before my interview with the FBI. You don't think I would be dumb enough to trust the government again, do you?"

"Professor, I-I . . . "

"I also wired my library to produce an audio recording of the agents's interview. Again, I did it with Rose's oversight, so I'd be sure to maintain the chain of evidence the agents claimed to be so concerned about. My attorney has the transcript. I think you'll want to compare it with the testimony your clients gave today, since my attorney will be making the same comparison for the court. I believe the appropriate term for their testimony is perjury."

Stern grabbed his files and shepherded his crew to the exit, "This deposition is over, counselor!"

A week later, John's attorney called Stern and delivered a settlement demand: ten million dollars and a personal apology from the President of the United States. By then the government attorney had recovered well enough to attempt to laugh at the demand and bluster in response.

"Burroughs, besides being a sandbagger you're quite the comedian! First of all, there's a daunting hearsay problem on the so-called CIA files, so no one can verify they're official records. Secondly, there's not an iota of collaborative evidence to support his claim. Thirdly, check out the *Feres* case. Even if these bullshit accusations are true, he was never discharged from the Air Corps, so it's a military matter, outside the scope of the Federal Tort Claims Act. Finally, on pretrial motions we'll knock the case out since we both know what you're really alleging is intentional misconduct, which isn't actionable."

"Stern, my client will pursue this if it takes a lifetime, and Church and the Senate will have no choice but to go after the Company after we withdraw from the confidentiality agreement and publish our story on the front page of the New York Times."

"We'll see how much credibility Redford has publishing it from prison, although he won't be there for long since Colorado has the death penalty. If he maintains his bullshit story, it provides a motive for killing Daniel Stegger."

"You can wipe your ass with motive without supporting evidence."

"I know, and that's why I feel so good about our position. See you in court!"

John had discussed the underlying dilemma thoroughly with his attorney, and he realized the files were a double-edged sword. They supported his claim, but also supplied a motive for Daniel's murder. He knew that, unlike Rose, a jury wouldn't give him the benefit of the doubt. If they proved he was at Stegger's the night he was murdered, he felt certain he'd be convicted, and he could be executed.

In fifty-five years, John had learned enough of the world to know that what actually happened often differed from what would have happened if justice prevailed. He knew, too, that his opponents wielded inordinate power and were unabashed to treat others as pawns to be sacrificed to suit their needs. Such men had stolen years of his life and victimized countless others, some in his experience and others in lives only connected to his obliquely: Native American Indians were displaced from their lands by whites founding his hometown of Kenosha; His old friend Slick's brother, Henry, was wrongfully killed by Irish police; the heirs of Hans Stegger were robbed with the help of Daniel's lawyer; the Nazis forced citizens to abide their immoral policies, abused their most vulnerable citizens, and slaughtered millions; U.S. airmen were wasted on ill-conceived missions; Europeans were slaughtered and starved in a war to end all other wars; unwitting men were given cancer by plutonium needed to build a bomb to kill even more men; innocents were incinerated by atomic bombs for the sake of show; a psychiatrist was killed, and another driven to exile in Brazil to cover up wrongdoing; young men were ground up like hamburger in Vietnam for no good reason; and a young woman died in a prehistoric time because she and her loved one refused to abide by the dictates of corrupt men.

Despite all of it, something inside Six/John continued to believe in an elementary cosmic justice that would keep him from being convicted of a crime he'd never committed. He drew upon such faith as he had left and told his lawyer to roll the dice. He wouldn't back down, no matter how little the government had to uncover to prove he'd been in Stegger's home on the night of the brutal murder.

The session between Stern and his clients after their deposition was full of such colorful expressions as men employ when seeing their lives crash down around them. The senior agent bore the brunt. "I can read men, you said, been doing it my whole career and Redford's too naïve to lie! He's too afraid to do anything with the file. You earned his trust. The delivery was spontaneous, you said, he decided on the spot to trust us, so we could bury it and be heroes! Jesus Christ, that was really spot on, you stupid shit!"

The senior glared back but had no response. They were in this together, had been from the time they'd agreed to help a friend in exchange for cash and upward mobility in the CIA. Now, he thought, *The only good thing is that no one knows we killed Blue to destroy the link to Frey, so we're not facing capital charges, just fucking perjury, destruction of evidence, obstruction of justice, and the end of our lifetime careers . . . shit! But we still have a chance since everything disappears if Redford folds his tent. He has to. He has to realize otherwise he'll go down for murdering Stegger. He's obviously the killer, after all, he had the damn files and fits the description of the attorney from Seattle perfectly. Once we prove it, everyone will shake hands and walk away. First, we need containment.*

"Look, Stern, this is how it shakes down. Remember who your clients are, us three, not the Bureau. If one word of this gets back to our superiors I'll have your license yanked for breaching attorney client privilege, got it? You just tell them it went fine. We forbid you to disclose anything else."

"Once the transcript is prepared, the deposition will become part of the official record and eventually they'll see it."

"We'll see, court reporters sometimes lose their notes."

"Look, if you're saying you're going to steal her notes . . . "

"Whoa, counselor, I'm not saying anything of the sort. I would never put you in the position of having to report a client planning a crime. Let's just say we could get lucky and she'll misplace them, or the transcript gets delayed, or the case simply drags on long enough to accomplish the same thing. It's already sealed tight, for Christ's sake."

"Burroughs will want to see the transcript and they're usually ready within a few weeks."

"Not a problem. I'll be in Colorado tomorrow, so very soon we'll have what we need to nail the bastard. When we show it to Stern he'll have to agree to a dismissal."

His partner agreed with what had to be done and the senior went to Colorado. Meanwhile, he'd work on Gail Stegger. The newest agent, Wilcox, said nothing. He thought he might throw up. He couldn't believe he'd gotten himself in this position. "It's how the game is played," they'd said, "we wash their laundry and they wash ours. Buck the system and we'll guarantee you're screwed." *Well, I feel truly screwed now. How can we nail a perp quickly on a case eight years cold?* He pictured himself being tossed from the FBI with a perjury conviction and his law license yanked.

Brad Frey orchestrated a successful break-in at the court reporter's office, but her deposition notes weren't there—the conscientious woman had taken them along to produce the transcript while vacationing with her folks in Maine. Frey became terrified when his agent buddy told him, "I'm not going down without you."

The FBI's focus on John Redford ended within just a few weeks: The senior agent went to Grand Lake and found that none of the fingerprints from the crime scene matched Redford's from Los Alamos; neither the proprietor of the motel where "Charles Smith" stayed, the Hertz clerk, nor the airline agent who sold a ticket to Seattle could recognize Redford as the man posing as Smith; and the sweet young waitress who'd been certain she'd recognize him again had died a year earlier in an unfortunate automobile mishap on an icy road. The only other items of tangible evidence were a third party's fingerprints that didn't match Redford's, and a size ten footprint from the scene; Redford's were a size smaller.

The senior partner interviewed Gail Stegger. The government file didn't help because it implicated the CIA, but if she verified the animosity between Daniel and Jack they might parlay it into a motive for murder. "Think back," he said, "search your recollection. Take as much time as you need and tell me whatever you can, Ms. Stegger."

"I never heard Daniel refer to Redford in any way before, during, or after Los Alamos," Gail said. "I was surprised to learn they worked together at all. As far as I know, Nathaniel never heard of Redford, and had no reason to target his family other than for their wealth . . . I can't imagine anything more unlikely than John Redford being involved in Daniel's murder.

No, I've never spoken with John about anything related to Los Alamos or shortly after the war. Goodness, I first met him only recently! All I really know about him before Lake Forest is that he taught at Columbia before coming to Northwestern.

I'll never understand why Nathaniel was at the party. He was so drugged up I wonder if he even knew. I don't have a clue since he broke off all contact with us long before. I only did what I had to do to protect Rose. I would have done the same thing if anyone else had attacked her."

Gail was scrupulous and moral, *but if God has any mercy and forgiveness,* she thought, *He'll absolve me from lying to protect John.* She vowed to confess her transgression in church the following day.

With all leverage gone, like rats on a sinking ship, the time had come for the agents to scramble. By the time the senior agent returned from Colorado, the newest agent, Wilcox, had confessed and cemented a deal to give his testimony and resign, in exchange for retaining his law license. *I'd rather practice divorce law in Bum Fuck North Dakota than spend a moment in jail.* His confession led to the arrest of the senior's longtime partner, who in turn accepted a recommendation for a reduced sentence in exchange for his testimony about the killing of Blue to cover up for Frey.

The senior agent spent the remainder of his life in prison in Fort Leavenworth, Kansas. Brad Frey ran off to Colombia, but this turned out to be a poor choice: nineteen months after fleeing the country and asking the Cartel for help in gathering his worldwide funds, they confiscated every cent, minced him up and threw him into the ocean, saving the taxpayers extradition expenses.

John Redford and his attorney had a cordial visit with President Gerald Ford and CIA Director William Colby in the Oval Office. John received a check for ten million dollars and a tardy apology "from a grateful nation." In exchange for assurances that the abuses of Chatter and MKULTRA would result in reformation and congressional oversight of the CIA, John agreed to keep his story confidential for the customary thirty-year period. They claimed, correctly he believed, that at least that much time would be needed to root out the abuses, repair the CIA's reputation, and regain the public support needed for its admittedly essential mission.

———

The hoopla over the strange events of the Fourth of July faded away and life proceeded apace for the Redford family. Rachel and Abe were married in a lovely, low-key service in Lake Forest, in December, 1971. In late 1972, Alexie and Tolo had a daughter, Abigail Atia Rivitolo, and Gail and John exchanged winks as agreed upon. In 1973, Adie and Hal had a surprise child, Hannibal ("Hanny") Joachim Marshall.

Mary and Lizzy treated with Rachel for a short time, but by the time of John's settlement in 1975, they were shining examples of youthful resilience—Mary was beginning her freshman year at Notre Dame, and Lizzy was thrilled to have been asked to her junior prom.

A week after John's settlement, the extended family gathered at Katya's to celebrate Hanny's second birthday. Rachel and Abe, married for nearly four years by then, announced her pregnancy and the expected arrival of their first child in May, just about the time Abe would graduate from Northwestern. It would be a girl, Rachel was certain, and no one would dispute her prediction. When they began discussing the child, Katya fetched a photo album from Rachel's childhood as they imagined how their daughter might look.

"This is my favorite photo of Rachel. We took it on the Milwaukee lakefront in '55 when she was eleven, trick-or-treating as an angel, wings and all. When I saw a painting called *Angel* a few years later, the resemblance struck me and I teased her about it, saying the artist must have had her in mind, and besides, she'd always been such an angel! It was painted by a man named Thayer, do you know it?"

John and Rose exchanged glances. They'd never forget John's obsession with the Abbott Handerson Thayer painting. Studying the photo in the album, John found that he couldn't distinguish the image of eleven-year-old Rachel from *Angel,* or from his mind's eye vision of Azume: all three had the same thin and delicate face, high cheekbones, cupid-shaped mouths, and thick auburn hair framing slim and fragile necks—the same timeless visage that had long been more memorable to John/Six than his own identity.

19.

Capri Boy

Evanston, Illinois, 1969

John took comfort in listening to the recordings and learning that he took Azume's life as an act of love. But belief in the incident's reality required belief in reincarnation and suspension of his inherent scientific skepticism. Without any supporting evidence of psychosis, he came to believe, as Doctor Cowell espoused, "That once all other explanations are proven impossible, the logical one remaining, no matter how implausible, is correct."

Dreams were important in reaching his conclusion, especially the persistently recurring ones, like the dream he experienced the night before confronting Daniel Stegger, years after first experiencing it before the Ploesti mission in 1943, a dream of reunion with Atia. As he'd explained to Cowell while speaking as Six in one of his final sessions, "It didn't make sense that I would soon be reunited with a woman from my past; at twenty-three how much past could I have? But still, I was certain I'd known her before, and beyond that, being with her imparted a sense of intimacy far too intense to be spontaneous. I knew instinctively our meeting was the continuation of many other shared experiences that apparently occurred in Italy, a place I was sure I'd never been otherwise, and hadn't given any thought to since childhood."

"Did you know her name?"

"I'd known her name ever since I fabricated an explanation for the origin of my own. I'd predicted, I thought as childish fantasy, that 'Atia' had been part of my Roman past and we would meet again in this life."

"Did the name occur to you in a dream or in some type of vision?"

"I don't know, maybe I just heard it somewhere and liked the sound."

"Does the name Takla mean anything to you?"

"No, but it sounds American Indian."

"What about the name Azume?"

"No, it's not familiar either, but it sounds Indian, too."

At that point, Cowell began to tell Six the story of Azume and Takla growing up in the Colya clan, but he stopped when it became apparent that as Six, it meant nothing to him, even though he'd told Cowell the entire story under hypnosis just days earlier as Takla. Then Cowell described Azume as seen through the words of Takla, to see if his subconscious mind thought of her and Atia as the same woman.

"Does the description remind you of Atia?"

"No. Azume sounds innocent and unsoiled, almost ethereal. She seems alluring and desirable, but somehow not meant to be attainable except in a platonic sense, as if destiny or fate or just something in her nature would keep her beyond the grasp of ordinary men.

But Atia was earthy and sexual, mature and self-confident. She knew what she wanted and went after it without hesitation. Beyond that, we shared a tangible relationship begun long before, intimate, sensual and passionate, but not at all ethereal or fleeting, rather durable and sustaining. Something like Odysseus returning home long after the Trojan War ended, and finding Penelope had waited, so they might continue uninterrupted right from where they left off. But honestly, it seems like even more than that, like more than the familiarity that bonds a married couple who have only spent one single lifetime together."

In the recording that described Six's meeting with "Capri Boy" in Montenegro, he admitted he'd been stunned to realize she was the image of the Atia from his dreams.

"As we sat beside each other in the cellar, I feigned interest in her plans for reaching the American Command near Naples. I was preoccupied by our charged handshake and my feelings for her. Dim light masked my amazement, and her companions, Aldo and Roberto, blanketed themselves on the floor to get some rest. I was so engaged in analyzing the unlikelihood of what was happening that I didn't realize she'd stopped speaking until she placed her hand on my leg and moved her lips to my ear.

The touch of her fingertips and the heat of her breath gave me a jolt, eclipsing every other pleasurable sensation I'd ever known. I felt dazed, then her whispered words of promise made my spirits soar—like a blind man suddenly glimpsing the starry sky. *"Erant non adaequate percipere. Denique nos es vere una. Ego sudo vobis cras nos ero junctus ut unus iterum!"* *We're no longer dreaming.*

Finally we're really together. I swear to you, tomorrow we'll be joined as one again!

I squeezed her hand and held her against me for an intoxicating moment, then leaned back and closed my eyes. I was numb and astonished. I remember thinking tomorrow couldn't come soon enough.

We were within sixty kilometers of our escape point across the Adriatic, just west of Krute, but Atia calculated it would take four days of patient travel to reach it, since we had to cross Lake Skadar to avoid the civil war adding to the chaos of the Italian withdrawal and German reoccupation. So we were surprised when Atia had us stop after traveling only two hours. She ordered the others to remain at guard outside before leading me into an abandoned barn.

She pulled me into a corner and we embraced, then she spread her coat on the ground with obvious intent—she wasn't going to delay her eight-hour-old vow. We made love and the reality surpassed its promise. As I anticipated, it was passionate and fulfilling, but also comfortable, familiar, and as well-conducted as I'd dreamt. For a time afterwards, we spoke of our memory of the son we'd once had, but talk of any future had to wait until we made sure we would have one.

Roberto was shot and killed by a sniper two days later, soon after we crossed Lake Skadar. It happened on an early moonless morning, and we couldn't even determine where the shot had come from. Aldo mourned his companion and friend until he died, too, on a rocky beach near Krute two days later—it was my my fault. I'd intervened to spare a child of ten he suspected of collaboration and wanted killed. As it turned out, the boy died anyway. I shot him in a small arms exchange that also killed Aldo and three of the misguided child's Nazi heroes.

We landed south of Bisceglie, Italy on October 12, 1943. We were cold and exhausted, but our timing was peerless. We were in an isolated area controlled by the Resistance, with the bulk of the Germans pulled back to their winter line far north, near the mouth of the Sangro River. It was fortunate because I'd been wounded in the leg."

"When were you shot?"

"I took a bullet in our skirmish with the Germans. It bled a lot and I couldn't walk too well, but it passed completely through my calf and only took three weeks to heal. With Atia nursing me back to health and her friend, Carmella, acting as our cook and host, I felt like I was vacationing in a mountain resort."

"What did you mean about the son you once had with Atia?"

"Have you ever heard of an ancient Roman named Quintus Tullius Varo?"

There was a pause and audible shuffling of paper as Cowell apparently tried to find the name Six had used when speaking only classical Latin. "Please, tell me about him."

"He was a first century Roman and a legendary hero to the people of Atia's province. He came from nearby Puteoli and rose to the top of his world as an architect and builder—some say he designed the Pantheon—but he was admired more for his eccentricity and courage than for his architectural skill. Derisively called 'the dreamer,' he was preoccupied with visions he claimed came from a distant past. Contemporaries avoided his friendship because they thought being close to him might be dangerous. He was anti-authoritative and unconventional, and in a fatal challenge to the Emperor, he sued a close friend of his for corruption. He was murdered before the trial, and the failure to charge anyone with the crime scandalized Rome. But it didn't change anything, even though no one doubted Emperor Domitian had approved the crime.

The thing is, Varo and his wife had a precocious ten-year-old son, but he'd been lost along with Atia when Mount Vesuvius erupted in 79 AD and . . . Well, the thing is, she honestly believed she was that Atia to my Varo, and we were meant to recreate our child. I-I, well, I actually found myself forming a mental image of the boy." He laughed, but his tone suggested he didn't think it humorous. "Look, I know when things sound crazy. I'm a scientist, trained to use experimentation and controlled testing to root out fact, and I don't know of any scientific explanation for past lives or reincarnation. So, I approached the idea skeptically, and asked myself what I knew to be true: a young woman I murdered, who never ages, returns in my dreams and reminds me of a past we once shared, even as she directs and consoles me; and an intimately familiar woman returns to my life, and she's clearly the same woman I imagined as my Roman wife who died with our son in a volcanic eruption near our home. Then Atia tells me she's experienced similar visions and dreams, of living with me as Varo, an ancient Roman called 'the dreamer,' for experiencing unusual visions from the past.

Religion asks why, so if I approach these matters on a purely spiritual basis, with a belief beyond reason, the facts appear more consistent with Atia's thesis than with any other explanation. Putting it another way, it requires considerably less faith to believe I've been reincarnated than to believe in most Christian dogma, from the virgin birth to a whole host of miracles, to the resurrection and ascension."

"If you really believe that, then tell . . . " began Cowell when spool five ended.

John scrambled to engage the next spool. After thirty-five minutes of hissing, it started again, ". . . wait any longer. We'd been in Amantea hiding and indulging ourselves for two months, and Atia believed she was pregnant.

Atia's Aunt Eda stayed with a neighbor, giving us a final night alone to say all we wanted and to lose ourselves in each other. We trucked to HQ in Naples the following morning, ending our three-month reunion. We had two final days together in Sorrento, until January 10, 1944, when I had to return to the states and Atia would travel north to rejoin the Risestanza supporting the Allies near Anzio.

When I think back on our time together, I'm struck by the feeling of homecoming I experienced at once upon seeing Vesuvius overlooking the Bay, even though it looked diminished. I'm struck, too, by how little time I spent discussing anything of my life before our reunion. I think it was because revisiting our ancient life together was so delightful, but also because my upbringing and background was so irrelevant and comparatively boring, composed of what seemed merely necessary intervening events between our lives together. I never even told her as much as where I'd grown up. As for the Manhattan Project, I told her in general terms that I was returning to work on an ongoing important, secret project, but no more.

In contrast, Atia spoke of her background to reinforce our history. She spoke of her formative years in Spain, her passionate father, and their frequent discussions of inherited foresight. They both believed their insight stemmed from the accumulated wisdom of past life experiences. Atia rarely shared her beliefs with anyone otherwise, thinking few would understand.

Usually, she considered her gifts a blessing and she took delight in the wondrous things she foresaw, yet sometimes past and present became confused in her mind. Like me, she'd also seen troubling sights and apocalyptic events that filled her with anxiety. She wasn't religious, so she never thought of it as praying, but she sometimes invoked the intercession of an ethereal being to comfort and guide her through those difficult visions, a spiritual presence nearby and very much responsible for her extreme self-confidence. She never felt alone, always had what some would call an angel by her side.

I thought it might be impossible to leave Atia, but I believed what she foresaw in our future. So when she said we might try, but she doubted we'd meet again in this lifetime, I took it as painful fact.

She also foresaw that our unborn son would find his way to me someday by his own devices, and I took that as fact, too. 'Can you imagine after taking nineteen hundred years to produce another son that he wouldn't be capable of finding you?' she'd asked. I admitted I couldn't. When we parted, we'd come a long way from when I'd teased her by asking why she hadn't foreseen our initial meeting in Montenegro. 'I'm not perfect, perhaps next time around,' she'd replied, and I believed that as well.

As a keepsake, she'd given me a picture of her to hold dear, a lovely photo of her with the bittersweet image of Vesuvius in the background. I gave her the only gift I could, my most prized possession, a silver tetradrachm bearing the image of Alexander the Great, a twenty-two-hundred-year-old coin given me by my father when I went off to war. She said it was definitive proof of my identity, as it was the same coin Varo had carried after receiving it from his father nineteen-hundred years earlier. It was meant as a reminder that even those considered the greatest of their era leave this life with nothing more remaining of them than an image rendered in metal, yet all will be judged by whether they lived virtuously enough to rise again. In slaughtering thousands to achieve earthly greatness, Alexander the Great failed his test miserably.

On a dreary January day, we stood in the rain wrapped in each other's arms before I boarded the plane to America. We laughed at the spectacle we made with water pouring down off of us, still full of happiness from our magical time together. I remember our conversation verbatim: 'Be well for our son, you wondrous wet woman, tell him of his father.'

'He'll know his father for himself, and he'll bear his name as a reminder.'

'Sixtus Rivitolo sounds nice.'

'Varo Rivitolo is better, and more authentic.'

'I'll search for you after the war.'

'Yes, I know you will, but only in a way. Think well of me then as I will always think of you.'

'But I won't find you, will I?'

'I don't think so, but we can never be certain. Regardless, sweet man, you'll always find me in the shadow of our son's smile!'

"I kissed her cheek, told her to get herself out of the rain, and turned to run to my plane. I waved before entering the aircraft, and she remained motionless, standing still on the runway in a moment forever frozen in my mind. Soon afterwards we ascended above the clouds and arched out to the west, heading toward the setting sun and leaving Vesuvius and Atia fading away below."

"I can't imagine how you must have felt," said Cowell.

"Honestly, it was bittersweet. Sad, obviously, but I also felt content and satisfied. I'd learned what I needed to of my past, and knew I had to focus on the future if I was going to be of benefit to anyone in this life, and someday meet and assist our new son."

When John played the last and most damaged spool of wire recordings, he heard himself speaking as John Redford, sounding frightened, confused, and uncertain over the difficult search for his identity and the desire to reunite with his family. Cowell had recorded his own impressions after that. "It's apparent the subject was treated inhumanely by the application of mind-altering chemicals while in the custody of the government. Ironically, this abuse led to the discovery of past life experiences otherwise likely to have remained unknown. The difficulty will be finding a way to study these revelations while holding those responsible accountable. It will be impossible to find the data needed without utilizing CIA resources and Doctor Wright . . ." Then the spool ended, and John had learned all he ever would from his sessions with Dr. Graham Cowell.

John/Six thought that someday he'd write what he knew of his past lives. It might help others understand not only the need to behave virtuously to halt the evil otherwise constantly intruding, but also to find a means of atonement. If men acted on the insight he now possessed, he believed they might fulfill the obligation given them at creation as a condition of their mastery and majesty.

———

On April 30, 1976, Alexie gave birth to the Rivitolo's third child and first son, delivered precisely when expected, at Northwestern University Hospital. After taking the infant and Alexie home three days later, Tolo's first visit was to his favorite colleague at the University office.

John Redford hugged Tolo and offered hearty congratulations.

"Thank you, Professor, it's a wondrous feeling to have a son! May I visit for a spell?"

"Of course, make yourself comfortable," said John. "It's after four, I have wine, and a toast is in order."

"Most definitely!"

John poured from a jug kept in a small refrigerator and they touched two glasses of Chianti together. "God bless you and Alexie, Tolo. May your son be a dragon!"

Tolo smiled at the familiar expression. "I have another toast, Professor, but I need to tell you a brief story first."

"Certainly, please sit down and relax."

"A few months back you asked me to drop off a paper at your home so you could read it on your way to Washington."

"Sure, it was the piece about supersymmetry supplanting particle physics."

"Right, well, in your office there was a call slip beside it, with a name and a Wisconsin phone number. I couldn't miss it."

John remained silent.

"You'd had a call from Ralph from Kenosha, and I thought of the man I'd met a few times, the 'old friend' you introduced as Ralph Ehlers—I always thought he resembled you enough that you might be related."

Sensing where this was headed, John began, "Tolo, I-I . . . "

"The note said 'Ralph *Peeters* called,' and I thought, what are the odds? '*Peeters*,' an unusual spelling, and my father's name, my father who wasn't referenced anywhere I could find, even though they took great pains to return him from the war zone to work on a large-scale, top secret project, rather something like your work on the Manhattan Project. So I looked in the phone book and found two addresses for Ralph in Kenosha, Wisconsin, and I went to find him."

John folded his hands across his arms and leaned forward expectantly, unsure of what he was feeling.

"He lived in a lovely place on the lake, but he wasn't home. The other address was for a very modest older home across the street from a church and school. I found the home intriguing, vacant but like a shrine, down to the gold star in the window—I understand those were given to families who'd lost a son in the Second World War."

"Well, wouldn't you know it, there's this wonderful retired nun at St. George who knew the family, a Sister Phillip Neri who taught there as her very first assignment. She told me she'd never forget her favorite student ever, Sixtus, my father, one of the Peeters that lived in the home across the street. She told me all she remembered about him, and throughout her description I kept picturing you."

Tolo reached behind his collar and uncoupled a necklace holding a mounted coin. He held it in a closed fist and extended his arm out, palm upward toward his mentor. "Perhaps you'll tell me what you know about this coin, and then we'll have a proper toast. I'd wager you might even be able to guess my son's name."

They looked at each other with recognition evident in glistening eyes, the stillness interrupted only by the movement of the hands of a wall clock, ticking steadily on even as time stood still. Relief, pride, hope, and joy washed across John/Six, knowing Atia had been right, their son truly was destined to find him.

"I believe you're holding a twenty-two-hundred-year-old silver tetradrachm bearing the image of a young man said by many to be great. My father bore his name, and so will my grandson . . . Alexander."

Tolo opened his closed fist, and John/Six took the coin and gazed at it once again for a moment, before lifting it to his lips and kissing it. Then the two men rose as if one and embraced, their hearts swelling with love, understanding, and fulfillment.

EPILOGUE
A Final Gift

Lake Forest, Illinois, December 26, 2008

In the early morning, a man stands on the deck behind his home in a raging storm. Icy air laden with snowflakes swirls all around, wetting his silvery hair. The air smells fresh and clean and the whistling wind and roaring lake soothe his soul.

He looks across mounded snow toward the surrounding forest, a maze of tree limbs bowing under their heavy loads, and he smiles at the amber tint cast upon the otherwise wintry whiteness—colored like the pages of an ancient book by lanterns hung atop his pagoda. The structure reminds him of the miracle that saved his family, apropos, as he built it to symbolize a phoenix that rose from the ashes of evil.

He wills himself to stand ramrod straight in the storm, despite his consuming cancer. But he's comfortably warm, protected by a khaki-colored, wool-lined coat—United States Army Air Corps issue, circa 1943—regifted by his brother Ralph. Its label reads, "Peeters," an integral piece of a puzzle finally, fully known.

All in the home is still. The Christmas celebration has given way to an easy sleep for his loved ones. He's crying, but without sadness. He's relieved at having completed his gift in time for this final holiday: it's a book recounting much of his life, explaining his quirks and lapses, and divulging lessons he's learned. Some is known to his family already, but it also recounts marvelous, magical adventures long concealed and beyond their imaginations. By revealing the inner self which defined but long eluded him, he hopes his descendants will realize that the evil found throughout life might not only be overcome, but also be used as a pathway to truth.

His mind flips through the faces of the holiday—friends, in-laws, children, grandchildren, and great-grandsons, fifty-five in total, and all younger than he. Always the scientist, he calculates a nearly eight hundred percent increase from the first Christmas spent in this home with Rose and their five children, forty-seven years earlier. It seems like only yesterday, since his life no longer seems sequential. Dreams and visions have blurred his beginnings, and all of time seems an unending continuum, with the distinction between past, present, and future merely an illusion.

After extensive study and reflection, he believes his current existence is linked to at least two other lifetimes; what appeared to be lives's endings, were only temporary pauses before his core identity migrated into another body and was reborn. He believes science will eventually embrace the reality of reincarnation, a worldwide philosophical concept maintained since antiquity.

He sees evidence of reincarnation in the human aging process: the average cell of an adult body is only several years old, since over its lifetime a body continually changes cellular composition and form even while the conscious identity of its inhabitant remains unchanged. And although science cannot disprove reincarnation, the concept comports with scientific principles, and it has withstood rigorous examination by its proponents and opponents alike.

Reincarnation also explains the otherwise inexplicable for Six/John, especially why Azume and his life near Amar seem undeniable, and why, in retelling his time as Varo with Atia, he'd been able to recount verifiable historical events with uncanny precision.

He knows that energy and matter cannot be destroyed, but are routinely transformed. And his study of quantum physics, which itself accepts formerly discounted and mysterious mechanisms, provides clues to a possible pathway: energy and matter consist of waves and particles inexorably linked in the subatomic realm, no matter how distant from each other; he extrapolates that the energy and matter composing one life may well cause an effect in another, with past sensory impressions somehow transmitted into a new brain as subatomic energy, from wherever such experiences are stored away in a limitless universe.

Still, he knows that belief in reincarnation is difficult because it requires acknowledgement of the distinction between one's essence and one's body, an awkward thought even though it's apparent that one cannot simultaneously be both an observer and the object of one's own observation. Belief in reincarnation may also require personal remembrance of past lives, but such memories may be inhibited by religious belief, painful or harmful recollection, or by the lack of a triggering event. As with so many things, people often fail to see what is readily apparent, despite such common revealing experiences as déjà vu moments and shivers of premonition.

Acceptance of reincarnation is also hindered since its application likely isn't universal. Six/John believes it is self-selective as a matter of simple logic, since no purpose would be served in reincarnating those with negative karma—unworthy souls who fail to use their talents to act virtuously, or those so blinded by hubris and ego that they misperceive their fundamental human obligations and role, such as an ancient Lord or Shaman, military officer, government representative, a President of the United States, or a scientist or lawyer named Stegger.

He'd once thought all of his lives were unified by the constant presence of a single angelic spirit to protect and guide him. But he's become uncertain of that, wondering if perhaps his "angel" was a projection used as a means of bolstering his confidence when making life-altering decisions. Regardless, he's certain there *were* angels assisting him, as there are angels for everyone, although few recognize it at the time. Azume, Atia, Abby, Momma, Pop, Ralph, Katya and Rachel had all been angels for him. There were also some who helped simply by example, by a single word, or in a lone encounter—even some as unlikely as John the Bum, his neighbor Slick Retzling, and Ardell Dystre, who told him before he learned it otherwise that men exceeded natural limits at their peril.

His heart swelled with gratitude for all the angels in his life, but mostly for Rose, who shared half a century of unquestioning love and support, even through his darkest moments. She'd been an unwavering anchor, even knowing Azume and Atia remained forever in his heart. She'd deserved more than he'd given her in return, and he thought he'd trade the chance for another lifetime just to hold her once again.

The door opened behind him, and a woman called out, "John, please, you need to come in now!"

"Be there soon, Abby, I'm almost done," he replied, thinking he truly was exactly that, just about finished.

Abigail Marshall Stegger O'Connor was also finding it difficult to sleep that night. As he stood outside in the storm, she remained inside in his study, reminiscing as she studied the oldest memento in the room, an enlarged and prominently displayed, yellowed photo of the crew of the aircraft, *Maid in America*. In her mind's eye, Gail/Abby still saw Six as the youthful and powerful navigator so vibrant in the photograph, hands on hips, prepared to spring into action, seemingly able to vanquish even death itself. For her the line between past and present had also blurred.

She'd been a godsend: She'd saved Rose's life, and with the atonement money John gave her and Rachel, she'd co-founded the Koalition for Enlightened Government ("KEG"), a private consortium meant to be tapped to counter the ruling elite, the disguised, subtle manipulators endangering the citizenry for their own personal gain. Abe and Rose also worked for KEG, and by the time Rose died in 1997, it had raised millions of dollars and influenced the election of selfless candidates genuinely interested in serving the public. Their thousands of members were a valued resource for everyone favoring responsible government.

While working for KEG, Gail fell in love. In 1978, in her mid-fifties, she married Colin O'Connor, a colorful lobbyist representing the Republic of Ireland. She continued working for KEG from Maryland after they wed, and for eighteen years they lived an adventurous and fulfilling life together.

John and Rose loved Colin nearly as much as Gail, and the couples pub-crawled throughout Ireland and in countless places throughout the USA. They spent every Christmas together as part of the extended family celebrating the holiday at the Redford's home. By the time Colin died of a heart attack in 1995, Gail and John had become good friends, regardless of their wartime romance. Nothing could have been more natural for Gail than to move into the Redford home to help care for Rose throughout her long illness, and then staying on after her passing as caregiver and companion for John, as Rose had requested.

The snow stopped falling, and Six/John looking up at the clouds moving swiftly across the sky, considered his lengthy journey—from a time when primitive men believed invisible gods lived somewhere high above, manipulating natural phenomena and dictating human destiny, to a time when men believed they understood the natural laws of the universe. With such knowledge, men wielded godlike power, and sometimes presumed they too were gods, so blinded by their arrogance that they failed to see the deficiencies in their judgment. As a result, they acted in ways rarely heavenly and often abhorrent.

Six/John had worked in Los Alamos with Enrico Fermi, the Nobel Prize winner well known for positing the Fermi Paradox. His paradox referred to the statistical certainty that there were a staggering number of advanced civilizations in the universe, yet the earth had never heard from any one of them. He feared the answer to the paradoxical question of "where everyone else is," was best answered by the likelihood that other civilizations, with comparably magnificent technologies and godly power, had misapplied such tools and destroyed themselves, just as mankind might someday do.

Six/John understood that while the nature of science was morally neutral, it nonetheless required the use of moral wisdom in its application. Since men were increasingly secular, he wondered where such wisdom would now be found, and whether it would be acquired before politicians blundered or radicals acted, using the power revealed at Trinity and unleashed against Japan to destroy the earth itself.

He took a final look at his cherished yard, then he turned and tottered into his home. His final thoughts, before passing from this life later that day, were full of hope that those he left behind would heed the message inscribed many years before on the teak plaque near the top of his pagoda. In gold Japanese kanji and kokuji characters, encircling the image of a green dragon, it read, "Be worthy of the stars that God created."

SELECT CHARACTERS

John A. Redford of New York City

Sixtus Peeters of Kenosha, Wisconsin

Rosabella Tassi Redford, wife of John Redford

The Redford Family Children:

Absalom "Abe"

Mark

Mary

Elizabeth "Lizzy"

Timmy

———

Daniel Stegger of Chicago and Grand Lake, Colorado

Abigail ("Abby," "Gail") Marshall Stegger of Lake Forest, Illinois, former wife of Daniel Stegger

Nathaniel Stegger of Maryland, son of Daniel and Abigail Stegger, twin brother of Alexie

Alexandra "Alexie" Stegger, daughter of Daniel and Abigail Stegger, twin sister of Nathaniel

James Jackson of Grand Lake, Colorado, manservant for Daniel Stegger

Brant Frey of Washington, D.C., partner of Daniel Stegger

Bradford Frey of Maryland, son of Brant Frey

Doctor Edmund Wright, CIA psychiatrist

Doctor Graham Steadman Cowell, psychiatrist, University of Virginia

———

Fritz "Slick" Retzling of Kenosha, Wisconsin, childhood friend of Sixtus Peeters

Hans Stegger II of Racine, Wisconsin, cousin of Daniel Stegger

———

Walter McFarland, Director of Project Engineering, Sperry Rand Corporation, former Special Operations Director in the Office of Strategic Services ("OSS")

General William J. "Wild Bill" Donovan, Former Director of the Office of Strategic Services ("OSS")

General Leslie Groves, Commanding Officer, Manhattan Project, Los Alamos, New Mexico

———

Katyalina "Katya" Krause Weber, wife of Joachim Weber

Adalia "Adie" Weber, daughter of Joachim and Katyalina

———

Varo "Tolo" Rivitolo of Amantea, Italy, exchange student at Northwestern University

Rachel Hoffman Weber of Milwaukee, Wisconsin, psychologist and daughter of Bea Hoffman and adopted daughter of Katyalina Weber

Giovanni "Gio" Conforti of Cicero, Illinois, Private Investigator

Ralph Peeters of Kenosha, Wisconsin, brother of Sixtus Peeters

Atia Rivitolo of Amantea, Italy, Partisan Fighter aka "Capri Boy" and mother of Varo Rivitolo

―――

Arlen Christensen of Miami, Florida, Daniel Stegger"s attorney

―――

Azume, member of the Colya Clan

Oto, Clan Lord and father of Azume

Takla, Clan member

Shaman, Clan priest

Nambe, Clan member and son of the Shaman

―――

Harold "Hal" Marshall, physician of Chicago, Illinois, husband of Adalia Weber Marshall and brother of Abigail Stegger

―――

Sally Ann Duncan Moriarty of Los Angeles, California

Author's note to readers: I hoped you enjoyed this sequel to *Worthy of the Stars,* and I invite you to review my effort on Amazon.com. I welcome your critique, and I look forward to sharing the adventures of the next generation of *Worthy* characters. I'd guess that the descendants of such as Six, Abby, Adie, Rachel and Slick will live very interesting lives in the future awaiting us.

www.ingramcontent.com/pod-product-compliance
Lightning Source LLC
Chambersburg PA
CBHW051512250626
47156CB00001B/66